# MOJAVE RUN

## VOLUME 1

**JARED MARTIN**

*Book Cover Design by Jair*

Visit the author's official website for updates and social media links:
www.byjaredmartin.com

Or visit the official website of the publisher for special announcements and merchandise: www.blackwingbooks.com

*TO THOSE WHO MAKE MY LIFE WORTH LIVING*

# MOJAVE
# RUN

# MOJAVE RUN

A NOVEL IN THREE VOLUMES

**PART HEIST THRILLER.
PART MYSTERY.
PART WESTERN ALLEGORY.**

# CONTENTS

# BOOK ONE

## BILLY DAGGER AND THE TWISTED HAND OF FATE

# ONE

Billy Dagger always knew how he would die. His fate was told to him by a blind fortune teller at the old street market in Kingman, Arizona in exchange for a couple of crisp dead presidents, and he believed every crackpot word she spoke. She said he'd go out in a blaze of glory, which wasn't much of a stretch. He'd always lived on the edge. Close enough to see the other side, in fact. He could almost reach out and touch it. He knew it was only a matter of time before he finally crossed over. He figured it would be in a burning street-racer turned on its head beneath an outlaw moon, not in a hail of bullets in the blistering Mojave sun, but there he was, public enemy number one, an unlikely folk hero, fighting for something far greater than his reputation on the blacktop drag strip.

## The "Old World", 2049
### Mojave Desert, California

Billy's black '63 Chevy thundered across the earth like an angry shadow defying the light, scraping through sagebrush and the deadly spines of jumping cholla. The custom C10 pickup truck was powered by a 383 engine that pushed 600 horses and raised the dead when it growled, and as Billy shifted into sixth gear and stomped the gas he could feel the ghosts of the desert clambering for their graves. He spun the wheel and drifted onto the broken pavement of Route 66. The Mother Road. Her womb now barren. An aborted piece of American history. The asphalt was crumbling and the spidery cracks were sprouting lifeless brown weeds. There were no yellow traffic lines running down the center of the highway. The paint had already faded from human neglect. A common degradation. The world was only a few months removed from the Collapse, but society had been trending that way for much longer, and infrastructure was the first of many casualties.

He pulled onto Cima Road, an old dirt path that cut through the desert like a serpent looking for shade. The truck curved and thrusted for miles, with a long plume of dust fanning out behind it. He smashed the brake and slid to a stop just before a cluster of granite rock. The '63 Chevy sat there idling in a shroud of dust, her blood revving, spewing exhaust from the molten side headers, convulsing uncontrollably like some dark chariot of war come to life and gone mad with bloodlust. That's how Billy envisioned her now. As a beast of burden. A war machine. She was once a badass street-racer, but now she was a weapon of stark defiance. Her body had been punctured by bullets, scarred by battle, broken and hastily repaired so many times it was hard to remember that she was once a beautiful piece of custom work. In the days before the Collapse, Billy had customized her from the ground up and christened her *the Moon Runner*, in honor of his outlaw grandfather who ran moonshine out of Arkansas in the 1960s for a backwoods criminal enterprise. Her black shine and polish had faded from exposure to the elements, but the family business emblem on the doors still shimmered with the bold words *Dagger & Son Kustoms*, which encircled the image of a menacing skull in a bobber racing helmet hovering over a pair of crossed daggers. It looked like the Jolly Roger of some merciless pirate, and these days it invoked that same kind of terror.

Just months earlier, Billy had been a simple man who owned a custom auto shop in Kingman, Arizona and made an honest living there, rebuilding cars by day and earning a reputation on the drag strip after midnight, scorching the blacktop in the Moon Runner. Now he was an outlaw, like his grandfather, and like the six generations of Dagger men that came before him.

He shut the engine off and stepped out of the truck and dug his boot heels into the sand and gravel. He liked to feel the earth shift beneath his feet, as if he had some power over the ground he walked on. Some days his purpose felt divine. It was one of those days. He removed his black bobber helmet and goggles and wiped the sweat from his brow.

"Another day of reckoning," he declared to his chosen god, hoping to secure a little divine intervention on his own behalf. But the Good Lord didn't seem to have an inkling of mercy. The sun was devilishly hot, and there were no clouds in the sky to act as angels. That first day of August was a hundred and seven degrees of pure misery. A sweltering torment. The desert air felt like flames dancing around him, as if he were centerstage in some wicked ballet from Hell. But still, he remained as cool as ever. He wore jeans and biker boots and a black leather jacket with the *Dagger & Son* emblem on the back. That's all he ever wore, despite the brutal scorch. His face had once been handsome, almost devastatingly, but it was now darkened and cracked, looking like petrified driftwood from months of exposure to the unforgiving Mojave. His long blonde hair was bleached by the sun and dreadlocked with beads of gold, and the sunken crevices of his cheekbones were hidden beneath an unruly beard. As unruly as the man himself. He had the look of a ghost that couldn't shake the habit of living. His piercing blue irises were so possessed with purpose, and so glassy and sharp, that they were rumored to penetrate the souls of his enemies if he glared at them for too long. He was even rumored to be immortal. Some claimed he was God's own hand. That's how far his legend had grown. Songs of his exploits were already being sung. Someday they'd write books about him, or maybe even gospels.

But only some of it would be true.

He spit in the dirt and glared with contempt at a large cargo trailer that was sitting on flat tires in front of him. It was bright orange, peppered with bullet holes, and blasted by a sandstorm that had struck the desert the night before. The company logo imprinted on the side of the trailer was speckled and striped, but the image was still visible, and instantly recognizable to anyone in the world:

A shining halo of fire.

The word *Nimbus* printed below.

The corporation that started it all.

Billy slammed his hand down on the hood of the Moon Runner and said with a scowl, "Stop pouting and get your ass out of the truck."

The passenger door swung open. A disheveled-looking boy dressed in blue jeans and a tattered *Highway to Hell* t-shirt got out and walked around to the other side of the truck. His filthy blonde locks hadn't seen a pair of scissors in months, and his skin was burnt by the ferocity of the sun, which hung in the sky like an unburdened eye. This was Billy's only son. Little Bo Dagger, as they called him. He was only ten years old, but the weight of the world had already crushed the childhood from his soul. It was bleeding out one day at a time. His eyes were sleepless and sagging in dark purple circles, as if most of his life had already been lived and he was just trying to escape the reaper. There was a .22 revolver tucked into his waistband at the small of his back and a weary frown that was lurching across his baby face like some damaged old man. "I'm out of the truck," he snarled. "What's your big plan now?"

"Don't mock my plans," Billy said, his eyes alight with some beguiling impulse. "Men of vision always have a plan. We're the movers and shakers and difference makers."

Bo rolled his eyes. His father always had a way of making himself sound cool and exceptional, but he just wasn't impressed anymore. 2049 had been a long, dark and sadly unforgettable year for the boy. It was the year of the Collapse and the Red Death that followed. The year that he lost his mother and his sister. The year he lost his nerve. It was the year that Billy Dagger started being a hero to the world and stopped being a father to his only son.

"Time to prove yourself," Billy said. He pulled a revolver from the shoulder holster beneath his jacket. A Ruger Redhawk with a three-inch barrel and a handle made from buffalo bone. He thumbed the hammer back and raised the gun and fired a single shot without taking proper aim. The hollow point .357 Magnum ripped through the side of the Nimbus trailer, blasting a hole right in the center of the shining halo of fire. "That's your target, son." He handed the revolver to Bo and offered a warning. "Don't miss."

Bo looked surprised, harboring an unsinkable doubt at the shoreline of his eyes.

Billy nodded his approval. "It's alright. Take it."

Bo took the gun into his tiny hands and tightened his grip around the handle. He rested his finger loosely on the trigger. He was surprised by the weight of the gun, almost as much as he was by his father's unprecedented gesture. He had never been allowed to hold Billy's prized Ruger before.

But it wasn't a reward.

Billy removed a leather belt from the waistband in his pants and wrapped the buckle end around the ball of his fist, leaving a rawhide strap dangling as a clear reminder. "You miss the mark, and I'm gonna beat your little ass with this belt."

The threat was nothing new to Bo, but the fact that he couldn't bear the weight of his father's Ruger made him unsure of his ability to fire it accurately and avoid the lash this time. He took aim, trying nervously to steady the gun.

"Don't be scared," Billy said.

"I ain't scared," Bo snarled. "The damn thing's just heavy."

Billy scoffed at what he knew was a lie. "Steady hands, steady aim, dead bad guy. It's a simple equation, son. Do the math."

"Math?"

"That's right," Billy said. "Mathematics. Two plus two always equals four, and the better man always wins." He reached his free hand out to help tighten Bo's grip around the handle. "It's got a helluva kick, son. You're gonna lose your goddamn nose holding it like that."

Bo jerked the gun away. "I shot a wheelgun before."

"Okay, big shot." Billy raised a skeptical brow. "If you say so. But this ain't no twenty-two, boy."

Bo gave him a scornful look. He hated when his father called him *boy*. It was belittling, like a schoolyard bully throwing insults on the playground to make himself feel bigger. When Billy called him *son*, it was with some form of love, though unclear and underwhelming. But when he called him *boy*, it was with obvious contempt, and that was clear as day to Bo. This time he would prove his father wrong. He raised the Ruger Redhawk again and thumbed the hammer back. His hands began to tremble more recklessly. Not from fear, but from the sheer volume of the gun. As he squeezed the trigger, the gun fired with a deafening bang, and the unexpected power knocked him backwards on his heels. The bullet missed wildly, never even hitting the trailer, and as the massive gun recoiled, it slipped from his grasp and nearly hit him in the face. "Damnit," he cursed under his breath. Lo and behold, he had only proven his father right.

Billy swung the belt and whacked him in the ass. "I told you, boy. You almost lost your goddamn nose, didn't you? Now firm it up and hit the target."

Bo raised the gun again and tried to steady his aim, but his hands were trembling even more. This time from fear.

"Pull the goddamn trigger," Billy said with a grating rasp. "We ain't got time to aim in a gunfight. *Shoot*."

Bo couldn't recall ever being so nervous while trying to fire a gun, and for a brief moment his mind drifted, thinking of the next belt lash, and he suddenly forgot what he was even trying to do.

"Pull the goddamn trigger, boy." Billy whacked him in the ass with the belt again. "*Shoot*."

But the boy just froze in place, and his finger went limp on the trigger like a dead limb dangling from a wilted tree.

Then, like some frantic whirlwind cutting through the desert, Billy drew a Colt 1911 from his waistband and ejected the clip. Bo watched carefully in his peripheral, his eyes billowing outward in a slow-burning panic. Billy racked the slide and ejected the bullet from the chamber and cocked the hammer back. "Whatcha say we raise the stakes?" He pressed the gun barrel to Bo's temple and spoke softly into the boy's left ear. "Can you keep your head about you while everyone around you is losing theirs?"

Bo shrunk in his frame. His shoulders dropped and his mind began to unravel. An uncertainty rumbled in his gut. The acidic taste of fear assaulted his tongue like something corrosive. He knew the Colt wasn't loaded, but this was an unfamiliar tactic, a crazy one at that, even for his crazy father.

"Well?" Billy asked with a whisper. "Can you, boy?"

Bo drew a steady breath. He closed his eyes and tried to clear his mind. The barrel of the Colt was cold on his sweaty temple. As he found his wits again, his body loosened and his jaw tightened and his shoulders rose back up into place, and suddenly a youthful look of determination rimmed the whites of his eyes. He pulled the trigger and the gun recoiled wildly. The bullet struck the cargo trailer five feet off the mark.

"Christ," Billy said with a hostile groan. "Apparently not." He whacked Bo in the ass with the belt. "Shoot again, boy. This time hit the goddamn target or you're a dead man. You understand me?"

Bo shook the sting of the leather, and the sting of his father's foreboding words, and he thumbed the hammer back and took his time and steadied the Ruger. He fired. The bullet struck the cargo trailer even further off the mark as he over-compensated for the recoil.

"Not even close, boy. For Christ's sake. With aim like that you're a corpse." Billy swung the belt again. The leather cracked even harder on Bo's ass this time, causing him to yelp loudly like a dog that had just been kicked.

Billy clenched his teeth so violently it sounded to Bo's ears like a chair being dragged across a wooden floor. Then Billy went dark. His blue eyes turned cold and he began to shout at the boy as if they were enemies, "Shoot again, goddamn you, or I'm gonna pull this trigger and put you out of your misery.

You understand me? You'll be *dead*. *Nothing. Gone.* Just a hole in my fucking heart."

Bo's hands shook uncontrollably, his insides sloshing around like a paint stirrer. His eyes welled up with a tangled mix of emotion. Love and hate. Sadness and rage. A broken-hearted defiance. He had never heard his father speak to him so cruelly before. It hurt to hear such terrible things. He felt stuck in place, his own fear taking hold of him and forcing his body perfectly still, like some rogue planet being trapped by a gravitational pull.

Billy noticed the wetness in the boy's eyes, and he just couldn't take anymore. "Fuck it," he groaned. "You ain't got the sand for this." He dry-fired the Colt into Bo's temple. The loud metallic click startled the boy. "You're dead now, son." Billy snapped his fingers. "Just like that. *Dead.* No coming back. You understand?"

"Dad, *stop*." Bo lowered the gun and began to weep. "*Please.*"

"No, boy. Don't you speak to me like I can hear you. You're a ghost. You're gone. Gone from me. Gone from the world we love. Gone because you didn't have what it takes to fight."

"Stop saying that. *Stop*."

"There ain't no stopping, son. You understand that? It doesn't stop. None of this. It *never stops*." Billy reached out with his free hand and wrapped it around Bo's loose grip and clamped down harder on the handle of the Ruger and forced a steadier aim. "Shoot the goddamn target. In this life you don't get second chances more than once. This is the only one you get." He drew back his belt and whacked Bo on the ass as hard as he could. "Now hit the fucking target."

"Dad, please."

"Shoot the gun!"

"No, Dad!" Bo's eyes were giant circles of heartbreak. "Why are we doing this?"

Billy clenched his teeth, as if he were struggling to hold himself back. "Would you rather shoot at something that's got a pulse? I can make that happen."

"That's not what I mean, and you know it."

Billy blew the stale air from his lungs and pulled a loaded mag from his jacket pocket. "Are the stakes just not high enough for you, boy? Is that it?" He popped the mag back into the gun and racked the slide and sent a shiny little heart-stopper into the chamber. "Then let's try it the hard way instead." His blue eyes were somehow blazing like fire. "Shoot the target or I swear to God I'll put a bullet right through your fucking skull."

Bo began to sob like a boy standing over his father's grave. "Dad? What are you doing?" His body trembled. "Stop this. Please. You're scaring me."

"I'll split your head open," Billy promised.

Bo could hardly stay upright. "Why are you doing this to me?"

"Pull the trigger! Now!"

"No!"

"I said shoot, goddamn you! Shoot the fucking gun!"

"No! Please! Stop this, Dad! Stop! Stop! Stop!"

At the sound of Bo's unfettered grief, Billy snapped back to reality, his eyes ablaze but slowly being doused by remorse. His body sat there idling, like some loping engine about to stall.

"*Answer me*," Bo said with tears streaming down his cheek-bones. "*Why are we doing this?*"

Billy drew a shallow, exasperated breath. "Goddamnit, boy. You know *why*." He tucked the Colt back into his waistband. He took the .357 from Bo and placed it on the hood of the

Moon Runner and looked at the boy with a scathing bitterness. "Maybe you need to be reminded."

"No sir. I don't."

"Go to church, son."

"No sir. Please. I don't need reminding."

"The hell you don't, boy." Billy grabbed him by the collar of his filthy *Highway To Hell* t-shirt. "You need to see it again." He shoved the boy away and raised the belt once more. "Take your ass to that church before I really do give you a beating."

Bo turned and floated away, as if he were walking on air, his feet moving faster than the rest of his body. Once he'd put a safe distance between himself and the lash, he looked back at Billy. He saw his father with his head down on the hood of the Moon Runner, covering himself pathetically in shame. But there was no hiding. Bo knew he was crying. The tears always came after the rage, like some biblical flood meant as a punishment, destroying everything in its path, specifically Billy's pride. Bo never understood the man that raised him, and he figured he never would. His father was impenetrable, like the hardpan caliche at his feet. But somehow, that notion of never knowing his father didn't make him feel sad the way it should have. The boy was devoid of those feelings now. Truthfully, he didn't care about feelings at all. Not his or anyone else's. He only cared about surviving and seeing another sunrise. The problem was that Billy never *stopped* feeling, and Bo feared those feelings would be the death of them both. *If it wasn't for Billy Dagger's feelings*, he thought, *we'd be someplace else right now.*

*Someplace safe.*

# TWO

The small adobe church was located just off the dirt path of Cima Road in the Mojave Preserve. It looked like a natural part of the landscape, as if it had grown there over time from the ground up. But it was only a few months old and built by hand, out of desperation and need. The frame and the roofing were made from scrapwood, but the walls were made from packed earth. There were no windows and only one entrance.

Bo opened the two giant cathedral doors that once belonged to a Baptist church in the nearby town of Essex. The adobe shack was flooded with daylight. He stepped carefully onto the scraps of plywood, which were shuffled out in mismatched planks. Then he stopped himself, holding the doors at bay, not wanting to seal himself off from the outside world. He hated this filthy temple. Everything felt wrong to him. The church felt like an unholy lie. There were a few rows of stolen pews inside with stolen bibles tucked into the cubbies on the backside just above the kneeling boards. A large cross made from acacia vine hung on the wall behind a makeshift pulpit. It had been stolen too. Nothing felt honest. Not even the sunlight, which penetrated the cracks in the roof and illuminated the entire church in a holy shade of gold. The light felt more like a ruse than a revelation. He grimaced at the horrible odor. It smelled like death and broken dreams. He stepped forward and the giant cathedral doors slammed shut behind him. The dirt from the roof came snowing down to the scattered wood floor like a nuclear winter. Darkness swarmed inside the church again, which was lit only by the dull streaks of sunlight and the flickering glow of the medic's kerosene lantern. The adobe shack was crowded with warm bodies. A long twisted line of desperate boys, all weary and waiting impatiently for their salvation.

It wasn't God's grace.

It was something far more attainable.

A medic and his young female assistant stood near the pulpit in front of the large cross. They were surrounded by empty boxes and wooden crates and a cart full of medical supplies. They both looked exhausted, like they'd been there for days without a wink of sleep. The medic was a frail man with a weak jawline but a strong tongue and the courage to use it. "Keep a straight line," he commanded. "Everyone will get their turn, but if the line isn't straight and orderly I won't administer the vaccine. You understand?"

A short, chubby boy around nine years old stood at the front of the warbling line. He was waiting for the medic to work his magic, but he looked skeptical at best. The medic swabbed his skin with an alcohol wipe and jabbed a needle into his arm, but the boy still had a doubtful look on his face.

"It's a vaccine," the medic assured him. "Sort of like a cure. You won't get sick after this." He saw that the boy wasn't grasping the concept. "You're safe now, okay? You're gonna survive."

The boy nodded, but he still had a look of disbelief. The

medic's assistant placed a bandage over his needle wound and smiled haggardly. "You're gonna be okay now."

Bo had seen the assistant many times before. She'd been doing this job for weeks now, without fail, and without much rest. Her eyes were twitching severely. They seemed widened by a permanent state of anxiety. Her long, brown hair hadn't been washed or even brushed in weeks, and the blue scrub pants that were once too tight for the extra few pounds she carried were now slipping on her starved hips. She looked like death warmed over. But she was there, and that said everything. She could've volunteered to save her own ass instead and headed for the hills like everyone else, but she stayed. As Billy always said, true adversity weeds out the fake advocates. Everyone talks a big game when the cards are still in their hands, but the real players stay in the fight when the chips are down and all they can do is bluff. The young girl was living proof of that theory.

Bo turned his eyes back on the boys in the warbling line. He recognized a wild desperation in their body language. He'd seen it before in looters and scavengers that he and Billy had met on the road. The boys wouldn't be orderly for much longer. They were covered in filth and wearing threadbare rags that reeked of body odor, urine and shit. Their journey to the church had been long and devastating and the effects were still evident in their hostile demeanor. They'd seen terrible things, no doubt, and maybe even done terrible things to get to where they were. Bo was frightened of them. He could see they were powder kegs of anger just waiting to burst from their mortal barrels. Their fists were tightly balled by their sides and they looked as if they welcomed a fight, or had at least prepared themselves for the possibility of one. None of them spoke. They just stood there in dubious silence, with a brash resilience in their eyes and no desire to make friends.

Then one boy shouted, *"hurry up"*, while another boy asked, *"what the fuck's taking so long?"* Some of them began to push and shove, and the line began to surge.

"Calm down, boys," the medic said, "You're all gonna get the vaccine. I promise you. Please stay calm and orderly." He made eye contact with as many of them as possible. "You're only minutes away from salvation. Do you know what that means? *Salvation?* It means you're all gonna be saved."

The boys stopped pushing and shoving and the line settled again. They stood obediently after that, waiting for their turn. This was their new normal: salvation or death. They were lucky to get the choice. Most didn't.

The Red Death virus had shaken the world earlier that year during the hottest January in recorded history. The first case was reported in Nairobi, Kenya where locals gave it the name *Kifo Nyekundu* on account of the endless bleeding that each victim suffered before death. Patient Zero was a young, healthy woman in her mid-thirties working for a water management company along the river delta. She was found at the water's edge, bleeding profusely from her eyes, ears, nose and mouth. The unknown strain of hemorrhagic fever had killed her in less than 24 hours. The governments of the world responded with the usual obligatory orders: contact tracing and travel bans. 10 days later it was global. Spread from continent to continent. Even in the most remote corners of the world. Soon every scrap of land seemed drenched in blood. Victims bleeding from every orifice of their bodies. Blood droplets from their eyes. A soft trickle of crimson from their noses. A bitter, metallic taste in their mouths. Their ear canals suddenly clogged by pockets of bloody puss. Then came the raging fever and the convulsing and the sudden stoppage of the heart.

The Red Death brought the entire world to a screeching

halt. People crashed to their knees in prayer or rose to their feet in protest, not wanting to endure another senseless fury of mask mandates and stay-at-home orders. Panic ensued, as it always did. The virus raged on, and answers became fewer. The people began to rebel, with violence and social upheaval and demands that went unappeased. Governments felt their grasp slipping as law enforcement and military personnel became part of the daily death toll. Politicians felt lighter in their pockets and less powerful. They could no longer buy their way out of the crosshairs. So the finger-pointing began. Leaders blaming leaders. Nations turning against themselves. Threats of war. Followed by acts. Blood in the streets. Among citizens. Among brothers and sisters. The purest form of anarchy. Nobody was safe. The collapse was complete, and the clock just kept ticking. The last of the world's scientists still couldn't understand how the Red Death was spreading so rapidly across nations, through closed borders and proven quarantine strategies, to the most isolated regions of the world.

Then a team of researchers at the powerful Nimbus Corporation in Phoenix, Arizona discovered a curious thing: the virus wasn't a contagion at all. It wasn't being spread from person to person as they initially thought, and it wasn't novel. It had always been there, lying dormant within every single human body. Just waiting. Probably for ages. A cruel irony of evolution. Scientists always knew that the human body was teeming with thousands of mysterious, unknown bacteria and viruses, most unaccounted for, and none of them sufficiently studied, but they never imagined such a tragic scenario playing out: a simple microbe, seemingly harmless, becoming a killer from within. An ancient ruse, like a Trojan horse attacking and destroying the human body from inside its battered walls. Like the inglorious fall of Troy.

They never saw it coming.

All the Red Death needed was a trigger.

No one understood what triggered it, or why, after such a long spell of dormancy. Scientists speculated that the warming of the climate was what caused the virus to wake up and activate. Others believed it was just God's punishment and didn't need any further explanation. But Billy, and others like him, believed it was mother nature's fail-safe device. An evolutionary function of self-preservation. A button she could push if she ever needed to abort. If human beings ever grew out of control, or began to massacre the planet, or even each other, nature could protect herself by *pulling the trigger*.

And she did.

It wasn't long before the Nimbus Corporation developed a vaccine. In the absence of a working government, their CEO — Lucian Vanderbon — took it upon himself to lead the dying world out of what he called *the new dark ages*. One jab and the virus was eliminated from your body. But it had to be preemptive. Before the bleeding. Once you started bleeding, that was the end for you. Survivors all over the country flocked to the American Southwest in a mass migration that rivaled the Great Exodus. Phoenix became the new Jerusalem. A new Mecca of sorts. But the brutal truth was that there weren't enough vaccines to go around, and time was not on their side. So Lucian Vanderbon, in all his newfound power, decided to *sell* the vaccines instead, and only to the chosen few, with plans to establish a new society of survivors whom he believed were the most adequately prepared to thrive: the wealthy elite. Everyone else was left to die. He offered them nothing but prayers.

Billy Dagger offered them salvation.

"Billy, it's me. Do you copy?" The two-way radio buzzed with a friendly voice on the dashboard of the Moon Runner. "It's Levi. You there, brother?"

Billy and his best friend Levi Scarborough had been tied to the hip for thirty-three years, and racing their customized cars together for more than half that time. Now they were outlaws together, drifting along the edge of life hand in hand.

Billy reached through the open window and grabbed the walkie. "I'm here. Go ahead."

"They're on the move," Levi said. "Westbound. A big rig and a four Humvee escort." His stubborn Texas drawl still lingered from his youth, and every syllable was tangling with his mild inebriation. "They should reach the mark within the hour."

"The vaccines?" Billy asked.

"Got a full load of 'em."

Billy grimaced and spit in the dirt. "Let's go make it right, brother. The midnight dance at high noon."

Levi didn't respond with the usual bravado. There was an awkward silence instead.

Billy could hear the hint of heavy breathing. "Levi? Goddamnit, you hear me?"

Then Levi declared, "I'm with you, brother. Guns a' blazin."

"Uh huh," Billy huffed. "Just get your ass here."

"I've got it to the floorboard. I'll be there before you can roll those pretty blue eyes."

"I won't hold my breath," Billy said.

He ended the transmission. His emotions were still revved up and running through his heart like a street-racing phantom. He wiped the nagging wetness from his eyes and stared into the white heat, squinting in a sort of distant agony, as if he were searching for the impossible: a return to another place in time. His mind was still on the boy. Billy missed the life they'd had together. He wanted to be a doting father again. He didn't like what he'd become. Before the world went dark, he would've never raised a belt at Bo or screamed at him with such irrevocable rage. He certainly would've never put a gun to his head and threatened to kill him. It broke Billy's heart to hurt the boy like that. He hated to be so brutal, but he had to be the grindstone to Bo's dull blade. He had to be a reckoner. Not just for the boy, but for the thousands of desperate people who were depending on him for their survival.

# THREE

When the Nimbus Corporation set up their vaccine distribution zones, they made sure to set them up in the most remote locations possible, to keep desperate and dangerous people away from their border in Phoenix, Arizona, which was now secured by a 500-square-mile mix of shipping container walls and chain-linked fencing, with thousands of armed mercenaries standing guard. They chose the surrounding deserts, where people without means would struggle to reach. The burning Sonoran. The bleak Mojave. Unforgiving lands that were scorched by the sun. A nefarious strategy. The people who came to the distribution zones without authorization were often armed and dangerous and desperate for a vaccine they knew they'd never get otherwise. So it was crucial to limit their numbers. In order to reach such remote locations, they had to know how to survive the desert on foot, which was the most common means of travel after the Collapse. They flocked to the deserts like birds with broken wings. Most of them died before they were halfway there.

But Billy figured out another way. He'd always had a mind

to fix things, be it carburetors or shocks or failing transmissions. Anything broken on a car, he could make it work again, and if he couldn't fix it with his own two hands, he always knew someone that could. He used to have a metal sign hanging above the office door in his auto shop that stated the obvious to his mechanics: *FIX THE BROKEN PARTS AND THE ENGINE KEEPS RUNNING.*

The first time that he and his crew hijacked a Nimbus rig full of vaccines on the highway, it wasn't for a higher purpose. Billy just needed the jab for himself and his only son. He and his crew were only there to save their own. They weren't trying to be heroes. But once Billy had thousands of vaccines at his disposal, he began to think of all those unknown faces who would die an unspeakable death without them. Mothers and fathers and sons and daughters, all desperate to survive. With that one stolen shipment he could save fifty-thousand souls. He'd never had much use for God, but he suddenly felt chosen, as if he'd been called upon, and that was all it took to sink the hook into his thrill-seeking heart. He recruited more "Road Pirates" and soon they were hijacking Nimbus rigs all across Arizona and the deserts of California.

Before his forty-eighth birthday, Billy Dagger and his crew had saved over half a million lives. He'd become a living legend. A modern day folk hero. But to the wealthy elite that he was stealing from, he wasn't a hero at all. To them, he was a terrorist. A murderous thief stealing their only salvation. The survival they'd bought and paid for. Their families would die now instead. Billy never stopped to justify that. He simply picked a side and fought for them. He chose the side that couldn't fight for themselves. Those poor unfortunate souls without the financial means to procure a vaccine with what he considered to be *blood money*. The way Billy saw it, if there was going to be blood regardless, he preferred there was no money involved. It felt more honest. Suddenly, he was public enemy number one, and for the first time in his life, he had true enemies. He was doing God's work in a time when all others had abandoned their gods and their principles. They weren't willing to fight the good fight as their faith had promised. They just walked into the swirling black hole with open arms and bowed to the beast, and they became the chaos. But Billy never bowed to anyone. So when the world fell apart, he gathered his wits and grabbed a gun and he did what he'd always done: he tried to fix what was broken.

---

"Alright boys," Billy said. "Let's dance." He tossed the walkie onto the dashboard and slid into the Moon Runner and cranked the engine. He shifted straight into second gear. He never bothered with first. The man never eased into anything. He gripped the shifter like some holy amulet. It was custom designed with a real dagger and made to look like the blade had been stabbed into the console. A clever touch that he'd always been proud of. The blade was a cherished heirloom from the 1800's, originally given to his great ancestor, Bartholomew Dagger, as a gift of good will by a war chief of the Cherokee Wolf Clan, who himself had taken the blade from a French captain that he'd killed in a bloody skirmish on the Virginia frontier. Or so the story was told. The blade had become a sort of family crest over the years, handed down through seven generations of Dagger men. Billy always wanted to honor their legacy with his own, and now that he had the chance to do so he wasn't turning back.

He hit the gas and the Moon Runner spun donuts in the dirt. The rims sparkled in the sun, each one ornamented with chrome-plated crossed daggers spinning in the center. Another clever touch that always made him proud. There was no mistaking the Moon Runner, and no mistaking the man behind the wheel. Like Billy himself, the truck was a true original. Not some lame, unimaginative factory restore. His creation was a beautiful Frankenstein of a truck. He'd plucked the steering wheel from an old '53 Skylark convertible that he'd won in a midnight street race in Tucson. The dashboard wasn't factory either. It was a custom-fit panel from a '63 Mercury that he'd bought for $500 on the street. The glovebox was salvaged from a totaled Marauder that he'd found wasting away in the back of Tilly's scrapyard, and the gauges on the dash were digital and rated for speeds in excess of 150 mph, which Billy had superseded on one very reckless occasion. The bench seat was taken from a '56 Buick and re-upholstered with a mix of arctic white vinyl, tweed and dark carbon fiber. It was once immaculate, but now it was punctured with bullet holes and stained with Billy's blood. The 4-point racing belts were originally installed for those dangerous nights at the drag strip on the outskirts of Kingman, though the harnesses were proving better suited to the neck-breaking whiplash of the outlaw life that he was currently living. The truck seemed almost sentient at times, her headlights shining with some bright, supernatural purpose. They were factory replicas that seemed to be impervious to bullets. The side mirrors, however, had been shot to pieces and replaced with a pair of '57 Bel Airs. The taillights had been shot out too, and of course Billy took pride in that fact, claiming it was because his enemies were always a step behind, with no choice but to shoot at his six. He replaced the busted tails with a pair of frenched beams that were taken from a '61 Oldsmobile and welded into the housing. So far they were proving impervious too. Billy kept a classic look to the truck, with no dropping or bagging, but he gave her a slightly raked stance with 20-inch wheels in the front and 22's in the back, which made her lean forward with intent, like something eager to charge. One could almost imagine her digging her hooves into the ground and snorting like some wild beast of antiquity. Billy revved the engine. The Moon Runner howled, and he howled with her. It was his way of announcing their presence to the world.

Inside of the church, Bo noticed that one of the boys in line was already bleeding from his tear ducts. The poor boy hadn't even noticed yet. Bo felt compelled to tell him, but the words died in his throat, as they often did when the moment was too big for him. Instead, he just watched in silence, imagining how broken the boy would be when he finally discovered his irreversible fate. Sure enough, the boy wiped his eyes and saw the blood on the tips of his fingers and began to panic.

The other boys noticed. One of them shouted, "Oh fuck! He's bleeding! Jesus Christ! He's bleeding from his eyes!" The line suddenly formed a crater. Everyone moved away from the boy and circled around him, keeping their distance as if he could somehow infect them. The medic stepped into the circle to protect the boy from any malice, with his arms spread out wide like a cowboy trying to corral a herd of rambunctious cattle. "That's enough of that," he said. "This isn't catchy, guys. We know that."

Then one of the older boys said, "He's gonna die. It's too late. Don't waste the jab on him." He was around fifteen years old and already matured beyond his years, with muscular curves and obvious street smarts. His eyes were burning with combativeness. "Think about the rest of us." he scowled. "We should get first dibs."

The medic didn't immediately respond. He stood there lost

for words. He obviously knew the truth. Everyone knew the way it worked. Once you started bleeding, there was no way of stopping the inevitable. "We don't know that for certain," he said with a false certainty in his eyes. "This boy deserves a chance. Like the rest of you."

"No he doesn't," the combative older boy said. "It's a waste. We're all healthy. We should get the jab first."

The other boys agreed and erupted with shouts of protest.

"Knock it off," the medic said.

"He's already dead!" the older boy declared. "Send him to the back of the line!"

"Enough!" the medic ordered. "You're not making the rules here. I am." He eyed the combative older boy with a shaky authority. "This boy deserves a chance, and he'll get it. Just like everyone else. Is that understood?" He motioned for the infected boy to walk towards him. "Come here, little man."

The infected boy stepped forward with a look of pure dread on his face, his bloody eyes scrutinizing the other boys carefully, especially the combative older boy with the big mouth and the violent glare.

"This is bullshit!" the older boy shouted. "Any of us could start bleeding while you're fucking around with him! He's already dead!"

"No," the medic said. "That's not how it works. Don't believe all the talk you're hearing out there."

"We don't believe *you*!"

"Then why trust what I'm jabbing into your arm? Do you even know what's in these vials? It could be anything."

The older boy stopped protesting and began to think. So did everyone else.

"You trust me enough to jab you with this stuff," the medic said, "but not enough to tell you the truth?" He let his words resonate. The boys looked at each other, seeming to accept the infallible logic. "Now," the medic said, "can I get on with it?"

The combative older boy didn't protest any further. So neither did anyone else.

"Good," the medic said. "Now get back in line."

They slowly reformed the line, while keeping their eyes on the medic. As they organized themselves, some of the boys began to argue over their place in the pecking order. A few of them began to push and shove. The combative older boy raised a fist. "I'll crack your fucking skull!"

"Hey!" the medic shouted. "Enough! Everyone back in the same place you were in before. No cutting in line."

The older boy didn't throw a punch, but he didn't lower his fist either.

"If things get out of order," the medic said, "I'll kick you out and you'll be having words with Billy Dagger himself." He eyed the older boy in particular. "He won't tolerate disorder."

The boy lowered his fist and quietly gulped, not looking so combative anymore. He and the other boys knew enough about Billy Dagger to abide by his law.

The infected boy with the bloody eyes stepped forward.

"Don't listen to them," the medic said to him. "You have just as much chance of surviving as they do. And it's a strong chance. Okay?"

The boy nodded. The medic jabbed the needle into his arm and sanitized the puncture wound with an alcohol wipe. The boy quietly thanked him and moved to the back row of pews and sat down and stared at the cross on the wall with a look of sheer relief on his face.

Bo felt a gnawing sense of guilt as he watched. He wanted to tell the boy the truth. The medic was lying to him. The boy was going to die, with or without the vaccine. Bo thought it fitting that the medic lied at the pulpit of Billy's fraudulent church. Everything about the unholy shack was a lie. The place was no holier than the shop that Billy had built cars in. It was just a temple built to worship his own ego.

But Billy saw it differently. He saw the church as a temple of justice. A reckoning in God's honor. So to honor the Good Lord, he had christened the church *God's Alamo* and placed members of his crew on 24-hour surveillance, watching over the stolen vaccines and the two medics who had volunteered to help administer the drug. The church wasn't hard to find if you knew where to look, but it was in the middle of nowhere, located just off the old dirt path near Cima Dome, built next to an old cross memorial that had been hammered into place in 1969 and frequently removed and vandalized by protestors almost every year since. An ongoing political battle for the right to honor veterans and God on public land. Naturally, Billy was drawn to such a contested area, being a man who liked trouble, and feeling himself firmly planted on God's side now. So he staked his own claim in the fight. *"What better place to build God's Alamo?"* he'd once said. *"This may be his final stand."*

Bo watched carefully as the next boy in line walked to the fraudulent pulpit where the medic had told his big black lie. The boy was scrawny and sad-looking, and he seemed to be stripped of anything resembling life. Bo figured he was no older than thirteen. Maybe even younger. There was a wooden cross hanging around his neck on a thin braided rope. He was clutching the crucifix in his hand while saying a prayer under his breath.

Bo thought the prayer was a hopeless endeavor. God wouldn't answer the call.

The praying boy looked like he'd just been risen from the dead and was wanting to return. His hair was sprouting wildly and the strands were matted by a disgusting mix of sweat and dried blood. His face was a purplish hew and the meaty parts were pulp and appeared to be healing from a previous beating. Bo thought he looked broken beyond repair. *Not everything can be fixed*, he thought, despite what his father had always believed. *Some things, when broken, are broken forever.*

The Medic rubbed the praying boy's arm. "What's your name?"

The praying boy wouldn't say.

"I saw you with a woman yesterday. Was that your mom?"

The praying boy nodded, but he still wouldn't speak.

"Where is she?"

The praying boy pointed to a row of fresh corpses stacked in the corner of the church. They were haphazardly covered in plastic and the stench was beginning to seep through the cheap cellophane wrap.

The medic cringed. "I'm so sorry." He composed himself and took the last vaccine from a plastic container on the medical cart next to him. He looked at the remaining boys who had not received their vaccine. At least a dozen of them, waiting for their only salvation, and not looking too convinced. The medic gestured to his assistant. "More vaccines."

She took quick inventory of the supply, which was strewn across the floor in wooden crates, and turned back immediately with helpless eyes. "That was the last box."

The medic tried not to panic. He casually turned to Bo and whispered, "Go tell your father we've run out." Then he said with obvious trepidation, "Hurry."

Bo didn't budge though. He was transfixed by the rising tension in the church, watching the boys trade desperate looks as they realized that only one of them would be getting the last vaccine. Despite the legendary Billy Dagger and his heroic exploits, none of them knew if they'd see another shipment again or not, and they weren't willing to wait their turn any longer. Bo felt stuck, his fear like a mudflow forming around his feet. The praying boy looked at him, and he looked back, and they locked eyes as if they were one and the same. The praying boy clutched the wooden cross tightly. Bo was clutched by his own cowardice. A lifetime seemed to pass by in seconds.

Then the desperate boys trampled across the church in a raging horde and knocked the praying boy aside as they stormed the medic and bashed him in the head with sharp weapons made from rocks, splitting his skull right down the middle of his forehead. Bo's eyes leapt from their sockets, but his body was perfectly still. The young nurse cowered down in the corner of the church and screamed.

Outside, Billy drove up to the church in the Moon Runner and blew the horn, shouting, "Bo, let's go!" The Nimbus convoy was on the move, and timing would be key to their success. He blew the horn again. "Goddamnit, Bo. Now! Move your ass!"

But Bo couldn't hear the horn from inside, nor his father's frantic orders. The other boys were making such a violent ruckus that it drowned everything out, including Bo's own terrified thoughts. He just stood there mired in place as the boys growled and shrieked and fought one another tooth and claw for the last syringe. It dropped to the splintered wood floor. The praying boy pushed his way past bloody punches and kicks and reached for the liquid salvation, but the boys pummeled him and pulled him back into the fray. The wooden cross hanging from the braided rope around his neck was ripped away. It hit the floor and slid towards Bo's feet. Bo snatched it up and squeezed the cross to his chest in hopes that it would bring a miracle. One that he couldn't provide himself. The praying boy reached again for the last syringe. His fingertips barely scraped the glass vial as the other boys pounded him with their swollen knuckles and brutal kicks. They piled on top of him and gnawed at his back with their scuzzy teeth and clawed at his flesh with their sharp, untrimmed nails. The praying boy looked at Bo and pleaded. "Help me! Please!"

Bo reached for the handle of the .22 that was tucked into his waistband at the small of his back, but as the instinct to draw the gun and fire turned to pure contemplation, he froze again, caught in the gravity of his own fear. He just stood there helplessly, watching as the praying boy was beaten to a pulp. The distinctive thud of bone clacking hard against bare skin echoed throughout the church, silencing any last-minute thoughts that Bo had of intervening. He stood there feeling worthless of the Dagger name. His cowardice rumbled in his gut like rotten milk. He couldn't bear the feeling any longer. The gravity of fear pressing down on him. The unrelenting heat that never seemed to stop cooking his brain. The constant thump of savagery. The desperate pleading from the praying boy, who was still wailing, *"Help me! Please! Help!"* It all caused the contents of Bo's stomach to rise into his throat. He turned and ran and burst through the double doors, and the bright sun hit his eyes like a blinding light from a God that was trying to speak to him. But he wasn't one to listen to voices that weren't his own. He could still hear the praying boy wailing, *"Help me! Please! Help!"* He covered his ears, but he knew those words would linger in his mind long after the moment had passed. He knew the boy would be beaten to death on the floor of that unholy shack. God sure wouldn't intervene. The boy's prayers would never be answered. Bo looked at the wooden cross in his hand. It meant nothing. He dropped it in the dirt. It lay there unmistakably worthless.

Then the Moon Runner's beastly engine growled and the horn blasted and Billy yelled out from behind the wheel, "We're making another run. Let's fucking go!"

Bo ran to the truck, leaving the wooden cross in the dirt, discarded and forgotten, like the poor boy inside the church.

The Moon Runner pulled away.

Bo turned to Billy and protested with big watery eyes. "Dad, why can't we just leave?"

"You know why, son."

"Dad, *please*. We can still live. We can live like we used to. A normal life."

"*A normal life?*"

"Yes. Father and son. You and me."

"You think so? Barbecues and street races?"

Bo could see Billy's disdain for the idea, but he didn't let it diminish his hope. "We already got the jab. Why can't we just leave?"

Billy was silent, refusing to indulge the boy's fantasies.

"Come on, Dad. *Please*. We could go someplace safe."

"There ain't no place safe, son."

"We don't owe these people anything."

Billy slammed his hands down on the steering wheel and growled, "Goddamnit, Bo, what have I told you? It ain't about what you owe, son."

Bo withdrew and went cold. He'd heard this tired old sermon so many times it was etched into his brain for eternity, like the ancient petroglyphs of Renegade Canyon. *It ain't about what you owe, son. It's about what you can do. And you better be damn sure you can do what's necessary when the time comes to do it.* The words made Bo cringe and tighten his fist every time he heard them.

"We ain't gonna run and hide," Billy said with an ironclad

resolve. "We can't let the Nimbus Corporation decide who lives and who dies. What good are we if we do?"

Bo didn't say a word. He just did the usual. He folded his arms and watched out the window as the desert streaked by in a sunlit blur. The colorless monotony of burnt earth.

"Someday you'll understand," Billy said.

But Bo never did, and he figured he never would. He looked back at the church and stared at the giant cathedral doors as they shrunk in the distance, hoping to see the praying boy alive and defying the odds that seemed to be willfully stacked against him. But those were just the fantasies of a naive child, and Bo knew that all too well. Good things never happened to good people. Not in his experience. He knew the praying boy would die at the hands of those vicious older boys, and he knew it was all his fault. He didn't have the guts to pull the .22 and stop them when he had the chance. Now he'd have to bear the guilt of that, and acknowledging his own cowardice scared him even more than dying. As they drove away, he kept his gaze on the doors, his eyes sparked by some stubborn hopefulness that he always failed to extinguish.

But no one came out of the church alive.

Not a soul.

# FOUR

It all began with a friendship. A friendship that felt inescapable, as if it were mandated by the universe. *Billy* and *Levi*. A proud Dagger son and a bastardized Scarborough. They'd been inseparable since their days racing through teenage wasteland. Billy in his grandfather's old '63 Chevy, and Levi on his steel horse with the bad ticker that just needed a $1200 engine transplant. One man's story couldn't be told without the other. Billy always said they were opposite sides of the same lucky coin, and some unlucky god would eventually have to call heads or tails.

They met when they were freshmen in high school in the fall of 2016. Levi had just moved to Billy's hometown of Kingman, Arizona from the Texas Hill Country with his mom and his new stepfather. The two boys were an unlikely pairing back then. Billy was only fifteen, but he was already big for his age, and graced with the confidence of a devil, and he was already stealing virginities every Saturday night from a different girl or two. Levi, on the other hand, was slight of frame and socially awkward, but not shy in the least, and his boisterous personality and bold talk only invited the wrong kind of trouble. He was an unusual kid for sure, which made him the usual target for bullies. Billy had seen him come to class with bruises and black eyes and a limp from getting kicked in the balls so hard that he puked on himself, or so the Kingman High gossipers said. So one day Billy followed him home from school out of curiosity, and when the bullies appeared on Benton Street with their knuckles scabbed over and their big mouths spewing threats, Billy came out of nowhere and balled up his fists and went to work on them. The fight was long and glorious and bloody as hell, but the bullies got the worst of it. All Billy had was two broken knuckles and a black eye. The bullies had bruised egos and hospital bills, and none of them could walk straight for a week. Billy wanted to make sure they never kicked anyone in the babymakers again. That was how he was wired. He had principles that he'd learned mostly from his outlaw grandfather, who taught him that a Dagger man never pulls off that road once he's on it. So Billy never did. He spent a week in juvie, then the judge threw out the case.

And that's how Billy Dagger and Levi Scarborough officially met. A story as old as time. One boy sticking up for another. The two became fast friends after that, and Levi never stopped looking at Billy as if he were his own personal Jesus. They spent the rest of high school tied at the hip, learning the ropes, chasing girls, getting wasted, raising all kinds of hell and doing what they both loved to do most: fixing up cars and motorcycles and racing them on the weekends. They kept themselves busy working at Blake's auto shop, banging out custom rides during the week and banging potential prom queens in the backseat by week's end, unbeknownst to the car's owners of course. They worked to live in those days, not the other way around. And live they did. A dozen lifetimes before they were old enough to get legally shit-faced. Not that the law ever stopped them. While other boys were living their best lives through a pair of VR goggles — far too frightened to take part in the real world — Billy and Levi were making their fantasies a reality, and seizing every glorious minute of it. That's when Billy adopted the old Glenwood Green '63 Chevy from the man who'd helped raise him: his outlaw grandfather, Arlen Dagger. The Moon Runner began its life in Billy's hands as a backyard-engineered muscle truck with a rusted patina frame, a cracked windshield, ripped seating, and a V-8 engine on nitrous. She wasn't much to look at in those days, but the noise she made when she was launching down the road was like music to the ears of gearheads everywhere, and she only got louder with age and years of Billy's mechanical influence.

A decade later, he and Levi were scorching the blacktop all over the Southwest. The Moon Runner was a beautiful, heart-breaking street racer and Billy was breaking hearts behind the wheel, notching his belt in more ways than one. She was all he ever wanted — that truck — and all he ever needed. He couldn't imagine anything more thrilling than that beautiful '63 Chevy.

Then he met Amelia, and everything changed.

She was dirty blonde and dirty in bed, but she had dignity and genuine class, and Billy had never been with a girl that could balance all of those sins and virtues at once. He thought he'd found a walking anomaly, and boy did he love to watch her walk. He would've married her on the spot if he'd had the money for a ring. But he'd never worked that hard in his life. Six months later, he scrambled up a little street cash and slid one on her finger after she said *"why not"* to his *"will you be a Dagger?"* For ten years they rambled and romanced as Billy built cars for Ryland Blake and raced the underground circuit. Levi was the third wheel on the road, all too happy to tag along. But Amelia grew up, unlike the boys, and she grew tired of the life. She wanted something more. A family. A future that wasn't built on street cash. Billy wanted to carry on the Dagger name, so he obliged.

Early in '39, a year after their son Bo was born, Billy finally saved enough capital to branch out on his own. He left Blake's and started his own auto shop: *Dagger & Son Kustoms*. He hired Levi to be his main mechanic and his rebuild specialist, and in a short time their custom builds became a cult sensation. The pride of Kingman, as the local media had put it. Business was suddenly booming. They had capital, and gains to boot. Amelia quit her day job as a bank teller, and they opened a bed and breakfast next to the shop, where she ran the daily operations. *The Old 66*, as they called it, was built next to the Dagger & Son shop on their 5-acre plot of land between Kingman and the Hackberry General Store on Historic Route 66. All it took was a little elbow grease and some bank loans and they were in business. It was open 24 hours a day with a staff of ten, including cooks and house keeping. The building was a two-story wood frame home with a tin roof, twelve available rooms, a shaded courtyard with a wading pool, and a small cottage where Billy and his family lived on-site. They decorated the place with an obnoxious, mid-century modern style from the 1960s that would've made Elvis himself cringe. A neon sign towered above the dusty parking lot announcing *The Old 66* in bright, flickering red light. There were cool rock 'n roll vibes throughout the joint, a retro 1950s-style cafe with a working jukebox, and a shameless amount of automotive memorabilia cluttering up the lobby walls. There was even a wooden barrel of novelty flags for sale, with the skull and crossed daggers on a stick. They sold for $8.99. The place itself was a painful cliche, and Billy wasn't a fan of that, but it became a landmark on the Mother Road, so the money was good and his wife was happy. He used both of those profits to his advantage. To finance and pursue his true passion: the Moon Runner. The girl that got away. He still desired her. More than anything. The blacktop drag strip was always calling. He wanted nothing more than to blaze his own trail on the street racing circuit and leave a legacy in his wake. To honor the Dagger name. To make the ghosts of Dagger men rise from the grave and holler with pride. Six generations of them. They'd been soldiers, bank robbers, bare-knuckle fighters, moonshiners and stock car racers. They'd all scorched the Earth in some way. This was Billy's way of continuing the legacy. Life was good. For a time.

Then Billy got antsy.

He'd always been jumpy in the quiet life. He preferred to make noise, and plenty of it. So he put his shop in the hands of his best mechanics and began touring the country on the street-racing circuit at least a dozen times throughout the year, earning loads of cash on the drag strip, but blowing it on more fixer-uppers and car parts, not to mention the booze and the drugs and the women. Levi followed him into the fray with his hair on fire, like an unholy disciple that took everything Billy did as gospel. He loved the nomadic life, running with Billy on the street circuit. He loved roaming the country with that gypsy soul of his, wandering without direction, moving from place to place, causing trouble with MCs and outlaws, getting drunk and high, telling stories that were only half true, and womanizing like a horny demon. The two of them together were more trouble than most places could handle. So they kept moving from one place to the next, leaving the mark of Billy's legacy in their wake. The Dagger name was suddenly known from coast to coast. His reputation was growing, and so was his head. That's when the bad Billy rose to the surface. The arrogant, impulsive, reckless Dagger man that had to prove himself to anyone and everyone and walk on the edge of everything.

He pushed the envelope to the point where the envelope was empty, and then he came back home with nothing to show for it but his swelling pride. That didn't exactly work wonders for his marriage. Things were getting dicey at home. Money was tight and business was getting slower. The kids were constantly sick from school germs and the bills were piling up. Meanwhile, Billy was blowing whatever street money he earned on car builds and races. He and Amelia had a second child in those days. A beautiful little girl named Shelby, named after the old car company and the race car driver who founded it.

It was 2047.

Shelby was three years old. Bo was nine. Billy never forgot that year. It was the last good one before the Collapse. That summer the economy took a steep nosedive, the markets crashed and inflation soared out of the goddamn stratosphere. Billy was suddenly struggling to keep the red neon sign above the Old 66 lit up and flickering. Then the bottom fell out. He always said if that ever happened the bed and breakfast would go before the shop, and in late February of '48 he had to pull the plug on Amelia's dream to keep his own alive. The end of an era. That's when Billy began to feel the Big Crunch, as he always called it. The pressure. It was beginning to mount. For everyone.

# FIVE

The Moon Runner launched down the Mother Road like a spaceship fleeing a dying planet. 93 mph on the digital speedometer. A steady blur of darkness in the clear brilliance of high noon. Billy smacked Bo in the shoulder to get the boy's wandering attention. "Load the grenade gun. *Close range.*"

Bo reached into Billy's war bag on the floorboard and grabbed a 40mm grenade cartridge. The words *Close Range IED* were crudely written on the casing in black permanent marker.

Billy could see the boy was sulking again, lost in a mind that could never see beyond the worst-case scenario "What'd your mom always say?" he asked the boy.

Bo wouldn't answer.

Billy smiled, unconvincingly. *"Ride or die, son."* He drifted on a thought, and he seemed dismantled by it. "She would've been with us to the end."

Bo just looked away and slid the grenade into the rusted M79's barrel and snapped it shut as if it was something he'd done a hundred times. "Mom would've taken me someplace safe," he said.

The words were meant to cut, and they did, slicing through Billy's heart and bludgeoning him somewhere deep inside where he'd been hiding a dark secret from the boy all this time. A secret he'd kept since Amelia had passed. He turned his eyes on the road ahead, but his thoughts veered off into the deadly wasteland of his mind, thinking about the boy's mother and how she really died. It wasn't the Red Death that had taken her. It was her own hand. Bo never knew. Billy promised himself that he'd never tell. For good reason. Amelia was always the one that Bo ran to when he was afraid. Billy never made the boy feel safe the way his mother did. He never even tried. *To be safe was to live in fear*. That was Billy's misguided logic.

Bo hated that side of his father. The arrogant and fearless side. Billy was always the type to go first. He'd offer himself up like a social service. *I'll do it*, he would often say, just about the time that everyone else was taking a subtle step backwards in apprehension. That's just how he approached life. That's why they were heading south *towards* the fight and not *away* from it. Bo just wanted to run in the other direction. He knew that someday his father's winning streak would come to an end, and every day he believed it would be *that* day. He feared the blaze of glory. The old fortune teller in Kingman said it was fated, so Bo figured they were just racing to a red light.

"When this thing is over," Billy said with a simulated grin, "maybe we can race the boys down Cima Road again. Put another notch on my belt."

"Maybe," Bo muttered.

"What's wrong, boy? You worried your old man's gonna lose?"

"On the drag strip? No."

Billy was silent.

Bo looked through the window and his eyes wandered off as he woefully claimed, "You know we're gonna die."

Billy turned his blue eyes on him. "What'd you just say?"

"I said *we're gonna die.*"

"Why would you say that?"

"Because it's true."

Billy searched for a way out of the conversation and finally said dismissively, "Well, son, everybody dies, don't they? Not exactly a revelation."

"But we're gonna die *soon*," Bo said. "Maybe even today."

Billy's blue eyes flickered like a bad bulb. "Don't you say that. I don't wanna hear you say that again. You understand me?"

"But that fortune teller in Kingman said—"

"Bullshit. That old woman was crazy."

"That's not what you said before."

"It was all lies, son. She just needed money. Probably for drugs. So she gave me a line of bullshit. Something she knew a street racer would want to hear."

"Why would you wanna hear something like that?"

"Because..." Billy hesitated, reluctant to admit his own foolishness. "Dagger men walk on the edge of everything. That's just the way it is. It's a..." He wouldn't elaborate.

"It's a *what?*"

Billy was silent.

"It's *what*, Dad?"

Billy didn't say another word. He just sat there driving down the highway, navigating the canyons, and navigating the sharp curves of his own conscience. He was sick and tired of living like a nomad on wheels, skipping baths and meals, and barely surviving on jackrabbit and canned food. Most of all, he was tired of trying to outrun his own fate. He could feel it catching up to him, with its cold breath on his neck, turning his hot skin to shivering gooseflesh. The blaze of glory was coming. The blind fortune teller in Kingman never told him *when* it would come, just *how*, and he always believed that he could choose the *when* for himself. But Bo's cutting words had carved doubt into his soul, and now he was spooked. Billy was always the eternal optimist, but he wasn't a fool. He knew the only thing a man ever got from making his own plans was a hearty laugh from God. "We're not gonna die," he finally said with little conviction, as if he were defying his own beliefs.

Bo didn't respond. His father always said the same things. They both fell silent as the grave, and the hush was more deafening than the Moon Runner's grumbling engine.

Billy stared ahead at the road. He couldn't muster a single comforting word. He loved the boy. More than anything in the world. The boy was his light. He just didn't know how to make him shine anymore.

Bo turned away and watched the desert flash by like moments of the past, and something in the cold silence between them stirred up his unwanted memories. He thought of that ruinous day in the desert. The day it all began to end.

It was back in April of that year. They'd gone in search of the vaccine. He could vaguely remember the trek through the Mojave on foot. The Moon Runner hidden in a faraway mineshaft that was cut into a canyon wall. His father leading him by the hand across the scorched earth. His mother and his sister trailing behind, both exhausted by the sun. He could still feel the oppressive heat. The dried sweat on his skin. The raw nerves of fear blasting through his veins. The foul scent of desperation and days without bathing. Their clothes were wet, stinking rags and their stomachs were swollen. They hadn't eaten since the morning before. The hunger pangs in his belly were sharp and brutal. His little sister was crying of thirst. It bothered him that he couldn't help her. When they saw the distribution zone in the distance, it was shimmering in the desert like a mirage, and they feared it would disappear when they finally reached it, like some cruel trick of the devil. He could remember the Nimbus trucks and the armed military personnel on guard. Wealthy citizens waiting in long, protected lines inside the gates. The endless crowds of desperate souls outside pulling angrily on the barbed-wire fence. His father fighting through the mob and disappearing behind the swell of human bodies. The military personnel had their fingers resting nervously on the triggers of their rifles. The wealthy families were receiving the jab, their faces broad with relief, cashing in on the deal they'd made for their own survival. The people outside looked so hopeless. Some were lost in prayer to their chosen god. Some were pleading to Nimbus for mercy. Others had already accepted their fate. They knew that without the vaccine they were going to die. Bo knew it too. Their voices had gone unheard that day, as if they were already dead. He could still see the chaos unfolding in his mind, as if it were happening all over again. The Nimbus rigs firing up their engines. Humvees with .50-caliber machine guns thundering to life. Nimbus security guards screaming for people to back away from the gate. He could still feel the rising anger on both sides. The sway of the crowd pushing him like the over-whelming tides of the ocean. The feeling of drowning in the middle of them. He saw the terror on his mother's face as he looked to her for comfort. He was hoping for his father to rescue them, but he couldn't spot Billy in the crowd. All he could see were strangers closing in around him, nearly tram-pling him to death in a panic. He smelled their filth and felt their sweaty bodies brushing on his skin. He heard his sister screaming madly from somewhere nearby. He felt like he was going mad too. Then the gates opened and the Humvees barreled out in a fury, crushing people beneath the tires like boots crushing a swarm of cockroaches. He could still hear the horrifying cries of women and children. The frantic rage of men. The sound of bones being crushed beneath the weight. The angry mob of people storming the gate like a rogue wave, desperate and armed and lashing out. The startling pop of gunfire, crackling around him like fireworks. The crowd began to surge. Large bodies crashing into his, knocking him aside and underfoot. He cried out for his father, but he still couldn't find him. The thunderous .50-caliber machine guns erupted so loudly he had to cover his ears. Such a godawful noise. Like mechanical banshees. Almost deafening. His ears felt like they were bleeding. But he could still hear the madness. The unthinkable devastation. Nimbus bullets ripped through the crowd, thrashing random people, as if they were stuffed piñatas at a child's birthday party. Their clothes turned red. Their eyes were suddenly frozen in their skulls. Bo closed his own eyes, trying to blind himself to it all. Then he heard his mother scream. A blood-curdling wail that he could never get out of his mind, like the wailings of the damned in Hell. Something grim and eternal. He turned and saw her on her knees, holding a lifeless body in her arms. His sister Shelby was covered in blood. She'd been massacred by corporate bullets. Her eyes were already closed, like a locked door that could never be opened again. Bo's body went cold. He saw his father running towards them through the crowd. Billy's eyes were bulging from their sockets in unspeakable agony. He looked as if he might collapse and die himself. Bo felt a seismic shift in the universe. He watched as Billy fell to his knees, holding Shelby's head, sobbing in a way that men never do. Bo never forgot that look in his father's eyes. The man was broken, obliterated, like a watch that had suddenly stopped ticking.

"Goddamnit, Bo! You hearing me?"

Bo snapped out of the unwanted memory. The Moon Runner was rolling at 86 mph down the Mother Road.

"Weapons check," Billy ordered.

Bo looked ahead and saw they were almost at the ambush site. *That was fast*, he thought. *Too fast.*

"Damnit, Bo, check the weapons!"

Bo grabbed the war bag and began pulling the weapons from inside, making sure they were loaded, primed and sharpened. It was the usual drill. He'd done it so many times it was second nature to him. He never understood why Billy made him go through the motions. The man had already checked every single weapon himself at least a half dozen times that morning.

"Make sure everything's in order," Billy said. "Guns loaded. Safeties off. One in each chamber. I don't wanna die from negligence."

Bo missed the old Billy Dagger. The man that flew by the seat of his pants and didn't harp on the details. Gone were the carefree days of weekend races and drinking a beer with his dad when his mom wasn't looking. Gone were the Sunday morning breakfasts at the Early Bird where he and Billy liked to sit together with a fresh pot of coffee and dream out loud. Gone were the late nights working together in the shop, his father teaching him how to repair engines and polish sheet metal.

"Organize all the explosives too," Billy said. "I don't want you grabbing the wrong one in the heat of battle. One mistake could mean the end of us."

Bo didn't bother with the details. His mind was stuck on something else. The burial. Laying his mother and sister to rest in some random hole in the desert. Throwing dirt over their bodies and watching them slowly disappear beneath the earth, each grain of dirt erasing them from his life forever. He felt like he was still standing there sobbing next to that pathetic mound of dirt in the ground with no markings or crosses to memorialize them. The emptiness in his gut still lingered. He always wondered why his father never shed a tear that day when they laid their bodies to rest. Even Levi had cried himself silly. Billy just stood there at the grave looking unhinged and devoid of anything meaningful. A stone silence that Bo would have to carefully chip away at for months to come. There seemed to be some terrible purpose corrupting Billy's mind ever since. *That was the beginning of the end*, Bo thought. *That was the day that Billy Dagger stopped being a father.*

"This is it," Billy said. "This is where we make our stand."

He hit the brakes and brought the Moon Runner to a screeching halt, straddling the faded yellow line on the center of the highway. He turned to Bo and uttered the dreaded words, "Go raise the flag, son. Raise 'em both."

Bo felt a sudden fear take hold of his limbs. His will was practically immovable. His throat felt like he'd swallowed an invisible ball of cotton. "But Dad… you said no more killing."

"Then let's hope they surrender when they see the flags."

Bo didn't budge. He hated this part. It meant there was no going back.

"Go on," Billy said. "Stalling doesn't change the fact it has to be done."

Bo swallowed hard, trying to move the invisible ball of cotton from his throat. "Dad, I don't wanna do this."

Billy looked at him. "You think I do?"

"Don't you?"

Billy thought about it for a moment. "Just go raise the flags, son."

Bo slunk in his seat. He took a deep breath of courage and opened the door and slugged his way out of the Moon Runner, and then he made his way around to the bed of the truck, his steps much faster than he wanted them to be. He stopped and took a deep calming breath, hoping it would ease the trembling in his hands. But it didn't work. His fingers just kept shaking. He reached out and grabbed a thin rope that was tethered to a wooden pole which was sticking out from the bed of the truck. The pole had been lodged tightly between the sheet metal and the framing of the rear window. He pulled the rope, and a black flag rose up into the air like some wretched banner of war. The desert breeze caught hold of it, stretching it out wide and revealing the notorious *Dagger & Son* emblem with the skull and crossed daggers. Bo was always sickened by the sight of Billy's flag. The flag meant death. Maybe his own. He didn't want to go down with his father's ship.

Inside of the Moon Runner, Billy sat behind the wheel and closed his eyes and exhaled his unburied grief. His face softened, as if he were letting go of some loathsome burden. He pulled a small photograph from his jacket pocket. A candid photo of him and Bo and Shelby and Amelia. Taken years before. Together at the Bonneville Speedway. The salty drag strip where he'd honed his craft and won respect as a fearless street racer. Happier times. Smiling faces. The future still a possibility in Bo's sweet little eyes. Billy looked up from the photo and caught a glimpse of the boy in the rearview mirror. Bo was crying as he raised the second flag. The dreaded *red* flag. It was a warning to the Nimbus drivers: *surrender, or no lives will be spared.*

No lives ever were.

But Billy was sick and tired of the killing. He'd done so much of it in the past three months that he could hardly stomach it anymore. It wasn't in his nature to take a human life, but pulling the trigger nowadays took about as much cognitive effort as snapping his fingers. His conscience didn't even factor in anymore. He felt like he was going down the rabbit hole with everyone else. That scared the shit out of him. He looked down at the photograph again. *Such ignorant bliss*, he thought. He wanted to see the world that way again. He wanted his family back. He wished he could go back and rescue them from their fate. *Maybe then I wouldn't be here in this desert playing god*, he thought. Then he thought about Amelia.

The night after Shelby was killed by Nimbus bullets, he'd found Amelia in her sleep sack with her wrists cut and bleeding out. She was blue-lipped and lifeless and already gone from the world. He remembered his heart stopping, and wondering if it would ever start up again. He always knew that Amelia was too light-hearted for the darkness of the world. He knew once the darkness took hold of her, as it did that day at the distribution zone, she wouldn't be long for it. He held her body in his arms all night long, crying in absolute silence, his mouth agape and making no sound, like a silent film, devoid of both color and truth. He couldn't risk waking the boy. Bo could never know the truth. So he cleaned Amelia's wounds and hid the evidence of her wrists beneath her shirt sleeves and smeared blood on the orifices of her face. He kissed her goodbye and said he was sorry and cried like a child, his head resting on her chest in grief. When he finally mustered the courage, he woke the boy with a soft touch and falling tears, and he delivered the earth-shattering news. He told Bo that the Red Death had taken his mother to the other side. The boy was ruined. In ways that Billy wasn't prepared for. Bo told him that his body felt like some kind of prison that was keeping him from his mom and he just wanted to escape and be free of it. He wanted to follow her to wherever she was. Billy told him that was the easy way out. It was for cowards. But that was always Bo's instinct: the easy way out. That's why Billy could never tell him the truth. The boy and his mother were just too much alike.

"The flags are up," Bo said as he slid back into the truck. "Both of 'em." He was free of tears now and feigning toughness.

Billy turned away and wiped his eyes clean, feigning the same toughness. Every bit of it was fraudulent. It seemed that's all they ever did anymore: feign toughness. No words between them. Just a false, unspoken bravado. Each trying to outdo the other. Wasting precious moments in masculine silence. There weren't many of those moments left to waste, but despite that inescapable truth, the wasteful hush always endured. Billy looked at Bo without a word. He studied the boy's face. The boy had his mother's eyes. Her kind spirit. It felt to Billy as if he were staring into Amelia's eyes, and she was staring right back in judgment. He quickly turned his attention on the road ahead and focused on what was in front of him. Bo did the same. They didn't say anything else. They both knew what was coming, and there were no words that could stop it.

# SIX

"Billy, I'm in position." The man they called Reverend was hiding behind the graffitied ruins of a long abandoned gas station on Route 66. He spoke into a two-way radio. "No sign of 'em yet, but the Good Lord tells me they're coming."

He was a black ordained minister and self-professed gearhead who had joined Billy's reckoning upon *God's calling*. He sat there on his Indian bobber motorcycle with a Remington shotgun slung over his shoulder and no moral conundrums to keep him from using it. His coarse black hair was high and tight with a holy cross buzzed into the side, making his motivation clear to anyone who wondered. There was a mini Bible lodged into the back pocket of his blue jeans. He was waiting for the Nimbus convoy to pass the second marker, which today was the abandoned gas station.

The rest of Billy's crew were already heading for the mile-long Pike's Canyon just off Route 66, burning the breeze in their lowboys and rat rods, and straddling their custom choppers like wrathful horsemen of the apocalypse. They were armed like warlords, with machine guns, pistols, RPGs, and hand grenades. They embraced the name they'd been given: *Road Pirates*. But their loot was something far more valuable than gold. They were flying Billy's colors — black *Dagger & Son* flags — high above their rides, with outlaw pride, looking like a fleet of battered warships sailing across a swelling sea of broken pavement. Once they got to their position in the canyon, they were ordered to wait for Billy's signal to light the smoke barrels. They had lined the canyon road with a dozen barrels filled with smoke powder, each rigged with a 10-inch fuse. The smoke plume would be crucial to their success. It would provide a necessary cover for the ambush. The timing would have to be perfect. If the convoy saw the smoke too early, they would redirect and change their course, avoiding the canyon altogether, and sabotaging the only advantage that Billy and his crew had. If the smoke barrels were lit too late, there wouldn't be enough smoke for the ambush to be effective, and Billy and his crew would be sitting ducks. The vaccine shipments had been few and far between as Nimbus was fulfilling the last of their orders, and the well was drying up, so they couldn't allow a thing like poor timing to be their undoing.

Reverend heard the convoy approaching from a good distance. The military engines were resounding and distinct and he swore he could feel the earth trembling beneath his feet. He raised a pair of binoculars to his eyes to confirm.

"Billy, I got eyes on." He saw the bright orange Nimbus rig and the four Humvee escort heading his way. There were men onboard with M4s, AR-15s, mighty .50 cals and enough mags to fend off an entire militia. They'd only have to fend off eleven men and one very scared little boy. "They're fully armed. A mile and a half out from the marker."

"Right on schedule," Billy said on the other end of the walkie. "You see Levi?"

Reverend glassed the horizon behind the convoy. "No sign of him."

Billy fumed, "Damn you, Levi. Always late to the dance."

Reverend cleared his throat nervously. "Billy, you heard me say they were fully armed? They got fifty cals."

"Yeah, I heard," Billy said. "Is that a problem?"

Reverend shrugged. "Not for me."

"Good," Billy said without a hint of fear. "We're ready to roll on this end. Let me know when they pass the marker."

"Ten four."

Reverend glassed the horizon again, watching the Nimbus convoy approach. He never got used to seeing military vehicles protecting corporate America. It was so contrary to his idea of liberty. Nimbus was a global powerhouse of capitalism. The corporation had a market value that surpassed the economy of most countries. Trillions of dollars and public stocks through the roof. It was run by the world's wealthiest man: the first and only trillionaire, Lucian Vanderbon. He was their founder and CEO, and he was Time Magazine's Man of the Year more than once. He'd started the company when he was only 26 years old. A startup that sold common goods online at discounted prices with free shipping. Two decades later his company was building top secret weaponry and artificial intelligence for the government, while also developing life-saving drugs for the entire world, exploring outer space, and maintaining the indisputable title of most profitable publicly-traded retail company in the world. Lucian Vanderbon had built an empire. One that crossed all borders. He had politicians in his pocket in almost every country, and celebrities in his bed. He had the world by the short and curlies, and his reach was long enough to maintain his grip. The only thing that could've brought Lucian Vanderbon crashing back down to Earth was another equally powerful trillionaire with greater ambition, and that person simply didn't exist.

# SEVEN

Billy's crew was a mile out from Pike's Canyon. They were just a ragtag bunch of gearheads, outlaw bikers, ex-cons and certifiables. Over the past few months, they'd become a brotherhood, like modern-day Knights of the round table, but without the table, and certainly without the chivalry. Most of them were felons, with some misdemeanors here and there. But they'd all served time in some capacity. They weren't your typical heroes. In fact, they weren't heroes at all. But they all shared a common theme that drove them to fight for what was right. Every one of them had been broken by the system, and now they had the chance to truly burn it down. Billy had weeded out the really bad seeds, but his garden was still growing black flowers. Once nearly eighty strong, the crew had been diminished significantly over the past month, some having died heroically in battle during previous hijackings, and others simply abandoning the cause out of fear. There were only eleven men left in his crew now, but they had fast rides, potent weaponry and huge balls to boot, and Billy believed that was all they needed. The men were convinced too. Billy had a way of convincing people of their own power. A charisma and charm that would've served him well had he chosen to be a cult leader instead. Fortunately for the world, his passion rested on coil springs and four racing tires.

Levi was the first in a long line of undesirables in Billy's madcap crew. He was the right hand man. The VP to Billy's El Presidente. He had the intangibles that Billy valued above all else: loyalty and trust. A lifetime of it. But Billy was alone in that trust. None of the other crew members trusted Levi any more than they could pick his cowardly ass up and throw him. He was never going to put himself in harm's way, which to them meant his loyalties only went so far. The other men in the crew were different. They were reckless, like Billy.

There was Dice, who's real name was Bobby Walker. He was one of Billy's racing rivals from the old days before the Collapse. Since the shit hit the fan they'd been on the same side of the yellow line. Brothers in arms, flying the same colors, and riding on the edge of everything.

Then there was Hooligan, a foul-mouthed Mick with a messy Dublin accent and a canvas of biblical tattoos covering his body from his mohawk on down. Billy called him the Mad Irishman. That was somehow an understatement.

Then there was Flyboy, a former navy pilot and one of Billy's closest friends. He'd been shot down over the Kumgang Dam in North Korea during Operation Saber Strike, where he'd narrowly escaped capture by the ruthless Norks, but he'd never seen anything quite as hairy as fighting alongside the legendary Billy Dagger in the Mojave, and that was no hyperbole.

But not all of Billy's crew walked on the wild side. Some were just good old-fashioned working men who'd found them-selves at their wit's end and felt compelled to do something about it. The man they called Wisdom was a former history teacher before the Collapse made history of him. He'd forgotten more about the art of war than most four-star generals ever knew. So Billy brought him into the fold and made him a chief strategist, even if it was pure academia. Suddenly Billy was a warlord with wits.

Then there were the black flowers in the garden. Outlaws like Merlin, a former stalwart of the Devil's Diciples motorcycle club out of Cali. The only things more intimidating than his rap sheet were his braided locks and wickedly long beard, which gave him the appearance of a crazed medieval wizard. Hence the moniker bestowed upon him by his club. Nobody even knew his Christian name, and nobody had the nerve to ask.

The blackest flower among them was Monk, a dark-mannered felon with an even darker past who was now on the straight and narrow, or so he claimed. He was one of the more motivated men in Billy's crew. He'd lost everything to the Red Death. His new family. His repurposed life after serving hard time for murder. He blamed Nimbus for stealing away his second chance. So his motivation was simple: he just wanted revenge. If he died getting it, so be it. To him, every day was a good day to die.

From there the crew got a little squirrelly. Starting with the two "prospects", Fender and Palooka. Fender was a young rockabilly punk who was desperate to prove himself. He always carried a dark cherry Stratocaster and a massive Smith & Wesson .44. He also carried a massive hard-on for Billy. He was one of those impressionable types who looked at Billy like he was the second coming of Christ. Billy never bothered to dispel that blasphemous myth. Fender worshipped him, because Billy set his own moral compass, and he had no fear of where that might lead. That kind of raw freedom was infectious.

Palooka, the other "prospect", was more aloof than Fender. A thin, scrappy ginger with freckles who loved a good fistfight but never seemed to win one. Even Levi bested him with heavy gloves and a "lucky punch", and Levi was stoned and drunk at the time. So the nickname was inevitable.

Rounding out the list of undesirables was Johnny the Raven. A half-baked, half-blooded Apache from San Carlos with limited brain cells who spent most of his time downing hooch with Levi and jabbing veins with the Mad Irishman. Truthfully, he was just batshit crazy. Like the rest of Billy's crew. They'd all been shot, stabbed, scraped and beaten at some point or another over the course of their lives. Most of the men were glory seekers. Adrenaline junkies. Addicts that needed a new thrill in the absence of drugs and street racing and whatever gangland warfare they were once a part of. Men that would not go quietly or bow to the system. Men like Billy. In fact, the only thing that made Billy different from the ex-cons in his crew was that little invisible line between legal and illegal. After the Collapse, that line was gone, and so were their differences.

"Billy, we're moving into position," Dice announced. He was behind the wheel of a '38 Dodge pickup, chewing nervously on a cigar and armed with an uzi that once belonged to the now-deceased President of the Bandidos motorcycle club. "This is gonna be a good day."

A pair of plush dice hung from the rearview mirror and a pile of grenades were rolling around on the seat beside him, with the pins rattling in their pinholes. The phrase *HIGHWAY ROBBERY* was painted on the hood of the truck. Hooligan stood in the truckbed wearing nothing but a pair of tighty-whiteys and combat boots, with an RPG-7 in his hand and a pack of warheads strapped to his back. "Let's fookin' go!" he shouted, his accent muddled and twisting every which way.

The fleet of road pirates entered the canyon.

"The cat's in the cradle," Dice announced over the walkie.

Then Flyboy asked, "Who's the first to shit their pants today?" He was driving a slammed '29 Ford Tudor with pilot wings painted on the rear. "I'm guessing Levi. But he won't be around for any of us to see it." A stroked Cadillac 540 rumbled beneath the hood of the Ford, and the headers were glowing with a molten orange heat. Flyboy had one hand on the steering wheel and the other on an AK-47 that was mounted to the dashboard on a swivel, aiming it through a hole in a glassless windshield made of chicken wire. A pair of aviator goggles were keeping the dust from his eyes.

"My money's on Palooka," Wisdom said. He was Flyboy's wingman today, standing up through a punctured hole in the roof with an RPG-7 and a rifle slung over his shoulder. He was a part of history now, not just an observer.

"I think *all* bets are on Palooka," Merlin chuckled through his walkie. "He was the first to shit himself last time. And the time before that. And the time before that…" He was behind the wheel of a custom '55 Ford pickup. The truck felt like a sheetmetal coffin to him. He wasn't accustomed to cruising on four wheels with no wind blowing through his hair. For a life-long chopperhead like Merlin to trade in his beloved wheels for an overstuffed lead sled like the '55 Ford spoke volumes about how much he respected Billy.

"*Question*," Palooka said into his walkie. "If I already shit my pants, are all bets off?" He stood in the truck bed with an AR-15 slung over his back and an RPG-7 locked and loaded. He was feeling downright unbeatable.

Monk was following behind the '55 Ford, straddling his Fat Boy Harley, and armed with an uzi, extra mags, and a Glock 19 stashed away in a shoulder holster. If he was going down, it wouldn't be for lack of fire power. He wore a *Stars and Stripes* bobber helmet, because in his belief, *second chances only happen in America.*

Fender was flying solo in a supercharged T-Bucket Roadster that Billy had restored a few years earlier. There was an AR-15 across his lap, an Uzi strapped over his shoulder, and a shitload of handguns in a duffel bag on the seat. His dark cherry Stratocaster was spread out across the backseat like a horny pinup girl and his massive Smith & Wesson .44 was holstered to his hip.

Bringing up the rear of the fleet was Johnny the Raven, riding high as a kite on his Harley low rider. He was stoned as hell, probably on peyote, and looking unfazed by the possibility of death. He had a sawed-off Maverick 88 and a belt full of shotgun shells slung over his torso. There was an uzi and extra ammo strapped to his kevlar vest. The black paint on his face said it all: this was war.

They pulled off the road and lined the edge of the rocky wall just off the soft shoulder.

Dice informed Billy of their position over the walkie. "Hey Wild Bill," he said, "We're all dressed up and ready for the dance. Where's the music?"

They waited for the signal.

Inside of the Moon Runner, Billy grabbed the walkie from the dashboard and said, "Just hold tight, boys."

"Ten four," Dice said. "Just waiting on you."

Billy placed the walkie back on the dashboard and opened the glove compartment and pulled out a rusty can of white face paint that he'd made from soft clay and eggshells.

Bo grimaced. It was just a bullshit superstition that his

father had always used to justify his madness. Another lie to make the boy believe they were somehow invincible.

Billy opened the can and scooped out a clump of powdery white paint and pressed his finger to his forehead and drew a straight line down the middle of his face, right between his eyes, over the bridge of his nose, across his blistered lips, and down to the very bottom of his bearded chin. It looked like his face had been split in two. One half a broken father, the other half an egomaniac trying to fix what was broken. "Come get your racing stripe, boy," he said.

Bo reluctantly obliged. Billy reached out and ran his painted finger down the middle of the boy's face, drawing a sharp white line from his forehead down to his shivering chin. It was a tradition that Billy had started before their very first hijacking, claiming at the time that the stripe was an old native spell to ward off evil spirits in battle, and since they had survived that bloody day and were still very much alive, Billy now claimed it gave them a temporary form of immortality, making them invisible to Nimbus bullets.

Despite the promise, Bo was still trembling with fear.

Billy winked at him. "Now we're bulletproof, son. Don't you worry. They can't touch us."

Reverend's voice buzzed over the walkie. "Billy, they just passed the marker."

Billy sat upright and grabbed the walkie. "Alright, Padre. Another day of reckoning."

"God willing," Reverend said.

Bo felt his stomach twisting into painful knots.

Billy flipped the custom line-lock switch on the dashboard, locking out the front brakes separate from the rear. He turned to the boy with a reckless look in his eyes and said, "You better hold on to something." Bo gripped the door handle tightly. Billy stomped the gas and blasted off towards the canyon. Bo was forced back into the seat as the Moon runner launched down the highway, the speedometer ticking faster than his own fluttering heart.

Once they were at the mouth of the canyon, Billy hit the brakes and brought the truck to a stop. He pressed the washer fluid release button, which he'd manipulated with multiple hoses and connectors running beneath the truck like swollen veins. Bleach sprayed from a custom nozzle under the chassis, saturating the road in front of the rear tires.

"Two tire fire," he exclaimed. "Let's blind these fuckers."

He punched the gas. The rear tires spun against the asphalt. Bo gripped the door handle. The friction of the spinning tires mixed with the bleach sent a fog of white street smoke billowing into the air, expanding into a massive cloud of uncertainty within seconds. As Billy spun donuts, he and Bo were tossed around wickedly in their seatbelts. Bo felt completely out of control. Billy was possessed, operating on pure impulse. He brought the Moon Runner to a sudden stop and sat there waiting, his eyes sharply focused. Bo looked ahead for the Nimbus convoy, but he was blinded by the whiteout. The street smoke swirled around the Moon Runner, and terrible thoughts began to swirl around Bo's fragile mind.

Billy's dramatic burnout was the signal, which meant the crew would ignite the smoke barrels now, to blind the convoy. Then the battle would begin. Bo smelled the bleach in the air and suddenly felt nauseous. His eyes began to water. His head began to hurt. He swallowed while he still could. His lips were drying up in the desert air. The lingering toxin only made it worse. He just wanted to be someplace else. Someplace safe. He didn't care about saving a bunch of strangers. He only thought about the people he loved. His mother. His sister. He thought he might be joining them soon. Wherever they were. If such a thing was even possible. The afterlife seemed like a painful stretch of the imagination to him. He looked down the highway through the fog of smoke, but he was unable to see anything but his own terrified reflection in the glass.

Billy set the digital stopwatch to 60 seconds and gave the watch to Bo. "When I tell you to," he said, "push start."

Bo waited nervously with his finger hovering over the button. The whole thing would have to happen in 60 seconds flat. That's how Billy figured it.

Only 60 seconds.

Not a second more.

# EIGHT

The seconds were always ticking away on Billy and Bo, but they were too busy counting the days to ever embrace something as fleeting and insignificant as mere seconds. They were always remembering the past or imagining the future, but never living in the present. The tragedy of human cognizance. Never enjoying the moment until it's too late.

That's exactly what happened to society.

They blinked and it was gone.

The Collapse didn't happen overnight. It was a slow burn. Billy said it was like packing too many people into an elevator and killing the power. Most people could sense it coming, like dominoes falling one piece at a time across the globe. Billy called it the Big Crunch. A rising pressure that no one could escape. He could feel it squeezing the life out of him and everyone he knew. People struggling to make ends meet and keep their sanity. Human decency all but gone. People glorifying all the wrong things. Their logic skewed. Their reality dismissed if it didn't align with their fantasies. Everything was suddenly backwards and upside down. The collective mind seemed lost, and nobody escaped the madness. Lines of division were drawn like social graffiti. Fingers were used to place the blame rather than to make an honest living. Hatreds were fueled by talking heads and politicians, and people fell right into their trap: divide and conquer. It was way too easy. Throw in a little tribalism, a steady rise in global temperature, constant drought, wildfires and a goddamn culture war fueled by the internet, and humanity had cooked up a recipe for disaster.

Billy always said the shit would hit the fan when the blades were spinning the fastest, and on March 21st 2048, the shit went flying everywhere. They called it the People's Revolution. An uprising of angry citizens around the world who'd secretly organized a global coup with one common goal in mind: to bring down the entire system. The movement crossed borders and party lines and didn't discriminate against color or creed or lifestyle. They were unified and they were dangerous, and on that hot day in March, they collectively stormed their respective capitols, in one swift and coordinated attack, armed with guns and blades and pipe bombs, and they overthrew their corrupt leaders. It seemed the final domino had fallen. The entire system was bleeding. Then the whole thing collapsed.

Soon Billy and Amelia and the kids found themselves barricaded on their property, living on rations in the Old 66, defending their valuable goods from the looters and violent street gangs that seemed to come out of the woodwork whenever a little thing like law and order ceased to exist. Eventually they were forced to flee in the Moon Runner, with Levi following loyally on his steel horse. They lived like nomads out of the '63 Chevy, taking what they could get without compromising their principles. The world had gone completely insane. Pure anarchy of the soul. And that was just the tip of the spear. The final thrust would come from Mother Nature. No one — not Billy, nor the People's Revolution, nor the failing governments of the world — were prepared for what came next. A few months later, on the 12th day of January in 2049, the Red Death took its first victim.

---

"Dad, would you miss me if I died?"

Billy removed his eyes from the white plume of smoke in Pike's Canyon. "You plan on going somewhere?"

"No. I mean, I don't know. We can't live like this forever."

"No, we can't. But who the hell wants to live forever? The flash of life is what makes it special. A thing matters more when it can be taken away from you. You understand?"

"I guess."

"Life goes fast, son. So you better live faster."

"I just want things to slow down."

Billy shook his head. "That's not gonna happen."

Bo hated when his father dashed his hopes like that. Like dousing a tiny ember before it could flicker and become a mighty flame. The boy suddenly missed his home, where everything good in his life had happened. But that history was gone now. Burnt down by Nimbus. Nothing left but ash and fluttering memories. He and Billy had gone back to see the place a month earlier. The Old 66 and his father's shop had been spitefully destroyed. The business sign was still intact and standing tall, but it was charred by arson fire and dotted with bullet holes from Nimbus guns. That was Lucian Vanderbon's way of letting Billy Dagger know that the rumors of a bounty on his head were true. The word *TERRORIST* had been painted in big red letters over the Dagger name. It was the first and last time that Bo had ever seen his father scared.

"I don't wanna do this, Dad."

Billy looked at him, but he didn't say anything.

Then Reverend's voice crackled over the walkie. "Billy, they took the bait."

Billy's eyes began to burn with that terrible purpose. He turned to Bo and said, "It's time, son. Start the clock."

Bo hesitated, his heart bursting uncontrollably.

"*Now*," Billy snapped. "*Do it.*"

Bo pressed the start button on the stopwatch. 60 seconds turned to 59... then 58... then 57... His hands were trembling. "Dad, there's four Humvees. *Four!* This is crazy."

Billy rested the palm of his hand on the boy's cheek and tried to calm his fear. "Keep your head about you, boy." Then he reached down and grabbed an RPG-7 from the floorboard and quickly mounted the barrel with a warhead. He stood up through a large, jagged hole in the roof that he'd etched out with a sawzall. He steadied the RPG on his shoulder and aimed down the highway, careful to center his shot with the faded yellow line.

The radio crackled with Reverend's voice again. "They're in the smoke, Billy."

Billy fired the warhead into the white plume of smoke, figuring God would do the rest.

---

The warhead whirled through the smoke and struck the lead Humvee and the powerful blast lifted the vehicle off the ground. It flipped end over end, crashing down on its rooftop and crushing the fifty-gunner beneath it. The second Humvee bulldozed through the burning wreckage, knocking the lead Humvee aside with a steal battering ram attached to the bumper.

Billy saw the bright flicker of flame. It lit up the dense fog of smoke with orange and blue strobes, like lightning bolts flashing in a thundercloud. He dropped back down into the seat and put the truck in reverse and rode the brake, looking ahead through the swirling whiteout, waiting for any sign of the convoy. Perhaps a pair of headlights exiting the fog. Or the sound of diesel engines approaching. Or a flurry of bullets hissing by the Moon Runner.

The fifty-gunner on the second Humvee scanned the surroundings with the massive barrel, but there was no visibility through the smoke. Suddenly the '38 Dodge emerged, charging from the north. Hooligan fired the RPG. It struck the interior of the Humvee, exploding like an angry starburst, disintegrating the fifty-gunner and wounding the other security guards with shrapnel. Dice swerved away and the '38 Dodge disappeared into the smoke again. Johnny the Raven passed the Humvee on his Harley chopper and fired the uzi, killing the driver, who in turn fell into the steering wheel and caused the Humvee to swerve and skid out of control. The Humvee hit the canyon wall and sprung back into the path of the convoy. The Nimbus rig barreled through the wreckage, knocking the burning vehicle aside.

The ambush was working.

Two Humvees were down.

Two more to go.

But only 40 seconds left.

Bo saw the Nimbus rig emerge from the smoke ahead and threaten to slam into the front of the Moon Runner. His eyes jettisoned from their sockets and he gripped the door handle and braced himself for a brutal end. But Billy stomped the gas and pulled away in reverse and floored the pedal. He pulled the handbrake and jerked the steering wheel to the left and spun a slick one-eighty. He shifted gear mid-spin and stomped the gas again and the Moon Runner launched forward as the Nimbus rig brushed the rear bumper. Bo felt the entire truck shuddering beneath him, and in his fragile mind he feared the weldings might come apart at the seams. He could see the Nimbus rig's massive grille in the rear window, like a metal beast about to swallow him whole. Billy floored the gas and pulled away and the Nimbus rig disappeared into the smoke again. All Bo could see now was the future that awaited. The inevitable blaze of glory that was coming for Billy, and maybe for him too. Death had never felt so close.

The T-Bucket Roadster and the '29 Tudor sped away from their alcove in the canyon wall and chased after the rear Humvee, following it through the fog of smoke. The fifty-gunner on the Humvee heard the engines and spun the turret. Fender steadied his .44 Magnum and fired from the driver's seat of the Roadster. The bullets ricocheted off the armored turret. The fifty-gunner fired back and the massive .50 caliber rounds ripped into the Roadster's engine. Fender lost control and veered into the canyon wall. He tried to fire the Smith & Wesson, but the massive .50 caliber rounds had the final say. His body thrashed wildly and his blood splattered about like a sprinkler head and he slumped over in the seat. His awestruck loyalty to Billy Dagger had come to an unceremonious end.

The fifty-gunner spun the turret and saw the '29 Tudor approaching through the smoke. Flyboy fired the dashboard AK-47 through the chicken wire with one hand and steered with the other. Wisdom raised the RPG and fired and the warhead struck the rear of the Humvee, erupting and butchering the fifty-gunner and the guard in the backseat with a fatal dose of shrapnel.

***

Johnny the Raven charged at the Humvee on his Harley chopper, passing on the right side, and as the driver and the gunner in the front seat were still disoriented from the blast, the Raven took advantage and shot the gunner with an uzi and disappeared into the smoke again, like a bird disappearing in a moonless night.

***

Merlin emerged from the smoke in the '55 Ford, passing on the left side of the Humvee. Palooka raised the RPG from the bed of the truck and fired, blasting the front wheel well. The Humvee kicked sideways and flipped and barrel-rolled several times, sending shards of metal and glass hurdling into the air. It slid across the highway in a shower of sparks as Merlin pulled away. The ambush was working flawlessly, and it was almost complete. Three Humvees were down. One more to go. But only 15 seconds left before they cleared the smoke.

***

The last Humvee pulled alongside the Nimbus rig on the right side, looking for a tactical advantage. Billy and his crew wouldn't be able to attack from all four sides now. The smoke in the air was getting less dense and visibility was beginning to improve. Time was running out. Monk charged at the last Humvee on his chopper. He fired the uzi at the fifty-gunner in the turret. The gunner ducked and took cover inside. Another guard in the back seat fired at Monk with an M4. The bullets pelted the headlights of the chopper and struck Monk in the kevlar vest, but he stayed the course, firing his uzi without pause and pulling to the left. He never took his foot off the gas or his finger off the trigger. It was a good day to die. The guard in the backseat was shredded by the bullets. Before Monk could find cover again, the fifty-gunner rose back up into the turret and took control of the .50 caliber beast and blasted him with the massive rounds. Monk was dead before his body hit the ground. The impact with the highway knocked the helmet from his head.

---

Bo watched it happen from the Moon Runner. His eyes were big and round and rimmed with terror. The rear tires of the Nimbus cargo trailer barreled over Monk's body and spit the corpse out of the back like a slingshot. Bo watched the *Stars and Stripes* helmet roll down the highway. He felt his own hope rolling away with it. Fate was not on their side this time. Fate was coming to collect. He could feel it reaching out to grab them. This was going to be a massacre.

---

Johnny the Raven charged the last Humvee on his rat bike, firing the uzi wildly and blasting the fifty-gunner in the turret as he took a stray round to the leg. The fifty-gunner fell into the seat below, leaving the .50-caliber beast unmanned. The Raven's engine was smoking and leaking fuel, and his leg was nearly severed in half. He swerved and sped forward, passing the front end of the Humvee. The driver swerved into the bike and clipped the rear tire. The Raven lost control of the bike and toppled over, and as he and the rat bike slid across the pavement, he turned and fired the uzi wildly. The bullets shattered the windshield of the Humvee and struck the gunner in the passenger seat. The driver grabbed the dead gunner's M4 and swung the barrel forward, firing through the hole in the broken glass. When the bullets hit the gasoline-soaked pavement, they sparked, igniting a fire. The flames spread rapidly across the highway and consumed the Raven's body in seconds.

Bo watched in horror as the road pirate burned alive, his face contorted and grotesque and locked in a dreadful scream, his arms flapping desperately like a bird trying to put out the flames. The smell of fuel, smoke and gunpowder filled the air. The thought of burning flesh filled Bo's fragile mind. He could hardly take a breath. He just watched the Raven burn.

"Goddamnit, Bo!" Billy shouted. "Get your fucking head down!"

Bo felt a surge of adrenaline as the air returned to his lungs, but the resurgence was short-lived. He noticed something ominous ahead. The smoke was beginning to clear. They wouldn't have the advantage of cover any longer. They'd be easy targets, like fish being massacred in a barrel.

He looked at the stopwatch.

Only 5 seconds left. 4… 3…

"Dad, time's up!"

Billy just ignored him.

"They're all dying, Dad. We're gonna die too."

Billy's eyes were aglow, navigating the unseen road ahead.

"Listen to me, Dad!" Bo hit him in the arm to get his attention. "Get us out of here! They're gonna fucking kill us!"

Billy kept his foot on the gas. He drew his bone-handled Ruger Redhawk and aimed it through the open window and fired recklessly at the fifty-gunner in the last Humvee. He pulled away as the gunner returned fire, taking cover in the Moon Runner behind the Nimbus rig. "We almost got the sons a bitches," he declared. "Only one Humvee left, son. One!"

The alarm on the digital timer sounded. Time was officially up. But Bo could see it didn't matter to his father. Billy was possessed by that terrible purpose. The one he'd discovered while standing over the unmarked graves of his wife and daughter. There was no stopping him now.

Dice charged the last Humvee in the '38 Dodge as the smoke began to clear. Daylight was shining on all of them now, with an unmistakable brightness. Hooligan raised the RPG, but the Humvee driver spotted him and fired a handgun. Hooligan dropped to the floor of the truck bed, dodging the bullets as they speckled the old wooden rails. "Pull back!" he shouted. "Pull back!" The backseat gunner in the Humvee rose up through the turret and took control of the .50-caliber beast, sending a hail of massive rounds crashing into the '38 Dodge and striking Dice in the neck, nearly decapitating him in the process. Blood sprayed from his jugular as he fell dead onto the steering wheel. Hooligan rose with the RPG, but the .50 rounds tore through his body, removing chunks of flesh and bone with every nefarious thump. His bloody corpse dropped to the bed of the truck. The '38 Dodge veered aimlessly off the road and crashed into the final stretch of canyon wall.

---

Bo hated to be so right. This was going to be a massacre. The ambush hadn't happened fast enough. It was time to retreat. But as the Moon Runner exited the canyon and cleared the smoke, Billy stayed the course, charging the last Humvee on the left. He pulled alongside the driver and raised the Ruger Redhawk and reached across Bo's face with the massive hand cannon and shouted, "Get down!" Bo ducked and covered his ears as Billy fired through the passenger window. The Humvee driver was shot in the head. Billy hit the brakes and pulled away. The gunner in the passenger seat was covered with the driver's brain matter, but he quickly grabbed the steering wheel and corrected the Humvee's course. The fifty-gunner fired on the Moon Runner, but Billy had already swung around to the left side of the Nimbus rig for cover. The bloodied gunner in the passenger seat pushed the dead driver out of the Humvee and slid into the seat behind the wheel, determined to press on. He was now in control of the last remaining Humvee.

---

The '29 Tudor charged from behind. Flyboy fired the dashboard AK-47 through the chicken wire. The guard manning the last .50 caliber machine gun ducked and took cover inside the turret. Wisdom fired the RPG, but the driver swerved and dodged the warhead as it flew past. The guard rose back up into the turret and fired the .50 caliber beast. The bullets ripped through Wisdom's body. He dropped lifelessly into the seat next to Flyboy. His left eye was shot out and his cranium was split down the middle. The guard kept firing. A murderous racket. Flyboy hit the brakes and pulled away as bullets sprayed the hood and notched the broken highway ahead. There was no time to mourn the loss of his friend. He pulled to safety and grabbed the walkie. "Billy, Wisdom's dead. He's shot to hell." Billy didn't respond. "Billy, damnit! We're getting the shit kicked out of us! Let's get the fuck out of here, man!"

Merlin pulled the '55 Ford behind the Humvee and fired from the open window, blindly, trying to hit anything that could make a difference. He shouted to his wingman, "Palooka, I'm gonna get you in range for the RPG." But the guard in the Humvee blasted the truck with the massive .50 rounds. The drumming of bullets trampled across the sheetmetal body of the '55 Ford like a marching band, sending chills up Merlin's spine. It sounded like a doomsday hailstorm. He hit the brakes and swerved for cover behind the Nimbus rig as the Nimbus bullets shattered the windshield. He shouted into the walkie, "Billy. It's over, man. We have to bail. That fifty's killing us. We're pulling out." He drove away.

The Humvee pulled around to the left side of the Nimbus rig. The guard fired the .50 cal at Flyboy. The '29 Tudor swung off the road. Bullets pelted the back end. Flyboy hit the brakes and hunkered down in the driver's seat, covering his ears as shards of metal and glass exploded around his head. He grabbed the walkie and shouted, "Fuck this. I'm out." He looked at Wisdom's dead body. "I'm sorry, Billy. There's nothing more we can do."

<hr>

The Humvee drove on, searching for Billy Dagger and his Moon Runner.

<hr>

Merlin turned around in the driver's seat of the '55 Ford and looked for Palooka in the bed of the truck. "Southpaw, you alive back there?" Palooka didn't answer. Merlin craned his neck and spotted Palooka's shredded corpse. He was nearly severed in half, facedown in a pool of blood. "Jesus Christ!" Merlin grabbed the walkie and shouted, "Palooka's gone. He's dead, Billy." He punched the dashboard in anger and slammed his head into the steering wheel. He took a few unnerved breaths and spoke softly into the walkie, "I'm sorry, Billy. I got no magic left in me. It's over, brother."

<hr>

But Billy had no desire to retreat. He was too damn close to give up now, and far too short on opportunities. The Nimbus shipments had been running low, and he didn't know when they'd get another chance like this. As always, he saw the prize and nothing else. He pulled the Moon Runner alongside the Nimbus rig on the passenger side and locked eyes with the man who was riding shotgun. He was a rough-looking ex-con with face tattoos and a half-crazed smile on his face that suggested he was a wildcard in this game. Billy knew he'd have a weapon on hand. Probably a shotgun. Something powerful and visually frightening. He didn't want to give the man an extra second to consider using it. "Bo, give me the grenade gun."

Bo was too overcome with fear to react. He spotted something through the rear window. "Dad! Behind us!"

Billy looked in the rearview mirror and saw the last Humvee charging hard from behind. The guard was in the turret of the .50 cal, primed to fire. "Oh fuck!" Billy downshifted. "Hold on!" He swerved hard right as the guard unloaded. The massive rounds shattered what was left of the back window of the Moon Runner and ricocheted off the roof, sounding like a dozen thunderclaps. Billy stomped the brake. The Humvee passed on the left side. He swerved the Moon Runner behind and hit the gas. "Give me the gun!" He took the grenade gun from Bo's hand and aimed it through the side window. The guard spun the turret around to fire the .50 cal, but Billy fired the grenade first and the close range IED struck the turret and exploded. The guard was eviscerated by the blast.

Billy swung the gun back to Bo. "Reload. Close range."

"Dad, Flyboy's gone. Everybody's gone. They left us. Stop!"

"Reload, goddamnit! Now!"

Bo grabbed another grenade marked *Close Range IED*. His nervous little hands were shaking. He was clumsy as he loaded the barrel.

"Hurry the fuck up!" Billy shouted. He pulled the Moon Runner alongside the Humvee on the right. Bo snapped the rusted barrel into place and handed the grenade gun back to Billy. The wounded driver behind the wheel of the Humvee was steering with one hand and raising a sidearm with the other. He fired the pistol at Billy's head, but his aim was unsteady, and the bullet struck the door below the window, missing Billy's shoulder by less than an inch, but throwing paint chips and metal debris at his face. He didn't flinch. He fired the grenade. It slammed into the driver's rib cage. But the cartridge just bounced off his wounded body and fell to the floorboard and didn't explode.

Billy had seen duds before, but never at such a crucial moment as this. "No," he said, completely dumbfounded by his sudden stroke of bad luck. "Not this way, God." He went blank in the eyes. The driver painfully raised the pistol and aimed it at his head. Bo's eyes grew with terror in the passenger seat. He winced and raised his hands to shield his eyes from the inevitable. Then he felt a burst of hot energy swarm the interior of the Moon Runner. The grenade had finally detonated. The explosion engulfed the Humvee and tore through the wounded driver's body. Bo's ears were ringing. Debris slammed into the Moon Runner. A sharp piece of metal struck Billy in the arm, forcing him to drop the grenade gun on the highway.

"Shit!" He winced in pain and nearly lost control of the truck.

Bo couldn't hear. His ears were still ringing from the blast. But he noticed Billy's reaction. "Dad, what's wrong?"

"I'm hit."

"You're hit?"

"Shrapnel."

"Where?"

Billy didn't say. He grimaced.

"Dad, where are you hit?"

"I can't raise my arm, son." Billy kept his grip on the steering wheel with his good arm. He kept his eyes on the Nimbus rig. He saw the man riding shotgun peering down on him with a sawed-off scattergun in his hand.

Bo saw the two-barreled beast too. "Let's get outta here,"

he wailed, ready to tuck his tail between his legs and run. "Fly-boy's gone. Merlin's gone. We should be gone too. Let's go, Dad."

But Billy had no intention of tucking his tail and running. "Take my gun, boy."

"What? No, Dad. They're gonna fucking kill us! Jesus Christ!"

"Take it, boy! The Humvees are down. We got the sons a bitches. No turning back now."

Bo began to cry, not bothering to feign toughness or hide his tears anymore. "Dad, please." His voice sounded pathetic, and though he usually hated to hear himself like that, this time he didn't have any inhibitions about it. "No more, Dad. Please. Let's get the fuck out of here!"

"*Stop crying!*" Billy glared at him with steely blue eyes. "We got the fuckers. You and me. We don't need anyone else."

"They're gonna kill us."

"Stop crying and take the goddamn gun. We gotta do this, you understand? We're all that's left. We can't stop now."

Bo wouldn't reach for the gun.

Billy was fighting his own tears now. "Take the gun, Bo." His blue eyes were icy cold but watery, practically begging. "Ride or die, son. There's no other way."

Bo wouldn't budge. He was held in place by fear. A gravitational force holding him down in the seat. He wondered if his heart was even beating.

"Take the fucking gun!" Billy roared.

Bo lunged forward on instinct and took the gun from Billy's hand.

"That'a boy," Billy said, trying to calm himself and the boy too. "Now be a Dagger man and stand up through the hatch and shoot those sons a bitches."

Bo's eyes burst. "*What?* No."

The boy had only learned to shoot at paper targets just weeks earlier, and that was a .22 pea shooter. Now Billy was expecting him to shoot at a living thing? With a massive .357? A hand cannon which he could barely keep steady?

"Stand up and shoot 'em," Billy ordered.

Bo could feel a coarse, dry cotton ball lodging itself tightly in the center of his throat again.

Billy looked unconvinced, but he pleaded with the boy. "You gotta do this, son."

Bo had seen his father broken before, and now Billy was carrying that same hopeless look in his eyes, as if he were expecting to be broken again. Bo didn't want to see his father break. So he clenched his teeth and began to rise.

Billy looked almost proud, but not yet. "Let's make it right, son. Or it's always gonna be wrong."

Bo rose up through the jagged hole in the roof. He tried to steady himself as the Moon Runner shook from the turbulence of the crumbling highway below. The Nimbus rig was rolling alongside them, looking like a bad dream that he'd recently had. He steadied the Ruger, taking aim at the man with the shotgun, who now had the two-barreled beast pointed down at Billy's head. Bo's hands began to shake. The fear rippled up his spine and streamed down his face in falling tears. "Dad," he whispered, "I can't."

"They're gonna kill us!" Billy roared. "Do it, boy! *Pull the fucking trigger!*"

The battle flags whipped in the wind next to Bo's head, thumping at his fragile mind like some clumsy war hammer of the gods. The jagged edges of the hole in the roof were digging into his skin beneath his shirt. His finger was tight on the trigger, but the nauseating rot of cowardice returned to his gut. It tasted worse than before, like his soul itself had turned sour. He couldn't pull the trigger. He just watched helplessly as the man with the shotgun smiled and aimed the two beastly barrels at his father's head. He just couldn't budge. Fate had reached out and grabbed him with its twisted, gnarly fingers, and now it was squeezing the courage right out of him. He had seen this moment coming, the night before, and now it was happening just as he'd feared.

# NINE

The night before the ambush, Billy and his crew had a club pow-wow in the desert. The usual midnight binger on the eve of a hijacking. The party was lit by headlights and fueled by drugs and hooch. Bo had been sitting off by himself, angry at the world, and even angrier at his father. He didn't understand how Billy could be drinking and carousing and having fun when everything they ever loved was lost forever. He figured his father had been lost too. He sat there dreaming of ways to escape him.

Then Levi turned up like a bad penny, and every private thought that Bo had was suddenly evaporating. This was one time that he just wanted to be alone. But *sometimes*, as Levi used to say, *alone ain't the way to go*. That was Levi. Always talking to the people that didn't want to be bothered. He was the kind of man you'd find in a bar after closing time, blabbering on about nothing and expecting everyone to laugh along with him. That's all he ever wanted to do: laugh. If Billy was a king, then Levi was his court jester. Eccentric, that's how you'd describe him in a word. He just looked different than everyone else, yet he always looked the same. He wore the same exact thing every day. Gold sunglasses, black leather pants that were too tight in the crotch, snakeskin boots pulled over his pants, a yellow t-shirt with a smiley face that said *happiest when I'm drunk*, a dirty red and black flannel that he never washed, and a denim biker's jacket with more patches on it than a poor man's quilt. But the way you picked Levi out of a crowd was by the hat. He always wore a Mobil trucker hat with the red *Flying Pegasus*, or as he always called it, "a horse with wings". It was, and always would be, his lucky hat. He never went anywhere without it. Not even to bed. He always said that's the place he needed it most, especially when he was stumbling out of a strip club with a voluptuous dancer on his hip. That line always got a laugh from Bo, even though Levi had used it a million times. Levi was the crazy uncle that nobody wanted but Bo got.

The drunken fool stood there that night at Bo's side looking as aimless as ever. He was two sheets to the wind and high as a kite. He'd been drinking his usual twelve and smoking pot with the half-blooded Apache. Bo figured the pot was probably laced with Peyote. They did all kinds of crazy shit.

"What's the matter?" Levi asked. "Why you over here sulking like the world is ending?"

*Because it is,* Bo thought. But he didn't say it. He kept his eyes down, looking at his own feet, wishing they would carry him off to someplace safe.

"You scared?" Levi asked.

Bo didn't say.

"What are you afraid of? Your daddy?"

Bo tried to harness the truth and chain it down, but his wavering eyes set it free.

"You're afraid he's gonna get us killed, huh?"

Bo nodded.

Levi grinned widely and sat down next to the boy and wrapped his arm around him. He held a bottle of hooch in one hand and a big fat joint in the other, its dark ashes flaking off onto Bo's *Highway To Hell* t-shirt. "Let me tell you something about your daddy," he said. "I've seen Billy beat a supercharged Caddy five-hundred on nitrous with nothing but a plain Jane three-fifty and four bald tires from a beat up Mitsubishi. Hell, I've seen him rocket down a half-assed dirt strip with his hair on fire, while he was blind-folded, with one hand tied behind his goddamn back. True story."

Bo scoffed at the claim. Levi never told true stories.

"I've seen him make grown men cry, I'll tell you that. I've seen it with my own eyes. Now what kind of man can make another man cry? I'll tell you what kind. A genuine badass. That's what kind."

Bo shook his head, "I'm not talking about the drag strip."

"I'm not either," Levi said. "I've seen your daddy take on thirteen men in a fist fight, and so have you."

Bo rolled his eyes. "They beat the shit out of him."

"Of course they did. There were thirteen of 'em. But did Billy ever back down?"

Bo didn't roll his eyes this time.

"No," Levi said. "He didn't. Not once. Not for a second. The thought of surrender never even crossed his goddamn mind, and it never will. And what happened to those thirteen men after that?"

Bo sat there motionless, not wanting to indulge the folklore that always seemed to make Billy's head swell.

"You were standing right beside me when it happened," Levi said. "What'd they do after they'd beaten Billy so bad he shouldn't have been able to stand, yet he stood taller than any of 'em?"

Bo didn't say.

"They rode for your daddy the very next day, didn't they?" Levi wouldn't take his eyes off the boy. "Why? Why would they follow him? He was nothing but a car builder and a street racer. They were bonafide outlaws. Bad men who had done bad things and done hard time for it. So why?"

Bo shrugged.

"Because Billy's spirit could never be broken," Levi said, "and theirs could. They knew a goddamn alpha when they saw one." He beamed with envy. "Billy ain't the biggest man. He ain't the strongest. Hell, he ain't even the fastest. But you'd have to kill 'em to beat 'em, and everyone knows that."

"Yeah," Bo said, "that's what I'm afraid of."

Levi realized his poor choice of words. "Ah shit," he said. "I guess I walked right into that one." He looked at the bottle of hooch in one hand and the big fat joint dangling in the other and said, "Maybe I should start choosing one or the other, and not both at the same time."

Bo looked at him pointedly and asked, "Are you afraid of him?"

Levi was suddenly speechless, which was a rare feat, especially when he was piss drunk and high at the same time.

"Are you?" Bo asked, sensing he had Levi on the ropes.

"Yes," Levi admitted, finally throwing in the towel. Then after some thought he said, "But I'm a coward."

Bo loosened his shoulders. He felt a sudden kinship. "Maybe being a coward is just… a sign of intelligence?"

Levi laughed. "Well, if I'm any measure it ain't. I'm as dumb as they come."

Bo didn't laugh. "Do you trust him?"

Levi thought for a moment. There was an obvious doubt in his stoney expression. "I trust him to do what's right."

Bo shook his head. "He doesn't know what's right."

Levi didn't dispute the surly notion. Then he smiled and said, "Your daddy loves you, boy. You know that?"

Bo sulked. "He loves the Dagger name more."

"That's not true," Levi said, looking as serious as Bo had ever seen him. "And some day he's gonna prove that to you. Maybe even tomorrow."

Bo crumpled up with confusion. He just couldn't imagine what that meant.

# TEN

"Bo, please," Billy shouted from the driver's seat. "You gotta pull the trigger. *Please, boy. Pull the fucking trigger!*"

But Bo couldn't break free from the limbo he'd been trapped in since the night before. The gravitational force of fear was still holding him in place, as if he were fated to fail. He was a coward, just like Levi, and that was undeniable. He knew it, and his father knew it too. Now the legendary Billy Dagger would die because his son — the *boy* — wasn't man enough to save him. Bo took his finger off the trigger and lowered his father's Ruger, surrendering to his own breaking heart. Fate would have the final say now.

He could do nothing to stop it.

Then as the man with the beastly shotgun appeared to be engaging, the Nimbus rig shuddered and the air brakes screeched and the trailer convulsed on its worn out tires and came to a stop in the middle of the highway.

Bo shrieked in victory, "They surrendered!" His eyes sparkled like mirror balls. He hadn't had that sort of look on his face since Christmas of '45, when Santa brought him a sprint go-cart with a camo paint job and a two-stroke engine after his parents told him he wasn't ready for one yet. And that's just how he felt in the moment. Like a kid on Christmas morning defying the odds. He dropped down into the seat with a confused smile on his face, not fully trusting his sudden feeling of hope.

Billy hit the brakes and jerked the wheel and spun a one-eighty, and as the Moon Runner wobbled to a merciful stop, he and Bo turned to one another and exchanged looks of sheer bewilderment. The *Dagger & Son* flag went limp in the stillness.

Billy grabbed the walkie. "We got 'em, Levi!" He smiled and grabbed Bo and pulled the boy close, embracing him the way he once did. "Levi," he said again into the walkie. "You on your way?"

There was no response. Just pure white noise.

"Levi, do you copy?" As the walkie fell silent again, Billy's smile began to fade. "Levi, it's Billy. Do you copy?"

Bo noticed the frigid concern on his face. "What's wrong?"

"It's just Levi playing dead," Billy said, dismissing the boy's instinct. "Nothing unusual. The two of you are…" He stopped himself from being too brutal. "He ain't your kin, boy… but sometimes I think you take after him, I swear."

Bo's smile turned to a frown as he recognized his father's insult. Levi was Billy's best friend, but he was a coward, and Billy despised that side of him. Bo figured he despised him too, and for the same reasons. Then he noticed a change in Billy's demeanor. It looked a lot like fear. "Dad, what's wrong?"

Billy didn't even hear the question.

Bo felt his own fear crawling back up the rumpled edges of his spine. It felt as if the atmosphere had changed around them. Sort of like the calm that lulls you to sleep right before a storm comes raging across the sky. Then to his surprise, Flyboy drove up in the '29 Tudor. Billy's friend hadn't abandoned them after all. He got out of his rat rod in a hurry with his AK-47 aimed at the man with the shotgun, who'd already stepped out of the Nimbus rig with his hands empty and held high in surrender. Then Merlin drove up in the '55 Ford and stuck the barrel of his shotgun in the driver's face, who was already trying to talk his way out of it.

The battle was over.

They'd won.

Billy turned to Bo, but he didn't look as enthusiastic as before. His eyes shifted.

"Something's wrong," Bo said. "I can feel it."

"Nothing's wrong," Billy said, trying to force a smile, but with unconvincing effect. "We just can't let our guard down like that again." He looked at the Nimbus rig, his eyes searching for something unseen.

"The fight ain't over yet?" Bo asked.

"No," Billy said. "It ain't over until we're driving away with that rig."

Bo's stomach began to churn. He then realized just how close they'd come to death, and like Billy always said, once death was near, it liked to stick around for a while, waiting for another opportunity. Death was always lurking around the corner, waiting anxiously in the barrel of some unseen gun, or in the tip of a hidden blade, or in the soft powdery insides of a hand grenade that no one ever saw coming. The reaper was always waiting. Bo felt restless again. His skin began to crawl.

Then Billy said, "You know what you gotta do, son. If something happens to me."

Bo shook his head. "Don't say it, Dad. Not this time. Please."

"If something happens to me, you gotta ride, boy."

"Stop saying that. Nothing's gonna happen to you."

"Listen to me, son."

Bo shook his head again. It was another one of Billy's tired old sermons that the boy hated to hear.

"You gotta survive on your own," Billy said. "You understand? Whatever it takes." He raised his wounded arm and placed his hand softly on Bo's shoulder. "Live off the grid if you can..." He raised a crude branding iron from the floorboard, with the letter *R* on the brand end. "...or blend in if you have to."

Bo remembered his father explaining the significance of the brand. An *R* on his shoulder meant he was a recent runaway from the Nimbus detention camps. So the Nimbus guards would assume he was an escapee and take him right back to camp, never thinking he might be Billy Dagger's son.

"But never tell 'em your name," Billy said. "We're the enemy to them. I won't be here to protect you. The Dagger name dies with me, you understand?"

Bo nodded, reluctant to even acknowledge such a terrible thought. "Dad," he said with a shivering tone. "I got a bad feeling."

"That's because you wanna live," Billy said. "That's a good feeling to have."

Bo closed his eyes tightly in frustration. His father could never admit when something wasn't right.

"It'll be okay," Billy said. "It always is." He pried the bone-handled Ruger from the boy's grip. "You remember the cue?"

Bo nodded. How could he forget? His father had practically burned it into the pallet of his brain.

Billy smiled and winked, and then he echoed what the boy's mother had always said, "Ride or die, son." He ruffled Bo's hair with his hand. "Take the wheel."

Bo didn't want to. He felt something breathing down the back of his neck. Like something hidden and waiting to strike.

Billy turned and stepped out of the Moon Runner. He

stood there for a moment with his back to the boy, lost in some thought that seemed to paralyze him. Then he turned back to Bo with a look in his eyes that the boy hadn't seen in ages. He looked like a father again, his eyes doting and alive. "Keep my seat warm for me," he said. Then he turned and walked away as if they'd always been strangers.

Bo slid into his father's place at the wheel.

The seat was already cold.

---

When Billy met Flyboy and Merlin at the back of the Nimbus cargo trailer, Merlin spit tobacco on the road and wiped the remnants from his mouth and said, "Where's that good-for-nothing VP of yours?"

"You know Levi," Billy said. "He only shows up when the shooting stops." He pulled the walkie from his pocket and inquired again, "Levi? Do you copy?"

There was no response.

"Levi, you bastard, where the hell are you?"

Then Levi's voice burst through the static, "Where's the fire?"

"It sure ain't under your ass," Billy snapped back.

Levi didn't respond, but Billy could hear the same hint of heavy breathing that he'd heard in the conversation before the ambush. "Where you at?" The walkie just chirped with white noise and nothing more. "Goddamnit, Levi."

"Don't wait for me," Levi finally said.

Billy sneered. "Do I ever?"

Then he ended the transmission, figuring he wouldn't see Levi until they were rolling away safely with the Nimbus rig in their possession. He tucked the walkie back into his pocket and turned and pressed the barrel of his Ruger to the driver's skull and said, "Open the truck or I'll open your head."

The driver didn't hesitate. Billy's reputation always preceded him, so nobody balked at his demands. The driver quickly popped the lock to the cargo door and stepped back. The door slid open on springs. Billy was expecting to see a truckload of vaccines packed neatly inside of their sealed boxes and stacked in nice wooden crates as usual. Instead he was startled by armed security guards aiming their assault rifles at him and shouting, "Drop the guns! Drop 'em now!"

He went stiff. Their gun-barrels were shaking nervously in his face. He could see they were on edge. They were bad men. Not military. Nimbus often hired thugs and ex-cons and offered them a chance to survive if they used the gun and their street instincts on behalf of the corporation. Billy could always recognize a previously incarcerated man. They carried what they'd learned in their eyes. It was the same look in all of them. A glaring proof of survival. A silent dare to disprove it. The intense refusal to look away. Billy knew they wouldn't back down, no matter how scared they were. He wouldn't back down either. But the shock in his eyes was unmistakable, and it was about to take a darker turn.

He watched intently as an armed guard — who appeared to be the leader of the bunch — shoved a hooded man to the edge of the trailer and placed a gun to his head. The hooded man was wearing tight leather pants and a patched denim vest over a red and black flannel, and in his left hand was a Mobil trucker hat with what appeared to be a red *Flying Pegasus* on the front panel. Billy felt an unfamiliar thump in his chest as the security leader ripped the hood from the man's head and revealed what Billy had already feared. The man beneath the hood was the man who'd helped him raise his son, bury his wife and daughter, and win his reputation on the street circuit. The man that he trusted most in the world. "Levi?"

"I'm sorry, Billy." Levi stood there trembling with guilt. "You were gonna get us all killed. What else could I do?"

Billy couldn't speak. He stood there silent and ghostly, as if he were already dead. No one had ever seen the legendary Billy Dagger lose before, at anything, but there he stood, defeated. His eyes had suddenly lost the indisputable impulse that always drove him forward.

"Levi... what did..." He paused, struggling to ask. "What did you do?"

"We should've run when we had the chance, Billy." Levi was in tears now. "You're obsessed, brother. You've always known how this was gonna end. It ain't right to drag us all down with you."

The security leader reached out and covered Levi's mouth with his hand and spoke to Billy himself, "Give up the guns, Dagger. Or your friend dies. You'll all die if you don't do as you're told. Lucian Vanderbon wants us to bring you in alive. If possible. He wants to make a deal."

Billy took a moment to gather his demoralized wits. "I don't make deals," he finally said.

The security leader exhaled sharply, as if he expected such a bull-headed response. "Lucian Vanderbon doesn't want anymore bloodshed."

"Could've fooled me," Billy said, "with those fifty-caliber rounds ripping into my truck, and into my fucking friends."

"He doesn't want anything to happen to your son."

Billy clenched his teeth. He never liked when strangers spoke of his own blood. It seemed to be happening a lot lately. As if everyone had forgotten who the boy's father was. "Lucian Vanderbon has plenty of blood on his hands. Why's he so concerned for my son?"

"We've been instructed to take you in alive," the security leader explained. "That's all I know. Your son won't be harmed. Neither will you or your crew. That's the deal. Don't make that impossible."

Before Billy could contemplate his next move, a man's voice called out from behind the guards on the highway, declaring that, "Every now and then God surprises us."

The guards jumped and turned their guns on him.

It was Reverend. He was standing there on the highway with an uzi aimed at them. They lurched forward with their M4s in a panic and began shouting, "Drop your weapon!"

"Hold your fire!" the security leader shouted. "Just calm the fuck down. Everybody calm down."

"That's Luke one twenty, from King James," Reverend said calmly, quoting the good book. "God really is full of surprises, ain't he?"

He looked at Billy.

Billy nodded.

The security guards looked eager to shoot.

"You weren't chosen by God," Reverend said to them. "Lucian Vanderbon is just a man, and not a very good one." He eyed the guards with the all-knowing glimmer of a holy man. "God is on *our* side. Not yours."

Some of the guards looked spooked, as if they suddenly believed it.

Billy smiled gravely. "Rev... You with me, Padre?"

"To the end," Reverend said. He kept his eyes on the guards as he quoted the Bible once more. "Timothy, book two, chapter four, verse seven. I have fought the good fight. I have finished the race. I have kept the faith."

Billy nodded in agreement. Then he turned to his other friends. "Merlin? What about you?"

"I'm here, ain't I?"

"Flyboy?"

"Do you even have to ask?"

Billy looked at the security leader, his eyes turning to blue flame. "Ya'll prepared to go out this way? Because *we are*."

The security leader held a silent gaze, and then his eyes began to shift and he looked like he was asking himself the same question. "You'd be a fool, Dagger," he finally said. "Take the deal. They're giving you the chance to live."

"Not the way I see it," Billy said.

"Give up your guns, Dagger."

"Giving up ain't something I do."

Then Levi interjected with a distressing howl and said, "You wanna quote the good book, Billy? Okay, I got one for you. Proverbs, sixteen-eighteen. You remember that one?"

Billy knew the passage. *Pride comes before the fall.* He looked at Levi now as if his best friend had just become his worst enemy.

In response, Levi looked devoid of life, as if he'd been stripped of everything that ever mattered to him. "Don't do this, Billy. Come on, brother."

"Don't call me *brother*," Billy said. "Never again."

Levi was gutted, looking hollow and empty, like an old tree dying from the inside out. His shoulders slumped and his bearded jawline sagged in disbelief. He looked at Flyboy and Merlin, expecting his other brothers to offer some kind of understanding, but they had the same bitter look as Billy: contempt for the Judas standing in front of them. Levi looked away.

Billy glared at the security leader for a moment, his darkening blue eyes sharpening like glass, but oddly enough, not piercing a hole through the man's soul as was rumored to happen. He looked back at the Moon Runner where Bo was peeking through the busted window with his head ducked and barely visible. The boy must've recognized the look in Billy's eyes because he put his hand out in a panic and mouthed the words, "*No, Dad! Don't!*"

Billy turned his eyes back to the armed Nimbus guards.

Levi must've recognized the look in Billy's eyes too because he began to beg nervously, "Please, Billy. You gotta surrender."

"You know I can't do that," Billy said. "I'm not like you."

"You ain't no fucking martyr!" Levi shrieked. "For God's sake, put an end to this shit!" He looked as if he already knew Billy's next move. "You got a little boy, Billy. Think about your son."

Billy turned and looked back at the Moon Runner. He didn't hesitate. He gave the cue. A hand on his heart. Bo went pale as a ghost. Billy looked at him for a moment, with fatherly eyes, his fiery blue irises doused by something unknowable but true, and then he turned back to Levi and said, "I never stop thinking about my son," and without another thought, he raised his Ruger and shot the security leader in the throat. The other guards fired back in a wild frenzy, every single gun blazing.

Levi screamed out, "Billy, no!" He lunged forward with his hand reaching out for his friend as if he could stop the tragedy from happening with sheer will. But the bullets kept flying, and Billy was struck so many times that he looked like a spouting fountain. His upper chest was blasted above the breast plate. His shoulder was thrashed and left mangled. His gut was punctured. His body convulsed from the constant bludgeoning of Nimbus bullets. The same corporate heart-stoppers that had taken his daughter's life. He fell to his knees and toppled onto the highway. He lay there in a pool of his own blood, drawing haggard breaths.

Bo slammed his hands onto the steering wheel and

screamed in silence, his agony drowned out by the endless gunfire.

Merlin and Flyboy traded shots with the Nimbus guards, their guns blazing mercilessly. In the midst of the madness, Levi was knocked to the floor of the trailer. He rolled off onto the highway below, hitting the pavement like a bag of crumbling bricks. He lay there for a moment, his eyes on Billy, watching in remorse. He could see Billy was still alive, his chest rising up and down, practically convulsing, but still taking air into his punctured lungs.

"Billy, I'm coming!" He crawled to his best friend in a hurry while bullets hissed above his head. He staggered to his feet and pulled Billy to his knees. Billy spit blood from his mouth. His eyes wandered aimlessly from side to side. Levi wrapped his arms around his waist and pulled him to his feet. "Let's get you out of here." They made their way to the Moon Runner with arms locked and Levi carrying all the weight. "Stay with us, Billy. Don't go, brother. Not like this."

The gunfight was still raging around them like some bloody battle on the day of Last Judgement. Flyboy was shot in the kevlar vest, but he stayed in the fight and kept firing back. Merlin was blasted in the chest and knocked off his feet. Then another round of bullets shredded him from head to toe. His eyes would never open again. No more magic. Reverend was shot in the gut and bleeding out beneath his kevlar vest. He rested on his knees, repeating a passage from the Bible. The one about fighting the good fight and keeping the faith. A Nimbus guard finished him off with a bullet to the head. Flyboy traded shots with the few remaining guards, gunning them down as he gave what was given. He took his death standing up with his finger on the trigger and spraying bullets at the few guards that were left alive. They fell to the ground. If their wounds weren't immediately fatal, it wouldn't be long before they finally succumbed to them. This was a massacre, as Bo had predicted. There would be no survivors. Maybe not even him.

Levi opened the passenger side door. "You gotta get out of here."

Bo was in the driver's seat, lost in absolute ruin and looking paralyzed by the sight of his father's punctured body. Billy spit up blood as Levi helped him into the seat. His body hit the arctic white fiber and collapsed. His head bobbled on the headrest and his arms went limp by his side.

Levi looked at Bo with a crushing sorrow on his face. "It wasn't supposed to go down like this." He didn't try to explain himself to the boy or wait for forgiveness. He slammed his hand down on the roof of the truck and ordered him to, "Ride, boy. Go! Get the fuck out of here!"

Bo was jolted back to the cold reality in front of him. He gripped the steering wheel and shifted into first gear, his eyes focused on making his escape. He revved the engine and popped the clutch and stomped his foot on the gas. The Moon Runner launched down the highway as Nimbus bullets pelted the side of the truck.

Levi was shot in the thigh. He clutched his wound and fell to one knee and turned to see the shooter. It was the security leader that Billy had shot in the throat. He was pressing his hand against the bloody hole in his neck. Levi tried to muster enough courage to engage with him. The security leader threw his empty handgun aside and swung his rifle around on the shoulder strap. The blood poured from his open wound. He took unsteady aim at the Moon Runner as it fled down Route 66. Bo's head was in the trembling crosshairs. Then a shot rang out and the security leader's chest burst open and his dead body hit the pavement.

Levi had blasted a hole straight through him with Billy's

Ruger. It was his attempt at a quick redemption, though he knew it wouldn't be that easy for him. He clutched his thigh and turned his eyes west, looking for the Moon Runner and making sure that Bo had escaped. The truck was fleeing down Route 66 at lighting speed as it disappeared behind a wall of granite rock. Levi sat down on the blood-soaked highway and closed his eyes in remorse. Then he felt the exhaustive sting of a guilty conscience, and he knew it would be eternal. Something that he may never escape, in this life or the next.

———

Bo had the pedal to the floorboard. His rattled mind was spinning like fresh cheater slicks. His eyes were bouncing recklessly in their sockets, searching for a way out. He just wanted to find someplace safe. A place where he could nurse his father back to health. He rocked the dagger-handled shifter into fifth gear and pushed the limits of his own skill. He just wanted to be free from the bullets and the blood and his father's fateful legacy. But he could feel something on their six, trying to catch up, breathing down their necks like some unseen hand, and suddenly a dark whisper of smoke began to rise from the engine block, obstructing his view of the highway ahead, as if to say, "*Sorry, Kid. This is the end of the road.*" He could feel the twisted hand of fate wrapping its crooked fingers around his heart and squeezing. He panicked and downshifted and pulled off the highway where the massive wall of rock ended. He brought the Moon Runner to a stop just off the shoulder, straddling the cracked pavement of Route 66 and the crusted earth of the Mojave. He turned to Billy's aid. "Dad, are you..." He could barely get his words out. "What happened?"

Billy couldn't speak at all. The blood was swelling into his esophagus, slowly clogging his airway.

"Dad, tell me. What happened?"

Billy gurgled and pushed his strangulated voice through the dense pocket of blood. "The bastard... he betrayed me."

"Who?"

"Levi," Billy said, struggling to make himself heard. "He... the son of a bitch sold us out."

Bo sat perfectly still for a moment. He wasn't surprised by the betrayal. Just heartbroken. He wondered how his father could be so blind. *How could he not see this coming?* Levi was his best friend, but the drunken coward couldn't be trusted to have anyone's back. Not even Billy's. There must've been signs. Obvious tells. But Billy would've missed them. He always had a weakness. A blindspot. Too much pride and trust that everyone around him would follow him without question, *ride or die.* He never looked in the rearview mirror, he just changed lanes at will, expecting everyone to move out of his way or fall in line behind him. Bo understood why Levi had betrayed his father, but all he could think about now was being left alone.

"Dad, please," he cried. "Don't leave me like this. Please don't go. I can't do this alone."

He checked Billy's wounds, which were too many to process. Blood was seeping from his gut. An expanding puddle of crimson. Bo pushed the black leather jacket aside with his hand and saw more bloody holes. From what he knew of bullet wounds, these couldn't be healed. Not with any instruments or drugs or stitches, and certainly not with divine intervention. The wounds were fatal. Every single one of them. Like it was meant to be. As if each bullet had Billy's name engraved on it, masterfully written in God's hand. Bo felt helpless to stop it, like fighting against a fate that had already been predetermined, perhaps years ago at that Saturday street market in Kingman, Arizona. The old blind fortune teller lady wasn't so crazy after all. "What should I do?" he asked in a panic.

Billy pulled him closer. He stared into the boy's eyes like a doting father again and whispered the only thought he had left. "Don't tell 'em your name, son."

The words came out almost silently, but Bo heard them loud and clear. They were the words he never wanted to hear. *Don't tell 'em your name, son.* It meant he'd be left in this terrible world alone. "Dad, please... *Don't.*" Then he watched in horror as Billy drew his final breath. A terrible gasp. A painful strain for more life. Billy's eyes glazed over and the last bit of air rattled from his lungs. Bo cried out like a child, "No! Daddy!"

The mysterious spark of life inside of Billy Dagger had suddenly gone dark, and so had the dull flicker of Bo's internal light. He was just an empty, unlit vessel now. For a moment he remembered the father he'd once loved. The man that held him in his arms when he was a little boy. The man who shielded him from the world when it became too cruel to endure. The man that taught him how to ride a bike, throw a baseball, flirt with girls, drink a beer and race cars. The man who used to love him above all other things. He grabbed a fistful of Billy's leather jacket and shrieked, "You can't do this to me! You asshole! Don't leave me!" He shook Billy's body, trying desperately to bring him back to life. "Wake up, Dad! Please! Wake up!"

Billy's head fell backwards against the headrest and bobbled like something inanimate, his dead eyes rolling around in the sockets like a doll. Bo suddenly felt untethered, as if he could float out into the universe aimlessly and out of control and without any kind of purpose or meaning. His heart was pounding harder, but he could hardly feel the perilous thump. He just wanted his heart to stop altogether. He wanted the pain of life to cease. He sat there for a moment, lost and confused and crumbling into unrecognizable pieces, like some glass sculpture being shattered. Then suddenly, as if letting go of something he'd once held precious, he felt nothing at all. Not even the numbness of grief. He came crashing back down to earth, feeling crushed by an unbearable weight. His father's fate had always been inescapable, and now he'd have to accept the finality of it. Billy Dagger wasn't coming back.

"Dad," he whispered, "why'd you do this to me? I told you to take me someplace safe."

He closed his eyes and fell back into the driver's seat and refused to look at Billy's corpse. They sat there motionless, the father and the son, only one dead but both already ghosts. As the warm desert breeze swirled through the Moon Runner, howling like a devil in victory, Bo sat there behind the wheel staring into some uncharted oblivion. He always knew the Moon Runner would be his father's tomb. He'd seen this moment in his dreams. His father lying dead in the seat. His eyes devoid of spirit. No words spoken between them. Just a cold silence, as harsh and unrelenting in death as it was in life. *How could you let this happen to me?* Bo asked in his fragile mind. *Maybe this is what you always wanted.*

The blaze had finally come for the legendary Billy Dagger, but Bo didn't see the glory in it. He grabbed the war bag and took inventory of its contents. A loaded Colt .45, a few extra bullets, some dented cans of food and the branding iron with the *runaway* brand on the end. He had a choice to make now: run, blend in, or just accept that he was fated to die too. Soon his agony turned to angst. He could see the bleak Mojave desert through the starry cracks in the windshield. The endless waves of earth were sprawling out before him like a sea of dirt waiting to pull him under the ground and drown him in the darkness below. He looked at Billy once more and whispered, "I hate you. I hate you forever."

He kicked the driver's side door open and got out of the truck and refused to close the door behind him, leaving his father's body exposed inside of the Moon Runner, to be discovered by Nimbus, and likely defiled, and probably paraded around in victory to deter any future uprisings or would-be heroes. It didn't matter to him anymore.

*Let them have the hero,* he thought. *This is what the bastard always wanted. His blaze of glory.*

Then he fled alone into the unforgiving Mojave with little more than a week's worth of food and only enough ammo to stave off a few ravenous drifters. It wouldn't be long before he was out of everything, hope included. The horizon looked out of reach to him, but he didn't expect to reach it anyway. The Mojave was nothing but a burial ground. A wilderness of death. It had swallowed his mother and his sister, and now it would swallow him too. He ran and never stopped, straying further from himself with every step, and losing a bit of his soul with every tear that fell, as if he were shedding his skin and rapidly morphing into someone else.

By the time the sun had disappeared behind the horizon that evening, Bo Dagger had disappeared behind his own eyes. Billy's son was gone for good, whether he survived the desert or not. There was nothing left of him. All that remained was a nameless shell. A fractured soul beyond repair. A runaway with no past and a future that was fading like his father's legacy.

# BOOK TWO

## SINS OF THE FATHER

# ONE

After two and a half decades of lies and embellishments, the truth about Billy Dagger had become a twisted, mercurial thing. There was never any proof of the outlaw's existence and no proof of his death. No photographed corpse or decapitated head on a pike. No dead body paraded around in victory by the Nimbus Corporation. No legendary Moon Runner to burn as a funeral pyre. No flying colors or crossed daggers. Nothing left of the *Old 66*. No relics of *Dagger & Son Kustoms*. No next of kin to carry on the Dagger name. Nobody claimed that birthright. All that remained of Billy Dagger were the stories. The lies and embellishments. Everything but the truth. The man of flesh and blood had become a myth. A dangerous name spoken only in secret.

### THE "NEW WORLD", 2074
### THE REPUBLIC OF PHOENIX

All across the globe the abandoned cities had become

ghosts. Decomposing bodies of steel and glass. Manmade skeletons. Their bones broken and partially buried beneath a jungly canopy. The infinite crawl of greenery blanketed the crumbling remains of human ingenuity as if Mother Nature were covering herself in shame. Wild animals roamed freely among the ruins without the burden of humanity to restrain them. Birds nested in shattered skyscrapers, their songs uncorrupted and carried on the breeze for miles. Windblown seed sprouted trees in strange places. Deer scampered through the city playgrounds where children once spent their Sunday afternoons wishing they'd never have to grow up and endure the chaos of their parent's failed society. Feral hogs hunted in wild packs down the main streets, having taken up the mantle of most destructive species on Earth. Animals, both wild and once held captive, had multiplied over the years, conquering a land that was foreign and dangerously unnatural to them.

As for humanity, they'd been all but wiped out by the Red Death virus. Some forty-million living souls had survived back in '49. How many still remained twenty-five years later was anyone's guess. Most of them roamed in primitive bands or lived in scattered colonies, either scavenging like vultures or cultivating the land with their own hands and protecting it with their lives. A return to simplicity. The earth had fallen silent around them. The city lights that once weaved their flickering web across the globe had gone dark. From outer space the world would've looked completely lifeless, if not for the incessant neon glow of one thriving city. The sole survivor among the ghosts.

---

Lucian Vanderbon stood alone in the executive boardroom on the top floor of Nimbus Tower One. He was seventy-seven years old and still CEO of the corporation that he'd founded in his garage over fifty years earlier. His ancient eyes peered through a wall of picture windows, staring down at his boldest creation of all: the Republic of Phoenix. The prosperous city that he owned. The last city on Earth. He whispered, "Rise up, my beloved beast." But the words felt impure, as if he were mocking the sentiment.

The suffocating metropolis was spread out in all its glory, like the wings of the mythological bird from which it took its name. Lucian could see everything from his perch on high. His eyes traveled miles in mere seconds, from border wall to border wall. He watched the bustling productivity unfold, as he did every morning before his daily briefings. It reminded him of why he existed. The order among the disorder. The oversight of the human cogs that kept the well-oiled machine pumping. Public transportation vehicles cruised freely down the orchestrated web of roadways without blockage or interruption or the bottlenecking effects of poor infrastructure. Maglev trains reached their planned destinations in record time, like bullets fired on magnetic rails. Shipping lanes buzzed with the latest and greatest of retail and technology. People in the streets below walked to work with heat resistant umbrellas blocking the brutal scorch of the sun. They looked like tiny ants commiserating in their sacred colony. Everything was in its right place. Upright and pure. Lucian was there to keep it all from collapsing again.

The new Phoenix had been rebuilt over the old infrastructure at a frantic pace, on a foundation of paranoia and reclusion. A compressed, urban squeeze of a city that was walled off in '49 and isolated from the outside world ever since. They'd always had the same problem: too many people in too little space. 12.3 million people to be precise. All squeezed into five-hundred square miles of compact living. There were seven main regions of the city. The neon-lit vertical dwellings of *Sky Haven*, the urban sprawl of the *Boroughs*, the suburban opulence of the *Vale*, the ecoTowers and vertical farms of the *Green District*, the brick and mortar strip of the *Industrial Zone*, the heavily guarded *Border Province*, and the imperious *Corporate Sector* on the southern border where business was always in full swing. At the center of the corporate sector stood the Nimbus Towers, all three of them encompassed by a massive halo made of steel and orange neon tubing which lit up the night sky, shining like a celestial body and captivating the entire Republic below. The "burning" orange halo of the Nimbus Towers could be seen for miles, from the flats of the Boroughs to the rolling valleys of the Vale. It was the glowing icon of Phoenix.

Everything branched out from Corporate Square. Lofty office buildings jutting upwards like monoliths growing out of the earth, as if they were an ancient gift from some extraterrestrial civilization. All the branches of Corporate operated within those glassy high-rises. Treasury and Finance. Marketing. Manufacturing. Asset Management. Business Development. Engineering. Technology. Product Distribution. Risk Management. So on and so forth. A department for everything. No details went uncrossed or without dots. Nobody went unmonitored. Nimbus Security was always watching. Control was a precious commodity. The city they were protecting was nothing short of a miracle.

Lucian was lord over all of it. The President of the Republic. Everything fell on his slinking shoulders. The past twenty-five years had been good to him. He'd lived the excessive lifestyle of a single, womanizing trillionaire before the Collapse, and in the decades that followed, he'd lived as the most powerful man in the world, with zero limitations, and no need to buy loyalties or climb political ladders. He'd made the kings of history look like peons, and the gods he didn't believe in look like mortal men. He was the imperious but charming face of Nimbus that everyone knew and loved. But he hadn't aged as gracefully or as fruitfully as he'd lived. His head was a silvery splotch of thinning hair and his face was wrinkled and leathery and suffering the duel effects of time and gravity. His gaze didn't carry the same conviction as it once had. He looked defeated around the sockets. Too much indulgence and too little time to exorcise the demons that always remained in the wake of such excess. He was suffering now from multiple sclerosis and nagging arthritis, and those were only the ailments that were made official. He was still capable of his trademark charm, but he pulled no punches these days. Especially behind closed doors. In fact, his old age and decline in health were making him swing even harder.

As the board room door opened behind him, he practically roared, "The meeting begins in thirty seconds, not a moment sooner. So whoever you are, *fuck off.*"

Another, less distinguished executive entered the board room wearing a dark blue suit and a bright purple tie. His brown hair was slicked back and well-groomed and his chiseled face was free of the usual sag and blemishes that one might associate with middle age. His name was J.W. Pharaoh. The Vice President of the company.

Lucian frowned at his nagging presence, "If I'd known it was you, I would've locked the door."

"I see we're still on shaky ground," Pharaoh said, his voice a raspy timbre, audibly unique and distinguishable from all others.

"Steady as can be," Lucian said. "I'm too old to hold

grudges. I just value my solitude, and you seem to purposely disrupt it every chance you get."

Pharaoh scoffed with his usual smugness. A trait he could never dismantle. He was forty-nine years old that morning and every single one of those years had been a battle for respect. He'd come from absolutely nothing. An orphaned weed in the garden with no roots to keep him planted in the soil. That was his lifelong war: self-ascendance. You could practically see the vigilance in him. He was short on people skills, but a political scrapper. The kind of man that would kick, bite and claw his way to the top, and he'd done just that. "I know that troubled look, Lucian. The last time I saw that look, you voted to pass legislation for refugee healthcare. I hope you're not about to make an even bigger mistake."

Lucian kept his attention on the city below. He and his right-hand man had a tumultuous working relationship of late. But the bitter silence between them was new.

Pharaoh uncoiled, and the words rattled off his tongue like something venomous. "Were you planning to consult with me before you offered it up to the board? Or is my council just a mere formality at this point?"

His question went unanswered as the double doors swung open and five other businessmen entered the room. They took their seats around a long, rectangular table with a mythological Phoenix carved into the wood, its body engulfed by chiseled flames. Pharaoh eased into his chair with his eyes still on Lucian. The executives waited patiently for their CEO to speak. There were seven board members in all, including Pharaoh and Lucian himself.

Galen Spade was the bulldog of the board. The man with the loudest bark. He never saw an argument that he didn't immediately want to win. He even looked like a bulldog. Short, stout, with a square jaw and dull eyes that didn't seem to carry the same weight as his loaded words.

Ravi Patel was the mediator of the board. A diplomatic man who never liked to rock the political boat too much for fear of actually having to swim. He had dark, intimidating features that often veiled his cautious demeanor.

Lawrence B. Billings, on the other hand, veiled nothing. He had little patience for diplomacy, and no qualms about voicing his displeasure. But unlike the others he delivered his scathing rebukes with etiquette. He had intellectual toughness. Lucian always appreciated that.

Charlie Ming was the one Lucian trusted the most. A life-long businessman who only saw the bottom line and did everything he could to raise it to more tolerable levels. It was just business to him and nothing more.

Then there was Jordan Ambrose, the *black sheep* of the board. The thorn in their side. The youngest member, and the most recent addition to the table. He was thirty-five years old and full of unwelcome idealism. Lucian saw an infinite amount of potential in him, but sadly, the young man had yet to maximize it beyond partying and politicking for the cameras. As Lucian had always told him, the cameras were just a tool. The boardroom was the workshop. You couldn't make good use of one without the other. But Jordan Ambrose never heeded the wisdom.

Lucian stood there with his back to them as they traded looks of curiosity, wondering why their President was so withdrawn and staring out of the window as if he'd finally lost his aging mind. "Our city is being crushed," he finally said. "The feeling of suffocation and implosion is growing among our citizens. Tensions are rising." He took a breath to ease the rise of his own. "Inequalities that were once conveniently ignored are now being exposed. The people are drawing lines of division among themselves and choosing sides again. A return to something we've always fought to eliminate. Political turmoil."

The executives seemed to agree, their heads nodding in unison like pre-programmed automatons. Refugees had been smothering their border for decades in the refugee camp just outside the western wall. A place commonly known as *Brimstone*. The presence of refugees was nothing new, but their numbers had been increasing at an alarming rate over the past few years, and so had their social influence over the citizens of Phoenix, who had recently begun to voice their grievances and wishes in ways which they never had before. The corporate structure of the Republic was at risk of turning into another open democracy of conflicting ideologies where people made demands and responded to any refusals with protests and riots and acts of political violence. No one wanted that. Society had been crippled by that kind of raw liberty before.

"Gentlemen, we've reached another milestone," Lucian announced. "Unfortunately it's not the kind of milestone that warrants a celebration or a pat on the back." He turned to address them, his eyes cast upon them like a disappointed god. "There are now *two million* refugees living in Brimstone."

The executives didn't seem provoked by the news. It wasn't exactly a revelation.

Lucian displayed a descriptive chart on the wallscreen. The latest statistics. Their refugee problem was becoming undeniably vexing. The social issue of their time.

"That's two million refugees and counting," he said. "All receiving free corporate healthcare on a daily basis. All receiving free worldly goods from our manufacturing plants and our markets. That's two million pairs of shoes every six months. Two million pairs of socks. Not to mention all the fresh clothing we provide annually. That's two million mouths to feed. Two million asses to wipe. Are you recognizing a trend?"

No one answered the question, recognizing the rhetorical nature of it.

"That's forty two million pounds of food rations a week. Thirty million gallons of drinking water a month. Not to mention the recycled bathing water and the constant costs of sewage and sanitation required to keep their conditions livable." He paused for effect, as he often did, allowing the executives to take note of the staggering numbers, which they'd always conveniently ignored. "We burn almost a billion kilowatt hours of solar electricity each year just to keep Brimstone running. We have to power the ration center, the field hospitals, the fire stations, the border patrol facilities, and the fucking *five-star* embassy. The cost in labor alone to keep that refugee camp operable is beyond astronomical. We're spending billions in corporate profit to keep these refugees fed, clothed and healthy." He paused for effect again, then he simply asked, "Why?"

The executives sat there looking glib. They turned to their Vice President, J.W. Pharaoh, who just shrugged with a bitter indifference.

"That's an actual question," Lucian said. "Not a rhetorical. Don't let it linger in the air like flatulence. Why do we continue to accommodate these people at such a great cost to our corporation?"

The executives traded a series of reluctant glances, each avoiding eye contact with Lucian and hoping someone among them might have a canned answer at their disposal.

Then Spade leaned forward and said something he and the other executives would immediately regret, "Sir, do we have a viable alternative?"

Lucian's face tightened, looking like worn leather being

stretched to its breaking point. "That's the problem with this board. You just answered a question by asking another fucking question."

The executives were glued to their seats, not wanting to stir the pot any further.

All but one.

Jordan Ambrose, the black sheep, leaned forward and said, "It's because we're afraid of losing the status quo."

The other executives glared at him as if he were a traitor that had just been discovered among them.

"Ah, there it is," Lucian said. "The undeniable truth."

Then the room erupted with protests and verbal assaults, all of them targeted at the black sheep.

"You're part of that status quo, Ambrose, you pretentious hack,"Spade said.

Pharaoh scoffed dramatically and added, "Yeah, for Christ's sake, Ambrose, don't leap into the saddle of your high horse just yet."

"What can I say?" Ambrose smirked. "I'm a political cowboy."

"Then consider me a fucking Indian," Spade grumbled.

Lucian just sat there shaking his weary head. "A little finger pointing, and some feather ruffling, and suddenly the cocks are ready to crow."

And crow they did, every one of them lambasting the black sheep. Jordan Ambrose was a constant target at these meetings. The other executives never liked how he'd come by his seat at the table. His father Byron Ambrose had been a respected oil tycoon before the Collapse who had then served faithfully as the seventh member of the Nimbus board for twenty years until his death. When he passed away in '66, Lucian named Byron's only son Jordan to replace him at the table, without consulting the board, and without respecting their misgivings. So they always had an outspoken contempt for the *"son with the silver spoon dipped in crude oil."*

"I'm perfectly content to rewrite the status quo to better serve the people," Ambrose said in his own defense. "Whether I'm part of it or not."

Pharaoh snickered. "You've forgotten who you're advocating for, Ambrose, you spoon-fed daddy's boy."

Ambrose's role was unique to the board. A chosen advocate for the people, or as Pharaoh still called them, *employees.*

"I'm an advocate for the truth," Ambrose said. "No matter which side of the wall it falls on."

"You've never been on the other side of that wall," Pharaoh snapped.

Lucian slammed his gavel down on the wooden block. "Enough crowing." He sighed heavily. "Someday I'd like to get through one of these meetings without getting our hackles up."

The board quieted down, but Pharaoh's impudent eyes lingered on the black sheep.

"Our own people are out there protesting," Lucian said. "*Protesting.* That's not supposed to happen in a well-oiled machine. Discontent is society's achilles heal. The crowds are getting larger every day. Their voices are getting louder. Do we really believe that's going to change?"

"I'm of the opinion that they'll lose interest," said Patel.

Lucian shifted his eyes. "Lose interest?"

"People follow trends," Patel explained. "They move in fleeting crescendos, like blips on the radar. This will fade."

"And what happens when they lose interest? The two million refugees at our border wall just vanish into thin fucking air?"

Patel withdrew his poor effort.

"This problem won't go away," Lucian said, "whether our

people lose interest or not. It's a logistics problem. A financial problem. A self-preservation problem. We've created a monster that we now have to appease in order to escape its bite."

Ming leaned forward in his chair and asked, "Why should we continue to be the hand that feeds them?"

"Great question," Spade said. "They're robbing us blind. We should deport them all back to the Blaze."

"Indeed," said Billings. "That's the simplest solution."

The Blaze, as they called it, was everything outside of the Republic, from the territorial lines on the map to the coastlines in all directions. It was rumored among the citizens of Phoenix to be a scorched land where nothing could grow in the soil and animals were scarcely found. The Great Plains were black now, left in ash and dry soil. The parts of the Blaze that weren't burnt by wildfires were plagued by locusts and endless drought and murderous gangs.

Ambrose practically snarled. "We can't unleash two million desperate people back into the Blaze. They'll have no viable home, no way to produce food, no available water, and certainly no will to act civil."

The room erupted again, the insults so abundant they sounded more like an incomprehensible drone than a series of cutting words.

"*He's right*," Lucian announced, cutting through their noise before their sharp words could draw blood. "They'll come right back to our borders, but this time with anger, and quite possibly with weapons. It won't end well. Not for anyone. Lest we forget, we're vulnerable right now."

The executives conceded to his point. Half of their security forces were currently spread out across the continent on newly established mining and recovery operations in rotting big cities like New York, Chicago and Washington D.C., protecting the Nimbus workers while they pillaged for historical artifacts, documents, art work and anything else of relevance that should be preserved on behalf of humanity. An order of business that they'd all agreed upon. So the Republic of Phoenix and its borders weren't as well-guarded as usual, which meant any war, big or small, would be costly. Their city would be an easier target. They'd found a way to make themselves even more vulnerable than they already were.

"Then keep the refugees right where they are," Spade said, "but cut their rations and accommodations by half."

"Half rations?" Ambrose rolled his eyes. "You know that won't work."

"Force them to make a hard choice," Spade insisted. "Either live like beggars at our borders, barely scraping by on half rations, or go make their own way in the Blaze."

Ambrose huffed. "Many of these people *were* making their own way in the Blaze before they came here."

"Oh here we go," Pharaoh said. "The people's advocate has spoken."

"That is until it became too hot, too dry, too burnt by wildfire to sustain their agriculture."

"Spare us the theatrics," Pharaoh said. "You're not in front of the cameras, Jordan. Have you forgotten that the jurisdiction of your moral support ends at our border wall? You're an advocate for our employees. The people who provide legitimate services. Not to the refugees, who *by the way* are constantly undermining the efforts of the very employees you're trying to protect."

"They had no choice but to embrace a shadow economy," Ambrose argued. "So they wouldn't have to be dependent on our corporation."

"And look at them now," Pharaoh said with a scoff. "They can't take a piss without our help."

Lucian slammed the gavel onto the wooden block again. "All that matters is what our citizens think." He eyed Pharaoh and Ambrose until their eyes met his, and then he continued his lecture. "There are dozens of new refugees flooding into Brimstone every day from the Blaze. That won't stop, no matter how many border patrols we station in the Rim. They'll keep coming, and the people will continue to voice their concern as Brimstone becomes less sanitary. It's a breeding ground for disease. The people are growing weary of the constant quarantines. They want change, and these protests won't remain civil for much longer if their demands continue to fall on deaf ears."

"They're just taunting us with these protests," Pharaoh said bitterly, "and you're falling for it. It's bad optics, nothing more."

"Bad optics?" Lucian pointed to the wallscreen, which was now broadcasting live surveillance footage from a boomerang drone. "That's not a taunt. That's not bad optics. That's a fucking *movement*."

The executives watched the unsettling images of the current protests in the Border Province. People shouting their pent-up grievances, holding signs and demanding change with a primal urge to lash out. The Border Patrols that were tasked with keeping them calm were on the verge of losing their cool and creating more problems.

"We keep hoping that they'll give up and go home for good," Lucian said, "but they never do. It's only a matter of time before these protests turn violent. When that happens, we will have lost something that we may never regain." The executives already knew what he was referring to, but he said it anyway. "*Control*."

Control was everything to Corporate. It was the ghost in their precious machine. The very thing that made the engine run. If people started believing there was a better way to set themselves in motion, the engine would fail, the Republic would break down, and the Nimbus Corporation would crumble to pieces. That's why Corporate always had men in place to ensure those pieces remained intact. Men with badges. Men without scruples. Men like Brixton Grace, their golden boy of law enforcement.

# TWO

Brixton Grace had fallen so far from glory that he'd forgotten how it felt to be glorified in the first place. To have his name spoken with such reverence and corporate pride. To be the center of attention when he walked into a room full of Nimbus royalty. To have women throwing themselves at him, walking around with the mattress practically strapped to their backs. Now he had to pay for that kind of pleasure. Now when he walked into a room, the needle on the record scratched and everyone stopped and stared in apprehension, as if something unfortunate was about to happen, and when they spoke his name, it was with contempt and a predetermined sense of dread, as if his reputation preceded him just to clear the room. *My how the mighty have fallen.*

### BRIMSTONE REFUGEE CAMP
### THE WESTERN BORDERLANDS

When the Republic of Phoenix disposed of trash, they transported it first to the Nimbus Waste Management Facility in Brimstone, just on the other side of the border wall to the west, along the defunct stretch of 19th Avenue. The facility had been converted from an old railroad plant into a holding area for waste. Trash from the city. Sewer drainage from the slums of the refugee camp. Any and all human filth. The trash was then sorted by workers and transported by garbage trains to locations far from the city walls, out into the endless sprawl where the Nimbus Corporation had set up landfills and dump sites among the suburban rot. It wasn't the most environmentally sound form of waste management, but at least the people of the Republic didn't have to look at their own trash or smell the stench of their own leavings. So no one complained about the logistics.

That morning Brixton's Volt-22 police cruiser was parked in the scattered trash just outside of the holding area. The engine was running idle and ready to leave in a hurry if necessary. He knew they could be watching. The Volt-22 was an electric-powered, aerodynamic piece of futuristic machinery, with sharp body lines and sporty curves, and the engine fluttered almost soundlessly as it idled, like the rapid wings of a hummingbird. The official emblem of the Republic was emblazoned on the sides. A burnt orange mythological phoenix rising out of burning flames. There was a shining halo of fire around its head. The words *Phoenix Police Department* and *Border Division* were inked in black. Brixton sat behind the wheel with his biomask on. The glass faceplate was fogging up from his rapid breathing. His amber eyes were scanning his surroundings nervously, as if he were waiting for something unfortunate to happen. His hands were gripping the steering wheel with such unnecessary force that it was threatening to rip the plastic of his skin-tight biogloves. The AC was cranked to sixty degrees. Outside it was already approaching one hundred. Despite the morning heat, Brixton wore his usual detective garb. A white dress shirt, pleated pants, a matching coat, and a bland-looking tie that looked like all the other bland-looking ties in his wardrobe. It was department code to look like an asshole. The only thing missing was a fedora, but Brixton didn't wear one of those. Only douchebags wore those. He might've been a colossal asshole, but he was no douchebag.

He was a detective by virtue of the job description, but not in name. In the Republic of Phoenix they were called Inspectors, not detectives, but the job was pretty much the same: figure shit out and bust some heads. That's how Brixton put it. Though today he was more worried about his own head. "Where the fuck is that asshole?"

He checked the time on a small, translucent device in his hand. The digital clock said: *7:36 AM.* The device was part smart phone — with calling capabilities and limited information technologies — and part police radio — with a two-way dispatch and a live feed that was broadcast 24/7 from the many surveillance drones that monitored the city. It sent signals via the Nimbus Mercury 5 Satellites that orbited the earth. Only cops and corporate suits carried these satellite phones. Not the general public. The common people of the Republic didn't have access to such powerful tools. Those types of limitless technologies had been the downfall of society once before, so that would never be allowed to happen again. Not on Corporate's watch. The phone couldn't even record sound or video. In fact, there were no recording devices allowed in the Republic of Phoenix at all, except for the surveillance drones and hidden security cameras, which were all controlled by the corporation. Brixton checked the time again on his SAT phone. It said *7:37 AM.* "Ah Christ," he groaned. "Where is that fucking slum bunny?"

That slum bunny — otherwise known as a refugee — was slugging his way through the flood of trash flowing out of a massive sewage pipe. He had a long brown beard that looked like the fine bristles of a broomstick with the dirt still swept up and clinging to the bristly hairs. His belly was plump and round like a certain man in a big red suit, and though he didn't have the sleigh or the eight tiny reindeer, he was just as jolly and giving. Everyone knew him as Gypsy, the man who could get you anything. A Merchant for the Bloody Knuckles crime organization. A cog in their black market. But he ran his own operation on the side, with select clientele: citizens of the Republic. Mostly authority types. Cops. Firemen. Health workers. Even some low-ranking businessmen. Whoever needed his services and could pay a premium. He didn't discriminate.

He shook a rat from his dirty pant leg and stomped at it with his mismatched rain boots. The rat scurried away. "I'll eat you later, you filthy little fuckstew." He carried on through the disgusting heap of wet trash, sloshing through the refuse with long deliberate steps. A marsh of human neglect at his feet. When he finally reached daylight at the end of the pipe, he shielded his eyes from the rising sun and was immediately startled by a small flying object. A boomerang drone. It swooped down with a whirl and hovered in front of him. The drone was shiny and black and shaped like a crescent moon, or more accurately a boomerang. Its carbon fiber body was sleek and almost seamless, with no buttons or protruding electronics. Smooth as beachstone. The rotors were hidden within the wings, spinning and pushing air through a ventilated frame. But the attributes that always caught Gypsy's attention were the two electric blue eyes glowing on the face of it. The eyes were oddly alive and responsive to stimuli, looking like the cognitive orbits of a sentient being or some technological demon. It spoke with a simulated voice, *"Refugee, state your name."*

"My name's Everett. Everett Waltz. But everyone just calls me Gypsy."

*"What is your purpose here?"*

"I'm just trying to survive, man." He displayed a handful of rotten food that he'd snatched up from the waste pile below, each piece dripping between his fingers in a gross, unidentifiable slop. "Gotta eat, man. I'm out of rations."

The drone scanned his face with its bright blue lasers. The electric eyes doubled as a camera system, recording everything the drone saw, and sending a live feed directly to Nimbus Security, where it was monitored day and night at Surveillance Headquarters in the Nimbus Towers.

"I'm just hungry is all." His eyes drifted to the tip of the boomerang's face, where just below the eyes was a lethal shock device crackling with 20,000 volts of fireblue electricity. Refugees called it the *kiss of death*. One zap from the deadly coils and you were in oblivion. Gypsy feared oblivion. But what frightened him most about the boomerang drones was their intelligence. The drones were fully automated. Controlled by sophisticated computer programming. Operated by an onboard processing chip. A computational brain with extreme awareness and deductive reasoning skills. They could perceive, learn, react and solve problems on the fly, and that miraculous feat of engineering always creeped him out. He stood there perfectly still as the drone examined his retinas, studying the data through its onboard operating system. He finally heard a comforting noise. A simple *ping*, which meant he was verified. His identity confirmed. The boomerang drone flew away without further questioning and disappeared from sight. Gypsy breathed easy again and checked his surroundings. All clear. No more boomerangs. No workers either. The facility was closed for the day. He slugged his way through the open trash pit, his rain boots swamped and nearly mired in place by rotten food and bacterial water. The smell was toxic and nauseating, but he was used to the stench. His stomach didn't turn. He didn't even bother to hold his nose. He sucked the odor into his lungs with pride. After all, this was his trading ground.

Brixton spotted Gypsy from the cruiser and lowered the side window. "Hurry the fuck up! I've been waiting for ten minutes!" He hated refugees. They were filthy people. No hygiene. Poor health. Every season they spread some common disease. The liver bug. White lung. Spots. Scarbug Syndrome. Even genital herpes. You name it, they spread it. The Republic lived in fear of their uncompromising germs.

Gypsy approached with a disgruntled look on his face. "It's really insulting when you wear that biomask around me, man. I'm no pariah."

"What the fuck took you so long?" Brixton asked.

"A boomerang spotted me."

Brixton looked around nervously, his eyes scanning the clear blue sky.

Gypsy assured him, "It's alright. It's gone. Don't be so damn paranoid."

Brixton eyed him for a moment, cementing his authority with an undisputed glare, and then he shoved a black plastic bag into the refugee's bulging gut.

Gypsy looked inside and his eyes lit up with joy. "That'll do," he said. "That'll do just fine." He handed Brixton a clear plastic baggie in exchange. There was a sand-colored powder inside. A drug of some kind.

Gypsy beamed. "16 grams of Sidewinder, man. That's black market approved, grade A dynamite dust. Shame it's gonna go to waste."

Brixton scooped out a clump of the powder with the tip of his finger and touched it to his tongue to confirm its authenticity. He knew the bitter taste of Sidewinder. It couldn't be replicated. This was the real thing. But it wasn't the thing he was really after. He dug through the powder with his hand and pulled out the real prize: a wallet that was hidden within the powder. A relic of the old world. He sealed the baggie and tossed the Sidewinder onto the passenger seat as if it were something to be discarded. He looked at the wallet for a moment. His eyes shifted, dancing uncomfortably in their sockets. He seemed unsteady. Struck by some unknowable emotion. His eyes glossed over and his face loosened in a sort of misplaced grief.

"You alright?" Gypsy asked.

Brixton fidgeted and tucked the wallet into his coat pocket. "I'm fine."

"Ain't you gonna open it?"

"No."

"You a collector?"

"Something like that."

Gypsy chuckled foolishly and said, "Well you better hope that crafty old coot Lucian Vanderbon doesn't find out about—"

Before he could finish his sentence, Brixton grabbed him by his filthy brown hair and pulled his head through the open window and pressed a corporate-issued Rapid 9 handgun to his temple. "You don't say a fucking word about this to anyone, you got me?"

Gypsy's arms flapped at his side like a frightened goose. "It's cool, man. I ain't gonna say shit. I wouldn't even know who to say shit to."

"What'd they do with the body?"

Gypsy looked confused. "The body?"

Brixton eyed him sharply and rammed the gun into his ear.

"They *burned everything*," Gypsy shrieked. "There's nothing left."

Brixton let go and holstered his Rapid 9 and stared off into the void for a moment. His eyes were no longer dancing, and his body had gone as stiff as the dead.

"What's wrong with you?" Gypsy asked.

Brixton glared at him again, with a forced authority that seemed to be questioning itself, and then he shoved the filthy refugee away from his cruiser. "You can go back to whatever hole you crawled out of. If I see you again, that's bad for you."

Gypsy staggered backwards. "Yeah, sure. Whatever, man." He rubbed his sore head. "Always a pleasure, Inspector."

# THREE

Vice President Pharaoh leaned forward with a disparaging eye. "These protests began when we started calling Phoenix City the *Republic* of Phoenix, and started referring to our employees as *citizens*. Now they call themselves *the people*. It was only a matter of time before they started demanding more individual rights and giving less effort in maintaining our collective prosperity."

"Who's being theatrical now?" Ambrose asked.

"I'll remind you," Pharaoh boasted, "I was the only executive to oppose such a radical change in corporate policy. I told you what would happen, and now it's happening."

Lucian scoffed and leaned back in his chair. "We're not measuring dicks, J.W." He offered a sly grin. "If we were, I'd win."

The executives laughed. A needed moment of levity. But it wouldn't last.

Pharaoh uncoiled again. "Will we be laughing when our power is stripped away and handed over to our employees? That's quite a business model."

"The people have a voice," Lucian said. "Whether we like it or not. They need executives who will listen."

"That sounds an awful lot like democracy," Pharaoh snickered. "What's next? Elections and four year terms?" His chin lifted in the air as if he were reminding Lucian that he was his right-hand man and not some unsophisticated dolt in a suit. "Democracy doesn't work. It's cannibalism. Eventually the people eat their own. We've built an empire, Lucian, and you just want to hand it over to them?" His eyes narrowed with an accusatory gaze, and he made sure the look was seen by the other executives. "Or does your intention go even further?"

The ambiguity of the question stirred the board's curiosity. They all looked at Lucian, their eyes expecting an explanation.

"Go on, Lucian," Pharaoh said. "Tell the board what you were too reluctant to tell me."

Lucian leaned forward and placed his elbows on the table. His face turned predatory for a moment, glaring at Pharaoh, who refused to be his prey. As their wordless exchange grew more hostile, the executives grew more concerned. Then Lucian turned his eyes away and reached beneath the table and flipped the switch to a holograph projector that hung from the ceiling like a chandelier. A three-dimensional map of the entire North American continent was suspended in the air in front of them. The glowing green image hovered above the long table like a ghost. A hologram of undeniable truth. Lucian pointed to the territory controlled by Nimbus on the map. "Look at that pathetic little spot. The *Republic* of Phoenix. All the land on this continent — nearly ten million square miles of it — and we only control one percent. The *outlaws* control the rest. *One fucking percent.* We're a coffee stain. Not an empire."

The executives were well-aware of their geographical percentages, and they'd always been content with that one percent, as long as they were sitting on top of it. Lucian was just using it to set up his shot. It was a long one, and he'd need every bit of informational ammo he could muster. "Our border is being choked to death by these refugees," he said. "We keep them contained in Brimstone so they don't gain self-sufficiency in the Blaze. We feed them and clothe them to keep them content. So they don't rise up against us. So they don't leave and form an army to resist us. Meanwhile, the Bloody Knuckles and their black market are thriving in Brimstone, undermining our very own economy. But we're afraid to lose control of the status quo, so we never expand our horizons." He shrugged. "That's not the makings of an empire. For fuck's sake, that's not even good business." His face softened, losing the steely conviction that he'd previously held in his eyes, as if he knew that what he was about to say would be met with shock and immediate protest. "I'm proposing a detailed plan for expansion."

As expected, the room fell silent. The executives sat there in shock, forgetting to breathe. The protests would be next.

"Expansion?" Spade gasped.

"Yes," Lucian said. "Incorporate Brimstone and give the refugees full citizenship."

The executives froze like wooly mammoths in a sudden ice age, their bottom jaws hanging loosely as if they'd just been walloped by a left hook.

"The refugees *will* rise up," Lucian explained, "and so will the people. That's inevitable. I'd rather they were with us than against us." He could see the weary executives weren't buying in, nor were they keen to even shop the idea. "We'll debate this more intimately in the coming days. I just wanted you to kick it around a bit before you decide if you're with me on this vote."

"My god," Ming said with a stutter. "You… You've already decided?"

Lucian nodded.

Spade threw his hands up in disbelief. "It's too early in the morning for this kind of fuckery, Lucian. I'm not amused."

"That's a radical idea," Billings said. "Not something I'd expect to come from you, Lucian. And I see you've been weighing it on your own. Without our knowledge."

Patel shook his head. "Lucian, you're a reasonable man. This can't be the answer."

"It won't work," Billings declared. "Our shareholders won't go along with this."

The shareholder argument was a common one in the boardroom, often used in desperation. But it had no bearing on Lucian's decision-making whatsoever. Shareholders were comprised of the wealthiest one percent of citizens in the Republic, each of them with a financial interest in the company, which supposedly gave them a say in things. But in truth, being a shareholder was more of a formality and a mark of status rather than a procurement of legislative power. They had sold themselves and their souls to Nimbus just decades earlier for survival and a chance to start anew. Whatever power they had before the Collapse was now and forever in the hands of the corporation.

"Our shareholders will go along with anything I suggest," Lucian said. "I've had them eating out of the palm of my hand for twenty-five years. Don't expect that to change."

Pharaoh interjected his will, "I'm in agreement with the board, Lucian. It won't work. Refugees live by a lower standard. They won't be able to rise to ours."

Then Ambrose leaned forward, eyeing Pharaoh in particular, and said, "You say *the board*, as if we're all in lockstep here. But you know where I stand. You know Lucian and I see eye to eye on this vote. I'll be voting *yes*."

"So we're voting today then?" Pharaoh asked provocatively. "Then I vote *no.*"

"I vote *no* as well," Spade declared.

"*Stop.*" Lucian slammed the gavel to the block. "No one is voting today. No one is to cast their vote until we hold an official referendum. This is a proposal day, nothing more."

"Christ, Lucian," Pharaoh said through clenched teeth. "Ambrose has put some crazy ideas in your head before, but this one takes the cake."

"It takes the whole fucking bakery," Spade added.

Lucian scoffed. "You give the black sheep too much credit. Don't flatter the young man. This was not Jordan's idea. Nor is it his proposal."

The executives looked at Ambrose. The black sheep shrugged with a look of pure innocence. They looked back at Lucian, who suddenly winced in pain and placed a hand to his head. His physical agony was obvious.

Ming offered his concern. "Lucian, are you…?"

"I'm *fine.*"

The executives traded looks again.

Then Spade said carefully, "Lucian, I'm not trying to insult you, but… how do we know that this radical idea of expanding our borders is not just some… *side effect*… or some debilitating consequence of your condition?"

"My *condition?*" Lucian asked, looking even more combative than before. "You mean the cancerous tumor that's slowly eating away at my brain? That *condition?*"

This was the glaring elephant in the room. The dark secret that the people of the Republic could never know. The unofficial ailment of their all-powerful CEO: a cancerous tumor growing rapidly in his brain. Only his executive board knew of the torrent condition. The people of the Republic had no idea. That's the way Lucian wanted it. He needed to maintain his superior presence, even if he didn't feel the loftiness anymore. Life had given him everything. Now death was slowly taking it away.

Billings leaned in, and while maintaining his usual etiquette, he said, "Lucian, we're all concerned for your health. Don't take our misgivings as a sign of disrespect. But perhaps your mental faculties have been compromised."

"My *mental faculties*?" Lucian sat upright and strong. "Am I not making myself clear? Am I stumbling over my words? Am I blabbering on about nothing like some mindless old fuck? Do you see a decline in my cognitive function? Are any of you willing to challenge my *mental faculties*? If so, stand up and be heard."

No one stood up.

He glared at them in the way that he used to. With overwhelming authority. *Lucian the Imperious*, as they'd always called him, had just returned from the proverbial dead, and he was wielding that same old iron fist. "Don't forget who built this company," he said with a shout. "Don't forget who brought you to the table to begin with."

The room was so quiet that one could hear a pin drop.

"I will not be a scapegoat for your fears," he continued. "We're afraid of everything outside of our walls, and that's why we never change. My decision to expand is good for business. There's nothing more to it than that. Don't politicize my professional ambitions." He grimaced in pain again, closing his eyes and wincing in discomfort. As the pain subsided he opened his eyes and spoke more calmly, "The refugees might not be so dangerous if we put a tool in their hands and paid them to do a job."

Pharaoh hawked his eyes with no sympathy for Lucian's suffering. "If we put a tool in their hands, they'll turn it into a weapon and use it against us. They'll rise up, Lucian. We'll lose control of everything. My God, know your history."

"I know my history," Lucian said, trying to regain his power. "When the will of the people is ignored, nations fall."

"We're not a fucking *nation*," Pharaoh said. "We're a *business*."

The other executives raised their brows at the unhealthy tension that was brewing between their President and his right-hand man.

"No," Lucian said. "We're history repeating itself." He glared at Pharaoh, who glared right back. Neither of them looked away. Nor did they say a word. But the bitter silence between them spoke volumes.

Then Lucian turned his attention on the others. "I've given my proposal," he said, "and I'll have seven days to solidify it. We'll have our official vote a week from today. You can each expect to hear from me on this subject in private. If I have to enlighten each of you individually, without the restraints of your collective mind getting in the way, then so be it." He tapped the gavel softly to the wooden block. "This meeting is adjourned." He placed his hand to his throbbing head. "I wish to be alone with my thoughts."

The executives sat there looking at him as if he were something to pity.

He slammed the gavel down on the wooden block. *Clack! Clack! Clack!* "That means *fuck off*. All of you!"

They rose to their feet and hurried out of the double doors, exchanging veiled looks of frustration.

Pharaoh didn't budge. He stayed in his chair with his bitter eyes glued to his mentor. "Democracy is the greatest disease that this company faces, Lucian, and even you can't deny that. Your beloved city will crumble."

# FOUR

Brixton pushed a button on the dashboard of his police cruiser, initiating the self-quarantine system. A fine, wet vapor blew in through specialized vents. A sanitizing Mist. 99.9 percent effective. It was overkill, but Brixton was fugeephobic, which meant he was afraid of refugees and their uncompromising germs. That was what they called his particular form of bigotry: fugeephobia. The vapor was sucked out of the cruiser like an air vac, leaving everything bone dry, including Brixton's sweaty neck. The onboard computer confirmed: *Sanitation Complete.* He removed his biomask and inhaled the clean, fresh air. He fixed his hair, which was dyed platinum blonde and swept to the side, cascading across his head like the crest of a summer wave. The long strands in the front were hanging over his eyes, creating a sense of mystery that he always strived for. It drove the ladies crazy, which was something he never failed to exploit. His proverbial belt was filled with notches. The sides of his head were shaved close to the scalp and skillfully faded, making him look like some gallant G-man from the Prohibition Era in the Roaring Twenties. A time which he knew nothing about. Though being a Border Inspector in the Republic of Phoenix in 2074 had its similarities. Keeping the castle clean. A battle for morality. In this case, keeping the immoral refugees from breaching the walls of Phoenix and making a mess of their beloved city. Sure, alcohol was prohibited, as it was in that long ago world, along with cigarettes and drugs, and even pain killers, but not strictly. There was always a way. He brushed the hair out of his eyes and marveled at his own presence in the rearview mirror. Every strand of platinum was perfectly oiled with pomade and shining like hot wax. A mark of status in the Republic. As he stared into his own eyes, the amber was glowing like warm butterscotch. He glimmered at himself and declared, "You're Brixton *fucking* Grace."

But the name didn't give him the usual surge of pride. It used to mean something. Now it didn't have the same ring, nor the same spark of confidence. He drew another breath, this time to reassure himself of his own importance. He pulled the wallet from his coat pocket and studied the relic with a sharp reluctance. But before he could pull the flaps open, his SAT phone buzzed with police dispatch. "Inspector Grace. Do you copy?"

"*Fuck.*" He fumbled with the wallet, as if it were hot to the touch, and then he shoved it back into his coat pocket.

"Inspector Grace? Do you copy?"

He grabbed his SAT phone. "*Copy. Copy.* This is Grace. What the fuck is it?"

"We've got a possible security breach in progress. Probably illegals. Sapphire Moon Apartments in Westborough. Over."

"Copy that," he said with a grimace. "I'm on my way." He tossed the SAT phone onto the passenger seat and exhaled. "Fuck my life." He shifted the Volt-22 into drive and sped away. The tires spun and kicked up the trash that loosely covered the road. He pulled out of the facility and raced onto Main Street heading towards the Immigration Center and the massive border gates that stood guard over the city in the distance. The sun was getting higher in the sky. It was going to be another scorcher.

"Why do you insist on harassing me?" Lucian asked his petulant Vice President. "I said I wanted to be left alone."

Pharaoh inched closer on the caster wheels of his chair. "I always admired you, Lucian. Your boldness. Your brutal honesty. That silver tongue of yours always came with an iron fist. Nobody fucked with you."

"Are you speaking in past tense?" Lucian asked.

"At your age, everything is past tense."

Lucian chuckled, but only because he wanted to steer the conversation in a less harmful direction. "We've clashed over many things lately, J.W. You know I prefer straight talk. Stop dancing around with your words and say what you mean to say."

"Your old age has made you affable, Lucian."

The words were meant to sting, but Lucian chuckled in good humor, refusing to take Pharaoh's insult as anything more than bait on a very sharp hook. "Affable?"

"You're more inclined to appease the people's wishes now, rather than dictate what's best for the corporation."

"The corporation serves the Republic," Lucian said. "It serves the people. Not the other way around. That's how it is now. Was that not always the goal?"

Pharaoh sneered. "Those are the words of an old man

who has lived a long and fruitful life at the top. I'm glad you exploited your power to the fullest while you had it."

"If there's something you wanna say," Lucian said, "say it plainly."

"You're expecting the rest of us to cash in early," Pharaoh admitted. "To bow out of the game. You're a hypocrite."

"Is that how you see it?"

"I have younger, *healthier* eyes, so yes."

Lucian laughed at the idea of old age and bad health being his downfall. It had been the story since his most recent doctor visit. "Only the young are foolish enough to dismiss the wisdom of old age," he said playfully.

"You make light of it," Pharaoh scoffed, "but I'm serious."

"I know you are. I am too. But you're blaming my desire for change on a phantom diagnosis. And that's why it's so hard to take you seriously."

"Phantom diagnosis?"

"You believe my cancer is causing dementia."

"Your doctor believes it's causing dementia. I'm just responding to his diagnosis."

"That was no diagnosis," Lucian said firmly. "Certainly nothing official. It requires further testing. The cancer is in the early stages. The tumor is still small. There's no certainty that dementia is, or will be, a factor. And besides, dementia doesn't cause one to suddenly want to rectify their past mistakes. The wisdom of old age does that."

"Listen to yourself," Pharaoh said. "Don't deny what's clear and obvious to everyone around you."

"Which is?"

"You won't be at the head of our table for much longer. We both know how this ends. You'll lose your grip on reality, and then your grip on this company."

Lucian's mood turned pensive. Not only did he refuse to

die prematurely, but he refused to be unseated from his position before he died.

"I'm sorry, Lucian," Pharaoh said. "But this is a conversation we need to have."

"Does this conversation include the board now?" Lucian asked with suspicion. "Is that why they're beginning to question my cognitive functions?"

"No," Pharaoh said. "I wouldn't betray your trust. I told you I wouldn't say a word to the board until your diagnosis was official."

"Then let's save this conversation for that day. If it ever comes."

Pharaoh shook his head. "I implore you to reconsider your vote on this expansion. At least until you've been officially diagnosed."

"Why wait?" Lucian asked, already knowing the answer.

"If you're diagnosed with dementia," Pharaoh explained, "you'll be required by executive order to step down. Then it won't be your decision."

"How convenient that would be. No mess."

"Don't insinuate something like that," Pharaoh said, taking insult. "Respect the process. That's all I'm asking. You know we wouldn't be able to reverse such a radical change in corporate policy. The people would surely riot."

"Yes, they would," Lucian said, "and that only proves my point."

Pharaoh dismissed the shaky logic. "If the diagnosis is favorable, then I'll stand aside and I won't protest your desires. You have my word on that."

Lucian chuckled in a way that suggested a sense of frustration rather than amusement. "There's one thing for certain that I've learned about you through the years, J.W."

"What's that?"

"You'll politicize anything to get what you want."

"Funny," Pharaoh said. "That sounds an awful lot like you when you were my age."

Lucian couldn't dispel the notion, so he didn't bother.

Pharaoh frowned. "I've heard enough *wisdom* for one day. I'll leave you to your scattered thoughts." He rose from his chair in a hurry.

Lucian rose to meet him. "Don't run from this, Jay."

Pharaoh turned back to him. "Why do you mock me? I've always had the best interest of this corporation *and* our employees in mind. Everything I do is on their behalf. I'm not you, Lucian. This company doesn't serve my lifestyle. I serve this company." He sulked, looking hurt. "I thought that's what you admired about me."

"J.W., you're missing the point."

Pharaoh didn't allow Lucian to make it. "You built this company, Lucian, and you know I respect that. But don't ask me to stand aside and watch you let it fall apart. I won't help you hide your condition. You'll have to answer for that *now*. Not when it's too late." He held his gaze on Lucian, though it quickly faltered, and then he turned and walked away.

Lucian raised his voice to reach Pharaoh's fleeing ears, "You can't stop change, J.W. Men who believe they can are always on the wrong side of history."

Pharaoh left without a retort, and the door closed quietly behind him.

Lucian sat down and began to sulk. He rubbed the aging craters of his temples with his fingers. He could feel his blood rising and his head begin to ache even more. Every conflicted thought he had was bouncing around violently in his cancerous brain like a pinball machine. The disease would eventually become too crippling to hide. A tumor the size of a walnut that was only growing larger by the week. The corporate doctors said it might prove fatal sooner than later. He pulled a powdery white pill from his pocket and swallowed it down with a glass of water. A pain killer. The light was hurting his eyes. He drew his wrinkled eyelids shut like privacy curtains and everything around him went dark. Then he said to himself in a haggard whisper, "We're history repeating itself."

# FIVE

As Brixton reached the border, he drove past the newly constructed refugee hospital, where healthcare was provided daily, mostly with lackadaisical effort and little funding. It was more political appeasement than altruism. He passed by the border patrol headquarters, where grunts were trained to abuse the law in such a subtle manner that it could hardly be recognized or prosecuted by law. But subtlety wasn't a given trait of Nimbus border patrols. They never could hide their hatreds. Brixton could see them plain as day. He passed by a fire and rescue station, where firefighters and EMTs worked to contain the constant threat of urban wildfires that often spread in the endless summer heat. He looped around the domed ration center in the heart of the Border Province. It was an old sports stadium that had been stripped down and transformed into a massive distribution hub. There was a long line of sweaty refugees outside waiting for their weekly rations. This was where they received their food, water and clothing. Today it was food, but Brixton questioned how edible it was. He watched as the violent border patrols stood guard over the refugees, waiting for any of them to step out of line or break a rule just so they could bust some heads or zap someone with a shock stick, or, if they were really lucky, blast one of them in the back with a shock round from their BP12 shotguns and watch them crash to the concrete like a corpse. Border patrols always got a kick out of that. The abuse seemed to happen every time Brixton was in Brimstone. Probably because it was a daily occurrence there. Lo and behold, as he drove by, it happened again. A young boy no older than ten snuck out of the nearby alley and snatched a handful of rations from an unsuspecting refugee woman who had just received her official allotment. The boy ran back towards the alley with a biodegradable bag of slop in his hands. Naturally, a border patrol in a biomask raised a shotgun and fired, and the rubber shock round struck the boy in the middle of the spine and knocked him to the concrete. The shock caused his body to go limp. Temporarily paralyzed.

Brixton cringed. He didn't like seeing the abuse. He hated refugees just as much as the border patrols did, but he couldn't stand how the mindless grunts of Brimstone treated the women and children in the slums. It was a step too far. Brixton was proud to say he had never hurt a woman or a child. He'd never cross that line. That poor little boy was just hungry. He probably had no caretakers. He probably lived alone in the slums. So he probably gorged his way through the weekly rations out of desperation, to cure his hunger pangs, and now he had nothing left but the prospect of thievery. Brixton thought it was unfair. *Just feed the damn kid, for Christ's sake.* The boy lay there on the concrete with blood streaming from his head and drool spilling from his mouth. Brixton didn't think the punishment fit the crime, but that was the law of the borderlands, and truthfully, the boy knew the consequences. That was just how the *garbage men* — as Brixton referred to border patrols — took out their trash. He turned his eyes on the road ahead and kept driving. The refugee boy was already gone from his mind.

He soon passed by the embassy, which was far too nice for the slums. He laughed to himself every time he saw the building rising up like a five-star resort in the midst of the corrugated metal shacks that were scattered about like human wreckage. The embassy was where any grievances or concerns could be officially lodged by the refugees. The poor boy with the bloody head and drool spilling from his mouth would likely never get his chance to be heard. If a refugee voice could be silenced in Brimstone, it always was. Brixton drove on, approaching the massive border wall and the impenetrable metal gates of Phoenix. It was a sophisticated piece of defense. There were personnel lanes for maintenance crews and border patrol, as well as fire and medical. But a man of Brixton's stature just drove straight through the exclusive VIP lane. It was reserved for Corporate, and for their golden boy of law enforcement. The main building in the Border Province was the Immigration Control Center, which was split down the middle by the border wall and secured by numerous high-security checkpoints. Anyone coming and going had to pass through customs, which included medical checks and security scans. Their body temperature had to be tested, and the microchip in their wrist had to be verified. Their health and identity had to be confirmed before being allowed into the city. Immigration Control was the final line of defense. Inside the building were holding cells for violators, and outside there were large-scale quarantine capabilities for emergency epidemics. It had a recruiting center for potential citizenship and a facility for preliminary job training. They called it the refugee pipeline. The next wave of workers. When someone died inside the Republic, there was always a fairly-qualified refugee to take that person's place. The machine had to stay in perpetual motion.

After Brixton scanned his wrist at the biometrics station, he drove through the gate. He passed by a loud smattering of protestors on the curb who were holding signs and screaming at him to stop torturing refugees and make them citizens of the Republic. He agreed with the first grievance. But there was no way in hell that he'd share personal space with those filthy bastards. If they didn't like their accommodations in Brimstone, they could take their sorry asses straight back to where they came from: the Blaze.

*Good luck and good riddance.*

He had no patience for the protestors. A self-serving lot in his eyes. He blew his horn and flicked them off and shouted, "Go to work, you fucking imbeciles." He knew they wouldn't listen. The problem was they were protesting in their own spare time. Nimbus allowed them to choose their leisures when they were off the corporate clock, and as of late the people chose to spend that time voicing their conflicting opinions in the form of protest. Brixton couldn't understand why Corporate allowed such openly defiant behavior.

*Big mistake*, he thought. *They're just stirring shit up.*

He pulled away from Immigration Control and blasted down Main Street, the electric engine of the Volt-22 police cruiser buzzing more harshly now, like the fluttering wings of a bumblebee. He passed through the outskirts of the vertical city known as Sky Haven. It rose up from the senile decay of old Phoenix like a middle finger rising up from a closed fist, and with the same youthful disregard. Skyscrapers, some fifty stories high, were interconnected by hundreds of pedestrian skywalks and a skytrain for urban transport. It was a cluster of intertwining high-rise condominiums. Glistening steel and glass bodies, replete with rooftop pools, party patios, posh clubs, exclusive restaurants and high-quality retail. The residents of Sky Haven existed high above the working class of the Boroughs below, both geographically and socially, and they were never shy about flaunting their godlike presence on the southern horizon. Each night the obnoxious glow of Sky Haven engulfed the Boroughs in a blinding tapestry of neon light. Flickering swirls of pink and blue. Sparkling flashes of every color on the spectrum. There was no escape from the sensory bombardment, and that was by design. A constant declaration of the vibrancy and status of life in the vertical city. Everyone wanted a place in the sky.

Brixton had one. A penthouse in fact. With one hell of a view. But unfortunately, he was heading for the other side of things at the moment. The lowly Boroughs. The flat, uninspiring urban sprawl of the city. A place that he hated with a passion. Two-hundred square miles of neglected infrastructure. Single-family homes that were retroactively split into duplexes. Corporate housing projects that were constructed in haste and scarcely maintained. Low rent apartments that were stacked one on top of the other like a child's building blocks. Public transportation that was outdated and unreliable. Crumbling streets that were lined with fast food, small businesses and cheap retail. All corporate-owned. All monitored and regulated by Nimbus. There were no private owners in the Republic of Phoenix. Only operators. Citizens had ownership of nothing. Everything was borrowed from the company. On corporate credit. They called it Nimbus Coin. The people's line of credit. It was the only currency in the Republic. As long as you stayed in the black, you had a home and enough allotted credit for food, clothing, rationed solar electricity, and even some personal luxuries if you were lucky. Whatever you needed was available. But find yourself overspent, in the red, and all of that was stripped from you. Citizens could find themselves in a loss prevention program, where the final strike was exile. Their citizenship revoked. Cast out to the Brimstone refugee camp, living on weekly rations with the refugees. Then they'd be sleeping among the diseased and the criminal elements in the corrugated metal shacks that choked the border wall. A cycle of borrowed lives, living on borrowed income, like children given a steady allowance and a roof over their head in return for their unquestioned obedience. The people were content to oblige though, since their needs were so well-stocked. That was life in the Republic of Phoenix. Contentment or bust.

Brixton drove on, pushing through the mangled guts of the Boroughs, wishing he had a hot coffee in his hand. He was heading for Westborough, and any coffee he found in that cesspool would be burnt and tasteless and probably under-caffeinated. "Goddamn ghetto," he said as he turned onto the fractured pavement of 38th Avenue. "Can't anyone ever commit crimes in the Vale?"

The Vale was another story. It's where Corporate and the wealthy elite resided. A suburban paradise. Brixton hadn't been there in ages. Nothing bad ever happened there. At least nothing that was punishable by Nimbus law. In the Republic of Phoenix, there were laws for Corporate, and then there were laws for everyone else.

# SIX

Lucian was still sulking alone in the board room when his headache began to subside. He was trying to enjoy one last bit of solitude before the day got out of hand. *Maybe I could enjoy a moment of clarity for a change*, he thought. *How welcome that would be.* Then the door opened slowly and his personal secretary, Thomas Barkley, stuck his head inside the room. A sheepish, gangly man in his forties, Thomas had been Lucian's secretary for ten years. He wasn't the most forward man, but he kept things in order, and he was also a male, which kept Lucian out of trouble. Lucian had bedded more of his female secretaries than his aging mind could remember. He'd grown tired of the carnal drama and the problems it created, so Thomas Barkley was the solution.

"Sir," Thomas said carefully, "there's a raid currently underway in the Boroughs. A possible security breach."

Lucian moaned and hung his head, which began to hurt again, this time with a different kind of pain. He had a suspicion but he asked anyway. "Whose operation?"

"Inspector Grace, sir."

*Wonderful,* Lucian thought, *my other loose end.* "Thank you, Thomas," he said. "That'll be all."

The secretary left the room and closed the door behind him.

"Just what I need," Lucian said with a deep sigh. "Brixton *fucking* Grace."

---

Brixton's Volt-22 barreled down Main Street in Westborough, an over-populated ghetto assigned to the *worst of the working class*, which meant the least essential. The west side was notorious for being two things: tasteless and undesirable. The residents were crude and the living conditions even more so. If you lived there, you were on the receiving end of the totem pole. If you ate there, you'd soon be on the toilet with a bad case of diarhea. Unfortunately, Brixton's gut was rumbling. He hadn't had breakfast or coffee. Now he was searching for both in the worst possible part of the Republic. He drove past the mess of shady storefronts and fast food joints that lined the road in cluttered agony. Privately-operated businesses, but all owned by the Nimbus Corporation. He passed by Birdie's Grocery where they sold expired milk and under-cooked nourishments, then by a rundown thrift store called Barlow's Antiquities, which he thought was a creative way of renaming other people's junk. The 8-Ball pool hall next door was closed during the week. *Good times,* he thought. He had busted a perps nose there a few weeks earlier. With a pool cue. While he was in cuffs. A perk of the job, being the golden boy and all. Abuse without legal consequence. But he only abused the people who deserved it, so he had no remorse. He was too busy thinking about breakfast anyway. He passed by the Yellow Dragon Sushi Bar which he'd eaten at before. It was total shit. Nothing like the Red Dragon in Sky Haven. That place was pure quality. He hit the curb of a Boltz Burger as he turned the corner. Boltz Burger wasn't bad, just bad for you. But he could tolerate it in a pinch. Their breakfast burgers were gut-busters, but they had decent coffee in the mornings. A little burnt, but laced with caffeine, and that's what he needed. But as he was just about to turn the wheel his breakfast plans were upended. He found himself driving through an inquisitive crowd of people that were standing outside of the Daily Resource, blocking the road. They surrounded his cruiser like a pack of braindead zombies. "Oh come on, you fucking imbeciles. What the fuck are you people doing? Move!" He blew the horn. "Get the fuck out of the way!" They finally scattered. "Goddamn gutterbugs."

He hated the Daily Resource, and the mindless "gutterbugs" who shopped there. It was nothing but over-priced garbage. But the "Resource" was easily the most popular retail store in all of the Boroughs. At least three storefronts in Westborough alone. The place was a big moneymaker for the Nimbus Corporation. Anything you needed, they had it on their shelves. Cheap prices and even cheaper quality. All profits straight into Corporate's pocket and redistributed. As he turned the corner he saw the Sapphire Moon across the street from the Daily Resource and realized why everyone had been standing around. "Oh you fucking rubberneckers. That's what you people are doing. *Rubbernecking.* Get to work! Or go clean something, for Christ's sake. Brush your teeth. Wipe your ass. Maybe scrub the shit off your shoes."

He hated the hygiene of the people in Westborough. They kept nothing clean, not even themselves. But at least there were no vagrants or street urchins to deal with in the Republic. No beggars and drifters. The Republic of Phoenix operated like clockwork, with all the cogwheels turning in a synchronized rhythm. Everyone had a designated occupation, assigned to them by the single, uncontested company at the top. Everyone had their place, and they stayed in it, without question, and without defiance, or they'd have no place at all. Brixton passed through the crowd of zombified rubberneckers and arrived at the Sapphire Moon apartment complex. A shady conversion piece that used to be a warehouse. It had a brick and mortar exterior. The windows and the apartments inside had been retroactively built within the existing framework. He saw the police were already on site, armed and standing guard. Flashers so vibrant and visually obnoxious they were likely to cause a seizure in the crowd at any moment. There was a big yellow quarantine bus parked at the entrance. "Not too subtle," he said with disbelieving eyes. Dozens of curious citizens watched from the other side of the street behind a barrier of caution tape. He dodged the chaos as he pulled into the parking lot. "So much for the element of surprise," he said. "Another win for the bad guys."

He parked and turned the ignition off and grabbed his biomask and got out of the cruiser. His frame was lanky and athletic, standing six-feet tall in his shoes and filling out his tapered suit with lean, optically-pleasing muscle, which he carefully molded in the gym at least once a day. He tucked his biomask under his bicep and held it there while he pulled a fresh pair of white biogloves from his pocket. He started putting them on, sliding his fingers into the disposable plastic sleeves one digit at a time. It was protocol. Nimbus had a security measure for everything. Precaution was the rule in the Republic of Phoenix. Never take chances. He walked past the numerous onlookers and police officers with a confident swagger, feeling their eyes on him and figuring they were green with envy. He canvassed the building up and down, taking particular note of the fire escapes and any other possible exit points.

Then he was greeted by his unexceptional partner, Inspector Nile Wambasa, who said mockingly, "The golden boy is here. Somebody roll out the red carpet."

"Wow," Brixton declared with pleasant surprise. "That's a decent shot across my bow. You're finally loosening up."

Nile was a serious-minded black man with a slowly developing sense of humor since partnering up with Brixton just a few months earlier. He was clean cut and meticulous, always playing things by the book, and always cautious. Brixton, on the other hand, always flew by the seat of his pants, and Nile always took exception, usually with a motherly gaze that Brixton always found patronizing.

"Don't give me that look, Nile."

"It's a bad time to be late, Brix. Corporate's watchdog is on the hunt."

"Arroway?" Brixton chuckled. "He's just chasing his own tail. As usual. It'll take him a few weeks to realize he's been sniffing his own ass the whole time." He took the biomask in his gloved hands. "Give me the rundown."

"A dozen refugees hiding inside," Nile explained cautiously, reluctant to reveal the source. "According to the… *tip* we received."

Brixton sighed. "Another tip? Jesus Christ. Anonymous I'm guessing?"

"Bingo."

"It just gets more embarrassing every time. Corporate didn't learn from the last two?"

"Maybe the third time's the charm?"

Brixton shook his head. "Fool me once, Nile. It's bullshit."

Nile pulled a solar scroll from his coat pocket and unrolled it, revealing a flexible 10-inch screen, which was completely translucent, like a soft panel of glass. "The anonymous tipper says they're hiding in apartment 407. It's registered to a Raymond Prisco. Male. Fifty-two years old."

Nile displayed the image, which was projected above the device like a holograph. An official Citizen's Profile. Private information and personal history. The picture of a man with dark, curly hair and thick reading glasses. "He's the landlord," Nile said. "Just another happy Nimbus employee."

Brixton pulled his Rapid 9 handgun and popped the loaded magazine out and placed a yellow magazine full of shock rounds into the housing instead. "Well," he said gleefully, "if the guy fucks with me he's gonna be unemployed."

Nile didn't laugh. He was still working on the whole humor thing. "Corporate called in the cleanup crew," he said. "I had them prep for a level three quarantine."

"That's a waste of time," Brixton assured him. "It's just another bullshit tip."

# SEVEN

Vice President Pharaoh and the other executives were watching the events at the Sapphire Moon unfold on a massive wallscreen in the Surveillance Headquarters on the third floor of Nimbus Tower One. The large room was dark, save for the glow from the cluster of wallscreens and rows of translucent computer monitors. This was their base of operations. Open only to drone pilots, surveillance operatives and personnel with top level security clearance. Nimbus Security agents were hard at work there, watching live security footage from all over the city every hour of the day. The Inspector General, Benjamin Ryker, stood at his podium overseeing the operation. He was in his late sixties and nearing retirement age, but the idea of retirement to him was akin to suicide. He wore a black suit and tie, like his agents, and he carried a Rapid 9 in his side holster beneath his coat. He had a head full of gray hair, a steadfast glint in his eyes, and a singular focus: to protect the Republic of Phoenix at all costs.

Lucian entered the room like royalty, cascading down the

stairwell one unhurried step at a time. Everyone nodded their obligatory respects.

Pharaoh greeted him with the same bitterness as before, but with another bone to pick. "Have you made your decision on Inspector Grace yet? Or will that require its own vote too?"

Lucian didn't answer. The golden boy Brixton Grace was on a short leash these days, and Lucian was the one holding the other end of it.

"You know our verdict," Pharaoh said. "We're just waiting on yours."

"I'm well aware of that, Jay, but thank you for the clarity."

Pharaoh followed after him like a dog chasing after a car. "He's one mistake away from disgracing his entire legacy. You could save him from himself."

Lucian turned with a probing eye. "You seem to be obsessed with that idea lately. Saving people from themselves."

Pharaoh stood there for a moment looking unsure of how to respond, and then he turned and walked back to the cluster of executives. Lucian turned and leaned against the railing just behind the computers and watched the operation unfold, hoping *something* would go his way today.

---

Brixton and Nile approached an armored SWAT team. The officers were decked out in full battle gear, carrying riot shields and assault rifles. Brixton slapped the Commander on the ass and said, "Listen up, you badge-carrying thugs. False alarm or not, we use shock rounds only. No live ammunition. If there *are* slum bunnies in there, the last thing we wanna do is spill their blood. You never know what kind of shit these people are spreading."

Then before he could make an off-color joke about the

refugees, a voice interrupted him, declaring loudly, "No chemical weapons this time."

Brixton turned to see a familiar face: Agent Arroway. An Internal Investigator with Nimbus Security. The most hated snitch in the department.

"*Arroway. The watchdog.*" Brixton's excitement was an obvious mockery, and he was sure to make it even more obvious than it already was. He exhaled theatrically, feigning sheer relief. "I think I speak for everyone when I say we're all feeling much better now that you're here. I mean really, we may as well close the fucking case. Nile, call off the SWAT team. Send all the units home." He turned to the street units that were keeping order among the onlookers. "Guys, Arroway's on it. We're good here. Everybody go home. No, really. No bullshit. I'm calling it off."

Arroway wasn't amused. He stood there with a deadpan look on his face.

Brixton hated to look at him. It was nauseating. Arroway had a pale, almost plastic complexion. He wore black-rimmed spectacles on a naturally bald and remarkably bulbous head. Brixton always thought he looked like a light bulb in a suit, but with the coil burned out. He'd hated Arroway for as long as he could remember. Ever since their days together at the academy. To Brixton, Arroway was just an academic with a badge, and quite inexplicably, a gun. His corporate-issued Rapid 9 was locked safely in his side holster, looking just as polished as it had the day he graduated from the academy. The guy had never used his gun in a real world scenario. Not once. Instead, he always carried a legal pad and a pen.

Brixton chuckled. "I see you brought your weapon of choice."

The officers laughed nearby.

Arroway brushed the insult aside. "There are hundreds of

law abiding citizens in that building, Inspector. Corporate doesn't need another PR disaster."

Brixton shrugged. "I still don't get what all the fuss was about. No one was injured. They took a little nap is all. They should be so lucky."

"That's not true," Arroway said. "About the injuries."

"Headaches don't count."

"They had head *injuries*, Inspector, not *aches*. From their *fall*. Fourteen admitted to the hospital." Arroway puffed up with authority. "No chemical weapons today. That's a corporate order."

"Jesus Christ," Brixton snarled. "Did they send you here just to bust my balls?"

"No. They sent me to ensure you follow protocol this time, Inspector. I'll be watching every move you make."

Brixton chuckled again, unable to help himself. "You've got your head so far up Corporate's ass I doubt you'll see a thing."

The officers laughed again. Then a boomerang drone swooped down from above and focused its camera lens on Brixton's face.

"Oh," said Arroway with his own chuckle, "they'll be watching too."

***

Inside of Surveillance Headquarters, the entire executive board was looking at Brixton's smug face on the massive wallscreen. A live feed from Arroway's drone.

"Really?" Brixton asked with a narcissistic grin. "They're watching me?" He looked directly at the camera. "Then let's give 'em a show." He winked at Corporate and smacked

Arroway on the ass with more force than necessary. Then he kept walking.

There was a collective sigh among the executives. They were tired of his antics. Lucian sighed too, though he tried to keep it discreet. Brixton's behavior didn't reflect well on him. It was Lucian's idea to give the golden boy another chance at respectability. So far that was proving to be a mistake.

Nile followed after the golden boy and shook his head so hard with disapproval it looked as if it might come rolling right off of his neck. "Are you trying to *impress* Corporate," he asked, "or just antagonize them?"

"It doesn't matter," Brixton said. "Either one works for me."

Then he and Nile and the SWAT Team took the stairs to the fourth floor. Agent Arroway and his boomerang drone took the elevator.

When Brixton and Nile arrived on the fourth floor with the SWAT team, Arroway came out of the shadows where he'd been safely waiting. He followed behind them, making sure to shield himself behind as many warm bodies as possible. His boomerang drone hovered over them.

Brixton snarled at it. "Get this fucking thing off my op, watchdog."

"It's not your op," Arroway said. "It's Corporate's. The boomerang stays."

Brixton swallowed his pride. Some fights were futile from the start. He walked the hall swiftly, with Nile hustling by his side. They passed by apartment 406, expecting to see apartment 407 next, but the wall was bare and longer than it should've been, and somehow they arrived at apartment 408.

"What am I missing here?" Brixton asked. "There's no 407."

Nile was miffed too. "Is somebody playing a joke on us?"

"Maybe."

"You telling me they just forgot an entire apartment when they built this place?"

"I'm guessing it's not a construction oversight."

"Probably not. But at the rapid pace these buildings went up, nothing would surprise me."

Arroway pushed through the SWAT team and said, "What's going on?"

"Police work," Brixton said. "You wouldn't be interested."

The SWAT team chuckled unprofessionally. Arroway withdrew with a sour look on his face. Brixton studied the wall where a door should've been, gliding his curious fingers across the area where he imagined the door jambs would be.

"Seamless," he said. "If this was a renovation, it's solid work. Not something that was done hastily or kept from the neighbors."

"So it was probably a construction error?" Nile asked. "You think someone's playing us for fools?"

"I think we *are* fools," Brixton said. "But I'd like to know for sure."

"Should we get thermal imaging?"

Then Arroway said, "I'll order the boomerang to—"

"No," Brixton interrupted. "Fuck that thing. Stay back and let me do my job."

Arroway conceded, but with a showy smugness. "Be my guest."

Nile asked, "You wanna check the surrounding apartments?"

"Yeah," Brixton said. "If I'm a fool, then I'd like to go all the way with it. I never half-ass anything, you know that."

"I'm learning," Nile said.

Brixton grinned. "I'm either a complete fool or none at all."

"My money's on complete fool," Nile quipped.

"Wow," Brixton said, impressed again with the decent shot across his bow. "That's two for you this morning. Well done."

"Should we split in teams?" Nile asked. "I'll take 408? You take 406?"

"No. 507."

"507?"

"Yeah, the apartment directly above. Who's it registered to?"

Nile pressed his finger to the solar scroll and navigated through the Citizen's Profile software. "It's registered to Raymond Prisco. The Landlord."

"Of course it is." Brixton had a curious look in his eyes. "If there's a hidden room behind this wall, then 507 is the entry point."

"You really think he's hiding illegals?" Nile asked.

Brixton started walking to the stairwell with his golden boy swagger in full swing. "Let's go pay him a visit and find out."

# EIGHT

Brixton loved his job. His badge gave him nearly unlimited power on the streets. He could kick down anyone's door if he had a mind to. There were no warrants, no Miranda rights, and no bureaucratic red tape to cut through. In fact, due process in the Republic of Phoenix wasn't much of a process at all. More of a *guilty until proven innocent* type of thing, which meant Brixton was free to follow whatever reckless impulse he had. When he and Nile arrived at apartment 507 with the SWAT team, he motioned them forward. Their P-16 rifles were ready. Their riot shields were in place. One of them swung a handheld battering ram and busted the door clean off the hinges. They charged through the door with their assault rifles scanning the room. Brixton was at the forefront with his Rapid 9 handgun aimed directly at the landlord. "PPD! Get on your fucking knees!"

The landlord, Raymond Prisco, was sitting in a chair at his dining table in front of a glowing heat lamp. His coke-bottle glasses were hugging his face and his eyes were large white circles of fear behind them. "Whoa, *easy*." He dropped an artist brush on the floor and raised his empty hands in a panic.

The boomerang drone surveyed the living space with blue lasers, lighting it up like a midnight discotheque. The SWAT team scoped the entire apartment. The kitchen, a bathroom, and a bedroom with closets stuffed to the brim. "*Clear. We're secure.*"

At the sound of "*we're secure*", Arroway finally entered the apartment.

The place was a dump. Stacks of dirty dishes in the kitchen sink. Blankets thrown recklessly in piles on the couch. The scent of eggs and rotten milk emanating from the trash can. Too much mess for one man alone.

Brixton headed straight for him. "Where are they, Ray?"

"Who?" The landlord pushed his thick glasses up onto the bridge of his nose.

"Don't fuck with me, Ray." Brixton's eyes were still adjusting. The curtains were drawn, and the drone had stopped scanning, and the only light was coming from the bright heat lamp on the table. Brixton motioned for SWAT to pull the shades back. When they did, a blinding flash of sunlight entered the living space and everyone shielded their eyes.

Brixton put the gun to the landlord's head. "A shock round to the head at this range would kill you, Ray. If you don't tell me where they are, you'll go to your grave an attempted murderer."

"Murderer?" The landlord was baffled.

"You came at me with a kitchen knife, Ray."

Nile grabbed a kitchen knife from the block on the counter and held it up so the landlord could see. It was a cheap tactic, and one that Nile despised, but it always worked, so he usually played along.

Brixton pressed the barrel of the gun harder to the land-lord's head. "I had to defend myself. You tried to stab me."

"You can't do that," the landlord said. "I have rights."

"You lost your rights when you chose to hide illegals."

Then Agent Arroway stepped in and said, "Inspector Grace, this man has rights. Stop abusing them."

Brixton huffed and ignored the bloviated order. He holstered his Rapid 9 and pulled a shock stick from his holster. He grabbed the landlord by the shirt. "Aiding and abetting refugees is a corporate crime, Ray." He shocked the landlord repeatedly, with the shock stick set to the lowest output, just to give him a scare and nothing more. "You'll be exiled. We'll throw you to the fucking rats in Brimstone!"

"Inspector Grace!" Agent Arroway shouted, "You're violating this man's corporate rights."

The landlord recoiled from the electric shock. His body was convulsing, as if he had just been pulled from the Arctic Ocean. Brixton checked the setting. "Ah fuck me," he said softly. The shock stick wasn't set quite as low as he'd thought. "That probably hurt."

"I'm not hiding refugees," The landlord exclaimed, "*Look around. There's nobody here.*"

Then the SWAT Commander said, "The apartment's been cleared, Inspector. There's no one here."

Brixton calmed himself and let the landlord go. The land-lord straightened his shirt and steadied the coke-bottle glasses on the bridge of his nose again and complained, "You're shaking me down for no reason. I'm a law-abiding citizen. I keep my credit in the black. I don't even exceed my energy allowance. *Ever.* Check the records."

Brixton regained his composure and slid his gloved hands through his pasty hair and shrugged apologetically. "Sorry, Ray. I had to know for sure."

The frightened landlord settled himself. Then he looked around the room, taking note of the exceptional firepower. He looked straight ahead nervously and didn't say a word.

Brixton noticed that something was amiss. He studied the dining table. He was curious about the mess on top. A litter of art supplies. An old 3D printer, containers of paint, plastic trays, cloth towels, a tube of crazy glue, and a handful of sculptured miniatures. Tiny figurines. He figured it was Raymond Prisco's hobby. "I have a question," he said, curling his brow in confusion. "Something is puzzling me. You only have one table in this entire apartment. How do you ever eat? It's an absolute mess."

The landlord was caught off guard by the trivial question. "Oh, I just... clean it off every evening before dinner... and... well that's that."

"It's that simple, huh?"

The landlord shrugged nervously.

"Are you nervous?" Brixton asked.

"Just shaken up is all."

"I understand. I was a little rough, wasn't I?"

The landlord didn't say.

Brixton studied the miniature sculptures. "You're into models and figurines and shit, huh?"

The landlord was flustered. "Oh, yeah, just a hobby. To pass the time. Being a landlord has its perks, but it's more often a mundane job."

"I would imagine so," Brixton said. He picked up one of the figurines and held it between his forefinger and thumb and studied it closely with inquisitive eyes. The paint job was nearly perfect. Not a single imperfection that he could see. "Impeccable detailing," he said with a spark. "You're very meticulous. That says a lot about a man's character. I consider myself to be very meticulous." He turned to Nile.

"Wouldn't you say I'm meticulous, Nile? I mean *Inspector Wambasa.*"

"Sure," Nile said dismissively. "Very thorough."

Brixton turned back to the landlord and scrutinized his unsteady resolve. Then he flicked the figurine across the room and the miniature hit the wall and rattled around on the dirty floor. It was a replica of a soldier. From the Restoration Wars. Patriot's Defense of course. Painted quite accurately. Brixton could see the arm had broken off from the force of the impact. The landlord didn't bat an eyelash when he saw it break. He wasn't angry or surprised. He didn't protest fervently or claim that his rights were being violated. He didn't balk at all. Brixton thought that was curious. *Why so forgiving?* He tried to pick up another figurine, but oddly enough, the tiny soldier was glued to the table. It didn't appear to be a mistake. He looked to the landlord for an explanation.

The landlord shrugged. "I must've been careless with the glue."

"Really?" Brixton asked. "Careless with the glue? That's surprising for a man with such a meticulous nature. That just... doesn't seem right." He turned to Nile again. "Does that seem right to you, Inspector Wambasa?"

Nile raised a brow in frustration. "Brix, are we finished here or what?"

Brixton looked back at the landlord. "Are we?"

The landlord shrugged. "Sir, I've told you everything I know. It was a bad tip."

"Tip?" Brixton stiffened. "Who said anything about a tip?"

"I just... I assumed."

Nile was getting impatient with Brixton's antics. "Brix, you were right. It's a bullshit tip. Let's go."

Brixton kept his gaze on the landlord. "Well, I guess I *was* right. *Again.* A bullshit tip. Sorry I was so rough with you, Ray.

I'm just *meticulous*, ya know? It's a curse to be so obsessed with the details." He smiled through his biomask. "No hard feelings?"

"No, sir. Of course not. You were just doing your job."

"I was. Thank you for being so understanding. It's not often I meet someone so forgiving after I zap the living shit out of them." Brixton forced an insincere laugh, keeping his eyes locked on the landlord. The landlord just sat there sweating profusely. The awkward moment was a great discomfort to him. Then suddenly and without provocation, Brixton lifted the table with his hand and flipped it aggressively onto its side and it came crashing down onto the hardwood floor. The landlord jerked backwards in his chair.

"Oops," Brixton muttered, feigning remorse. "I think my glove got stuck to the table. You put so much glue on the goddamn thing."

"*Inspector*," Arroway shouted. "That's enough."

Brixton shrugged innocently. "I just tried to pull my hand away and the fucking table flipped with it. Not my fault."

Nile grimaced. "Christ, Brix."

Brixton looked around at the mess he'd made. The floor was speckled with debris. Several models and figurines had gone flying through the air and onto the wooden planks. Paint had spilled onto the colorful Persian rug. A few soiled brushes were tossed onto the nearby couch. But surprisingly, the 3D printer was still attached to the tabletop, which was odd considering the table was lying sideways and the printer, by the strict laws of physics, should've fallen right off. He saw that it was bolted into place. There were also several figurines stuck to the table. Some were standing upright and a few were lying on their side. He saw a few brushes and paint trays stuck to the tabletop as well. "Careless with the glue again?" he asked.

The landlord was too nervous to answer.

"That's pretty fucking careless." Brixton knew the landlord had glued it all down for a reason, and suddenly he knew why: so the table could be easily moved, while looking practically immovable. He shoved the table aside and kneeled down and pulled the Persian rug back and was only mildly surprised to see a hidden doorway cut into the wooden floor beneath it. The door was bolted with hinges.

The landlord tried to rise from his chair, but the SWAT team grabbed him and pulled him back.

Brixton blew the vexing heat from his lungs. "You lied to me, Ray." He gestured to the SWAT team. "Stand clear of him." He pulled his Rapid 9. "I don't like being lied to."

Agent Arroway moved in, "Grace, *don't*."

But Brixton raised the gun and fired a shock round, and the electric bullet struck the landlord in the center of the chest, causing him to convulse and fall to the floor with his eyes bulging and his body temporarily paralyzed.

"That was unnecessary," Arroway said with a scowl.

"So put it in your report," Brixton snarled. He turned his attention back to the hidden doorway. He raised the inset handle and lifted the door slowly. His Rapid 9 was aimed and ready to fire at whatever was down there. He flicked the gunlight on and shined it at the mysterious gloom of room 407, and suddenly his trademark swagger turned to a look of pure dread. His eyes expanded like two white balloons behind the faceplate of his biomask. He saw a dozen refugees huddled together in the room below, their eyes weary and engulfed by purple flesh. Filthy men and women with their arms held out wide, protecting something that was hidden behind them.

"Step aside," he ordered, his gun threatening to fire.

They wouldn't move.

"I said *step aside. Now!*" He squeezed the trigger to the break.

The refugees separated, parting like the Red Sea. Brixton spotted what they'd been trying to protect: a sick little boy. He was maybe seven years old, lying in a bed of wet sheets in the center of the room. His lungs were wheezing harshly, like sandpaper grinding on a piece of coarse wood. A woman stood by his side, holding his hand and refusing to let go. Her eyes were wet with tears. Brixton knew she was the boy's mother.

She cried out, "They said we'd get meds." Her voice was hoarse and broken up by mucous and thick phlegm. "They *promised*," she screeched. "Please help us. *Please*."

Brixton could see they were *all* sick. Pale and feverish, and suffering from whatever terrible respiratory issue the boy had. Their chests were rising up and down rapidly, struggling to draw a healthy breath. He was suddenly afraid. He'd seen the White Lung and Scarbug Syndrome, but those common respiratory illnesses were treated daily in Brimstone. This was something else. Something new. Something dangerous. "Nile," he said with terror in his eyes, "alert the cleanup crew. Have them quarantine the building."

---

A troubling hush fell over the darkened room at Surveillance Headquarters. The executives sat there with their mouths agape and their eyes stuck in their orbits. Lucian couldn't feel his feet. They'd gone numb. His head began to ache more. The implications of Brixton's discovery were staggering. A worst-case scenario had come to fruition. Nimbus had always prepared and planned for something like this, but nothing of this magnitude had ever happened before. These refugees were deathly ill, with only God knows what, and they had crossed the border unimpeded. The only way that could've happened was if someone had turned a blind eye at Immigration Control, and that someone would've been on the take. *But for who? And why?* Lucian raised his palms to his face and closed his eyes tightly behind a wall of wrinkled fingers. So many questions. *Who promised these people meds? Someone on the inside? Why is Corporate in the dark? What else don't we know?* His mind was spinning with endless possibilities. Too many questions. Too many doubts. There was only one certainty: this mystery illness was unprecedented, and that was going to change everything. Everywhere. Even out in the burnt wilds of the Blaze.

# NINE

Croix Youngblood had only one unshakeable belief: that God is a sucker puncher, and a man better keep his goddamn guard up. So he never let his guard down. That's how he lived his life. Keeping everyone and everything at arm's length, with his hand on his holstered gun, his eyes watching with caution, and a bullet waiting eagerly in the chamber. He lived by the self-preserving motto *shoot first and ask to be forgiven later*. He figured he'd need to be almost clairvoyant if he was ever going to compete with the cruel, unpredictable world that his former God had wrought. So he did his best to plan for everything, and prepare himself for anything. He made sure he never had to rely on recklessly trivial things like happenstance or luck. To him, happenstance was lazy, and luck was just plain dumb.

Croix Youngblood was neither.

### THE BLAZE
### GRANITE VALLEY, FORMER CALIFORNIA

Mornings in the valley were deceptively calm. If a man

wasn't careful, the charming blush of dawn could be down-right beguiling. A dangerous seduction of pink watercolored clouds and golden streaks of sunlight that could weaken a man in the knees and wilt his fertile judgement. He'd be an easy mark for the gangs and scavengers that roamed the territory. Then his beautiful world would turn cold and dark with a dull blade thrust into his back or a bullet lodged in his brain while he was thinking about the meaning of life or something. That was always nature's cruelest trick: disarmament. This morning was no different. The low golden sun was spying over the powdery White Mountains with a curious eye, its soft bronze glow piercing the smoke of wildfires in the distance and casting a beautiful spell on the serrated edges of the western Sierra. A breathtaking dreamscape of razorblade peaks and evergreen pine that only planet Earth could provide. The jagged crest of Mount Whitney jutted up from the molten rock like a witch's finger, sharp and pointed and dangerously bewitching. All was quiet and motionless in the valley, looking unspoiled by man, as if the earth had been cleansed of its dirty past.

Then a 500-pound bengal tiger leapt from the brown needle grass and turned the picturesque valley into a crimson battleground. Blood trickled down its faded stripe-coating. It darted frantically across the valley floor heading for the maze of granite boulders known as the Alabama Hills. The beast was wounded and bleeding from its side, and by all accounts it was running for its life. A hunting dog chased after it, snapping at the tiger's heels with sharp, filed teeth. A Rhodesian Ridgeback. A guardian hound with a light wheaton coat. A slender frame, but packing a strong, inherited wallop. Ridgebacks were once bred to hunt big cats in Africa, and now one of their descendants was hunting a wild tiger in what used to be Eastern California. A feral-looking horse followed. A battle-scarred golden palomino with a pure white main and tail and white blazing on its face. A rugged man was in the saddle, looking even more feral than the horse and digging his heels into the mustang's flank. His blue eyes were predatory and set ablaze. His rowdy blonde locks were shaded by a dirty brown Stetson that barely clung to his head as he burned the breeze. He was armed with an impressive arsenal of guns and blades and improvised weaponry, stuffed into leather holsters and saddle scabbards and roped over his back.

This was Croix Youngblood, and as the tiger had learned, once you crossed the man, your days on Earth were surely numbered. The tiger's number appeared to be up.

Croix pulled an Apache throwing star from his leather saddle bag. An improvised weapon made of two crossed sticks that were carved to a sharp point at all four ends and tied together by duct tape, looking like a wooden X with bladed tips. He threw it, and the deadly star swooshed end over end. The sharp arrowhead tip struck the tiger's hind muscle and splayed it open. Blood spurted from the wounded beast like a geyser. The tiger began to hobble, but it kept its frightened pace. The predator had become the prey. The Ridgeback, named Patch, bit at the tiger's hind legs. He growled viscously, but he was disciplined enough not to bark. Croix had taught him well. There were two things that drew unwanted attention in the barrens of the Blaze: gunshots and barking dogs.

Croix tossed another Apache star. It spun through the air and struck the tiger's rib cage. The sharp arrowhead tip was embedded deep in the marrow. Croix threw another, with polished skill and precision, striking the tiger's hind leg as the beast leapt into the sharp rock formations and disappeared into a maze of granite. The dog leapt after it, disappearing too. The golden palomino seemed eager to follow, but Croix jerked the reins and the horse dug its heels into the ground and jolted to a dusty stop at the foot of the rocks.

Croix stepped down from the saddle. He had the look of both cowboy and Indian. An untamed banditry in his blue eyes and a savage wildness in his heart. His face was rough-hewn and molded by the valley sun, and his clothes were scrubbed clean and always drab, perfect for camouflaging himself in the desert terrain. His unkempt stubble barely covered the brutal knife scar that was trenched across his left cheekbone like a fault line. He wore a bulletproof kevlar vest with the faded words *Southwestern Guard* painted across the chest plate in red lettering. A Maori tribal tattoo ran the entire length of his left arm down to the tip of his trigger finger, which was resting anxiously on the *Crazy 8* revolver holstered to his hip. A .357 caliber hand cannon made by *Chronos Arms* in the old world, circa 2043. It was gunmetal gray with a dark wooden grip and an eight-round cylinder, carrying two more rounds than his other revolvers. The extra shots always seemed to save his ass at just the right moments. The infallible *Crazy 8* was practically an extension of his arm. It may as well have been welded on. He relied on the heavy wheelgun as much as he relied on his own wits.

But a .357 was no match for a 500-pound bengal tiger. Even one that was badly wounded and limping. Croix wasn't gonna take that chance. He was never one to play with fire in hopes of not getting burned. These desert beasts were man-eaters, and his skinny white ass was the only meat currently on the menu. He pulled a pump shotgun from the leather sheath on his saddle. A rare 12-gauge *Breckenridge Hydra 300*. A triple-barreled, vertically-stacked boomstick with three mag tubes and a 30-shell capacity. There were only a thousand of them made before the Collapse. His was the only one he'd ever seen. There was a noise suppressor attached to the barrels. A necessity in the Blaze. Shotgun blasts travelled far, and they lingered long enough for curious ears to locate the direction from which they came. In the healthier parts of these barren lands there were plenty of scavengers and gangs that were waiting for any sign of opportunity, or perhaps a senseless mistake that they might capitalize on. Croix never made mistakes. He never fired a shotgun that wasn't muzzled. The *Hydra* was loaded with homemade shells filled with his own powdery mix of *tiger shot*.

He tugged on the horse's bridle. "Stay here, Hop. I'm fixin' to dust it up with that beast. I don't want you getting in the middle of it."

Tigers were a menace in the Blaze. Before the Collapse, there were over ten thousand of them held in captivity in America. After the Red Death, they were all set free by animal rights activists. Free to roam among the living and the dead. They outlasted the black rhinos and the elephants, who were both easy targets for human hunters, and even the lions, who lived in packs and made themselves vulnerable to trackers. But the tigers were ghosts, living alone in the forests and deserts, always in motion, in hiding, avoiding human bullets, and breeding at their leisure. Now they were multiplied, and adapted to the hot new world, having lost their typical body mass through daily consumption of their own fat cells. The lighter frame helped them to better regulate their body temperature in the extreme heat. They were quicker now and more aggressive, hunting Bighorn sheep and living off cactus water and bacterial sludge. They slept in caves and long abandoned mineshafts where they could cool down and rejuvenate in the shade. Tigers were nearly atop the food chain now. But not quite.

Croix turned and saw the Ridgeback tracking the tiger's blood trail through the rocky terrain. The dog disappeared again behind the massive boulders. Croix entered the daunting maze of rock with his wits squarely on his sleeve. His eyes were sharp and his ears even sharper. He heard a soft thumping noise and swung the shotgun in that direction. It was just a black crow that had landed in the dirt to swallow a crusty earthworm. The crow flew away, its wings fluttering loudly, casting an ominous shadow across the granite wall as it coasted on the wind. Then Croix heard footsteps coming from the rocks behind him. He swung the shotgun back around and his eyes went from craters of fear to slits of anger as he saw the Ridgeback standing there panting. The dog had backtracked, following the tiger's blood trail right back to where Croix was standing.

"Goddamn dog," Croix hissed.

Then suddenly the dog coiled up and bared its sharply filed teeth, hawking its eyes and growling viscously. Croix heard a noise that pattered behind him and saw a dark shadow blotting out the sun at his feet. As the dog panicked and barked, Croix spun a one-eighty and swung the shotgun upwards, and the tiger, which was just a dark orange silhouette, leapt from the rock above him. Croix's trigger finger twitched and he fired the shotgun by accident and blasted the tiger in its underbelly. The wounded beast landed on him, knocking the shotgun from his grip and pinning him to the ground. The tiger's breath steamed onto his face, smelling of blood and raw meat. Its teeth snapped just out of reach but clacking ferociously. Croix slid his hand under the tiger's chin and pressed upwards with every bit of strength he had, struggling to keep the killer beast at bay. He pulled a Bowie knife from his kevlar vest with his free hand and thrust it into the tiger's neck. The killer beast roared, and Croix's eardrum nearly ruptured. Blood splattered onto his face like hot red paint exploding from an aerosol can. The dog ripped into the tiger's hind leg with its filed teeth and shredded the striped coating, pulling skin from bone. Croix squeezed a handful of the tiger's furry coat in his grip while he stabbed it repeatedly in the neck. The tiger shrieked. Croix wrenched the Bowie knife from its neck and drove it into the top of the tiger's skull. The ravenous beast stopped chomping, like clockwork grinding to a halt. Its powerful jaws lay slack. Its tongue fell limp, hanging loosely from its bloody mouth. The 500-pound man-eater was dead.

Croix wasn't.

He could hardly believe it.

The Ridgeback relented, pulling its filed teeth from the tiger's flesh. The proud hunting dog walked circles around the defeated beast, panting in victory. Croix mustered what little strength he had left and slid his body out from under the crushing weight of the tiger's corpse. He lay there a moment regaining his composure and refilling his lungs with air. "That sure as hell didn't go as planned," he said to the dog, glaring defensively. "Don't you tell anyone about this."

Everything had happened so quickly, but already Croix was replaying the steps in his mind, and he was embarrassed by how easily he could've been killed. *How the hell could I be so careless?* The tiger had outflanked him and outsmarted him. That in itself should've been a fatal mistake. Had the dog not been there at just the right time, he would've been nothing more than tiny particles of human flesh acidifying in the tiger's gut. He'd barely gotten the shot off in time before the tiger landed on him, with just enough weight not to crush his ribs and puncture his lungs and leave him there to die a slow death. The tiger's jaws had been snapping less than an inch from his face. Any closer and he would've been mincemeat. Everything had to align just perfectly for Croix to still be lying there breathing. That made him contemplate things he never had before. Trivial things. Suddenly he was in unfamiliar cerebral territory, his mind spinning silky webs, his soul getting caught in the stickiness of it. Then he heard the sound of equestrian hooves moving across the valley floor. He looked up into the sun and saw the dark silhouette of his golden palomino standing over the top of him. "Oh now you show up," he said indignantly. "Helluva horse you are."

The mustang blew at him and stomped its hoof into the earth, as if to say *I told you so.*

"Sure," Croix said. "You're always right." He reached out and pulled a hand-rolled paper cigarette from the threaded clutches of his back pocket. It was made from the fading page of some meaningless old book. He pulled a cracked zippo from the same pocket and grimaced from the pain in his shoulder. The lighter was filled with mash liquor that he'd brewed for himself earlier that spring. He flicked the spark-wheel with his thumb, then lit the cigarette with a dull yellowy flame. Then he took a deep purposeful drag of homegrown tobacco. It never tasted so good. He lay there thinking about the futility of his own life. Not something he made a habit of doing, but this was unavoidable. He had almost lost his ability to contemplate anything at all. Only inches away from mindless oblivion. That kind of thing could put the zap on a man's head. He thought maybe it was the unfortunate timing of it all, and nothing more than that. He would be a father soon, and the prospect of fatherhood had dulled his double-edged senses. He never wanted to bear fruit, but his tree was suddenly blossoming. His instincts were a step slower since he found out they were expecting. His mind was cluttered. He hated to admit it, and probably never would, but had he not been so goddamn lucky that morning, his unborn son would've been fatherless, and that was something that he feared more than tiger teeth.

After he smoked his hand-rolled cigarette down to nothing, he grabbed a machete and severed the tiger's head from its body. Just a few hard strikes, and a few splatters of warm blood, and the beastly prize was his. He strung the head with rope and tied it to his saddle and let it dangle there like a trophy of war. The flies swarmed around the eyeballs, which were still lost in their predatory gaze. This was a victory that Croix wanted to remember. He placed his left foot in the stirrup and gripped the saddle horn to pull himself up, but he stopped mid-legswing as he caught a glimpse of something in the distance. Something eerily familiar. A strange-looking rock formation, towering above all the others. A circular hole in the granite that he'd always called *Lover's Arch*. "I'll be damned," he said to the horse, looking a little uneasy. "Didn't realize where we were."

The arch was a natural curvature in the stone that formed a complete but imperfect circle which from his vantage point framed the jagged peak of Mount Whitney perfectly within its granite ring, like a living canvas framed by nature's own hand. He stood there for a moment, reluctant to let his feelings guide him. Then he wandered over to the arch and placed his hand on the rock, its massive frame curving upwards and over the top of him and casting him in a cool shadow. The unheated granite gave him a reprieve from the crippling onslaught of the sun. He ran his fingertips across the rock, his eyes searching, until he found what he was looking for. A bittersweet memory, etched into the stone:

*Croix kissed me here*

*2053*

## – *Zee* –

He held his hand over the crude engraving with his eyes closed, and his heart stammered like it had back then. A fleeting joy that he knew would only harm him. He jerked his hand back and hissed and turned away with a blankness in his eyes. He walked back to the horse and hopped back in the saddle and clicked his heels harder than he should have. "Let's go," he said. "Gotta keep moving." He didn't want the memory to linger. Memories were a trap that a man could never escape once he was locked inside. His head had been zapped enough already that morning. He rode on, staying alert in the saddle, his head on a swivel like always, trotting north through the lusher parts of the valley. The Ridgeback followed him through the repurposed land. A deep rift, resting quietly between the Sierras on the west and the powdery White Mountains on the east. They called it the Granite Valley. But it was once called something else.

Before the Collapse, on the old paper maps, the land was called *Owens Valley*. A dry stretch of infertility haunted by dead soil and swirling ghosts of dust. The valley's water had once been stolen way back in 1913 by the booming city of Los Angeles and their corrupt power brokers. The lifeblood of hard-working farmers and cattlemen was then diverted through a manmade aqueduct that carried their precious water from the Owens River to a massive reservoir located 233 miles away in the city of angels. Los Angeles prospered. The once-thriving Owens Valley was raped by the big city and left to die. Seventy-five miles of fertile soil left barren. The Owens Lake decayed into a lifeless bed of earth, and the people of the valley were suffocated daily by inhospitable dust. The farmers and cattlemen eventually left. The wildlife too. The lush, green land they once dubbed the *American Switzerland* was vanquished by the backwards notion of human progress. Thievery disguised as business. Nothing grew in the valley after that but the bitterness of the earth.

But a century and half later, everything changed. After the Collapse, and after the bloody carnage of the Restoration Wars, the lifeless land of the valley was resurrected by members of the newly disbanded Southwestern Guard. A militia that had formed during the wars to protect the free people from Nimbus rule. When the war ended, and the New World Order peace treaty was signed, establishing the Blaze as an independent land, the southwestern guardians inhabited the dry valley and raised her from the dead, bringing the land back to life like an earthen Lazarus. They renamed it the Granite Valley and established colonies along the river and among the foothills. They destroyed the murderous aqueduct that carried the valley's stolen lifeblood to Los Angeles, dynamiting the main intake, destroying all 14 hydropower plants, and demolishing several siphons and conduits and tunnels along the way. Soon the deserted city of Los Angeles was transformed back to its natural state: a desert plagued by drought, dead vegetation and constant dust storms. A total reversal in the order of things. A natural reclamation of nature's original purpose. That's how Croix saw it. The Granite Valley was built on revenge.

After that, the water slowly returned to the valley from the Sierras, cascading through the Owens River, saturating the valley floor, replenishing the parched earth, and clearing the suffocating dust from the air. The Owens Lake on the southern tip of the valley became a large body of standing freshwater again. The people of the Granite Valley dug complex irrigation ditches and spread the river's water throughout the decomposing rift, healing the land that had been sick for so long. The hard, encrusted, granitic soil was reformed into a soft, nutrient-rich breeding ground for life. A triumphant return of bacteria, fungi, earthworms, and pill bugs. The vegetation exploded upon the landscape like fireworks. The spark of goldenrod, pink checkerbloom and white lupines. Rainbows of summer florals in bloom. A lush greenery blanketing the valley floor. The wildlife returned too. Mule deer and Tule elk came down out of the mountains to forage and drink from the cool waters. The founding motto of the Granite Valley had proven true: *Water is life.* It was now a lush garden of eden.

The river flowed mightily through the heart of it, slithering from north to south in twisting, serpentine shapes, cascading from the mountains, and flowing with wild trout and bluegill. The cottonwood trees were abundant along the riverbanks, their crooked arms outstretched towards the sky in yearning. Their leaves like bright yellow fingertips. The grass of the valley was tall and dancing in the breeze. The blades were greener than the darkest jade stone. Wild irises poked their purple heads from their stems like bright neon bulbs. The scent of summer lavender and bristlecone pine hung in the air. Shadows of crows floated across the granite rock like dark ghosts chasing their haunts. Bighorn sheep wandered out of the forest for a dip in the clear waters. Black bears, whose coats were now sparse and brown and desperately endangered, splashed in the shallows and trapped fish beneath their paws in the stoney brooks of the river. The people of the colonies had done what so many others were unwilling to do. They saved a dying piece of the earth and made it their own. Now they had to fight tooth and nail to preserve it.

There were thirteen colonies in all.

On the southern tip of the valley was Darwin's Ghost, a small colony built over the old ghost town of Darwin in the sloping hills of the Great Basin. The people there repurposed old machinery for the criminal enterprise known as the Bloody

Knuckles. They bought and sold parts on the black market in Kelso.

Then there was Baytown, a few miles west on the southern bay of the reclaimed Owens Lake. It was famous for being the first bartering post in the valley back in '54, before the Bloody Knuckles established a hold on the area a few years later and disrupted the valley's lucrative trade economy. Now Baytown was just a survivor's fort like all the others.

Then there was Bulletwood, founded by the war hero Sam Borland who built the colony's first cabin with timber from the ancient bristlecone pines that he and his guerrilla fighters used for target practice during the wars. Whenever the colonies called for a helping hand in battle, Sam Borland and his *Bullies* were always the first to arrive, climbing down from the Inyo Forest with guns and blades and unbreakable loyalty to the valley.

Golden Peak was a colony of reclusive foragers that sat high up in the foothills of the Sierra. Their stone dwellings were built in the shadow of the sunlit mountain peaks. They hunted black bears and Tule Elk among the evergreens and ate straight from the earth. Nobody heard much from them anymore. But they were there. You could see their fires burning at night.

Further up river was Ponderosa, home of Walton Hutch and company, the largest cattle breeder in the valley. The lush farmland lay among the scattered fir on the west side of the Owens just a stone's throw from the river. He supplied the Bloody Knuckles with beef. They supplied him with the upper hand over everyone else in the valley.

Birdsong was built under the shade of pinyon pines where the sandpipers sang their chirping melodies. Most of the huts in the colony were treehouses on stilts with walking bridges extending from one hut to the other on timber planks connected by rope. The strategic elevation kept the residents safe from the bears and man-eating tigers that often wandered out of the forest looking for a quick meal.

The colony of New Hope lay on the winding riverbank just west of the White Mountains in the flatlands. The people there were evangelical types with bibles stacked on bibles and judgmental fingers to thump them with. But they were good souls, if not a little too righteous for the valley.

Then there was Cotton Creek, founded by Bonnie McMasters and her two husbands. It was a small colony of fist-fighting artisans that was built among the dense forest of yellow-leafed Cottonwood trees. Nice people. So long as they weren't piss drunk and frolicking around naked in the light of day. That happened often.

Then there was Cathedral, built on the crest of the Sierra in a nest of beautiful, misplaced willows. Their beloved church was built before anything else. A tall, glorious stained-glassed house of God. But they weren't righteous at all. Most of them were more inclined to raise hell than cast stones or quote the good book. The celebrations in Cathedral were said to be legendary. In fact, Cotton Creek and Cathedral had an unofficial joint celebration every fall called *Hooch Fair*, to see which colony could consume the most backwoods hooch in a fortnight. Two straight weeks of getting hammered and clamoring the hills with unruly shouts and wild music.

A few miles northeast was Little Switzerland, the most breathtaking colony in all of Granite Valley. They had the enviable luxury of location. There was no better spot in the entire strip. The grass was greener than the greenest grass on earth. The mountains on both sides were magnificently close, towering with powdered majesty, like it belonged on another planet, or at least in another country. Though the beauty hid a troubling darkness. In April of '71, a terrible massacre had taken place there. A violent civil war between factions. A conflict of leadership. Their chosen leader Arturo Langley was killed in a bloody mutiny. Amidst the turmoil, everyone lost their way, each one turning on the other, until no one was left and the entire village was burned to the ground. Now Little Switzerland was a deserted ghost town, save for the ashes of the dead.

Shining Star was the northernmost colony in Granite Valley, resting along Crawley Lake in the ancient caldera near the Glass Mountains. They were a community of fishermen living off the abundance of trout and bluegill that inhabited their waters. The village was nearly wiped out by an epidemic of white lung a few years earlier and now their population was down to six living souls, all struggling with the lingering effects of the disease. So it wouldn't be long before the valley's shining star burned out.

In the Wild Canyon below them lay Wellspring, a colony of self-proclaimed healers who lived among the temperamental hot springs. The healing powers of their mineral oasis was a perennial attraction to the rest of the valley. Colonists came from all over the land to take a curative dip in the warm, miraculous waters of the village. For a cost of course. Nothing of value was ever rendered free in the valley. Trade was the currency. For a time they'd all worked together to ensure they had a sustainable economy. Then the Bloody Knuckles stuck their crooked hand into the pot and every colony but one was in their grasp.

The lone holdout was Revival, the first of the thirteen colonies to be settled back in '53. It lay at the center of the map, in the gorgeous flatlands, just off the mighty riverbank. The people there were impervious to just about everything. They called themselves Revivalists. Like the prehistoric granite peaks that stood guard over them, they were eroded by time, misshapen and scarred, and their souls were constantly chipped away by the inescapable horrors of the new world. But they were also immovable. A permanent fixture of the landscape. It would take an act of some terrible god to force them from their home. Nothing had even come close in twenty-three years.

As Croix approached, he passed by a large wooden sign. There was a friendly warning carved into the cottonwood planks: *Welcome To REVIVAL. We're armed and we don't suffer fools. Respect our way of life or you WILL die. Plain and simple.*

He rode onward and soon passed by a small wooden shack with a tin roof and an old screen door. There was a less prominent wooden sign with a much friendlier message: *SHARE SHACK. Help yourself. Take what you need. Leave what you don't.*

Croix was happy to be back.

Revival was his home.

It felt like a warm pair of arms waiting to embrace him. But to strangers, Revival was anything but welcoming. In fact, it was downright cautionary. A militant fortification that seemed impenetrable. Croix passed by the old crumbling stone wall that encircled the entire compound. There wasn't much left of it. The leavings looked like the ancient ruins of some lost civilization. It was the first wall of Revival. A remnant of the Restoration Wars. Built decades before. Now a worthless artifact. Most of the ramparts had been ravaged by warfare and broken by the cruel hands of time. The wall no longer served a purpose. Nothing more than a constant reminder: *Never let your guard down.*

Revival was protected now by a solar electric fence made of chain-link and curled barbed-wire at the top. Anyone that touched the fence was shocked by 10,000 volts of electricity. Anyone who made it past the shock was sliced to pieces by the sharp metal barbs. Anyone who made it past the sharp metal barbs was faced with a dozen armed Revivalists. Anyone who was spared by their bullets was judged accordingly and sent to the gallows. If someone made it that far, they were as good as dead anyway. There was no going back. At that point, it was between them and their chosen god, and that often meant nothing.

There was a retractable gate on the south side of the fence just beyond the share shack, and several gunner posts rising up at each of the four corners with protective turrets made of crumbling stone and timber. They stood two stories tall and twelve feet wide and offered a strategic mode of defense. Inside Revival, a deep channel of battle trenches ran parallel to the perimeter fence, offering an even more strategic mode of defense, and looking like the Western Front in the war that failed to end all wars. As Revivalists knew all too well, war *never* ended. It just found new vessels to carry on its misguided glory. That was human nature. To divide and conquer and defeat and then wonder why the circle of madness was never broken. So everything in Revival was designed with survival in mind. The place was a fortress, but only because the people there were willing to protect it with their lives.

They had much to protect. There were two rows of timbered A-frame cabins, thirteen in all, each with steep metal roofing that reached all the way to the ground and were covered in solar panels and tubes for collecting rainwater. A large two-story headquarters cabin stood at the end of a long, brick path that cut between the dwellings. Inside was their meeting room, the well-stocked galley, more living quarters, and the indispensable communications hub, complete with every possible *old world* communications technology that could be scavenged and looted over the past two decades.

To keep the place safe, there was always a set of eyes in the sky. A five-story lookout tower called the *crow's nest* rose up from the center of the compound like a ship's periscope. It was built from timber and secured with metal bracing. The tall, rickety ladder was daunting enough, but the pole slide down was even more ominous. There was a large emergency bell hanging from the rafters, with a rope attached to sound the alarm. One ring meant that a friendly was approaching on the horizon. Two rings meant it was time for an emergency meeting. Three rings meant grab your weapons and stand guard. Any more rings than that meant something really bad was about to happen and you better be ready to fight for your life.

That morning the bell only rang once. Croix approached the gate with the bloody, flyblown tiger head dangling from the saddle on a tie wire.

"*It's Croix*," someone announced. "He's *back*."

Wade Gunderson sat up in the crow's nest watching through the scope of his M40 sniper rifle, his finger resting loosely on the trigger. He was the *Watchman*. That was his primary job in Revival. The other was keeping tabs on his fellow colonists. Nobody liked that. He was a one-eyed cyclops of a man, with an eye-patch and a staggering limp and a bad attitude that never brought much good to anything. His hair was already a wiry patch of gray and his body was already decrepit and feeling broken, despite him being only forty-nine years old. Life had taken more from him than it had given, and he was still holding a grudge. He spotted Croix in the crosshairs. He didn't remove his finger from the trigger. There was always a temptation to squeeze, or at least a secret desire. The two didn't get along. But that was nothing new.

The people of Revival were a mashup of colors and cultures and histories and differing beliefs, but they all shared a common goal: survival. The ultimate equalizer. A bond stronger than the dividing forces of any petty differences they may have had. They were a tribe. The only family they had left. But that didn't mean everything was sunshine and roses between them. More often than not it was thunderstorms and weeds. The pesky kind of weeds that just keep coming back after you pluck them from the ground, roots and all. Their family was a dysfunctional mess. A beautiful imperfection. But it had been working like that for twenty years and counting.

Wade grabbed a remote control that was hanging from the rafters by an electrical cable and pressed a red button in the center of it. The electric gate retracted. The Ridgeback sprinted through the gate and into the perimeter run, storming the kennel looking for food and water and a place to lay its weary head. No time for pleasantries with the other dogs.

Revival had everything a survival compound needed. A wooden aqueduct snaked its way from the Owens River straight through Revival to the power station, where a wooden hydroelectric waterwheel powered part of the compound. Scattered solar panels powered the rest of the compound through an underground cable grid. There was a secret armory buried beneath the earth with hidden access points, storing thousands of weapons, from assault rifles to pistols to blades of all shapes and sizes. There was a small infirmary made from a shipping container and a makeshift quarantine with no yellow flag in the window. There was a prison cage made of timber which was used for punishment and a wooden gallows with three nooses and a drop deck that was used for penance. A crowded graveyard loomed on a nearby mound. Several cross headstones marked the burial ground of past residents. It was sacred. That's where Revivalists were buried. The bodies of fallen enemies were buried in the foothills with no markings or words spoken over them. There was a storehouse filled with food, and a root cellar, and a workshop, and a tool shed packed with tools. There were hoop houses for seasonal crops, and a greenhouse for medicinal herbs. They had a large outdoor garden too, with colorful fruit cages. There was a muddy pig pen filled with swine, a covered chicken coop with fowl, a manmade fish pond, and a goat house right next to the sheep yard. Revival wasn't just a fortress. It was a farm, and their work was never done.

Horses whinnied from the stables and ran free in the turnout. Spotted appaloosas, pintos, paints, geldings, mares and several wild mustangs. The kennel was overrun with Ridgebacks and one very commanding Australian cattle dog. The rabbit hutch was alive and hopping with a new litter of pure white New Zealands. Rainbow trout swam cluelessly in the makeshift pond waiting for the unlucky day when they'd be next on the dinner plate. The corpses of brown trout hung from the front porch of the headquarters cabin on hooks, covered in salt and drying out in the summer heat to be used for jerky. Livestock roamed and fed on grass in a small cow pasture that was fenced by electric wire. Milk cows, which were rare and precious. Meat cows, mostly Longhorns and mini Herefords, which had been bartered for in Ponderosa. Their unlucky day would come eventually too. The smell of blood and raw meat drifted on the breeze from the slaughter-house. Meat was on the menu tonight. The Revivalists had just slaughtered a mini Hereford.

Croix approached the open gate with his head high and looking triumphant. Two of his fellow Revivalists, Tavo Kelton and a man named Skinny, were waiting for him just on the other side of the gate, rubbernecking as they often did. Their eyes spotted the trophy that Croix had brought back with him.

"I'll be damned," Tavo said with a smile. He was a high-spirited black man in his thirties who claimed to be born laughing. No one ever doubted that claim. He never heard a joke or an insult or a snide remark that he didn't get a charge out of. He just looked for the humor in all situations, and he believed that all situations could use a little humor. Despite his silliness, he was built like a dark bronze adonis, his muscles bulging through his shirt. He could fight with the best of them. To look at him, you'd think he'd never lost a fight in his life. In fact, he could only remember losing *one*, and that was to the man who was currently riding through the gate with a severed tiger head dangling from his saddle. No shame in that.

Skinny, on the other hand, was a tall and slender man with virtually no muscle at all. A literal string bean. There was no irony in his nickname. When he turned sideways, you practically lost sight of him. His legs were like the pegs of an old wooden chair. His arms like tiny white strings hanging from his shirt sleeves. His lack of bulk was only bested by his lack of intelligence. He was a dim-witted country boy from some backwoods town in the Ozark Mountains, and not a day went by where he didn't say something foolish. He looked at the tiger head and asked, "You don't think that damn thing can still bite, do you?"

Tavo rolled his eyes in disbelief.

"Well damnit," Skinny said defensively, "a *rattlesnake* can still bite you with its head cut off."

The gate closed as Croix entered, retracting on the wheels that were housed in the metal track. The electric lock engaged.

Tavo studied the bloody tiger head with a beaming satisfaction. "That bastard won't be nosing through our share supply no more." He held his hand out in victory. "Pay up, Skinny." He waited for his winnings, his smile turning to a boastful smirk.

But that smirk quickly dissipated as the bossman of Revival approached from the headquarters cabin, not looking too keen on their gambling ways. The bossman was sixty five years of Polynesian spirit, but despite his age, his hair was still as black as it was when he was born. He was kingly, with an aura about him that made most people fall right in line whenever he spoke. His name was Ru, short for some long Polynesian name that was hard for everyone else to pronounce. A Maori tribesman from Hawke's Bay, New Zealand who came to the states on a student visa years before the Collapse and made a life there. His face was adorned with tribal tattoos and his arms were shamefully spotted with Mongrel Mob ink. But he'd come a long way since his days spent gang-banging as a troubled youth in Hastings. He was the chosen leader of Revival, going on twenty years. He had the look of a cowboy now, with an American glint in his eye, but there was still a bit of Polynesian warrior in him. He studied the tiger head. "Is that what I think it is, mate?"

"If you're thinking it's a tiger head," Croix said.

Ru glared at Skinny, then at Tavo, who expected another painful lecture on gambling. But the usually serious-minded leader of Revival surprised them all and said, "Pay the man, Skinny."

Tavo was all smiles again. Skinny was all frown. He reluctantly paid Tavo his winnings, but with a pout on his face. The jackpot was just random junk, scavenged and collected over time, but it was practically gold to them. A few shiny things, some of which might've been jewelry.

Tavo gloated. "Croix, you should've bet on yourself."

Croix shook his head, "It ain't sport to bet on something when you already know the outcome." He stepped down from the saddle, looking victorious.

Skinny puffed up to him, looking a tad salty. "I know I'm supposed to be the stupid one and all, but… that was stupid going after that tiger alone. You're lucky to be alive."

Croix pulled the bloody Bowie knife from his sheath. "Luck didn't have a damn thing to do with it."

Skinny saw the blood on the knife and his eyeballs nearly

sprung from their sockets. He'd seen Croix take down a Tule elk with nothing but a pocketknife and a well-placed punch, but a tiger was something entirely different. Skinny never thought it possible. He quickly withdrew his criticism and stood there in blank-faced awe.

Croix didn't bother to offer him the truth.

Then some obnoxious kid yelled out from the cage, "*Hey. Let me see it.*"

Croix looked at the kid with exhaustion and turned back to Ru and asked, "What's shit-head doing in the cage?"

"He tried to run again," Ru said with similar fatigue. "Caught him trying to shut the fence down."

Croix glared at the cage. "Goddamn it, Kid. What have I told you?"

"Don't waste your breath," Ru huffed. "I've already said it all. Didn't make a dent."

The kid had no real name. They simply called him Kid. He was thirteen years old, or at least that was everyone's best guess. He'd just hit puberty a few months earlier, so thirteen seemed about right. He'd only been a Revivalist for a year and a half and nobody knew his history. He had pimples and a few scattered pockmarks, but other than that he was a decent-looking young man with soft brown eyes and olive skin and surprisingly good teeth. The only other disturbance to his decent look was the cringeworthy gash in his forehead. The shallow crater was fully healed now. At least on the outside. He was missing part of his skull on the inside, and with it the part of his brain that produced memories. Sadly, he didn't possess a single memory from before the accident. That made him an open book. One which needed to be filled with endless curiosities. One that Croix often wanted to close. "*Let me out,*" Kid shouted. "*I wanna see the tiger.*" He shook the timber bars of the cage. "I won't run again. I swear. Come on, Ru." When his plea to Ru didn't work he chose another target. "*Hey Croix. Come on. Let me get a look at it.*"

Croix shook his head, looking more defeated by the kid than by the man-eating tiger that had nearly taken his life. "Thanks to you, Kid, we'll be running another security drill today. I'll fit it into our busy schedule somehow."

Tavo stomped his foot. "Damn you, Kid."

He hated Croix's security drills.

They all did.

"In the meantime," Croix said, "this tiger can keep you company." He tossed the decapitated head towards the cage. It landed just outside the timber-framed door with a heavy thud, swarming with flies and reeking of mangled flesh. Kid reached through the cage bars carefully, looking mesmerized, but reluctant to touch the beast, his hands dancing around the fangs carefully.

Croix chuckled. "It's dead, Kid. Ain't gonna bite you."

Kid slowly ran his fingers across the tiger's bloody fur, in awe of its orange and black-striped majesty. "It's a shame you had to kill it."

"It's a dangerous animal," Croix said.

Kid shook his head. "Hard to believe something so beautiful could be so dangerous."

Croix chuckled again. "That's because you never been with a woman. Wouldn't be so hard to imagine after that."

Tavo and Skinny laughed, both enjoying the moment far more than they should have, considering their heavy workload was currently being ignored.

Croix wasn't one to let a good laugh linger in the face of backordered chores. "What the hell ya'll standing around laughing for? Ain't no shortage of work. Get to it. And take that goddamn kid with you."

Kid stood up, looking bright-eyed.

Tavo and Skinny weren't so amused anymore. The Kid was a pain in everyone's ass, full of angst and mischief and always in some kind of trouble. That seemed to be his role at Revival. The whipping boy. When anything went wrong, he seemed to get the blame. Though most of the time the blame was justified.

Ru lingered at Croix's side. "Speaking of dangerous women..."

Croix nodded. "Yeah I know. She hates when I go out alone." He looked nervous. "Hell, ain't sure why she cares so much. We've hardly spoke a word in months." He was reluctant to ask, but he couldn't tame his own curiosity. "She still pissed at me?"

Ru smirked. "Hell has no fury like a woman scorned by you, Croix. She's practically growing horns on her head."

"Yeah," Croix said with a frightful grimace. "A baby in the belly does that to a woman."

Ru laughed. But Croix wasn't laughing. He was the one who'd have to endure the fury.

# TEN

Zee Hendricks didn't know how much time she had left before the baby inside of her finally broke free from its uterine prison. All this pregnancy stuff was guesswork to her. The baby had begun to drop into the cavity of her pelvis two weeks earlier, and she figured it wouldn't be much longer before her cervix did the rest. So when she felt a sharp pain and deep pressure in her lower belly that morning she panicked and called for Hickory over the walkie. The cervical spasm had started before she even had the chance to wake from her uncomfortable slumber. No time to even brush her teeth or fix herself up for company. Not that anyone would ever notice. She was stunning with or without maintenance. She had a natural beauty that had proven itself incorruptible by the brutalities of life. Her hair was a dark auburn mess, but she was still glowing with maternal glory. She had soft white skin, emerald green eyes and a gorgeous smile that could charm a rattlesnake. But her tragic past had left unsightly scars on her face. Knife wounds that slithered across her cheek like the devil's claw-prints. Like a mark of his constant torment. Despite her tragic blemishes, she was always alight with some kind of purpose, as if she was out to prove the impossible. All she ever proved was that she was impossibly stubborn. Nobody even tried to change her mind once it was set in motion. Least of all the man who'd accidentally knocked her up. She was Croix's *"on again off again"* companion, girlfriend, partner, pain in the ass, whatever they were calling it these days. Nothing official, but it had been set in stone for years.

She was definitely feeling her torment today, in her third trimester of Hell. She lay there in her daybed, belly up and grimacing, her face an awful shade of red. "Damnit, Hickory. Take it easy with them boney old fingers." She grasped at the bed sheet tightly. "I hate this worse than pulling teeth."

An elderly man named Hickory sat at the foot of her bed with his gloved fingers inside of her, feeling her cervix. He was eighty-five years old and looked every bit of it. His red, irritated eyes were scratched by crow's feet and suffering from glaucoma, and the spectacles on his face were as thick as a bottle of sarsaparilla. Everything sagged on his body and his bones were like brittle corn, but his hands were steady as ever. In his youth he was a certified veterinarian for a cattle ranch in Montana who also liked to cowboy on the side. Now he was the closest thing Revival had to a real doctor. "I'm sorry, Zee. I'm just tryin' to be effective is all."

"Well, you poke me like that again, you're liable to get a heel upside your head. How'd that be for effective?"

"I'd rather not find out."

"Then hurry it up."

"I'm going as fast as I can, believe me. This process ain't much less painful for me. I'm sitting on boulders here." He was referring to the two massive hemorrhoids in his ass. "Too many years riding horseback I suspect."

Zee grimaced. "Well stand up, Hickory. For God's sake."

"Then I gotta stand on my two bad knees." He was referring to his arthritic joints. He shifted on the hard, wooden stool to relieve the pressure from the swollen veins in his anus. "When you're as ancient as me, you gotta pick your poison."

Zee laughed. "You're impossible."

"And you're laughing," Hickory said. "So that part of my job is done."

"You always have a way of bringing me back down to earth, don't you?"

"I figured I better soften you up before I let Gin take over. I don't want her to get the heel upside the head."

Zee exhaled. "I'm sorry, Hickory. This baby's got me foaming at the mouth."

"That's expected," Hickory said with a sweet demeanor. "Don't you fret about it." He removed his fingers and grabbed a hand towel. "Alright, Gin, you wanna feel?"

Gin Sweeney sat nervously in a chair beside him, waiting for her chance to play midwife. Her flowing blonde hair sparkled. Her silvery eyes did too. She was sixteen and still shedding her youth at a snail's pace, her gaze fraught with a deadly sense of wonder. But there was no time for wondering. Her days were spent learning the medical trade, to carry on the practice when Hickory passed, which looked like it could be sooner than later. She looked at Zee to get her blessing.

Zee gave it to her with a nod.

Hickory moved aside and let Gin take the reins. "You know what to do," he said with a punchy tone. "Get on in there and do it."

It was a tad indelicate, but that was Hickory. Not one for delicate sensibilities. Gin was a determined young lady, as Hickory had always told her, but she was filled with self-doubt, and that was something they'd have to remedy.

She stuck her gloved fingers inside of Zee and felt around

for the cervix. She wiggled her digits nervously. Her eyes seemed lost as she tried to register what she was feeling.

"Well?" Zee asked, squirming with discomfort. "Whatcha think?"

"About two centimeters," Gin said, her declaration sounding more like a question than a point of fact. She looked at Hickory for assurance. "Maybe?"

"That's right," Hickory said. "Don't question it." He turned to Zee. "You're about two centimeters dilated. Your cervix is softening. That means you could have the baby any day now."

Zee swallowed nervously. "Any day? Like tomorrow?"

"It could be tomorrow, or it could take weeks. It all depends on your cervix. But it's high time."

Her eyes were big and round. "I guess there ain't no stopping it now."

"No ma'am, there ain't."

---

At first glance, Croix's cabin looked exactly like everyone else's. The same A-frame construction. The pitched roofing with solar and rainwater collectors. The small galley kitchen that he kept clean and tidy. The loft where he kept his bed neatly made. The solar shower that he kept spotless. The composting toilet that practically sparkled. He even had the stone fireplace and a chair to enjoy the nighttime warmth of a crackling flame, just like everyone else. But there was one exception. He had a large shed built onto the back of his A-frame, creating a sort of elongated spine that made the cabin look like a large wooden beast that was stretched out on its belly and napping on the valley floor. It was Croix's sanctuary. An ammo factory, a metal foundry, and a training shed all in one. Those were the things that preoccupied him during his long, sleepless nights: security and self-defense. In fact, that was his job. His official title in Revival was *Guardian*. He took his job as seriously as everything else in life. His cabin was proof of that. A literal workshop for survival. The shed at the back was covered by shredded tarpaulins to keep the space well-ventilated. The process of melting lead for casting bullets was a toxic one, and Croix spent a lot of his time making homemade ammo. If he wasn't making ammo, he was forging blades and improvised weapons in his steel forge, which he'd made from an old brake drum with metal legs welded to the sides for support. He could be heard hammering away on his anvil at all hours of the night or crafting handmade bullets in the old reloading presses that he'd looted from an abandoned gun shop in the ghost town of Lone Pine. There were piles of lead ingots for casting bullets and scavenged metals for forging new blades. Metal was easy to come by. Lead not so much. He scavenged lead from all over the Blaze. Wheel weights from dilapidated automobiles in salvage yards. Range scrap from abandoned military bases. Roof flashing from tumbledown homes. Random antiques looted from shops in the ghost towns. Old scuba diving equipment and boat ballasts and keels from their wanderings to the Pacific Coast a few years earlier. He even had some radioactive isotope cores that he'd scavenged carefully from a radio pharmacy during their perennial scavenger hunt. If he saw a piece of lead, he snatched it up and carried it home, regardless of the weight or the inconvenience. He did whatever it took to preserve their way of life in Revival. Lead was like water to him. He knew Revival would never survive without loads of ammunition. So he casted every bore possible in his factory. Bullet molds of every caliber. Stacks of meticulously crafted ammunition. Precise, powerful and deadly accurate. But bullets don't work without gun powder. So he made that too. From potassium nitrate, charcoal and sulfur. He had the chemical formula etched in black letters on his cottonwood wall: 75% KNO3, 15% C, 10% S

He collected those elements as obsessively as he collected metal and lead. Potassium nitrate from sunflowers, spinach, buckets of urine, and limestone caves, where bat droppings would mix with the rain-soaked limestone and become evaporated salt. He made the charcoal by burning wood without oxygen. Willow was best, from the Sierra Mountains, but pine cones worked too. He extracted the sulfur from pyrite. Fool's gold from the rivers. Steamed in a makeshift, hollowed-out heating pipe, then released into a basin and left to cool. All he needed after that was a pestle and a mortar and some late night diligence and he had barrels full of gunpowder. They stocked his gunpowder and lead like it was something sacred. A true ambrosia. Their *life insurance*, as he always called it. Defending the fortress was a lifestyle for Croix. A Spartan motivation. The shaping of blades and bullets felt like mastery over the world and its elements. Turning something formless and void of purpose into something strong and useful. When he wasn't making weapons, he was breaking them in. Always practicing. Always perfecting his fighting skills and sharpening the uncompromising instincts that he'd developed after the Collapse. The bloody chaos of the Restoration Wars, and every terrible thing that followed in the subsequent years, had shaped him into a human blade. A weapon that was also formless and void of purpose until he was forged into something strong and useful. Now he was an instrument of war, plain and simple. But he didn't fight because he loved it. He fought to protect what he loved.

That morning he felt like he couldn't protect anything. The near-death experience with the man-eating tiger had really made him think. He stood there in the solar shower scrubbing the dried blood from his skin with rock salt and calendula oil. The cold water from the broken thermosyphon tank trickled down his spine in bloody streaks, turning his skin to gooseflesh. His naked form was slim but muscular, and it was covered in bad history. There were battle scars all over his body, from his head to his toes, criss-crossing along the flesh like winding rivers in a search of an ocean. His skin a canvas of scars. A gritty, abstract work of art. Dotted with puncture wounds, all splattered in dark pink lesions. Swollen ridges of flesh and gradient scar tissue, raised from the skin like a topographic map. The grueling work of enemy blades and bullets. A litany of lashings and beatings and burns. A body misshapen by the jagged protrusions of broken bones. Breaks that were improperly healed. The savage markings of a man who'd been to Hell and refused to stay there. But he wasn't just marked by the wounds of battle. He was marked by his own militance too, in bold pronouncements, as if he wanted the world to know where he stood on matters of war and peace. There was an elaborate tattoo inked across his back in bold lettering. The Latin phrase: *si vis pacem para bellum*. If you want peace, prepare for war. Croix lived with the knowledge that evil never ends, unless you put an end to it yourself.

He watched the tiger's blood swirl around in his cupped hands. He could see his own reflection in the crimson swell. His eyes looked unchanged but he was wondering if something hadn't shifted inside of him. The bloody water escaped between his crooked fingers and was washed away. He wondered how many times he'd done that in life. Washed it all away. The blood. The killing. The sin. The remorse. Like none of it had ever happened. Then his mind flickered to a memory. Something unwanted. He suddenly remembered the desert of his youth. The brutal Mojave sun scorching his back. The red badge of death on his young hands. A pocketknife covered in someone else's blood. His tiny, boyish limbs stabbing the knife into some unknown boy's gut. He could still hear the boy screaming. He shivered and flinched at the echo in his mind, his memories like vicious claws digging into the back of his head. He could still feel the nauseating guilt in the pit of his stomach. The unbearable sorrow of a broken promise. A promise he still hadn't kept.

Then the memory flickered and stopped, like a film reaching the end of its reel. He covered his eyes with his clean hands as if that would make him blind to his past. But a man is always tormented by one of two things: the things he's done or the worries of things yet to come. He began to think about his unborn son, and the unformed memories inside of that uncharted soul, floating around cluelessly in the safety of Zee's womb. Croix hoped the boy would never have to do the terrible things that he'd done. He'd have to teach the boy how to navigate the deadly seas of life, or the boy would capsize and drown in them. That's just how the ebb and flow of life goes. Any which way it wants. So Croix figured he better get a jump on this fatherhood thing, one way or another. He shut the water off and grabbed a towel. His mind was hemor-rhaging on Zee and their tumultuous relationship of late. It was time to make amends with the mother of his unborn son. Time to gain her forgiveness, without actually asking for it, if possible. The thought of reconciliation made him nervous, and suddenly the near-death experience with the man-eating tiger seemed like an evening stroll among the cottonwoods. There was nothing in the world quite as dangerous as Zee Hendricks on a hormonal kick.

"*Damnit, Hickory,*" Zee shouted. "What else could you possibly need to poke at? You been nosing around between my legs for thirty goddamn minutes."

Hickory shifted on the wooden stool. His gloved hands were still poking around her lady parts. "Patience is a virtue in this world," he said. "One to strive for in fact."

Zee was just striving for a healthy breath. Her uterus was pushing on her diaphragm and her diaphragm was pushing on her lungs. She only had so much room in her tiny frame to accommodate another life form. "I think my virtues are all tapped out," she said, nearly breathless. "I ain't got much left to give."

She could feel the usual aches and pains, which seemed constant nowadays, and seemed to emanate from every square inch of her body. She loved the fact that there was a new life blooming inside of her, but she hated being pregnant. Her body had changed in so many unforgiving ways she felt like she was in someone else's skin. Her blood pressure was so high it was causing headaches and blurry vision. Her back hurt like hell. Her gums were always inflamed. She had stabbing pains in her pubic bone and soreness in her ribs, and even tightness in her bowels, where her chronic constipation was threatening to form hemorrhoids like the ones that Hickory was always complaining about. She had spells of sciatica and leg cramps, which seemed to alternate on cue, never giving her lower half a moment's comfort. She was angry half the time and depressed when she wasn't. Her digestive system was even more temperamental than her mood swings. She had heart-burn after every meal, and every meal that she was scarfing down lately was larger than anything she'd ever eaten before in a single sitting. Eating for two was a chore, and it was down-right nauseating. At least three hundred extra calories a day. Her stomach felt like a lead balloon that would never pop no matter how much it expanded. And that was just her insides. Her outward appearance had changed too. Her breasts were larger now, and the swollen veins were making them look like a pair of extraterrestrial cocoons. Her deep auburn hair was thick and impossible to tame and she thought the ridiculous poof on top of her head resembled a palm frond. Her once unblemished skin was covered in new moles and unsightly tags that clung to her flesh like bloated ticks. *Where's that special glow that everyone's always rambling on about?* She sure as hell didn't see it.

*Maybe my eyes are just too swollen*, she thought.

Everything on her body seemed to swell over the last two weeks. Her feet looked like surgical gloves that were filled with water and ready to burst. That's exactly how her bladder felt too. Even her face was swollen beyond its limits. Her nose looked bigger in the mirror now, so she avoided her own reflection like the plague, even more so than before. She thought it looked like a man's nose. She hated the masculating effects of pregnancy. There was nothing feminine about this glorified process. She even had severe bloating and gas, which in her experience was a realm of uncouthness that was usually dominated by men. But men could never handle pregnancy. That she knew for sure. "How much longer are you gonna poke and prod me down there?" she asked Hickory.

Before Hickory could explain his deliberate pace, Gin turned to him with a sudden giddiness and asked, "Can I tell her?"

"Tell me what?" Zee asked.

"Go on," Hickory said. "You can tell her."

"Tell me *what*, goddamnit?"

Gin grabbed Zee's hand and grinned mischievously. "We got a surprise for you."

Zee wasn't in the mood for surprises, or mischievous grins.

Then Hickory pulled a handheld electronic device from his medical bag and Zee was suddenly intrigued by the sight. It was a cylindrical wand with a small video monitor attached to the end by a long spiraling cord. Old world technology. But Zee had an idea of what it might be.

"It's that old handheld ultrasound we've been trying to salvage," Gin said with excitement. "Elmer got it working."

Zee's scowl melted away. Her green eyes lit up like phosphorescent algae. "I can see my baby with that thing?"

"We're gonna try," Hickory said. "If you want to?"

"Well *hell yes* I want to." She looked as giddy as Gin all of a sudden, staring at the monitor that was propped up on the bedside table by a stack of old books. Hickory fired up the strange-looking device. A black and white image appeared on the tiny screen. Nothing recognizable to Zee. Just a wavy blur of colorless distortion. Hickory moved the cylindrical end around, scanning different areas of Zee's belly, until he saw what he was looking for.

Then Zee saw it too. "Oh my God," she said, not believing her eyes. It was a vivid, three-dimensional image of a living baby, and the baby was actually moving. Alive inside of her. She'd never seen anything like it. "That's my baby," she said with happy tears forming in her eyes. She placed her hand to her mouth in surprise. Then she drifted on a thought. Something that made her sad. "I wish Croix was..." She stopped herself short of admitting her foolish desire.

Hickory recognized her sadness. "You know, Zee, I may be able to see if it's a boy or girl. If you wanna know?"

"I already know," she said, looking sure of herself. "I've felt it in my heart for a while now."

"That's called a mother's intuition," Hickory said.

Gin squeezed Zee's hand tightly and looked at her with a

gaze fraught with wonder. "I'd sure like to know, if you're alright with it. Can we?"

Hickory looked to Zee.

Zee gave her blessing with a nod.

"Alright," Hickory said. "Let's do it." He scanned her belly on the right side, searching for the baby's genitalia. Any clue that might tip him off to the baby's gender. "I just gotta maneuver this thing around a bit. Sometimes it works out. Sometimes it don't. Sometimes it's pure luck. Hope you're feeling lucky." He moved the device around to the other side of her belly. The image was still distorted. He moved it again and suddenly it became clear, like a winter's morning. He squinted behind his thick glasses. "If I can just get the angle…" Then he spotted it. "Oh boy," he said, cringing in disbelief. "Ya'll seeing what I'm seeing?"

Gin pointed to a dark spot on the screen. "*There*. You can see between the baby's legs."

Zee squinted, her eyes on the struggle. "Ain't nothin' there."

"Nope," Hickory said through clenched teeth. "There sure ain't."

Zee was straining to see. "Hold up... is that a...?"

"It sure is," Hickory said. He bared a slight grimace, as if he knew the gender reveal wouldn't be well received. He was waiting for another angry tirade, or the heel upside the head. But Zee was speechless. Her eyes were locked on the screen in a mild state of shock. Some dull, shatterproof daze.

"Ain't what I was expecting to see," she said, looking foiled by the universe. "A mother's intuition my ass."

# ELEVEN

Croix made his way to the fence line and pulled a handful of flowers from the wet soil. The latest bloom. Purple irises. Zee's favorite. He figured it wouldn't work, but it was worth a shot. He'd need all the sappy reinforcement he could get, shameless or not. He stood there mustering the nerve to pay her a visit. Then he made his way towards her cabin. He walked slowly. *Very* slowly. Then he stopped for a moment and decided to take the long way around.

Zee sat in her daybed looking ready to quarrel, despite her mental exhaustion. A duality of emotion that seemed to characterize her these days. The bitter morning had already stirred her hormones, and now the surprising revelation of her baby's gender had left her feeling more volatile than usual. Despite the painfully large baby inside of her, she was still impetuous and energetic, and certainly not one for self-pity. Her impervious constitution didn't preclude her from bouts of pouting on occasion, but no one ever saw her feel sorry for herself. It wasn't in her nature. She hated spending her precious energy on such prideful things, so she tried to keep her mind where it belonged: on her work. Now that Hickory and Gin were gone, she could get back to it. Her fingers wrestled with a needle and thread, stitching a pair of wool pants by hand. She was the artisan of Revival, always making useful and inspiring things. Clothing. Candles. Soaps. Crafts. Her cabin was provisioned accordingly. Baskets of wool and homespun thread, and several repurposed sewing machines. Wooden shelves packed with containers of mud and clay and bark and countless other earthy substances. She had stacks of collected leathers and hand-threaded baskets. Her small galley kitchen was tailored more for crafting than for cooking. The countertop and dining table were covered with paints, animal hides, beeswax and dyes rather than food or decorative flowers. Her daybed was the only clean spot in the cabin. Even the loft upstairs was a workspace, where she most often found her creative inspiration while catching wondrous glimpses of the valley through the antiqued windows. She had a hundred different projects going at once. A whirlwind of production, even with a bun in the oven. An imaginative soul in an unimaginative world. Her free-spirited creativity sometimes got her in trouble, at least with the more practical types who didn't bother with such trivial things like art and freedom of thought. If only she hadn't hitched her romantic wagon to one of those types.

---

Croix approached her cabin with a brooding sense of dread, as if the feeling itself were a living, breathing creature growing inside of him, curling its gnarled fingers around his beating heart and crushing it into a bloody pulp. His imagination could be so vivid, especially when he was fearing for his mortal soul. He was a man that feared no other man, but he lost his wits entirely when he was around women, especially Zee. Women made no sense to him. They were emotional acrobats and unpredictable scrappers, and he had no effective tactical strategies to counter their surprise attacks. Dealing with women was like guerrilla warfare. They'd just hide out in some proverbial bushes somewhere and wait for the unsuspecting male to wander aimlessly into their trap. Then they'd fire without warning, and usually without a lick of sense. No one could defend against that sort of thing. So he always kept his head on a swivel when dealing with the opposite sex.

He stepped onto the front porch of Zee's cabin, trying to compose himself. The flowers were being crushed in his hand. He felt like an absolute fool for even considering a peace offering. He knocked on the door and took a few healthy steps back. He waited, his chin high, ready to face her with confidence. Then as he imagined the unfavorable outcome, he panicked under the weight of his own doubt and tossed the flowers into the half-filled rain barrel by the porch steps.

The door opened and Zee stood in the doorway like an angry St. Peter guarding the Pearly Gates. The scars on her face were contorted by her hostile expression.

Croix expected her worst. "Hello, Zee," he said, sounding uncharacteristically meek. He immediately raised his hands in self-defense. "Now don't go slamming the door on me."

"Whatcha want?" she asked with a well-harvested scowl.

Even with that ugly look on her face she was still a thing of beauty, and Croix wanted to press himself against her swollen body and kiss her on the neck, and that wasn't all that crossed his mind. "I just thought I'd talk to 'em. The baby. Introduce myself or something." He was unsure of his own words, feeling way out of his comfort zone. Only Zee could make him feel so uneasy. "You said he can hear my voice now, didn't you?"

"I told you that months ago. Why the sudden interest?"

Croix moaned in surrender. "Never mind." His rage was pulsating through his hyper-tense veins. "This was a goddamn mistake." He turned to walk away.

But Zee opened the door wider and said, "You got five minutes."

Croix stopped in his tracks and turned back, surprised by her mercy.

Zee started for the daybed so she could rest her swollen feet. She waddled like a wounded penguin. Croix followed her into the cabin, nosing around like always, looking to see what she'd been doing to pass her time in stubborn reclusion. He saw baskets of light wool sheared from the Dorset Horn sheep. There was a set of tarnished dyeing pans on the table surrounded by a cluster of onion skins, black currant, weld, and willow root for making the dye.

"You shear all that wool yourself?" he asked.

Zee didn't respond. Her silence was ominous. Croix suddenly felt targeted, like prey just waiting for the ambush. It would be a surprise attack, no doubt. An emotional outburst. An angry tirade. Conflict with her seemed obligatory these days. Then he noticed a bassinet that she had made from wicker. It looked sturdy. He was quite impressed. "I see the baby ain't slowed you down none. You never been one to pity yourself. I'll give you that."

Zee rolled her eyes as she often did when he spoke. "Is that your idea of a flattering word? Hope you ain't here to woo me. 'Cause it ain't gonna work."

"Hell, girl. I ain't delusional."

"Good. Then do whatcha come to do and get it over with."

*So much for mercy*, Croix thought. She may have been from the antebellum south, but she was no southern belle. Or as he often put it, *her Georgia was no peach*. He followed her to the daybed, his eyes watching carefully, and ready to bail at the first sign of trouble.

Zee laid herself down on the daybed, belly up, with her sore back propped on a few soft pillows stuffed with crow feathers.

Croix thought about his brush with death earlier that morning and inexplicably asked, "Can I say something without you getting mad?"

"I don't know," Zee said. "Can *I* say something without *you* getting mad?"

"Never mind," Croix said. "I'll just talk to the baby."

"Well go on and do it then."

He conceded to her unshakeable will. He kneeled down next to her belly, his eyes trying to convince her of his sincerity. He wasn't there for any other business. She watched him skeptically as he moved his hands slowly to her side. He was nervous all of a sudden. "So how do I do this?"

"You just talk to my belly, fool."

He cleared his throat. Several times. A nervous tick that always gave him away.

"What the hell you doin'?" Zee asked.

"I'm thinking," he shrugged. "Ain't sure what to say."

"That's nothin new."

"Well not everybody's got your big mouth."

"Don't start, Croix."

"You started. I'm just finishing."

Then Zee felt the baby kick. It was an angry jolt, as if the baby had joined the conversation with its own grievances to air. "Now look whatcha done, Croix." She placed her hand on her belly. "All your hollering got the baby stirred up."

"Whatcha mean *stirred up?*"

She grabbed Croix's hand and placed it on her belly. He felt the warmth of her skin. The supple temptation of her flesh caused a sudden tingling in his pants. The very thing that had gotten him to this regrettable point in the first place. Then he felt a hard, punchy kick and his mindless sexual urge was vanquished. He drew his hand back. "What the hell was that? Something wrong with him? That ain't normal."

"It's alright," Zee said. "She's just kicking." Then her eyes went wide as she recognized her unfortunate slip of the tongue.

Croix's mood suddenly changed, his brow furrowing into curly blonde ribbons. "Whatcha mean?"

"I said *it's kicking.*"

"No, you said *she*. Whatcha mean *she?*"

Zee stiffened. Then she unloaded the unfortunate news. "It's a girl, Croix."

Croix's eyes sharpened and his ears seemed to pin back like a horse just before it swings its head around and takes a mighty chunk from your leg. But it was more than anger brewing inside of him. It was bitter disappointment. A deep concern, bordering on fear. "You don't know that," he said, holding out for an alternate possibility.

"I seen it with my own eyes," Zee assured him. "Elmer got the ultrasound working."

He shifted and rocked backwards and his eyes dropped to the floor with a vacant stare. "This was a goddamn mistake." He rose to his feet and started making his way to the door in a hurry.

Zee sprung from the bed like a woman scorned and waddled after him on her swollen feet. "There you go again, off and running."

Croix stopped and turned to face her and snarled. "Don't

you turn this on me. You bushwhacked me with this whole baby thing, and now you're just shoving the blade in deeper."

"I'm sick of your same old accusations."

"Tell me the truth then," he said. "You just used me to get this baby, didn't you?"

Zee didn't say a word. She just stood there with a stubborn look in her eye.

Croix nodded and said knowingly, "Uh huh… and I'm sick of your same old response." He turned his back to her again and headed for the door.

She shoved him from behind. "Then stay the hell out of my life if you don't wanna be a part of it, you son of a bitch!"

He stumbled out of the door and gritted his teeth and tried to get control of his boiling rage. He turned to get the final word, his lips pursed and everything, but Zee slammed the door shut before he could even push the air from his lungs. He scowled helplessly and stood there for a moment just glaring at the door. Then he turned and walked away, stomping off with heavy, awkward steps and calling her dirty names under his breath.

Zee peeked through the curtains that covered the cracked window, trying not to be seen. She was pissed that he was just walking away without conflict or concern or a single cross word. The bastard didn't even look back. She winced and pulled the curtains closed with a sharp tug, and that was that. It always ended that way. That was how it was between them. Their relationship in a nutshell. As volatile as the random universe from which they sprung, and as painfully senseless as their subsequent existence. They just weren't meant to be. Somehow everyone saw that but them.

When Croix retuned to his cabin, Kid was standing on the front porch looking guilty of something. The door was wide open, as if someone had been inside rummaging around, and Croix jumped to the obvious conclusions. "Goddamn you, Kid. You been going through my shit again?" He charged at Kid with a mindless impulse, his blood still thundering beneath his skin like an active volcano.

Kid threw his arms in the air to protect himself. "I didn't touch nothin, I swear."

Croix grabbed a bag that was slung over the kid's shoulder. "Stay out of my things, you little shit."

Kid pulled the bag away. "I ain't no thief. I didn't touch nothin. I didn't even set foot inside once I seen you wasn't home."

Croix grabbed him by the sagging neckline of his shirt and pulled him upwards onto the tips of his toes. "Get the fuck off my porch," he said with a simmering growl, "and get your ass to work on something. *Anything*. I don't even care what it is. Just get the hell away from *me*." He let go of Kid's shirt and turned his back and fumed quietly in the doorway of his cabin, looking for any disturbance to his precious belongings.

Kid stood behind him. "What's got into you anyway?"

Croix held his tongue.

Kid pressed. "What was all the hollering about between you and Zee?"

Croix still didn't answer. His blood was too hot to offer any meaningful words.

"Ya'll at it again?" Kid asked. "That's all ya'll seem to do anymore is argue. That's the last thing Zee needs with her belly about to pop. Maybe you oughta think about that."

And that's when Croix felt the hot-blooded flow of lava surge from his black heart through his burning veins to the fiery synapses in his brain and back into his reckless extremities, which were already moving on their own free will. A gushing kinetic energy with only one place to go. He charged at Kid with a murderous rage and shoved the mouthy little fucker off the porch and sent him crashing to the ground with a brutal thump. Croix stood over the top of him with a clenched fist in the air and a vicious blue glow in his eyes and said, "Learn when to shut your fucking mouth." He turned away and stormed into his cabin and slammed the door shut so hard that the window panes rattled like trembling victims of an earthquake. He carried his rampage inside, stomping the wood floor and taking his murderous rage out on any soulless objects that he could get his hands on. Ceramic plates, old pressboard cabinets, and finally his muleskin punching bag that hung from the rafters like a piñata waiting to be punctured. That's how it was when he lost his temper. Everyone felt the tremors. Nothing escaped the fallout. His demons ran deep, and once they were set loose, they were deadly.

Outside, Kid staggered to his feet and brushed himself off and whispered angrily, "I *did* go through your shit, asshole." He stood tall and victorious and pulled a piece of fabric from his shoulder bag and unfurled it with a vengeance, revealing his stolen loot in all its outlawed glory: a tattered black flag. The fading remnants of a skull and crossed daggers. The white ink dulled by time and looking more like ancient bone. The words flaking away, but still formidable: *Dagger & Son Kustoms.*

# TWELVE

The lobby of the Sapphire Moon in Westborough was a chaotic web of yellow *crime scene* tape. Gossiping officers stood guard over a wobbling line of disgruntled residents that were being escorted out of the building in their biomasks. There were men in yellow hazmat suits coming and going through the main entrance, carrying rolls of clear plastic sheeting. They were the Cleanup Crew, quarantining the area. Level Three. The big one.

Brixton and Nile were waiting for their chance to investigate the crime scene and interrogate the sick refugees that they'd discovered in Apartment 407. Brixton's mind was spinning with endless questions. *Who helped smuggle these refugees through the border gates? Why were they here for meds? Who promised to help them? Why the hell would anyone do that?* He could hardly wait to get answers. But he'd have to wait until the Cleanup Crew finished testing the area. Both Apartment 407 and Apartment 507 would have to be officially cleared and given the green light for investigators. Then the landlord Raymond Prisco and the refugees he was hiding would be at Brixton's mercy. The golden boy had none. He couldn't wait to get answers, by any means necessary.

Nile seemed to have different questions on his mind. The kind of questions that were personal and not relevant to the investigation.

Brixton offered him a chance to commiserate his feelings. "What's rolling around in that analytical mind of yours, Nile?"

Nile didn't say. He just stood there looking mentally bankrupt for a moment, and then he asked, "How'd you know about the hidden doorway in the floor?"

"I didn't," Brixton said.

"When did you figure it out?"

Brixton shrugged. "When I pulled the rug back."

Nile shook his head, clearly expecting a different answer.

"Maybe it was the figurines being glued to the table that tipped me off," Brixton theorized aloud. "It seemed curious. So I wanted to know why."

"But you didn't know before you flipped the table?"

"No. I had a strong suspicion I guess. But I didn't *know*. Maybe I just wanted to see his fucking reaction when I flipped the damn table over."

Nile cringed at Brixton's negligence.

Brixton cringed at his discomfort. "You think too much about consequences, Nile. Don't think too much. Sometimes you're right, sometimes you're wrong. Who gives a fuck?"

Nile frowned, as if the badge he wore made no sense to him.

Brixton knew what was bothering him. They'd only been working together for a few months now, but Brixton had picked up on Nile's deficiencies, both in life and on the job. The thing that afflicted Nile the most was his own ineffectiveness. Nile had yet to prove himself in his new role as an Inspector. It was becoming well-known that he was a stickler for the rules and not one to get dirty and get the job done effectively, and that meager reputation stuck in Nile's side like a thorn.

"Listen," Brixton said to him, "the reason I'm better than you at this job isn't because I'm smarter, or more perceptive. I'm not. It's because I don't care about the rules or people's rights. Empathy doesn't cloud my judgement like it does yours. Neither does my intuition." He shrugged. "I don't outright violate their rights, but I bend the shit out of 'em. And guess what… it's effective. When I want answers, I get answers, despite the rules and… people's rights."

Nile shook his head. That wasn't what he wanted to hear. But Brixton was Brixton, and that's how it was with him. Right or wrong, Brixton Grace was the golden boy with the fabled legacy and he could get away with walking that fine line between ethical and unethical.

"You would've picked up on it too, Nile, if you weren't so concerned with hurting the landlord's feelings. You're always consumed by the wrong questions."

Nile didn't argue the point. The job required a particular skill that he didn't possess: indifference.

"Inspectors," a voice said from behind. "We're ready for you."

---

The dark chamber of apartment 407 was blacked out by cardboard and old paper clippings that were taped over the windows. The refugees were still huddled together, struggling to breathe and surrounded by a human wall of hazmat suits and armed police officers in biomasks. Boomerang drones buzzed around the apartment, scanning the rooms with beams of blue lasers. The boy in the bed was deathly ill, lying there in puddles of feverish sweat and struggling to draw a breath. The medical team had him on oxygen. They were preparing to move him and his family to the quarantine chambers at the police station. His chest was convulsing even with assistance, and his airway rattled every time he sucked air into his lungs. His mother held his hand as he tried to tell her something, but he couldn't speak through the oxygen mask. She fought back tears and tried to calm him. "They promised us meds, baby. We're all gonna be okay."

Then a boomerang drone scanned their faces. The sharp blue lasers began to survey their retinas to document their identities for the Nimbus records. The mother gripped the boy's hand even tighter. "It's okay, baby. It won't hurt us."

Brixton approached the woman like a vengeful wraith and grabbed her wrist and turned her arm over. To his surprise, there was a blue light glowing beneath the skin. He was shocked to see it. The blue light could only be caused by one thing: a microchip. "Nile, look at this."

Nile looked and was immediately bewildered by such an improbable sight. "What the…? How'd they get…?"

---

"Microchips?" Lucian asked as he sat upright in his chair in the surveillance headquarters. He looked to General Ryker for answers.

General Ryker took a deep breath and said with a calm suspicion, "Sir, I think we just found our missing microchips."

Brixton turned to the camera on Arroway's boomerang drone. His mixed expression of insult and surprise was projected on the wallscreen in glorious Technicolor. "Missing microchips?" he asked. "What missing microchips?"

"For Christ's sake," General Ryker snapped at his agents, "Turn off our audio feed."

No," Lucian said. "It's alright."

Brixton continued to press, "Sir, missing microchips?"

"Yes," Lucian said carefully. "Five days ago, dozens of microchips were reported missing from our factory."

Brixton felt a sudden punch to his ego. He felt violated by the secrecy of the revelation. "I was never informed of that," he said, sounding more irked by being kept in the dark than by the unprecedented threat to his company's security.

Lucian didn't offer him any consolation. He watched the live feed on the wallscreen as Nile scanned the mother's microchip with his solar scroll.

Surprisingly, an official citizen's profile appeared on Nile's screen. "Whoa," Nile muttered. "Brix, look at this."

Brixton looked at the profile on the solar scroll and immediately froze. "What the fuck?"

"Forgeries," General Ryker surmised.

Lucian turned to him with shock in his eyes. "Forgeries?"

"Has to be, sir. The stolen microchips had no software installed on them. They were clean at the time they went missing. Factory settings. The only explanation is some sort of forgery."

"How?" Lucian asked, clearly vexed by the cluelessness of his security team. "How the hell did they create forgeries?"

---

Nile studied the profile on his solar scroll. "Sir," he said cautiously, "if they're forgeries, then they've been uploaded with fake profiles using some sort of bootleg software. I'm looking at it now. It's an exact replica of our operating system. If I were hard-pressed, sir, I wouldn't be able to tell the difference." He shared the contents of his solar scroll with Corporate through the camera on the boomerang drone. "I assume this is how they passed inspection at the border, sir."

Brixton was still frozen, standing there speechless. A state of professional impotence that no one had ever seen him in before.

———

Lucian rose to his feet and began pacing the room, his concern unraveling one strand at a time. "An exact replica? That means they're undetectable?"

"It would appear so," Nile said timidly through the drone's live feed. He seemed overwhelmed by his newfound authority. He looked to Brixton with hope that his partner would say something — *anything* — but Brixton was no help. He just stood there like a stone carving waiting for the sands of time to devour him.

Lucian staggered on his aching feet. "So more refugees could be slipping through the border as we speak?" He turned to General Ryker, who had no answers, and then he turned to Pharaoh and declared, "This will prove to be the worst security breach in our history."

"I think it already is," Vice President Pharaoh said.

"I wanna know what's going on out there," Lucian demanded, "and I don't just mean in Brimstone."

Then Jordan Ambrose, the black sheep of the board, leaned forward in his chair and said, "We should get more eyes in the sky."

"Yes," General Ryker said. "Drones. I agree."

Pharaoh nodded, "Absolutely. We need optics."

"Do it," Lucian said. "Deploy the boomerangs." He took a

moment to ponder his next move. "It's time we expand the surveillance zone."

The executives traded looks of unbridled concern. Lucian's order to expand the surveillance zone was unprecedented, and recklessly impulsive. Lucian had no authority to make that call without an executive order, which could only happen through an official vote.

General Ryker asked, "What's our new search radius, sir?"

"Everywhere."

"*Everywhere*, sir?"

"The *entire continent*," Lucian roared. "From sea to shining sea!"

Ambrose rose from his chair. "Sir, with respect, I meant Brimstone. Not the Blaze."

"I'm aware of what you meant, Jordan. Sit down."

Ambrose reluctantly withdrew his weightless opinion and sat back down in his chair. He straightened his tie, tugging at it to vent his frustration.

"There are questions that need answers," Lucian said. "Questions that we don't even know to ask yet. How'd the Bloody Knuckles get access to this sort of technology? How far have they gone with it? Do we have any idea? A single fucking theory?"

General Ryker didn't appear to have one.

Pharaoh didn't either.

"Why are we in the dark?" Lucian asked. "Anything we don't know is dangerous. They could be forming an army in the Blaze and we wouldn't even know it."

Ambrose leaned forward and spoke out of turn again. "Sir, I'd be remiss if I didn't voice my concern over this order."

"Not now, Jordan."

"Sir, sending drones into the Blaze is a calculated security risk. We've already lost one drone in Brimstone. Number 88 is still unaccounted for. If the outlaws or the Bloody Knuckles get their hands on these things, they could—"

"Thank you, Jordan. I'm well aware of the fucking risk." Lucian turned to General Ryker and gave a stern command, "Deploy them."

"Now, sir?"

"*Yes. Now. Right now*. Am I not making myself clear?"

Ambrose rose from his chair again, pleading, "Sir, please… let's just take a moment here. This is a direct violation of our peace treaty."

"We're the ones who've been violated," Lucian said with a muted growl.

"We don't know the source of these forgeries, sir."

"The source?" Pharaoh asked, interjecting.

Ambrose nodded, "How were they taken from the facility without our knowledge?"

Lucian's eyes narrowed. "You're suggesting someone from the inside had a hand in this?"

Ambrose nodded.

"I agree," Pharaoh said. "That's the most plausible scenario."

"Yes," Lucian said, pacing the floor, "I also agree… and that in itself is troubling enough to declare a state of emergency. Which is what I'm officially doing now."

The executives traded those same looks of concern again.

"Lucian," Pharaoh said with shock, "we have to be sure this is the right course of action before we—"

"We're not sure of anything," Lucian groaned, cutting him off. "None of us. But you can be damned sure the Bloody Knuckles are the ultimate source of these forgeries… and this *fucking* security breach."

Ambrose interjected once again, "Sir, I'm sorry, but we should take a moment to strategize this."

"Jordan, I'll have you removed from this room. Do not undermine me again."

"But sir, this could trigger a war that we don't want."

"As far as I'm concerned, Jordan, the war has already begun." Lucian slammed his hand down on one of the tech stations and scanned the room with his imperious eyes. "Forged microchips? On our turf? Does anyone really believe we're in control here? It's already out in the open. The public will catch on soon enough. We have to get ahead of this."

Ambrose surrendered. He stormed away in anger, looking at the other executives in sheer exhaustion and throwing his hands up in defeat. They shared the same weariness. The situation was unravelling so quickly, and so chaotically, but there was nothing they could do at this point. Lucian was CEO, which meant he was the commander of military operations, and that gave him undisputed war powers in a state of emergency, which he had just declared. The board had no authority to intervene for 24 hours. There would be no vote. Only Lucian's raving impulse. "Search every corner of the continent," he ordered. "Shore to shore. If the drones turn up anything suspicious, I want boots on the ground."

General Ryker nodded. "We'll scour the earth, sir."

# THIRTEEN

Brixton finally woke from his state of professional impotence and charged at the refugee woman and grabbed her wrist and flipped her arm over. "How'd you get this in your wrist?"

Her eyes shifted from side to side.

He squeezed her tightly. "Who put it there?"

"I don't know," she said through nervous tears.

Nile carefully intervened, "It's in your best interest to tell us now, ma'am. Later won't be so easy."

Brixton shoved him aside and glared at the woman. "You said they promised you meds. Who's *they*?"

"I don't know," the woman said. "Please. We just need help. My son needs medicine."

Brixton scoffed and turned to the officers and said, "Take these people to the quarantine chambers. It's gonna take more than simple questioning."

"Please," the woman pleaded. "My son is dying."

"That's not our problem. You're not citizens."

"Please," she begged. "We just need meds. We'll go back to Brimstone, I swear."

Brixton pulled her closer. "If you want help, then tell me what you know."

Agent Arroway placed a hand between them. "Grace, let her be. Leave this to Nimbus Security."

"This isn't your case, watchdog."

"It will be if you keep violating people's rights the way you're doing."

"Screw you, pencil dick. This is beyond protocol."

"Nothing is beyond protocol." Agent Arroway offered a cryptic gaze. "Maybe someday you'll learn that."

***

As Brixton and Arroway argued over professional ethics, Nile began to wander off from the confrontation. But not to avoid it. He had just heard something curious coming from another room. His ears were perked up, listening carefully to a strange rummaging noise that was emanating from the darkened bedroom nearby. An unclear sound that he couldn't identify at first. It sounded like the crumbling and tearing of paper on holiday mornings. Then it dawned on him. *The windows.* He suddenly heard what he immediately knew to be the screeching clatter of an old window being pushed open in a hurry. The commotion of the street noise outside rushed in like a radio being turned all the way up. He took a quick step sideways and looked in the bedroom. The window was open and a lone foot was just clearing the sill on its way to the fire escape. "Brix, *the window.*"

***

Brixton's SAT phone buzzed with the frantic voice of an officer in the alley below. "Inspector, we got a runner. Fire escape." Brixton hustled past Nile, running to the open window. He looked up and saw a male refugee climbing the stairs to the rooftop. "I'll pursue."

"Brix, *wait*." Nile tried to run to him and grab him.

But Brixton didn't wait. He made his way out of the window and up the fire escape.

"*Grace*," Arroway shouted from the safety of the darkened room. "Wait for your backup."

Brixton raised the Rapid 9 to fire at the fleeing refugee, but the man stepped onto the rooftop and disappeared from his sight.

Nile made his way through the open window and onto the fire escape platform. "Brix, I'm coming."

Arroway stepped onto the platform behind him. "Let's get eyes in the sky," he said over dispatch.

The boomerang drone flew out of the open window and headed for the top.

Brixton stepped onto the rooftop alone. It was cluttered with lines of hanging laundry. Cheap clothing and frazzled quilts and stained sheets that flapped stiffly in the wind. The boomerang drone flew past him and rose into the sky above.

When Nile and Agent Arroway reached the top of the stairwell with their guns drawn, Brixton was nowhere to be found. He had already disappeared behind the hanging linens. Arroway went left. Nile went right and raised the SAT phone and spoke over dispatch. "Brix, we're on the roof. Where are you?"

Brixton heard the two-way transmission, but he ignored it, keeping his focus on finding the refugee who could at any moment leap out and attack him. Refugees were good at hiding, and most officers had to learn that the hard way. Brixton bobbed and weaved through a fluttering maze of white sheets. They flapped in his face. He tried to rip them from the line but they wouldn't budge, having been tied in place. "Fucking gutterbugs!" Then he was startled by a sharp whirling noise. He pulled the sheet away from his face and turned to fire at the source, but he stopped when he saw the boomerang drone hovering beside him and buzzing with power. "Get this fucking drone out of here!" he roared into the SAT phone.

The boomerang drone pulled away and rose above the action again, its camera lens still surveying the rooftop from the sky above. Brixton knew that Lucian and General Ryker and those nosey executives would be watching his every move on their wallscreen at Surveillance Headquarters. He didn't like being monitored. Having that on his mind was a distraction. A distraction that could get him thrown off a roof or beaten to death by a desperate refugee.

---

Agent Arroway pushed through a clutter of dense clothing on the lines. Brown dress slacks and torn jeans. Colorful blouses and heat-resistant jackets. He was alone and looking afraid, his bulbous head sweating profusely beneath his biomask. This was not his element. In the field, stuck in the middle of a real world scenario, with his gun drawn for the first time since the academy. He heard footsteps. His eyes wandered frantically. As he cleared the line of clothing, he was struck from behind and his gun was knocked from his hand. Before he knew it, he was wrestling with the refugee on the gravel rooftop, and he was already losing. The refugee was on top of him, clutching the lapels of his suit and slamming the back of his bulbous head into the concrete. The only thing keeping Arroway's skull from being cracked open was a thick piece of rubber on the back of his biomask.

"*Backup*," he shouted through the voice box of his faceplate. "I need *backup*."

The refugee grabbed the biomask and tried to rip it from Arroway's head. Arroway tried to shove his gloved fingers into the refugees eye sockets, but the refugee swatted his arms away and ripped the biomask from his head and tossed it aside.

"*Backup*," Arroway shouted. "*Backup!*"

The refugee raised a rusty old hatchet and reared back to strike, but before he could bring the blade down on Arroway's head, he saw Brixton in his peripheral approaching through the flapping linens with his gun aimed. The refugee stood in a hurry and dipped behind the sheets.

Brixton fired and missed. "*Fuck.*" He spoke into the SAT phone. "He's armed with a *hatchet*. A hand axe. I repeat, he's got a *fucking hatchet*." He lowered the phone and swiped the translucent screen and opened the Surveillance App. "Punch the live feed into my phone. I need eyes." The drone's live feed appeared on the screen of his SAT phone. A high-definition image of the rooftop as it was being filmed by the drone from above. All he could see was himself, surrounded by a cluster of flapping linens, his distant body looking like a tiny dark spot on a large white bed. Then his eyes ballooned outward as he saw another dark spot on the screen. It was moving among the white linens, charging at him from behind. He dropped the phone and swiftly turned to fire the Rapid 9, but the refugee swung the hatchet and struck the faceplate of his biomask. The impact knocked Brixton backwards, his feet staggering beneath him. He couldn't see through the streaks of cracked glass and the rusty blade that was stuck in his faceplate. He fired the gun wildly. Shock rounds spiraled in every direction. The refugee tackled him, knocking the gun from his grip and taking him to the ground. Chips of glass fell into Brixton's eyes. As the refugee pulled the hatchet from the cracked faceplate and drew back to strike again, Brixton punched him in the chest, knocking him backwards. The refugee raised the hatchet again, but Brixton pulled the backup gun from his ankle holster and fired a live round. The bullet ripped through the refugee's chest, opening a hole the size of a small fist. His blood splattered all over Brixton, contaminating his hands, his clothing, and his compromised faceplate. All he could think of was the severed glass and the refugee blood and the possibility of deadly pathogens that could be seeping through the cracks. The refugee staggered to his feet and stumbled backwards and finally dropped to the rooftop. He was motionless. As Brixton focused his eyes through his cracked faceplate, he saw Agent Arroway standing there just beyond the refugee's body. "Oh shit."

Arroway's unmasked face was covered in the refugee's blood. He was frozen in a panic, looking at the blood on his hands. He touched his face with a shriek, realizing the blood was already in his eyes and mouth.

Brixton's faceplate began to crack even more from the stress, snaking across the compromised glass. His vision was fractured too. Just altered pieces of color, like a broken kaleidoscope.

Nile arrived, and when he saw Arroway covered in blood he spoke frantically into his SAT phone, "*Medic*. We need a medic. To the rooftop. Suspect is down. Officer wounded." He holstered his gun and moved to assist.

Brixton sprung to his feet in a hurry and grabbed him. "Nile, stay back. It's not his blood."

Arroway staggered toward them, his eyes glowing white with fear.

Brixton pleaded, "Arroway, don't come any closer." He pulled a gun from Nile's holster and aimed it at Arroway, eyeing him through the webbed glass of his biomask.

"Arroway, *don't*." The gun was loaded with shock rounds and Brixton was eager to fire.

General Ryker's voice came roaring over the radio. "Grace, it's Ryker. Stand down. That's an order."

Brixton ignored the order, keeping his fractured eyes on Arroway, who looked distorted through the broken glass. All Brixton could see was a scattered puzzle of crimson and black, and it was getting closer and closer. "Arroway, you could be infected. *Stop*. Don't come any fucking closer"

General Ryker's voice roared again over dispatch. *"Stand down now, Inspector. Holster your firearm. That's an order."*

*"Arroway, stop,"* Brixton shouted. *"Stop!"*

But Arroway didn't stop. He was in a trance of pure terror, unaware of the immediate threat that he was posing. He just kept walking toward Brixton like a zombie with his bloody hands held outwards for help.

Brixton was only concerned with helping himself, so naturally he fired a shock round. The electrified bullet struck Arroway in the chest, and as the hated snitch convulsed, he dropped to the rooftop floor, his cheekbone and skull crackling as he hit the graveled concrete. His body went limp and temporarily paralyzed, and his eyes were bulging from the sockets like a squeeze toy.

Nile looked at Brixton in disbelief. His partner had just shot a superior officer. Shock round or not, that was an indefensible violation of protocol. He eyed Brixton, castigating him with that disparaging motherly gaze that seemed to be asking, *What the hell were you thinking?*

Brixton shrugged, but with no arrogance this time. He was absolutely petrified. His one visible eye was glowing white hot behind the broken glass, and suddenly his trademark swagger had vanished, as if all that remained of his golden boy legacy had just been expelled with that shock round.

# FOURTEEN

The slaughterhouse in Revival was located right next to the cattle pasture, which seemed a cruel intent, though it was completely unintentional. It just worked out that way. No malice in it. There was only so much space in Revival to work with. Fortunately, the cows weren't smart enough to figure out that they were being bred for their eventual slaughter. There was always a dead meat smell coming from the wooden structure that housed their dismembered peers, but they never seemed concerned, even when they were obviously next to meet the blade. They weren't the only hoodwinked fauna. The sheep, chickens and rabbits were clueless too. Their ignorance was bliss.

The slaughterhouse, like most every other structure in Revival, was made of timber from the forest. Pinewood in this case. The ventilation was good, but the blowflies were always a nuisance, with their metallic bodies buzzing through the air like falling ash. They weren't the only breed of flies either. There were house flies, soldier flies, black flies, and even stable flies that often found their way over from the barn to the local all-you-can-eat diner and nesting ground. So Revivalists peppered the entire slaughterhouse with an overwhelming amount of herbs. Scents that nauseated the flies. Peppermint, basil, rosemary, pine, lavender, eucalyptus, and bay leaves. Tacked in the doorways and crevices. Their vines hung from the ceilings, emitting a wonderful, fly-deterring concoction of odors. They hadn't had a major fly problem in years.

That morning, a black woman in her mid-thirties stood there hard at work, her face free of blowflies, and her hands sawing the tender flank from a newly slaughtered mini Hereford. Meat that would last them for weeks if stored properly or cured into jerky. The woman's real name was Naomi Brooks, but everyone called her by her chosen nickname: Memphis. She had the most universally cherished skill in all of Revival. The woman could cook like nobody's business. A culinary artist. Not just patties on a firepit grill or a pot of bland lentil soup in a hearth. She was a bonafide gourmet chef. Food for the soul. Smoked brisket, scalloped potatoes, roasted beet jewels, toasted corn on the cob, asiago salad, and a pitcher of sweet lemon tea. And that was just Monday night's meal. They had the entire month's menu to look forward to. Everyone indulged her culinary talents, for obvious reasons. If she needed a vegetable or a fruit, they seeded it and grew it in the garden and plucked it from the earth and made sure it was cleaned and washed and ready for storage. If she needed a plant spice, they hiked the hills with guns and totes and foraged it from the mountains with their own two hands. Memphis always joked that the people of Revival didn't love her for her soul, they only loved her for her soul food. But whatever it took to survive. She'd been surviving the hard way since she was five years old in the ghettos of North Memphis, after her drug-dealing father murdered her mother right in front of her eyes. She was subsequently raised by her grandparents, who made sure she didn't get swallowed up by the streets. It was her grandmother who taught Memphis the culinary traditions of the deep south, and who'd given her the will to survive in a world that seemed out to get her. Not surprisingly, Memphis was the strong and proud type, with a brazenly upright posture and broad shoulders. She had beautifully-shaped cheekbones, and her eyes were a soft, creamy hazel. They glimmered against her dark skin like two hypnotic spirals lulling you into a false sense of security. But despite her disarming allure, she was deadly with a set of butcher knives. She even had a special belt made to holster them during battle. She carried herself like some African goddess, both dignified and sensual, yet a force to be reckoned with. Her sprightly hair was kept in dreads and she always kept herself clean and looking respectable, even in the slaughterhouse where she spent most of her time. Her apron was covered in blood that morning, her face was dripping with sweat, and her hands were caked in unrecognizable meat particles, but she was still a sight to behold. Especially to one tirelessly passionate man in particular.

Tavo entered quietly through the open doorway behind her with a mischievous look on his face and a perpetual desire to pounce on her.

She stopped cutting and said, "I can hear you coming from a mile away."

He grabbed her around the waist and pressed himself against her backside. "Maybe I like getting caught."

She turned her eyes on him. "Don't come in here with that smile on your face. I told you to stop gambling our things away."

"And I told you every dog has its day. Even a mutt like me." He displayed a closed fist, hiding something within his grasp.

Memphis hawked her eyes. "You mean you actually won something this time?"

"I won *this*," Tavo said, opening his hand and revealing a large, sparkling diamond ring. "For *you*." He watched her reaction. She wasn't entirely impressed. Her eyes were unlit and looking severely underwhelmed. He tried to explain the significance to her. "I think it's one of those diamond rings that women used to haggle over in the old world. Skinny's been hoarding it in his cabin all this time."

Memphis took the ring and scrutinized it with educated eyes. She chuckled, covering her mouth politely with her hand. "That ain't no diamond ring, Tavo."

The silver band was a tarnished green color. The diamond a white sapphire knockoff. She knew the difference, even when it wasn't this obvious.

"Well I thought it was a diamond," Tavo said, looking wounded. "That should count for something."

"But I like it," Memphis assured him, her smile broadening into a deep blush. She slid the ring onto her finger and held her hand outward away from her body so she could see it sparkle in the sunlight that was streaking through the open doorway.

Tavo smiled and tightened his arms around her waist. "Nothing but the best for my queen."

"Oh please," she said. "Don't flatter yourself. It's the first gift I got in as long as I can remember."

Tavo rested his hands on her hips and nestled his chin into her neck and spoke softly into her ear. "You think there might be a little gift waiting for me in return? Maybe a little something later on tonight?"

Memphis flicked her eyes at him. "So you can't give a gift without getting something in return?"

He began moving his hips side to side and moving hers

right along with him, being more suggestive with his flirtations. "It's not like you ain't gonna enjoy it."

She smiled, her flattered eyes turning to a soft, alluring bedroom gaze. Soon enough, the two lovebirds were getting their feathers too entangled for comfort.

For Croix's comfort anyway. He stood in the open doorway and grimaced, his shadow cast over them in judgement like a Sunday school preacher. "How about keeping that business behind closed doors," he said, startling them both. "Ya'll may as well spend your nights with the bunnies in the goddamn rabbit hutch."

Tavo and Memphis giggled like schoolchildren. They didn't bother to appease Croix's prudish concern. They kept on, playfully teasing each other like teenagers in the backseat of their parent's car. But it wasn't for show. This was just how they were. Every single day.

Croix couldn't stand to witness it.

Memphis giggled as Tavo slid his hands down the front of her pants. "Stop it, baby," she said. "Save something for later. Stop."

"You know that word don't mean nothing to me," Tavo said, chuckling and grabbing her in places that made a certain onlooker feel uneasy.

"Well it means something to me," Croix said from the doorway. "When Zee says stop, I stop. It's what gentlemen do."

"Yeah, but Zee never says *go*," Tavo said, laughing boisterously and without caution. Memphis laughed too, but she tried to cover her mouth out of respect.

"I'll let that one slide," Croix said with a deadly glimmer in his eyes, "But any more disrespect and you and I are cross, got me?"

Tavo withdrew his laughter and put his hands up in

defense. "Easy now, Croix, I'm just trying to make time with my queen."

"Make time on your own time," Croix said. "Not on mine. We gotta stock the share shack. You wanna put those nimble fingers to work? They're better served on stocking empty shelves."

"I beg to differ," Memphis said.

Croix scoffed. Then he grunted as the lovebirds began to chirp at one another again. He scowled at them and made every repugnant noise he could think of in the moment, in hopes of ruining the mood.

Tavo kissed Memphis gently on the cheek, with a reassuring tenderness. That was his true nature. Sweet and romantic. Everything else was just play. "We'll continue this later?" he asked.

"To be determined," she said with a flirty grin.

Croix kicked a stack of utensils in a box and made them rattle around for a moment. "The work is waiting, Tavo. So am I. Get your hands out of her pants and let's get on with it."

Tavo backpedalled out of the slaughterhouse, his hungry eyes on Memphis. "Don't break my heart, woman. I'm expecting big things. You should be too."

Memphis beamed from ear to ear, showing her pearly whites. Then she looked at Croix and her smile receded to an awkward scowl. Croix shivered like he was disgusted by what he'd witnessed. It was maybe in good humor, but most likely sincere, and that left Memphis feeling resentful. Croix always stood between her and her man. He always squabbled at their affection. She gave him a disapproving look. He walked away in a hurry, pulling Tavo by the arm like a child. Tavo turned and blew Memphis a kiss. Croix tugged on his arm again. "For Christ's sake, Tavo, you're gonna see her again in two hours. Is that really necessary?"

"Yes," Tavo said adamantly. Then they both disappeared from sight.

Memphis looked at the cheap ring on her finger and smiled. She blushed like a young lover, her heart still fluttering from Tavo's charm, even after all these years. "Necessary indeed," she said.

# FIFTEEN

The share shack just outside of Revival was a simple defense strategy, not a gesture of good will or hospitality. The whole thing was Croix's idea, from concept to finished product. But admittedly, he wasn't motivated by a sense of altruism. He really had no desire to share the spoils of their hard work at Revival, or give handouts to anyone, especially to those who hadn't even tried to earn their own keep or carve their own way in the Blaze. He had no sympathy for the drifters who relied on other people's charity, and he rightly feared the desperate scavengers that often targeted the colonies of the Granite Valley. His strategy for the share shack was simple: to give those ravenous, greedy fuckers an alternative to raiding the colony for precious resources. He figured if they were offered enough of what they needed up front, it would keep them content and eager to move on, and not desperate to raid the colony for more. It was a small sacrifice in the greater scheme of things. So they stocked the share shack with everything a hungry, tired drifter or scavenger might need. Purified drinking water from the river was the first consideration, for obvious reasons. They kept the water in a large, plastic tank that couldn't be stolen or easily broken out of spite. Someone had once shot a .45 ACP through the tank, but Croix had heard the gunshot from the stables, and he settled the situation himself. The bodies were buried in the foothills. With no markings.

The second consideration was food. Hunger was a powerful motivator. It made desperate people do bad things. So the Revivalists stocked the shelves with fruits and veggies from the gardens and dried meats from the slaughterhouse to keep bad things from happening. A full belly wasn't nearly as desperate. Health was a third consideration. There was nothing more dangerous than drifters or scavengers who were sick or badly injured and felt they had nothing to lose but everything to gain by raiding the place. So the Revivalists stocked the shack with medicinal herbs from the greenhouse and some common medical supplies that could be used to keep wounds from becoming infected or fatal.

Sleep was the final consideration. Drifters and scavengers were usually tired from being on the move, so the Revivalists placed five reasonably comfortable sleeping cots in the share shack and bolted them to the floorboards and stuffed them with bird feathers in case anyone needed a little cat nap in the shade or a decent night's rest. Sleepovers were welcome. With shades of gray. Revival always had eyes on the overnight visitors. A micro-camera from the old world hidden in the wall. It sent a video feed to the communications hub in the headquarters cabin where someone was always on watch. Any funny business, and that sign out front that said *respect our way of life or you WILL die* was swiftly proven to be true. There were enough supplies in the share shack to please even the greediest of souls. Anything the Revivalists could stand to part with was offered up. What they *never* offered up were tools, weapons, ammo or anything that could be used against them in a raid. Those things would have to be taken over their dead bodies, and they were all still alive, which was a testament to Croix's strategy over the years.

That morning, after all the drama with Zee had subsided, Croix was in the shack with Tavo and Skinny re-stocking the shelves. Jagged clumps of jerky. Wraps of hard tack. Cracked mason jars filled with fruit and dried veggies. Clean jugs of drinking water that they'd collected from the river and purified for consumption. The usual chores. But today there was an extra chore added to the list. They'd have to clean the mess left behind by the nosey man-eating tiger that Croix had tracked down and killed in the Alabama Hills. The beast had ruined their latest supplies. It was all strewn across the floor in a fractured mess of glass. The spilled food was already crawling with ants. "That goddamn kid," Croix said. "He was supposed to clean this mess by sunrise. He's supposed to be helping us too. Goddamn tiger destroyed half our supply and the other half's gonna go to spoil because that little shit is so goddamn lazy."

"I told you I can clean the mess myself," Tavo said.

"No," Croix said. "That's the kid's job."

Kid was always off somewhere fooling around with nature or daydreaming in the shadows. Croix hated slackers, so the kid's whimsical approach to life always stuck in his craw.

"Let me clean it up," Tavo insisted. "It'll take me half an hour and I'll be done."

"No," Croix said adamantly. "We gotta restock all these shelves and still carry out our other duties by dark. So ya'll are gonna have to pick up your effort. I can't carry ya'll too."

Tavo and Skinny traded disgruntled looks behind his back.

Croix just couldn't keep quiet. "That goddamn kid," he continued. "He's a literal pain in my ass. I can practically feel him crawling around in there."

Tavo laughed quietly behind his back. It wasn't unusual for Croix to be in a foul mood or to rant with even fouler language, especially after an unfavorable exchange with Zee, but lately those exchanges were getting more volatile, and so were Croix's subsequent mood swings. Sometimes he'd sulk in silence. Other times he'd rant. Today he was ranting.

"It really sticks in my craw," he continued, unable to work in the silence that he usually begged for. "The idea of that kid doing nothing I ask him to do. *Nothing.* Not a goddamn thing. He don't do nothin but cause trouble and exhaust my fucking nerves."

"Probably shouldn't have brung him here then," Skinny said without a single cautious thought. As Croix turned to him with a deadly blue gaze, he tried to reverse course. "I mean, I'm just sayin… you're always complaining about… well, I mean… it's like beating a dead horse."

Croix's eyes turned fiery blue, as if something impossibly hot was about to burst from the unimaginable depths. Skinny recoiled and shrunk and looked down at his own hands as he continued to pull stock from the wooden crates. Fortunately for him, Kid walked through the door and intercepted Croix's wrath at just the right time.

"Sorry I'm late," Kid said. "I had to go… uh…" He stopped himself, recognizing the tension in the room. "What's going on here?"

Croix slammed a plastic jug of water down on the wooden shelf. "It's about goddamn time you showed up."

Tavo smirked, already amused by the comedic potential of such a dicey situation.

Kid was curious why he was so amused. "Whatcha smiling about, Tavo?"

Tavo glared at him and shook his head firmly.

"It's Memphis, ain't it? She's always got you smiling."

Tavo gestured for him to shut up, but Kid was oblivious to the danger, as usual.

"It's nice to see a man and a woman get along for a change," the kid blabbered on. "You wouldn't think it'd be such a hard thing to accomplish."

Croix started throwing insults, which was much safer than what he usually threw. "Goddamnit, Kid. I sometimes wonder if there's even *half* a brain in that mangled head of yours."

"Why would you say that?"

"Because there's work to be done, that's *why*, and the work ain't gonna do itself, and we ain't gonna keep doing it for you. So I suggest you stop flapping your gums and get to work before you give me a reason to get angry."

But Kid didn't heed the advice. He just picked up a handful of supplies and rattled off another zinger. "I think you were born angry, and you'll probably die that way too." Then he went and made things worse by saying, "Hey Tavo, tell me something… how is it that you and Memphis are always doting on one another, but Croix and Zee are always at each other's throats?"

Suddenly a loud *thwack* startled his young ears. It was the sound of Croix stabbing his old Bowie knife into the wooden shelf.

Kid gulped and said, "I'm sure that temper don't help."

Tavo lowered his head, shaking it from side to side in utter disbelief. The kid just never knew when to shut up.

Croix threatened the kid with his eyes. "You were supposed to get a jump on the shack this morning. We're all sick and tired of having to pick up your slack, Kid. You don't earn your keep, but you seem to keep an awful lot. It ain't right, and I ain't gonna stand for it no more. You don't do a goddamn thing around here."

"That ain't true."

"*Yes it is.* How am I ever gonna teach you to be a guardian of Revival if you can't even keep our food supply safe from ants? I told Ru you ain't the one. You're just proving me right."

"I don't need another tongue lashing from you."

"No you don't," Croix huffed furiously. "You need a different kind of lashing. The kind that leaves your fucking ass red."

Tavo and Skinny couldn't help but chuckle aloud, which only made matters even worse.

Kid dropped the handful of supplies onto the wooden crate and whined, "I'm tired of being treated like I'm somebody's bastard. You're always ripping me up and beating me down with your words. It ain't my fault you and Zee ain't getting along, you son of a bitch. So don't take it out on me."

Croix wrenched the knife from the wooden shelf and launched it in Kid's direction and the blade struck the wall near Kid's face.

"You asshole!" Kid shouted. "It ain't my fault you don't wanna be a daddy!"

Croix grabbed a mason jar full of dried berries and launched it at Kid's head, but Kid had already stormed out of the shack, so the jar just struck the wall and shattered, exploding like a dead star. The broken glass flung through the air and fell to the ground with a reflective taunt.

Tavo and Skinny traded looks of concern. The situation wasn't funny anymore. They looked at Croix and waited for the inevitable fallout. He was fuming, slowly erupting like Mount St. Helens, and that never ended well. He could go either way. A silent rage or a volatile outburst that would leave the share shack in much worse shape than they'd found it.

"That little shit doesn't know when to keep his fucking mouth shut," he fumed. "I should've left his ass for dead. Should've left 'em right there to die on the cold fucking ground. We'd all be better off." He slammed his fist into anything that looked durable enough to tolerate the abuse. The sturdy wooden shelf took the brunt. The supplies shook and clattered as he punched down on the plank. After a few brutal strikes, he stopped himself and steadied his hand and said, "Ya'll better just leave me be for a few. I'll finish up myself. Go on now. Get out of here."

Tavo approached him cautiously, "Croix, that's a lot of work for one man to—"

"Leave me be, goddamnit!" Croix's head whipped around and his blue eyes flickered. "I'm not fucking around."

"Alright," Tavo said, carefully withdrawing. "We're going."

He and Skinny placed their supplies on the table in the center of the room and casually made their way out of the share shack. They didn't push any further. Croix was dangerous in those moments, like a wounded animal lashing out, and Tavo and Skinny knew better than to stick around for the bite.

Once they'd left him alone, Croix stood there with his blue eyes burning and his hands trembling out of control. The room felt ten degrees hotter than before, and he was dripping with remorse. He had his work cut out for him now. Not just straightening up the share shack. He had to straighten up his own affairs. *The clutter of his own soul,* as Zee had often put it. The disordered ramblings of his troubled conscience. Wrestling his own demons was a herculean effort. A supernatural battle for the ages. One he often lost.

# SIXTEEN

After he straightened up the share shack but failed to straighten up the clutter of his soul, Croix made a beeline to the greenhouse in dire need of some herbal relief. He grew tobacco in a small planter box inside, but that's not what he was after. He needed something to secretly calm his mind. Something more potent. They didn't grow things like marijuana in Revival. They didn't forage for hallucinogenic mushrooms either. That was their law. No head-spinning drugs of any kind. But Croix would never mess with that kind of stuff anyway. Mash liquor was the closest thing they had to a vice. The only thing to alter their minds. But it was only used as lighter fluid. Croix didn't mess with firewater. That stuff made a man affable and witless. It impaired his judgement. Croix always made sure that he was the most dangerous man in the room. He couldn't be dangerous if he was too busy stumbling around and laughing at nothing in particular. What they did grow at Revival was natural remedies, and if they couldn't grow them, they foraged them from the earth with their own two hands. Things like Holy Basil, Hawthorn, St. John's Wort,

Elderberry, Passionflower and Skullcap. Croix would need lots of it to get his mind right and his blood pressure down to healthier levels.

As he entered the greenhouse, a gloomy woman in her early sixties was clipping petals with a pruning knife and watering the plants in the garden troughs. She had long black hair that was overrun with dead, silvery strands which were splitting at the ends and pulled back in a pony tail with a coarse rubber band. Her clothes were bland and soiled by the dirt. She always looked like she didn't give a shit, and that was by design. Her name was Teardrop. That's what they called her anyway. She was a voluntary mute who never spoke a single word. She only communicated through improvised sign language, or with dirty looks, or with furious scribblings on her little slate chalkboard that often hung around her neck by a rope. As far as everyone at Revival knew, she was perfectly capable of speaking, she just wasn't willing to, as if she were defying the universe or God by refusing to use the gift that she'd been given. Something had brought her to that certifiable level of spiritual protest. But nobody knew what had driven her to such extremes. She'd been living among them for seven painfully silent years, ever since she came to Revival. Despite her stony bitterness towards life and everyone around her, she always had a soft spot for Croix.

"Teardrop," he pleaded desperately, "I'm about to burst through the goddamn roof. I need something to calm my nerves."

She turned to him with a look that said a million things at once but nothing at all. He could never read her. Nobody could. She grabbed her chalkboard and a piece of chalk that Zee had made from eggshells and grain flour, and she began to scribble furiously.

Croix sighed. He knew what was coming. A handwritten

lecture, veiled as advice. She held up the chalkboard. It read: *Zee did this to you! I told you she's bad luck!*

Croix chuckled. Teardrop always used oversized exclamation points to express her anger, but she really didn't need to. The scowl on her face and her unmistakable body language always made the point loud and clear. "Come on," Croix said, brushing it off. "You know I don't believe in luck. Good, bad or otherwise."

Teardrop erased the board with her shirt sleeve and began scribbling furiously again.

Croix sighed, his blood only rising. "I just need something to calm me down, Teardrop, and you and that goddamn chalkboard are just making me crazy."

Teardrop erased her scribbling and shook her head and began scribbling again. She held the chalkboard up: *No! Zee's the one making you crazy!*

Croix chuckled insincerely. "To be perfectly honest, I was born crazy."

Teardrop looked at him with contempt, as if to say *don't be an ass*.

He chuckled again. "My crazy just don't compete with *her* crazy. Or *yours* for that matter."

Teardrop gripped the chalkboard tightly and began scribbling again.

"I know what you're gonna say," Croix muttered. "You're gonna say Zee's bad for me and I shouldn't let her lead me around by the nose. Am I right?"

Teardrop stopped scribbling and clenched her teeth and quickly erased what she'd written. She began to write something else.

"Easy with the exclamations," Croix said.

She stopped and erased her exclamation point and went back at it furiously with the chalk.

Croix marveled at her diligence. It would be so damn easy to speak instead of carrying on the charade of silence and writing maniacally on her little chalkboard every damn time she had a sudden thought to share.

She held the chalkboard up: *You don't owe her your soul. She tricked you into this. She's not what you think she is.*

Croix scoffed heavily. "I've heard all that before, Teardrop. But what am I supposed to do?"

Teardrop erased the board and scribbled furiously again and held the board up: *Be a man!*

"Jesus Christ," Croix snapped. "That's what Zee always says to me too. *Be a man.* One of you is gonna have to explain to me what being a man is all about, because apparently I don't have a goddamn clue."

Teardrop set her chalkboard down on the pruning table and grabbed Croix's hand softly, looking at him with a bottomless sorrow. Her sad brown eyes always made him feel somber. They seemed flooded with some unspoken tragedy. So inundated by hidden emotions that one could drown in them if they scrutinized her too deeply. But Croix always tried to see beyond her silence, regardless of the risk. She had a faded enchantment about her, as if she was once a vibrant, beautiful woman with a meaningful life and joy in her soul. Croix always wished he could know that side of her. Now she was unkempt and frail, as if she'd lost her life force and was just carrying on without it on some twisted principle, and that always made Croix feel sorry for her. She apologized to him with her sad eyes.

He looked at her with mercy in his. "Zee's not as bad as you make her out to be. I just ain't the man to make her happy, and maybe that's why I can't..." He stiffened and sighed and scoffed again, this time in surrender. "You know what... I think I'm good here. Maybe I just needed to open up and talk about it or something. Express my feelings. That sorta thing. I feel better already. So never mind the help. I don't need it." He tried to walk away but Teardrop grabbed his arm and spun him around. She shook her head and began using her own brand of sign language, which is what she always did when she was too angry to write. Croix had a mild comprehension of the hand gestures, though most of them looked like pantomimed gibberish. He thought she was trying to say something along the lines of *Zee broke our law and now she's trying to break you.*

Croix couldn't disagree with the first part. It was an established law in Revival. No breeding. No children. They all agreed long ago that bringing children into the world might be a cruelty considering their quality of life. Croix was young then, and things were worse, but he swore an oath to honor that law. So did Zee. That's why everyone in Revival was so damn mad at her.

"Look, Teardrop, what's done is done. Law or not. I can't change that."

Teardrop reached for her chalkboard, but Croix grabbed her arm and stopped her. "Goddammit, I just came to get some help from the garden, not for your handwritten advice. You got something more to say, you're gonna have to actually *say it*. Otherwise I ain't listening."

Teardrop pulled away and snatched the hand towel from her pruning table and whacked him across the chest with it and gestured something with her hands that he assumed meant *dumbass*.

He glared at her. "Do you have anything that can help me or not?"

She stood there for a moment, as if she were calculating her investment. Then she grabbed her chalkboard and scribbled out a question: *What needs fixing?*

"Everything," Croix said. "The usual. I can't sleep. My mind is slipping. I can't stay focused on my job. Which ain't good for any of us. I obviously can't get my rage under control." He exhaled with a furious twitch. "It's *everything*. Everything all at once."

Teardrop took his hand in hers and placed it over her heart. She smiled sympathetically, her face cracking from the resistance of a natural frown. She looked at Croix and said something with her eyes that he could easily understand this time.

He didn't smile back, but his eyes softened. "I know," he said to her. "That's why I come to you."

Her smile grew, broadening across her face with unnatural curves.

Croix nodded his gratitude and then lowered his eyes a bit and said, "I know I don't have to say it, but…"

Teardrop pantomimed like she was zipping her mouth shut and throwing away the key. She wouldn't tell a soul. Croix's pride was safe with her. He nodded his appreciation, and she began gathering the necessary ingredients to make a stress tincture for him. Something to calm his nerves, settle his blood pressure, help him stay focused, and put his dumbass to sleep. It would take a whole lot of everything.

# SEVENTEEN

The bright yellow quarantine bus parked outside of the Sapphire Moon apartment complex was already causing a small panic among the local residents. They were lining the streets where the police had blocked it off, standing there rubbernecking by the caution tape and traffic barriers. They were asking too many questions and getting no answers. Instead they were being told politely to go home or go back to work. It was a corporate matter. *It's being handled.* That's what they were told.

---

Brixton was in the bathroom of the bus scrubbing his hands with disinfectant soap and water, rinsing the intense fugeephobia from his forearms on down to his perfectly manicured fingernails. The bathroom was a sterile box, with plastic walls, faux white tile, a porcelain sink, plastic piping, a self-sanitizing toilet, some disposable hand towels, a biohazard trash can and a foggy mirror with Brixton's terrified expression reflecting back at him in the glass.

Nile peeked his head in through the door. "Brix, you alright?"

Brixton kept his eyes focused on his hands. "I don't trust this disinfectant shit they give us."

"You had your gloves on. Your mask."

"Yeah, but the faceplate was cracked."

"Cleanup Crew didn't seem too concerned. I'm sure you're fine."

"But you never know."

Nile hovered in the doorway with his usual distracted look. There was a question on his mind, and that was clear, but he was too reluctant to ask.

Brixton looked at him sharply through the foggy reflection in the mirror. "Do you want something?"

Nile hesitated. He craned his head back outside of the door to see if anyone was in earshot of their conversation, and then he stepped inside the bathroom and closed the door behind him and stood there with a reluctant stare.

"What the fuck is it, Nile? Spit it out."

"You've been under surveillance by Nimbus Security for weeks, and you still haven't told me why."

Brixton sighed. "It's best you don't get involved."

"You don't have to protect me, if that's what you're trying to do."

Brixton snickered. "Don't flatter yourself."

"We're partners, Brix. We're in this together."

"Don't play the partner card, Nile. We've only been together for three months."

"Four."

"Nah, the first month doesn't count. It's a grace period."

"Stop with the smart-ass buddy cop routine," Nile said sharply. "It's just a device to avoid real conversation."

Brixton wiped his face with a clean hand towel. "You moonlighting as a shrink now?"

"I deserve to know what's going on, Brix."

Brixton turned back to the foggy mirror and stared at his own reflection, which he thought looked pathetic. Just a pale, conflicted face staring back at him. His eyes looked ghostly, almost transparent, as if everything he used to be had suddenly escaped his earthly vessel. "Nobody ever gets what they deserve in this world," he said, keeping his eyes on himself. "You should lower your expectations."

"Are you talking to me?" Nile asked. "Or yourself?"

Then the bathroom door swung open and struck Nile in the back, knocking him aside like an autumn scarecrow. He managed to keep his balance somehow. A man entered the room. He was a hulking figure with a pure white military-grade haircut and a forehead like a brick wall. He was dressed in a white collared shirt with a badge pinned to his chest. His official title was Captain Darvish, their superior at Border Division. He saw Nile rubbing his shoulder from the impact. "You're not gonna file for disability, are you?"

Nile wasn't amused, but he offered a courteous grin.

Captain Darvish wasn't to be trifled with. He was a man among boys. Stout and barrel-chested. Built like a pit bull that had eaten too many kibbles 'n bits. His belly pushed out past his belt by a few inches. His bright eyes were sharp as a blade, and his hands were huge and hairy and wrapped in thick muscle like a gorilla. He hailed from the mean streets of Central Boston where he'd worked all those rough neigh-borhoods as a cop before the Collapse. He knew how to handle the worst of men, so he certainly knew how to handle a generic prima-donna like Brixton. "*Grace...*" he said, his voice resounding with unquestioned authority, "…you alright?"

"What the fuck's it look like, Cap?"

Captain Darvish scrunched his brow in sheer vexation. "I beg your fucking pardon?"

"Sorry, Cap. I'm just a little rattled." Brixton dried his hands on a disposable white towel.

Captain Darvish sneered at him, his eyebrows drawn together tightly like two white centipedes in the heat of battle. "Corporate wants your bloodwork."

Brixton whipped his head around. "What?"

Then, as if right on cue, a lab technician walked into the bathroom wearing remnants of a hazmat suit: a white t-shirt, yellow rubber pants, and Nimbus Lab credentials hanging from a lanyard around his neck. He was holding a needle and a vial and he looked eager to use them both.

"I'm alright, Cap," Brixton said. "I wasn't exposed."

"It's straight from the board of executives, Brix. Corporate-ordered."

"I had my gloves on. My mask."

"Don't argue with me."

"I'm fine, Cap. It's not necessary."

"*Goddamnit*, Brix, pull up your sleeve and let this man draw your blood."

Brixton finally conceded. He had no choice. The lab technician walked over and dabbed his arm with an alcohol swab and prepared the needle. Brixton began to sweat as he watched the needle penetrate his skin, and as the blood began to pulsate into the glass vial, he swallowed with a great gulping motion. His heart began to palpitate.

"You alright?" Captain Darvish asked.

"Yeah, I just don't like having my blood drawn, that's all. Do you?"

The Lab technician finished the job and placed a bandage over the tiny puncture wound on his arm. He said, "Thank you, Inspector," and then he left the bathroom.

Captain Darvish watched as Brixton struggled to compose himself. "Go home, Brix. You don't look good."

"Home?" Brixton looked at him defiantly. "Bullshit. I'm not going anywhere."

"The refugee that you shot didn't survive. You're grounded until they investigate."

"It was a clean shooting, sir."

"I know that, but you know the drill. They still have to run the investigation and do the paperwork before you can return to active duty."

"We've skirted this before, Cap. I've gotta question the refugees."

"No. They're in quarantine for at least the next 24 hours. They're off limits. Especially to you."

"This is bullshit, Cap. Let me do my fucking job."

"*Grace…*"

"Fuck this."

"*Brix… Go home! That's a goddamn order.*"

Brixton turned back to the mirror, barely able to contain his reckless defiance. The fog had dissipated from the glass, but the ghostliness in his eyes had not. Who was this frail creature he was looking at? He used to love to look at himself. The high cheekbones. The pouty lips. The amber eyes that shined like butterscotch. The undeniable animal magnetism that women could never resist. He couldn't see it anymore. None of it. His hands trembled for a moment, gripping the porcelain sink and trying to crush it between his perfectly-manicured fingers. Then he swung around in a visceral rage and kicked the plastic trash can across the bathroom floor. He chased it down and kicked it again, leaving a crack in the plastic. He stopped to draw a breath, slouching and placing the palms of his hands on his knees.

"You done?" Captain Darvish asked, looking quite peeved by the childish outburst.

"No, sir. Actually, I'm not." Brixton picked up the plastic trash can and threw it into the wall. It crashed to the floor. He stomped on it with his blood-stained dress shoes and smashed the label that read: *Biohazard*. He kicked the can once more. "Now I'm done," he said, and then he stormed towards the bathroom door.

Nile grabbed him by the arm, "Brix… hold on…"

Brixton knocked his hand away. "Get the fuck off me." He shoved Nile aside and hurried out of the bathroom, slamming the door so hard that the plastic walls were shaking.

Captain Darvish looked at Nile. "What the fuck was that all about?"

Nile just shrugged cluelessly and said, "Imagine being his partner."

# EIGHTEEN

When the mighty horde of boomerang drones flew out of Sky Harbor airfield at midday, they buzzed over the city like a swarm of giant black flies, or like some godawful biblical plague. The people stopped in the streets with their black umbrellas overturned and their eyes rising up to meet the brutal sun. No one had ever seen the drones deployed in such great numbers before. Hundreds of them flying urgently over the border wall, in all directions, at unusually high speeds. It was an extraordinary sight, and that was alarming. Anything out of the ordinary always meant something was wrong. They watched with concern. Some already had fear in their eyes. The next logical step would be absolute panic.

---

The board of executives were gathered around the long table in the boardroom on the seventy-eighth floor of Tower One. Inspector General Ryker was Lucian's unfortunate guest of honor.

"I want a full investigation," Lucian said, sounding more calm than earlier, but still scolding them like a disappointed god. "I want to know who's responsible for those stolen microchips. No scapegoats. This isn't about saving face. We're past that point. No **PR** moves. I want the truth. I want heads to fucking roll." He took a breath to curb his frustration. "What about the refugees we detained? Do they have a contagion?"

"They're sick, sir," General Ryker explained, "but to what extent, we don't know yet. Medical is in the lab testing the bloodwork as we speak."

"Anything on surveillance?"

"Nothing."

"Any leads on the stolen microchips?"

"Nothing, sir. I have my agents on the case. They're checking the log books again. The distribution sheets. You know we've already questioned everyone who was on duty at the factory that night when the microchips went missing. Everyone had clean alibis."

"What about the trafficking across our border?"

"I have agents heading to the border now, sir."

"Are we looking into the Bloody Knuckles in Brimstone?"

"Of course, sir."

"What about the refugees we detained?"

"They're in quarantine at PPD."

"Has anyone bothered to put a hazmat suit on and go question them?"

"That's not protocol, sir."

Lucian shook his head and tightened his fists. They hurt from the arthritis. "*Protocol*," he said, stressed by all the uncertainty. "We have protocols for our protocols." He raised the gavel and held it in the air for a moment. "Just to be clear," he said, looking directly at General Ryker, "you are the head of Nimbus *Security*, right?"

General Ryker didn't appreciate the insinuation of incompetence, but as always he maintained his respect and dignity.

"Listen to my words carefully," Lucian said, sure to make eye contact with each and every executive. "Heads *will* roll, gentlemen. One way or another. I hope you get my meaning."

He smacked the wooden block with the gavel. *Clack Clack! Clack!*

As the executives rose to their feet and began to leave, Lucian gestured for the black sheep Jordan Ambrose to stay behind. "I'd like a word with you in private."

Ambrose looked like a guilt-stricken child who knew he was in trouble. A *hand in the cookie jar* kind of thing. He nodded and sat back down in his seat.

Pharaoh lingered.

Lucian looked at his VP and said, "It's a private conversation, J.W."

Pharaoh tightened his face, looking suspicious of Lucian's intent, and then without argument he turned and left the room. But he eyed Lucian once more before closing the door behind him.

Lucian sat down next to Ambrose and rolled close to him on the caster wheels of his chair.

Ambrose seemed to know where the conversation was going. "Sir, I... I didn't mean to step out of line earlier. I just..."

"You doubt me."

"No, sir... but I... I question your..."

"My *what*? My cognitive function?"

"No, sir. Your judgement."

Lucian frowned. "Please elaborate."

"You didn't think it through, sir. You acted on pure impulse. Not on reason."

"Is this a recent development?" Lucian asked. "This lack of faith in your leader?"

Ambrose hung his head. "Sir, it's not… I've just never seen you so rash, sir. You've always been impulsive in your personal life, yes, but… never in business, sir. *Never.*"

"This isn't business, Jordan." Lucian exhaled and shook his head in obvious dismay. "This is the part of the job you'll never understand. We're in a state of emergency. One wrong decision could be the difference between the life and the death of this company. Of this entire city. And often times, death comes so deceptively that you fail to prepare for it."

"Yes, sir," Ambrose said. "I think that's the point I'm trying to make. To err on the side of caution, sir."

"But you don't understand the risks that come with making high-pressure decisions. The failure to act at the right moment is irreversible." Lucian paused. "You don't have the instinct for leadership, Jordan, so how could you have the decisiveness?"

Ambrose didn't say anything in response. He looked utterly indefensible.

"If you don't hone your instincts," Lucian said, "they fade away. Soon you have no instincts at all."

Ambrose just sat there listening, having enough instinct to know when he shouldn't talk.

"Jordan… I have such high expectations for you." Lucian didn't elaborate. He let the words linger.

"Yes, sir, I know you do," Ambrose said uncomfortably. "I'm sorry I stepped out of line."

"I'm not upset with your instinct to protect our political progress," Lucian said. "I'm upset because you question mine."

Ambrose sat there looking exposed.

"You're not a leader, Jordan. You're an instigator. But that's not a bad thing. In fact, it's why I gave you a seat at the table to begin with. But your instincts are still unpolished. You don't spend enough time in the boardroom to hone them. Making the right decision at the right moment is what will make or break us. Those are the moments you will have to learn to navigate if you're ever going to be a leader."

Ambrose looked at him with curious eyes.

"I want you to spend more time in the boardroom," Lucian said. "More time in your office. More time doing what's expected of you. Not just playing advocate to the people."

"Sir, I—"

"You won't last long at the table, Jordan, if you don't occupy the chair you were given. Someone else may swoop in and take it. Nothing is guaranteed in this business."

Ambrose looked shell-shocked, as if he wasn't ready to take his job so seriously.

"Don't disappoint me, Jordan. Your mother wouldn't like that."

Ambrose lowered his eyes. It appeared to be more sadness than shame.

Lucian placed a delicate hand on his shoulder. "How is she, by the way?"

"Not good, sir. Her body seems to be shutting down little by little. They say her organs are beginning to fail. They're medicating her. Making her comfortable."

"She's at the Institute?"

"Yes, sir."

"They'll take good care of her there."

"Yes, sir."

"I'll have to find the time to go pay my respects."

"She'd like that, sir."

Lucian nodded. "She's proud of you, Jordan. Your father would've been proud of you too."

Ambrose sat upright. His eyes sparkled. "Thank you, sir."

Lucian eyed him like a man who wished he had bore a son of his own. "Now I want you to make *me* proud."

Ambrose nodded.

"We have a job to do, Jordan."

"Yes, sir. We certainly do."

"So don't question my judgement again," Lucian said with a stern eye. "Not until you have the proper instinct to make your own."

# NINETEEN

Elmer Nash was a short, balding man of knowledge who was always the first person consulted whenever something inexplicable happened at Revival. Be it a sudden power failure, or a freak occurrence, or some strange, unexplained natural phenomenon that had everyone running for their firearms in a panic. He always had the solution to those problematic mysteries. He'd spent fifty-seven years on Earth and didn't waste any of that time on useless information or futile leisures. He was somewhat of a child prodigy, reading technology books by the age of six and building his own robots in his bedroom before his eighth birthday. Now that he was fifty-seven, there wasn't much in the field of mechanical engineering, or any type of science for that matter, which he didn't already know by heart. Before the Collapse, he was a professor at the Colorado School of Mines in the city of Golden, teaching mechanical engineering and advanced energy at the National Renewable Energy Lab. They called him *the mad professor*. The one the students always hoped they'd get. The man who went out and discovered all the answers if he didn't already know them. He wasn't afraid to set the classroom on fire or take the students off campus to really strange unapproved places, to do really strange unapproved things, which more often than not proved his scientific theories correct. You could say he was strange himself. That wouldn't be inaccurate. He had a fanatically curious nature, and all he ever did in his free time was salvage books, read them, learn from them, experiment with the knowledge he'd gained, and create something unprecedented with his newfound skill. That sort of reclusion didn't exactly sweeten his social palette. But it made him wise, and that was his gift to Revival: knowledge.

That evening he sat at his cluttered workstation in the communications hub vegged out in a sloven state, his sagging belly protruding through his tight shirt and the glasses on his face not magnified enough to keep him from squinting. His hair was thin and wispy and salted on top, and the dead follicles were threatening to infiltrate the rest of his head. But he had always been older than his age. Both in body and mind. The communications hub — his personal domain — was a darkened room located in the headquarters cabin just off the galley. It had no windows and only one door. The converted office was lit by flashing blue lights and little red blips, stacked with old radios, CB units, walkies, televisions, tape recorders, computers, handheld drones and cameras. Not to mention all the contraptions that he was always tinkering with. Mechanical inventions that ticked like a clock, or flew around, or rolled on wheels, or exploded when prompted. There was a barely-visible metal desk that he called his workstation, and a soft cushiony sofa in the back against the wall where he often slept, sometimes in the same clothes that he had worn the day before. The hub was a permanent mess, like a child's bedroom on the weekends. He was notorious for collecting junk. A recovering hoarder still in remission. A true scatterbrain. But Revival leaned on him, and his clutter, for all sorts of things. He had many jobs in Revival which required his intellectual prowess. Repairing PV panels, maintaining the power station, running system checks, keeping logbooks, and tallying up the percentages. He had a general working knowledge of almost everything. Though his most prominent and persistent role in Revival was communications. That included radio surveillance, which is what he was doing that evening, sitting there in his rolling chair at his desk, listening to the static on the old Kenwood HAM radio. The desk was stacked high with transceivers, amplifiers, a bundle of mics, and a very ancient computer that was used to log and store frequencies and channels. A multi-band setup. Duplex operation. Rigged with a thousand watts of power. That was a crucial part of his job. Listening for anything out of the ordinary. Anything that might give pause or raise concern. He proudly called it *surfing the radio waves,* as if it were some recreational sport. He even had a little bobblehead surfer glued to the desk next to his tabletop mic for good luck. He called him Little Kahuna and spoke to him as if he were actually listening. As the head bobbled on its springs, Elmer spun the dial clockwise on the HAM radio. "Quiet night, huh?"

His Little Kahuna nodded.

The channels were buzzing with only static. So far the evening was uneventful, and that was a good thing. No chatter whatsoever. He was just beginning to lose interest and about to sign off for the night when he happened across a sound that spooked him. A woman shouting hysterically on a UHF channel. He stopped to listen, his ears straining to hear what she was saying through the white noise and whirling frequencies. He could tell by the cadence in her voice that she was in distress.

"Hello?" he said into the microphone. "Is somebody out there?"

The woman shouted through the static, the words barely audible, but unmistakable to him, *"Help me! Somebody help me!"*

He gripped the tabletop mic tightly, "What's happening there? Hello? Miss?"

The woman shouted again, but it was inaudible. The signal was poor, fluttering in and out, probably coming from a great distance.

"Miss, where are you?"

The woman shouted inaudibly again, this time followed by a high-pitched scream.

"Miss, can you hear me?"

Then the signal cleared up for a moment and Elmer heard a man shout, *"Get the bitch in the dirt."* Then another man shouted, *"I get first go at her."*

Elmer heard the woman begging, her voice shrieking in fear. *"Please! Stop!"* He sat there frozen in his chair, his stomach turning in tight little knots and his eyes swollen with grief. The woman screamed louder, *"No! Please! Get off me!"* The hair on Elmer's neck stood up and he rose from his chair, shouting, "Hey! *Hey!*" He pulled the microphone closer to his lips. "Stop! Whoever you are, *stop this.* You hear me? *Stop this now. Leave her alone.*"

But it was futile. The woman was already at their disposal. Elmer could hear the distinct, repulsive sound of the men having their way with her. The horrible smacking of flesh against flesh, wild and without mercy. Her terrible cries were muted intermittently by the crackling of static. He could hear the men howling in diabolic arousal. The twisted sound of their disgusting moans. Their unthinkable laughter. He grimaced and covered his ears. Then suddenly, the unbearable noise stopped, the transmission ended, and all he heard was a long steady pulse of static. The bitter hiss of radio silence. He took a moment to breathe.

---

A few minutes later he was standing in front of Ru, Croix and Wade, telling them what he'd just heard. They were all visibly shaken. No one said a word. They just sat there looking disturbed.

Then Croix asked, "You think it happened here in the colonies?"

Elmer shrugged. "I suppose it could've been here. But judging by the poor signal I'm guessing it was much further out. The HAM can pick up crystal clear chatter as far as the Mojave."

"But you can't be sure it *wasn't* from around here?"

"No. That's why I'm telling you about it."

Croix exhaled, looking like he wanted to ride off and find the culprits and get his revenge.

Ru scratched at his chin vigorously and asked, "What else could cause a poor signal?"

"If it was a walkie," Elmer said, "then low solar batteries could do it. Maybe a poor antenna."

"So it could've been local?"

"It's possible."

"But your gut says *no*?"

"My gut is saying a lot of things right now," Elmer admitted. He held his hand to his mouth, his face pale and sweating, his insides rumbling.

Wade sat there in doubt. "You're positive that's what you heard, Elmer? I mean... a woman being... you sure you couldn't be mistaken?"

"Believe me," Elmer said, "I wish I hadn't heard any of it.

There's no mistake. My ears don't play those kinds of tricks on me. I know what I heard." He grimaced as he recollected the horror. "I can still hear it."

Croix clenched his eyes tightly in distress. "We should assume that it *was* here in the valley. That's the safest play. We should assume that whoever did this is still out there right now, roaming the colonies" He looked at Ru. "Maybe we should go on high alert?"

Ru nodded. "Probably. It's best to take precautions."

"Absolutely," Wade said. "Better safe than sorry."

"Then we go on high alert," Ru ordered. He turned to Elmer and said, "Let's contact the colonies. See if they've seen or heard anything."

"I'll get to it," Elmer said.

Then Ru turned to Croix. "Who's on watch tonight?"

"Gin," Croix said, looking unsure of her effectiveness in that role.

Ru recognized the doubt. "You don't think we can count on her?"

Croix shrugged, not wanting to say it outright.

Then Wade interjected and said it for him, "No, we can't. She ain't ready. I'll take the shift and save you two the trouble of having to make the right decision."

"No," Ru commanded, his voice booming. "Gin has earned her watch. We trained her and set her in motion, now we gotta let her be what we expect her to be. Our doubt is only gonna set her back."

Wade tensed up, "Look, no offense to Gin, but she's wet behind the ears. She's not one to take control of a situation either. She's too unsure of herself, and I'm not sure how well any of us are gonna sleep tonight with her on watch."

"I'll sleep fine," Ru said, his eyes unwavering. "The fences are fired up. The floodlights are working. The dogs will be roaming the perimeter. It's business as usual."

Wade shook his head in disagreement.

Croix nodded, agreeing with Ru, but still having doubts of his own. "Gin will be fine," he said, trying to convince himself. "I'll bring her up to speed."

"Better put a rush on that," Ru said, "The sun is getting pretty low in the sky. The day is almost gone."

"Yes it is," Croix said, "and that can't happen fast enough. This has been one hell of a day."

"Yep," Wade said, sure to get the final word. "Let's hope it's not one hell of a *night* too."

# TWENTY

Gin hated her lonely gig in the crow's nest. That night, sometime after midnight, when everyone in Revival was asleep, she was up in the lookout tower alone. Her fretful eyes were on high alert, scanning the surrounding area through a pair of binoculars with night vision. This was the *night watch.* Not for the faint of heart. Anything could be lurking out there. Or anyone. There hadn't been a night raid on Revival in quite some time, but old habits died hard in the Granite Valley, and the Revivalists kept the practice going, knowing that someday their streak of good fortune would end and their home would be targeted again. They never allowed themselves to be lulled into complacency. Battles were few and far between now, but war was eternal, and they lived by that notion. The battles would come, likely when they least expected it. They wouldn't be caught off guard.

Gin figured it would happen on her watch. That's how things always went for her. She'd be the notorious failure that didn't alert the others in time to save the place. She'd be the reason Revival was raided and destroyed, with everyone inside being killed and maimed or worse. She just wasn't ready for this level of responsibility. Her once-a-month shift had come early, and she was feeling doubtful about her ability to spot the crucial signs of danger and react fast enough. *What if I freeze up at the wrong time?* she worried. The backside of her ears were so wet she could practically feel them dripping. Croix had been breaking her in slowly over the past year, getting her used to the rigors of night watch before giving her the full once-a-week duties that everyone in the compound was tasked with. But he had just pulled the plug on that slow indoctrination a few hours earlier and now she'd been thrown to the wolves. She hoped she wouldn't see any of those. Wolves came around every so often. Coyotes too. She hated when they bared their fangs. It reminded her of just how violent the natural world was inclined to be. She got nervous at the thought. She scanned the horizon with the night vision binoculars again. The green glow in her magnified view created a ghostly image that sent chills up her spine. It always looked to her like some alien world, or some living Hell beneath the earth. She felt a little shiver, expecting to see a bad man, or maybe two, jumping out of the tall grass with their eyes shining red like demons and looking back at her with their guns aimed. She thought something might jump out of the brush at any moment. Then something did. A dark figure in the tall grass. It scared her half to death.

"Oh *you*! You... *darn* hog!" It was a wild boar scampering through the grass looking for food. "Stupid things. Nothing but a nuisance."

Feral hogs were the biggest threat to a colonist's food source and land cultivation, especially in the Granite Valley, where the violent pests roamed the nearby forests and foothills, eating natural herbs and other animals, including their own kind, and attacking any humans that got in their way. Gin hated the filthy cannibals. They were more numerous now than human beings. Some sixty million pigs were once confined in North America before the Collapse. Once they were left free to roam, they bred with feral swine, which created a crossbreed of leaner, meaner, and more mobile hybrids. These feral hogs had larger tusks now and a stronger desire to use them. Gin figured the boars had rabies. It was as common as the winter sniffles. She saw three more rooting around in the tall grass, snorting and fighting one another for dibs on a dead mountain beaver. She calmed herself. No reason to fear critters that were on the other side of the fence. Truthfully, unless they stood upright on two legs they weren't an immediate threat. Then, just as her heart began to settle, she heard a sudden creaking noise coming from behind her. She dropped the binoculars and spun around as fast as she could and huffed furiously when she spotted the source. "My God, Kid. You scared the crap out of me."

Kid was sticking his head up through the opening in the wooden floor.

*Just another kind of nuisance*, Gin thought.

Kid smiled at her, but the gesture was half-hearted. He seemed to be hiding a frown, like he was about to break some terrible news.

"What are you doing up here?" Gin asked. "You know the rules."

"I came to say goodbye."

"Goodbye?"

Kid swallowed nervously, his gaze captured by an obvious uncertainty. "I need you to do me a favor."

"What favor?"

"I need you to look the other way for a few minutes."

"What are you talking about?"

"I need you to look the other way while I power down the fence."

Gin looked at him with severe misgivings and felt a sudden urge to slap him across the face. "Why would you power down the fence?"

Kid meandered with his mouth open for a moment, then he said plainly, "I'm leaving, Gin."

"Leaving? To go where?"

"Doesn't matter where. Just not here."

"No way. You shut the fence down and Ru's gonna put you in the cage for good. Don't be stupid."

"Nobody's gonna know."

"They'll know when they see you're gone. Then I'll be the one that takes your punishment. *Thanks a lot.*"

Kid didn't consider her predicament. He was too consumed with his own. "I can't live in this goddamn place no more," he huffed. "I'm sick of everybody treating me like I don't belong."

Gin put a hand on each of his shoulders and squared him up so his eyes met hers. "They'll catch you, Kid."

"Not if you help me."

"Better hope it ain't Croix that catches you. He'll hang you from the noose."

"He ain't gonna find out until I'm long gone. The fence is only gonna be down for a few minutes. Come on, Gin. You can power it back up when I'm gone."

Gin didn't say no, or yes, or maybe. Her thoughts just wandered. No direction in particular. Conflict always demagnetized the compass in her mind.

"Unless..." Kid muttered.

"Unless *what?*"

"Unless you wanna come with me? Then we can just go together."

Gin furrowed her brow in near disgust, pulling her hands away from his shoulders, but doing her best to be polite about it. "I ain't coming with you. No way. Not a chance."

Kid looked determined despite her conviction, like a used car salesman on the lot refusing to give up on a tough sale. "I just thought... we... you and I... could maybe..." He stopped short of saying what he really felt.

"Maybe *what*? You gonna protect me out there?"

Kid puffed up, his head rising pridefully. "I'm more of a man than you think."

Gin rolled her eyes impolitely. "I don't think about you much at all."

Kid suddenly turned to stone. His emotions evaporated. His face was somehow expressionless. He sat there completely rigid for a moment, his mouth a perfect circle of resentment.

"I didn't mean it like that," Gin said, doing her best at damage control. But the damage was already done.

"To hell with this fucking place," Kid snapped. "I'm leaving with or without your help. Screw Revival. And screw you." He spun around in a flash and started climbing down the ladder. His feet stomped heavily on the old wooden rungs, his teenage angst being unleashed one step at a time.

"Kid, *don't*." Gin shouted as quietly as possible. "Don't be stupid."

She heard his feet hit the ground. Then the soft pattering of his footsteps as he scurried off towards the power station. She slammed the palm of her hand to her face and groaned. Conflict resolution wasn't exactly her strong suit. She gazed up at the emergency bell, pondering her options. Kid had put her in a precarious situation. Ringing the bell would raise all kinds of hell. But not ringing the bell could invite something far worse. She rose to her feet and grabbed the thick rope attached to the iron clapper. Her hand gripped the bottom knot tightly. But she didn't ring the bell. Instead, she made her way to the ladder and climbed down in a hurry.

---

Kid squatted in the shadows and powered down the electric fence. It went off without a hitch. There wasn't much to it. He just unlocked the electrical panel with the stolen key and flipped the big red switch that said *fence*. He trotted softly to the gate and slid it open on the metal track and stepped outside cautiously, entering the dark blur of the moonless night. He closed the gate behind him, making sure to engage the latch. He didn't want to leave his former family in harm's way. He looked to the crow's nest to give Gin a signal if she was watching, but she wasn't there. He hoped that meant she was looking the other way as he'd asked her to do. He studied Revival, looking for any sign of life that might be reason for him to fear for his own, or any sign of Gin giving him the thumb's up. But he saw nothing. Oddly, that made him worry even more. He gave a remorseful look, as if that were his private attempt at goodbye, and then he turned away and set out in the darkness alone, just a boy on a mission to prove himself a man. He sauntered into the share shack in the pitch black, carefree and quietly, as if he had nothing to worry about. He lit the spark on his zippo and lit a candle made of beeswax and the room was illuminated by a soft yellow glow, throwing shadows from wall to wall like phantoms playing chase. He set his old Taurus .380 pocket pistol down on the table and unzipped his shoulder bag. He grabbed a few mason jars full of fruit and dried veggies from the shelves and set them on the table beside the gun. He grabbed some jerky in cloth wrappings and stuffed it into his shoulder bag. He placed the .380 on top of the jerky. He turned to grab the mason jars filled with dried fruit and veggies, to pour the contents into his bag, but suddenly the wood floor creaked behind him and the candle went out as if someone had blown their breath on it. He scrambled aimlessly for the .380. His hands searched the table in the dark. Then a bright flash of light hit him in the retinas. He raised his arms to his face to shield his eyes. Then something grabbed a hold of him. Strong fingers pressing deeply into the flesh of his arm and pulling him backwards. Then a warm hand grabbed him by the back of his neck and forced him towards the cots. He spun his head around and saw a man with a potato sack over his head with maniacal eyes glaring through the eyeholes that were cut out of the hood.

"Where you going in such a hurry?" the hooded man asked with a high-pitched, nasally voice. The words twanged from his lips.

Kid felt shivers up and down his spine, and a sudden need to defecate himself.

There were two other men in the room, both wearing the same kind of hoods over their heads, one holding a shotgun, and the other shining the flashlight in Kid's face. They looked predatory. The whites of their eyes were bulging with hunger. They grabbed him and overpowered him and forced him face down on one of the cots that were bolted to the floorboards.

"Hold 'em down," the hooded man said with his high-pitched twang. "A pretty little thing like this should be deflowered properly."

Kid screamed out, "Help! Help!" His voice sounded like a steam whistle. The hooded man covered his mouth with his filthy hand. Kid nearly vomited at the foul odor. It smelled like gun oil and smoke and tasted like tobacco.

"Let's get his little britches off," the hooded man said. "I'll break 'em in for ya'll." He reached down and grabbed the shrinking noodle between Kid's legs, squeezing delicately through his pants, but with a threatening authority in his grip to let Kid know who controlled the moment. He unzipped Kid's pants. Kid fought back as hard as he could, his little arms swinging like the leafless twigs of a cottonwood tree in a windstorm, but the man resisted his punches with ease and pressed his other hand into the back of Kid's neck and pressed him down deeper into the mattress on the cot. "Hold still, you little fucker."

He pulled the back of Kid's pants down slightly, just enough to get the job done. All three of the hooded men put their hands on Kid's body, groping him wildly, like primates in heat. Kid tried to scream out again as his mouth escaped the man's oily hand, "Help! HELP!"

The man pressed the barrel of his gun to the back of Kid's head. "Shut your fucking mouth."

Kid couldn't see what kind of gun it was, or if it was even loaded, but he knew the feeling of cold steel pressed to his head, and he didn't want to die.

"Shush now, boy."

Kid went silent, his body trembling with a fear he'd never known, and his mind caught somewhere between fight and flight but incapable of either.

"You hear that, boy?" The man's twang was beginning to sound fraudulent, as if he were disguising his real voice. "That's total silence," he said. "Ain't nobody heard you. So ain't nobody coming to the rescue."

Kid tried to scream for help again but the man shoved his face into the mattress, and everything that came out of his mouth after that was muffled and indistinct.

"Don't make a fuss now, you pretty little thing," the hooded man said. "This ain't gonna hurt but once."

He shoved his knee into Kid's back with brutal force. Kid screamed into the mattress. His voice was muted, sounding like

an air conditioner on the fritz, humming and loping and struggling to come to life. Then he managed to turn his head sideways and his mouth broke free just long enough to get a few
words out, "Croix! Help me, goddamnit! Please! Help me,
Croix!"

The man turned him over and shoved a knee into his gut
and held him there for a moment, his maniacal eyes glaring in
a familiar rage. Then he slowly removed the hood that he'd
been hiding behind.

Kid almost wept when he saw the face staring back at him.
"Croix?"

It was Croix alright, and his eyes were turning that same
old fiery blue. He spoke with a simmering tone, his voice no
longer fraudulent. "So now you need my help, huh? You little
shit."

Kid refused to believe his own eyes at first. He felt trapped
in some diabolical nightmare. He just needed to be pinched or
slapped around and he'd wake right up. But this was no
dream. "Croix… what the fuck?"

The other two men removed their hoods. Kid was vexed
by the sight of Tavo and Skinny standing there giggling at his
embarrassing predicament and not even trying to hide their
amusement. That's when it finally dawned on him. Croix had
done this just to make a fucking point. "You sons a bitches.
You fucking assholes!"

Tavo chuckled, "Kid, you nearly got your cherry popped."

Kid began to cry in anger.

Croix pulled him to his feet. "That's just how it happens,
Kid. Lucky for you it was just a ruse and not a fucking
ravaging. Hopefully a lesson learned."

Kid rose to his feet and pulled his pants up in a hurry.
"Screw ya'll! Sons a bitches! I hope ya'll rot in hell for this!"

He wanted to lash out at Croix, but before he could even

consider throwing a single regrettable punch, Croix grabbed him by the back of the neck and shoved him out of the shack and into the blinding security lights of Revival, which were shining like the blind eyes of judgement. Every floodlight was on, pointing their accusatory beams at Kid. A bright glow highlighting his red-faced guilt.

"Looks like you woke the whole neighborhood," Croix said.

Kid tried to pull away from him, but it was futile. "Let me go. That hurts, you asshole!"

"You think that hurts? Taking it right up the ass from a two-hundred pound pedophile is much worse." Croix squeezed harder. "You go out into the world alone and you're gonna be hurting in ways that you can't even imagine." He jerked Kid around a bit to establish his dominance. "I've tried to tell you what the world is like out there, but you needed me to show you, didn't you? I could only go so far. You'll have to use your imagination for the rest. If you can." He shoved Kid through the open security gate.

Kid stumbled forward. He looked up and saw everyone standing there in disgust. The entire Revival family. They were clearly unhappy to be awakened at such an ungodly hour, all of them armed and still in their sleep clothes. Ru was standing at the forefront, his arms crossed angrily. Gin stood by his side, looking guilty, but not remorseful.

Kid winced at her, "You told on me, Gin?"

She diverted her eyes.

Ru glared at him. "You shut the fences down?"

"It was only for a minute, Ru, I swear."

"That's all it takes, Kid. You put us all at risk. We could've been raided and killed. We don't know who's out there waiting for us to make a fatal mistake. That fence is the only thing that separates us from the evils of the world."

"It was gonna be the last time, I swear. I was gone. On my way."

"On your way to what?"

"I'm sorry, Ru. But… I just don't wanna live here no more. Just let me go."

"Go where?"

Kid had no answer.

Croix clawed at the back of his neck. "So you're just gonna set off on your own, huh? Was that the plan? You think you can take care of yourself outside these walls?"

Tavo and Skinny walked up with Kid's shoulder bag.

Croix took the bag and unzipped it. "Let's have a look inside and see what kind of badass we're dealing with here." He pulled Kid's gun from the bag first. "I hope you have more than this pissant .380 to protect yourself. That's a goddamn toy compared to what they got out there." Then he looked inside the bag and his face shriveled up into a ball of kinetic fury, the skin tightening around his cheek bones like some lost submersible about to implode under the pressure of the deep blue sea. He turned to the others and flipped the shoulder bag upside down and poured the contents out onto the ground.

Everybody gasped, erupting in anger, each of them cursing the kid as they recognized their own belongings.

"You thieving little bastard," Wade said, limping towards him with a stringent look in his one good eye.

Croix put his hand up, stopping Wade in his tracks.

Kid hung his head. His eyes turned to the ground in shame, looking anywhere but at his accusers. The collection of things that were piled at his feet weren't even his. They were stolen. Personal items that he'd taken from seemingly everyone in Revival, without their consent. Keepsakes. Old photographs. Survival tools. Random objects of affection that he didn't even know the meaning of.

"You ain't no thief, huh?" Croix asked.

They all charged the pile and reclaimed their property, some of which were irreplaceable memories. They called Kid every bad word they could think of. But the word that stuck in his mind the most was *thief*.

"I was just borrowing it," he said.

"A night in the cage," Ru declared. "That's your punishment. For now. More to come."

"No, please," Kid pleaded. "Not the cage again. I learned my lesson."

"How's that?" Croix asked. "You ain't even served your punishment yet."

Kid groveled, "I'm sorry, Ru. You gotta believe me. I just wanted to leave is all. There's something better out there. Something better for *me*."

"This world ain't about *you*," Ru snapped, his voice rumbling like a storm on the rise.

Kid fell silent, looking heartbroken. He had never seen such a contemptuous look in Ru's eyes before.

Ru ordered the others to head back to their cabins. As they staggered back to their beds in their sleep clothes, they scolded Kid with their scathing looks, which quietly told him that he was no longer wanted in Revival. The only one who didn't scold him with her eyes was Gin. She refused to even look his way. That hurt him the most.

Ru nodded to Croix, offering him the reins, and then he headed back for the headquarters cabin, pulling his thick woolen robe around him tightly.

Kid stood there feeling abandoned, and feeling afraid of what Croix might do to him with no one around to keep his deadly rage in check.

Then Croix spotted something else in the bottom of the

bag and grumbled through his clenched teeth, "You little son of a bitch."

"Oh shit," Kid said.

Croix pulled out a piece of black fabric that was crumpled up into a ball. He unfurled the wad. It was the *Dagger & Son* flag that Kid had stolen from his cabin. "You *did* go through my shit."

Kid raised his hands in defense. "Don't hurt me, Croix." But Croix's angry claws were already digging into the back of his neck and pushing him towards the cage. "Stop squeezing so hard. It hurts!"

"I told you this flag is dangerous."

"Why?"

"It just is."

"Did you know 'em or not?" Kid asked squeamishly. "You knew Billy Dagger?"

Croix ignored him.

"Was he real?" Kid tried to plant his foot into the ground and stop Croix from shoving him into the cage. "Wade said the stories ain't even true. It's just some bullshit legend. He said you're full of shit, man."

Croix grabbed a knot of his filthy hair and tossed him into the cage. "Keep your thieving little hands off my things."

"I didn't steal it. I just borrowed it."

Croix slammed the door shut behind him. "It ain't borrowing if you don't ask. That's called stealing. And I don't think you had plans to return to Revival and give it back to me, now did you?" He locked the padlock and gave it a hard tug for good measure. There would be no escaping tonight.

Kid wrapped his hands around the wooden bars and pulled at the door. "Why don't ya'll just let me leave?"

"If it were up to me, Kid, you'd be swinging from the gallows. That'd be your only way out of here."

"Then why'd you even bring me here? You should've left me for dead when you had the chance."

"Hindsight is twenty twenty."

"What's that mean?"

"It means I made a mistake."

"So you finally admit it?"

"I admit that I bit off more than I can chew with you. But I'm the one that brought you here, so you're my responsibility now, and I don't shirk my responsibilities. *Ever*. I admit my failures, and I fix 'em too, and I'll be goddamned if I don't fix you."

"Well ain't you just so goddamn special."

"That's called holding myself accountable. You need to hold yourself accountable too. You remember what that means?"

"Yeah, it means I gotta be more like you."

Croix scoffed with a patronizing hiss, "You'll never be like me. Aim smaller. How about you just grow the hell up and stop acting like a goddamn child for starters."

"Oh yeah, God forbid I act my age. Could you imagine? A kid being a kid?"

"Don't give me that shit. Your goddamn balls have already dropped. You ain't a child no more. There's consequences to your actions, you little shit, and you need to learn that."

"*Learn?*" Kid began to quake with teenage angst. "I can't *learn anything* in this fucking place. Because nobody teaches me a damn thing except how to obey. *Obey! Obey! Obey!*"

"Keep your fucking voice down," Croix snapped with a heated whisper. He punched at the cage door. "There are rules in life, you little shit. That's always the first thing you learn. "

"I don't wanna follow your bullshit rules. Just let me leave."

"Where you gonna go?"

Kid didn't have an answer. He just stood there trembling.

"You don't even know what's out there, Kid. We're trying to help you understand the world, but you're too childish to accept that."

"So you're just gonna lock me up? That's your solution?"

"It's the only solution I've got that don't involve a noose around your scrawny little neck."

Then Kid erupted like a baby volcano spitting cold lava and kicked the cage door and stomped away, pacing in temperamental circles. "If you ain't gonna tell me the things I wanna know, then just let me leave. I'm better off on my own."

"Until you prove yourself to be a man," Croix said, "you're better off behind these bars. That's the plain and simple truth. It's time to grow up. Your childhood is over."

Kid shook his head in defeat. "I'd sure hate to see what your childhood was like."

Croix looked at him with a blankness in his eyes and said, "There wouldn't be much to see, Kid. It didn't last very long." Then he turned and walked away and never looked back.

Kid grabbed the cage door and shook it furiously, as if he were shaking the guilt from his own conscience. "It's just a flag, you asshole. A goddamn *flag*!"

# TWENTY-ONE

The night had been long and restless for everyone in Revival. Not much sleep at all. Too much adrenaline rushing through their veins. It was hard to put their mind at ease when they'd just been violated by one of their own. Kid had stolen their memories, all of which were precious to them, even if they never spoke of them. Thievery wasn't something they took lightly.

The next morning came early, but as usual, Croix had beaten the disarming glow of dawn to the punch. He'd already run his security checks and fed the animals before the lazy old sun even raised its head. Only one of those two jobs was actually his, but he was pulling double duty thanks to the thieving little shit that was still sound asleep in the cage. But Croix was content with that. It almost felt like Kid wasn't even around. No questions, comments or demands. No harassment, complaints or excuses. Croix was enjoying the calm. He shoveled the dog turds from the kennel without feeling the least bit degraded by the lowly job. He could just as well be sitting in the shade of the cottonwoods catching an afternoon nap. That's how peaceful it was. The dogs were busy jogging around the perimeter run, searching for little creatures in the dirt. Ridgebacks always kept their bodies moving and their minds on the prowl. They were bred for two purposes: hunting and standing guard. They were good at both. Croix usually tried to mimic their purpose, always on the move, in mind and in body, but this morning he was perfectly still, and imperfectly happy, even as he stood there lathered up in the oily skeeter repellent that Teardrop had made from witch hazel and lavender. He hated the stuff. But Mosquitoes were the deadliest creatures in the valley, especially in the bloodthirsty mornings of early August, with their stealthy attacks and a needle-like proboscis and a deadly malarial bite. Only the females of the species sucked blood though. Croix thought that was appropriate. It made him think of Zee. He figured she would ultimately be the death of him, with her constant nagging and her unrealistic expectations, stressing his arteries to the point of no return and sucking the blood straight from his body. He would likely die from a stroke or a heart attack, and it would be on account of the unyielding pressure that she always placed on him. He tried to reclaim the moment, compartmentalizing his thoughts and focusing on his work, but Kid shouted out from the cage, "Croix, let me outta here," and Croix sprung from his calm like a man leaping to his own death. "Goddamnit, Kid, you ruin every peaceful moment I get."

"Come on, Croix. Let me out. I served my time." Kid was swatting at the mosquitoes. "I learned my lesson. The goddamn skeeters are biting."

Croix felt his arteries begin to bloat. A smorgasbord of blood for the nagging little bloodsuckers that were buzzing around his sweaty head. He tried to ignore the kid's jawing, which seemed to carry on endlessly, like the droning of mosquito wings. One-thousand flaps per second.

But somehow, Kid's lips flapped even faster. "Croix, I'm serious. Let me out. I'm skeeter bait in here. Unlock the fucking door. Come on. Unlock it. *Please!*"

"*Alright, goddamnit,*" Croix swung the shovel and slammed the blade into the kennel wall. "*That's enough.*"

Kid went silent.

Croix stormed out of the kennel, pacing towards the cage with the shovel in his hand and looking as if he might just use it for nefarious purposes.

Kid backed away from the cage door.

Croix stood there looking deceptively calm. He handed the shovel to Kid through the wooden bars. "Here you go. Take it."

"I ain't shoveling dog shit," Kid said. "Not my job today."

"You're right, it's not, and I'm not expecting you to do it."

Kid grabbed the handle of the shovel cautiously. "Then what's this for?"

"You want out, don't you?"

"Yeah… so?"

"So… *dig* yourself out, you little shit."

Croix scurried away, feeling a mild sense of victory.

Kid kicked the cage door. "You asshole! Let me out of here!"

Croix disappeared around the corner of his cabin, drowning out the kid's bitter complaints with his own. "Sorry, Kid. Can't help you. I got shit to do, and unlike your job, my job never ends."

The storehouse was a 400-square-foot hut made with wood framing and walls of packed earth and kept cool and dry all year long. No windows, no light, no moisture, and no insects or rodents to contend with. Revivalists filled the place with sustenance. Salt, pepper, sugar, rolled oats, rice, yeast, all the staples. Some of which they'd traded for on the black market in Kelso, and others which they'd foraged from the mountains or plucked from the foothills or grown right there in their own nutrient-rich soil. They stored everything in metal cans, plastic bottles and glass mason jars. Stacked on old wooden shelves. Fruits like berries, lemons and apples. Veggies like potatoes and carrots. Herbs like echinacea and oregano. Flavor boosters and old-time remedies like garlic, onion, ginger, and honey from the bee keep. They stored buckets of hard tack, dried fish and jerked meat. Barrels of corn, grain, nuts and wheat. Maple syrup drained from the nearby Bigleaf trees, meadow barley, mint and purple sage. Every bit of it plucked from the earth. But not everything in the storehouse was for eating. They stored healing powers too. Hundreds of miracle plants like jimsonweed, skullcap, yarrow, elderberry and valerian root. They even stored jugs of purified drinking water from the Owens River, in case of an emergency or an unforeseen need to flee their home in a hurry. But the most precious commodity in the entire storehouse was the seed. Buckets of survival. Without seed, it would be impossible to keep all of these fruits and veggies and medicinal herbs growing and harvesting year after year. Without seed, Revival would be fruitless and bare. So the storehouse was life.

As Tavo stood outside the earthen hut tossing a bundle of logs onto the wood stack, the heat of the oncoming day was beginning to sting the back of his neck. "The morning sun sure is doing her best to challenge my good nature," he said, followed by a scowling yawp. He and Skinny were both dripping wet, stacking the firewood together under the overhang where the kindle was kept off the ground and kept dry under a tarpaulin. "Hard to believe it's only seven in the morning," he said as he wiped his brow with his forearm. The firewood bundles seemed to get heavier as each degree got hotter. Then he noticed that Skinny's workload didn't quite match his own. "What the hell, Skinny? You stacking one damn log at a time? You damn fool. I'm stacking bundles."

"I'm pacing myself," Skinny said casually. "So who's the damn fool?"

"Good point," Tavo said with a humorless self-loathing. "And here I thought *you* were the dumb one."

Skinny chuckled, always one to laugh at himself. He had obvious cognitive disabilities, but he was smart enough to recognize when something was funny, belittling or not. He may have been simple-minded, but as Croix had always told him, common sense didn't require a master's degree.

Suddenly, Croix approached them, looking pissed at the world and stomping across the ground like an angry bull. "Where's Ru?"

"Inside," Tavo said.

Croix studied their log count, as if he already knew to expect a disappointing number. "Ya'll still got twenty bundles left? Christ Almighty. I could've had this done before sunrise."

"Skinny's pacing himself," Tavo said.

Croix stopped in his tracks. "Pacing yourself, huh? Well, Skinny, I got three words for you, and I'll make 'em simple enough for you to understand…" He pursed his lips, probably about to launch into an angry tirade that would far exceed his aforementioned three words, but his voice was drowned out by the sudden ringing of the emergency bell in the crow's nest. A loud, panicky DING! DING! DING!

He whipped his head around and spun on his feet to get a

look and saw Wade ringing the bell frantically from the crow's nest and shouting, "Boomerang! Look out! Behind you!"

Croix spun around as a boomerang drone swooped down and buzzed by his head. A startling flash of shiny black metal. He ducked and nearly stumbled to his knees. "Holy fuck," he shrieked. "It's a goddamn drone."

Ru came running out of the storehouse, his eyes scanning aimlessly at the coral sky until he spotted the intruder. "Christ in heaven." He turned and shouted, "Shut the doors. Hide the weapons. Hide everything." He closed the door to the storehouse and ran for the headquarters cabin, putting his aging legs to the test.

Tavo ran to the slaughterhouse, charging at a sprint and nearly tackling Memphis to the ground as she stumbled out of the door in her bloody apron. "It's a boomerang. We gotta close the doors and windows."

Skinny and Croix ran to the cabins to alert the others, ordering them to shut their windows and close their doors. It was imperative that everything in Revival was closed off and kept from the boomerang's curious eyes. The camera on the drone would be recording, and anything the boomerang saw would surely be seen by the Nimbus Corporation too. Things the corporation might see as a threat. Weapons, trade goods, and anything that might suggest a defiant way of life. The boomerang would spot it all.

"What's it doing way out here?" Skinny asked

"I don't know," Croix said, looking frightened for the first time in years. "It's never happened before."

---

Kid had been in the cage trying to dig his way out with the shovel when all the commotion erupted. He'd seen Wade shouting the word *boomerang* and ringing the bell from the crow's nest. He spotted Croix running between the cabins and shouting for everyone to close their windows and doors. The word *boomerang* sounded familiar, but Kid couldn't quite place it. He couldn't figure out why everyone had suddenly lost their minds. There was no sandstorm kicking up in the valley. No band of scavengers. No gang of thugs. Nothing.

Then he felt the hairs on the nape of his neck stand up and begin to shiver, as if something was watching him from behind. He turned his head around slowly and saw the boomerang drone hovering just outside of the cage. A terrifying sight to his naive eyes. He had never seen such an ominous machine. The drone's sleek body was like a shadowy haunt in a fever dream, its blue camera lights glowing like two evil eyes. "What the fuck is *that?*" He could barely project his voice. "Cruh… Cruh… CROIX. What the fuck is this?"

The drone glided softly towards the cage, eerily rotating sideways and slipping between the wooden bars like some miniature flying saucer. Once it was inside, it leveled itself again and moved towards Kid with the stealth and scrutiny of a snake.

"Croix, *help*." Kid began to backpedal, his wide eyes unblinking. The boomerang flashed its blue lasers and began to scan his face. Kid stumbled backwards and slammed into the cage wall behind him. He was trapped with nowhere to go. The boomerang had him pinned. He gripped the handle of the shovel tightly as the drone inched closer to his face.

Croix ran for the cage, recognizing Kid's foolish intent. "*No*. Hold still, Kid. Don't move."

The boomerang drone ordered Kid to, "*State your name.*"

"Tell 'em your name," Croix shouted as he reached the cage.

But Kid was stuck in a deafening panic. "What the fuck is this thing, Croix?"

"It's a boomerang drone. I told you about these things."

The drone moved even closer to Kid's face and ordered him again to, "*State your name.*"

"I don't know my name!"

"Just tell 'em your goddamn name, Kid." Croix saw the drone moving in, only a couple of inches away from Kid's head and threatening to zap him with the shock device mounted on its face. The *kiss of death*. 20,000 volts of electricity. "Goddamnit, Kid. Tell 'em your fucking name."

The drone crackled a final warning, the coils sparking with a wicked blue promise.

"I'm *Kid!* They just call me *Kid!*"

Then Croix saw him raising the shovel by his side, about to strike the drone. "No. Don't do that, Kid."

But it was too late.

Kid whacked the boomerang drone with the metal end of the shovel. The drone somersaulted backwards in the air and stopped itself and flipped over and zoomed right back towards him in a blurry rush. The shock coils crackled with electricity, lighting up like a Tesla coil.

Croix drew the *Crazy 8* revolver from his hip holster and fired a single shot. The .357 round slammed into the boomerang, knocking it into the cage wall. The drone corrected itself and lunged forward in the air. Croix shot the padlock off the door and burst into the cage. The drone rocketed towards Kid with no mercy and the blue coils crackling, but before it could plant a fatal kiss, Croix grabbed the shovel and bashed it across the face with the blade. The drone tumbled backwards and rolled in the air and hit the cage wall with a fracturing thud. Croix raced over and hit it again, knocking it to the ground. The wounded drone tried to rise up, the blue coils sparking this time like a live wire, but Croix slammed the tip of the blade into the carbon fiber body and gutted the drone, splitting the shiny black surface and rupturing the mechanical entrails. The wires spooled out like colorful intestines. Croix struck it again and again with the cutting edge until sparks flew from the wound and the loud buzzing noise turned to a low inaudible shriek. Then he heard a final electronic gasp and the noise stopped altogether. He took a deep breath. The first breath he'd taken since he fired the first shot. The drone was dead.

Kid was still shaking with terror.

"It's alright," Croix said. "It's over." But the concerning look on his face suggested otherwise.

Ru stood outside of the cage now, huffing and puffing with his hands on the bars and holding himself upright. The running had nearly done him in. He looked at Kid and shook his head in a foreboding manner.

Wade approached them in a panic. "They'll be coming now."

"Who?" Kid asked.

"The border patrol," Croix answered with a frightened breath. "To recover their drone. They'll tear this place apart."

"Or worse," Wade said.

Kid sill hadn't blinked.

The Revivalists had all gathered around the cage in a broken circle of troubled faces, each of them on edge and fearing for what came next. They all had the disquieted look of soldiers preparing for battle. But in their case, preparation would be key to avoiding one.

Ru ordered them to, "Hide the contraband. The valuables. Secure it in the safe room. Hide our weapons in the armory. Leave nothing more than a few pistols and shotguns in your cabins. Nothing they'd see as a threat." His surefire voice was suddenly wavering. "But make it look like we have the means to protect ourselves out here. You all know the drill. Get to it."

Everyone sprang into action.

"Let's be quick about it," Croix added, looking to the southern horizon with an undeniable look of dread on his face. "They're already on their way."

# TWENTY-TWO

"This is Captain Vedder, Outpost 11," a voice declared over dispatch. "We're in route to recover drone number 147. *Hoorah.*"

The Draco hovership hummed through the sky like a heat-seeking missile targeting anything with a beating heart. It was a hybrid quadcopter with coaxial rotorblades and ducted fans with dynamic drive shafts. A sleek carbon fiber body, shaped like a bullet at the nose, with stubby wings on the fuselage. Capable of speeds of up to 500 mph. Like everything else in the Republic of Phoenix, the hovership was electric. It ran on a propulsion system that was powered by solar collectors and a host of nuclear batteries. The emergency reserves were stored in ultra-light hydrogen fuel cells. The airframe itself was made with sustainable, lightweight PV materials which captured solar energy and transferred it to the thermal core, effectively making the hovership self-sustainable. It could run constantly, on regenerated power, as if it had a pumping heart inside of it. Though the Draco was designed for platoon transport and cargo hauls, this particular model was repurposed by the Warhawks to be a bullet-proofed war machine. There was a belly turret and several weapon doors on the sides, and when the Warhawks lit the sky with their roaring machine guns, it was like some mechanical dragon reigning fire down on its enemies below, as if refugees in the Rim had gone through a time warp and found themselves running scared in some fantastical medieval kingdom. Now the mechanical, fire-breathing dragon was heading straight for Revival.

---

Wade shook an accusatory finger at Croix. "We're the only colony in the entire valley that doesn't trade with the Bloody Knuckles. If we had their protection, we wouldn't be in this mess."

"Don't give me that shit," Croix snapped. "Their protection doesn't mean a goddamn thing to the border patrol out here and you know it."

"I think we should consider wiping our hands clean," Wade said, staring with his one good eye. "Just give the border patrol what they want."

"You think we should give the Kid up?"

Wade nodded half-heartedly, not strong enough in his conviction to say it out loud.

"We ain't giving him up to those animals," Croix insisted. "No way in hell."

"What's the difference?" Wade asked. "They'll just take him to Brimstone and put him to work. Or they'll make him pull labor at their barracks. Either way, it's the same thing he's been doing here."

"No," Croix said. "Why would they bother with corporate policy out here? Ain't nobody watching what they do. They'll kill the kid on the spot. Just for the inconvenience he caused them. I've seen it before, and so have you."

Wade huffed. "If I thought they'd kill him, Croix, I wouldn't suggest it."

"What reason would they have not to?"

Wade shook with frustration. "The kid ain't even one of us."

"He's been here for a year and a half. Don't tell me he ain't one of us."

Wade raised the same accusatory finger again and said, "This is *your* mess, Croix. *Your* mess. You brought him here. Whatever happens is on *you*."

Croix moved closer to him. "Wade, you put that finger in my face again and I'll bite the fucking thing clean off your hand. We're not turning the kid over to them just to save our own ass."

"Alright, *enough*." Ru placed a firm hand between them. "Kid is a Revivalist, same as any of us. That's been established." He eyed Wade. "We protect him as we protect ourselves. And that's not on Croix. It's on all of us. We all agreed to let him live here."

Wade backed down.

"What have we always promised ourselves?" Ru asked rhetorically. "We're in this together. We're all Revivalists, or we're nothing at all."

"I'm just trying to protect that promise," Wade said. "I'm trying to protect our home."

"By throwing Kid to the wolves?" Ru asked. "That ain't who we are, mate. Besides, even if we give Kid up to them, that won't be enough. They're gonna punish all of us. That's the way it is. It's not about justice to them. It's about sending a message. They want to remind us that they're in control and we're not. And the truth is, they *are* in control. Wherever they set foot. We just have to hope they show mercy. That's how we protect this place. *Cooperation and resolve.*"

Wade nodded, but his eyes shifted, as if he wasn't onboard with Ru's strategy.

Then Croix said, "Alright, let's get Kid to the safe room."

The safe room was buried beneath the earth and hidden under a brick courtyard where several outdoor chairs were placed in a circle around a brick firepit. It was a simple place to relax, but with a catch. The firepit was fake. Not made for real flames. There was an access point hidden within it. The brick structure stood about two feet off the ground and was completely hollowed out beneath the grill top. The burnt logs had been pasted onto the grating to add to the authenticity. Croix pulled the faux top aside with very little effort, exposing the steel hatch that was hidden inside. A cheap metal door. It was circular and two inches thick, with a heavy duty handle, a key lock and metal hinges that had been retroactively welded on. Nothing impressive, but no one outside of Revival had ever discovered it, and hopefully never would.

When Croix pulled the hatch open, a musty odor hit his nose. He turned away and grimaced and waved Kid onward with his hand. "Go on, Kid. Get your ass down there and flip the switch."

Kid grimaced too, "Ah Jesus. It smells. What the hell is that?" He pulled his shirt over his nostrils.

"You'll get used to it," Croix said. He smacked Kid on the back and shoved him forward. "Get down there."

Kid already looked nauseous. He began his climb down the ten foot ladder, trying to hold his shirt over his nose at the same time. He nearly slipped on the metal rungs. When he got to the bottom he flipped a switch with his free hand, keeping his other hand over his nose. The lights flickered on and the room lit up in a fluorescent strobe. There was a steady hum of power, like the sound of a microwave oven. The entire safe room ran on solar electric from the PV panels and the power station above ground. Several fans began to spin quietly overhead. It was the climate-controlled air filtration system at work. Croix was happy to see it was still functioning properly. It had been a while since they'd operated it.

"That oughta help the smell," he said. "Unless the intake pipes are clogged."

Kid looked up at Croix with a rumpled forehead, "Intake *what?*"

"I'm sure they're fine," Croix said. "Your turn, Gin. Get on down there."

Gin was hovering over the open hatch and looking down with caution in her eyes. But it wasn't the safe room itself that had her in such a state of reluctance.

Kid shouted up, "Alright, Gin. Come on down." He looked curiously excited, his ignorance as blissful as ever.

Gin wasn't too thrilled to be locking herself in a room alone with a pubescent teen that seemed all too eager to share the tight space with her.

Croix nodded. "It's alright, Gin. You won't be down there for long. Not long enough to do any harm anyway."

She sighed and began her reluctant descent down the ladder, steadying herself on the metal rungs. Kid reached up to offer a helping hand, and inexplicably placed both of them right on her ass.

She smacked his hands away," What the hell, Kid?"

"Sorry," he said, looking embarrassed. "I wasn't aiming or anything. My hands just sorta went that way."

Gin rolled her pretty eyes. "I don't need your help. Get

away." She finished her climb down and shoved Kid aside like the unbearable nuisance that he was. She looked around the room with a curious eye. She'd never been down there before. Two years and three months living in Revival and not once had she seen the inside of the safe room. It was furnished with nine bunk beds, stacked by threes in a small sleeping area just behind the ladder. On the other side of the ladder, in the compact living space, was an old leather couch with holes in it and a queen bed with no linens. She looked at Kid uncomfortably, and he returned the same uneasy look. They both diverted their eyes away from the bed.

Croix reassured them, "You'll be safe down there. Don't you worry."

The Revivalists kept the safe room well-stocked, in the event of an emergency, which in their experience never announced itself. There was enough survival gear and tangible goods inside to get them through a week or two if necessary, and possibly a month if there were only a few people to accommodate and feed. They had a microwave, pots and pans, a pump sink, and cabinets filled with canned food and several jugs of drinking water. There were storage compartments hidden beneath the bunkbeds filled with rope, candles, a first aid kit, and several jars of medicinal herbs. The small bathroom had a hand-pumped toilet and a solar shower with just enough water to last a week. The large gun safe was stocked with guns and ammunition. Elmer's HAM radio was sitting on the desk with more than enough power to reach the other colonies. The solar battery bank next to it could store enough juice to power the safe room for a month. There was even a periscope that could be raised up to ground level to survey the area before they climbed out. They'd thought of every precaution.

But to really ensure the secrecy of the underground safe

room, they'd built another 'faux" safe room on the other side of Revival. An old yellow school bus that was dug into the ground decades before and compacted by the earth on three sides. They left it partially exposed. Just enough to draw curious minds. There was a poorly hidden ladder that led down to the rear door of the bus, which was the only entrance. Inside of the bus were some worthless items that would appear worthy to anyone else. A few old guns stuffed in a wooden crate, some dented cans of food, a jug of water that they often replenished just to keep up the appearance of freshness, some redundant medicinal tools, and a kerosene lantern that was half-filled. The ruse looked authentic enough. The thinking was if anyone raided their compound, the raiders would think the buried school bus was the only bunker in Revival, so they wouldn't snoop around for the real one. But they'd never had to test the validity of that theory until now.

Everyone gathered at the firepit and argued over who belonged underground and who should stand and face the border patrols with the rest of them.

Tavo was looking anxious. "The women need to be underground," he said. "All four of 'em. No questions asked."

"I agree," Croix said.

Memphis puffed up defiantly. "No. I'm not going in that safe room."

"You have to," Tavo said. "This ain't no time to be prideful, woman."

"No," Memphis demanded. "And it ain't pride."

"Memphis, please. I won't be able to stand aside and watch them hurt you."

"It ain't gonna look right. Nothing but men living here?"

"Who cares what it looks like? I don't want you hurt. Those bastards hurt women. Some of them do much worse. If they so much as look at you the wrong way I swear I'll lose my mind."

"It just ain't gonna look right," Memphis insisted. "A bunch of men living in this place with no women? They won't buy that. They're gonna search the place, and they're gonna find our things. They'll know there's women here. Then they'll search us out, and you know damn well they'll find us, and then they'll punish everyone here just for lying to 'em. And it won't be no simple punishment either."

"Shit," Croix said. "She's right."

"No she ain't." Tavo pleaded. "Memphis, you gotta go in the safe room. Please."

Memphis grabbed his hand softly. "Tavo, you know I'm right."

"No, baby. Please. I can't... you no I can't..."

She pulled him closer. "This has always been the plan if something like this ever happened. Stick to the plan."

"Memphis, no... you can't..."

"I'll be okay. I promise." She embraced her man, her disarming eyes speaking to him more effectively than words. "Who's to say it's gonna go the way you fear it will? They could hurt you just as easily as they hurt me." Her eyes turned to unbreakable stone. "I'm not going in that safe room."

Tavo stood there in silent protest, knowing he had no chance of breaking through.

Croix placed a hand on his shoulder. "She's right, Tavo. I hate to side against you, but she *is* right."

Tavo softened his posture, as if he were accepting the indisputable reality.

Then Ru gave his orders. "Only Gin and Kid in the safe room. Everyone else needs to stay above ground. That's how it's gonna be."

"Zee needs to be in that safe room, too," Croix said.

Tavo looked back at him with anger. "That ain't fair."

"She's pregnant," Croix said. "Whatcha think they're gonna do when they see there's a baby in her belly?"

Memphis nodded, "He's right, Tavo. Zee needs to hide."

Tavo looked at her disagreeably.

"She's got a baby inside of her," she said, looking conflicted by her own emotions. "My womb is empty."

"What does that matter?" Tavo asked.

"She'll be a target."

"No. This just ain't fair."

"Not everything is equal, Tavo. She'll be a target and you know it." She looked at him with her soft brown eyes.

After a stubborn moment he finally surrendered to her logic. "I'm sorry," he said. "My emotions got the best of me."

She kissed him on the cheek. "Your emotions *are* the best of you."

"Alright," Croix said. "No time for tenderness." Then he and Ru walked back to the open hatch and looked down at Kid.

"Stay put down there," Ru said. "No exceptions." He looked at Gin. "Make sure he stays put."

Gin nodded and said, "No exceptions."

Kid looked anxious. "Ya'll gonna fight 'em, Ru?"

"No," Ru said. "We can't fight the border patrol. If we do, hundreds more will come. They'll kill us all."

Kid looked away, probably pondering his own death.

"It's best we all stay calm and do as they say," Ru ordered. He turned his eyes on Croix, who was always the first to pick a fight in any situation. "That means you too."

Croix nodded, acknowledging the need for restraint. But Ru didn't seem too convinced. Croix already had a protective look in his eyes. He always had a preemptive scheme of vengeance. A readiness to retaliate at the first hint of injustice.

That's who he was. So Ru didn't exactly trust his ability to remain unprovoked. Nobody did. No more than they trusted a live wire not to shock the shit out of them. Croix was ruled by his rage, and when his rage was provoked, it was deadly to everyone. That's another reason they all agreed that Zee should be in the safe room. Her presence would be provocative, in more ways than one.

Kid raised his eyes at Croix. "How do you know they ain't gonna kill ya'll anyway?"

"They'll kill *you* if they find you. That's a guarantee. So stay down in the safe room with Gin until we say otherwise. You understand?"

Kid nodded. "I'll protect Gin. Don't you worry."

Gin rolled her eyes. "What about Zee?"

Croix looked to Zee's cabin. His stomach was already twisting into painful knots. "Don't worry about Zee. She's *my* problem."

Zee was kneeling at her daybed with her pregnant belly pressed against the side of the mattress and her hands pressed together in prayer. A tattered Bible lay face up on the ruffled sheet in front of her. She whispered to God, and it sounded like a huddle of angry hornets protecting their nest.

Then Croix barged into the cabin with a duffel bag. "Zee, we gotta get you to the safe room."

But Zee was lost in her whispered prayer, saying, "Oh that you would bless me—"

"Zee, stop talking to yourself and help me hide this stuff."

Zee didn't budge. Croix started gathering any valuables he could find in the kitchen. A few vital tools that Zee used for crafting, a loaded handgun that she always kept in her kitchen drawer, and anything that could be seen as contraband or considered dangerous by the border patrol. He shoved it all into the duffel bag. "Zee, come on."

But Zee just kept praying with a whisper, "Please be with me. In all that I do."

"Goddammit, Zee! Get your ass up and help me!"

Then her whispering plea turned to a combative shout, "*and keep me from all trouble and pain!*"

Croix charged at her and grabbed her by the arm. "*Damnit, Zee! Get up!*"

She slapped his hand away. "*Don't you touch me.*" She rose to her feet and met him eye to eye, her pregnant belly brushing up against the cold buckle of his belt.

Croix dropped the duffel bag at his feet. "There ain't nobody out there listening to your bullshit prayers. I can tell you better than anyone that God's book is empty. It's just a bunch of meaningless words. You're praying to a void. Look around you. *This* is the world we live in. It's meaningless and cruel and it's about to come crashing down on us when the border patrol gets here."

She pushed him away. "Don't talk to me like I don't know the world." She stood tall with her chin up and her eyes matching wits with his. "I know the world. I just ain't afraid of it."

"Because you think it's changed. But you ain't been out there in so long."

"You think I forgot?"

"I guess maybe you did. When you live this long behind fortified walls it's easy to forget."

Zee's lip began to quiver. "As long as I can see my own reflection, I'll never have that luxury."

"Then *why*, Zee?"

"Why *what? Why bring a child into this world?* Is that what this is about?"

Croix looked at the floor. "Forget it. I knew it would turn into this."

"There you go again. Ready to turn heel and run. You'd like to forget everything, wouldn't you?"

"Don't, Zee."

"You still can't forgive yourself, can you?"

"I'm warning you, Zee. Stop this."

"Because it's life, Croix. That's *why*. It's meant to be. I won't lose faith in that just because you have."

"Don't you fucking lecture me on faith." His face turned to a bitter cringe. "You can't just pick a book up off the shelf and call yourself a believer."

She shoved him away again. "You're just scared to be a daddy. Because you're afraid to love someone again."

Then his fury rippled across his face like a doomsday tsunami. "You ain't no saint. You're only doing this 'cause you're lonely, and you think that baby's gonna bring me closer. But it ain't."

Zee went quiet, her body perfectly still but trembling. "You goddamn coward." She hit him in the chest, with a reckless burst of grief, striking him repeatedly with the meaty undersides of her fists.

He struggled to keep her swinging arms at bay. "Stop, Zee."

She swung wildly as the baby kicked inside of her. "You're nothing but a goddamn coward, Croix. You fucking *coward*."

Croix grabbed her by her elbows and squeezed her arms against her sides, pressing them tightly to her body and forcing her into submission. "Enough!" She tried to break free, but he overpowered her. "Stop playin' the martyr, Zee. You ain't going through all this for *her*. You're only doing it for *yourself*. And she's gonna fucking *hate* you for it."

Zee gasped. Her body froze. The word *hate* had punctured her armor, and now her body was ossifying, as if a knife had struck her right in the heart. She went limp and sunk through Croix's arms and her knees crashed to the hardwood floor.

Croix didn't bother to break her fall. He just stood over her and drove his point into her brain like a nail being hammered into a warning sign. "This world ain't no place for a little girl, and you know it. She's gonna be a target her whole goddamn life, and I won't be able to protect her. That ain't no kinda life worth living. And you wanna bring her into *that*?"

Zee couldn't even look at him. All she could do was cry. Her ears were throbbing. The internal buzzsaw of her own corrupted thoughts were cutting her mind in half.

Croix backed away as if he couldn't stand to see her weeping so pathetically. His eyes shifted, looking anywhere but at the mess he'd just made. He grabbed the duffel bag and gazed at her once more with sorrow in his eyes. The words he'd chosen were weaponized and cruel, and she had been massacred by them. But he offered no remorse. "Get up and get to that safe room," he said, and then he stormed off, lugging the duffel bag and trampling down the steps of the front porch with his mind on protecting their home.

Zee was splayed out on the floor like human remains waiting to be buried, and that's just how she felt. Like death without dying. A soulless vessel. Everything went blank inside of her. An emptiness that she'd never felt before. She imagined it was how Croix must've felt about life. A nihilistic void. That's when she realized that Croix would never want their child, and for the first time since being pregnant she truly felt stripped of her maternal glory, as if bringing a child into the world was somehow evil or selfish. A cruel act blinded by righteousness. She just wanted to crawl inside of her own belly and wrap her arms around her unborn child and weep. She needed her child to know that she was wanted, and she wanted to feel needed by her child. It was something that Croix would never understand. Maybe no one in Revival could understand anymore. Their spark of life had gone out. They'd all gone cold long ago. But Zee could still feel the flame burning inside, even as she lay there completely void of everything else. *I'll be damned if I let Croix extinguish that*, she thought. She rose to her feet, her emerald green eyes shining defiantly through the murkiness of her tears. She was determined to prove the impossible. She was going to bring light into their darkened world, even if she was the only one who could see it.

Then as she hustled to the door, she heard the unmistakeable sound of a hovership approaching from the south, the rotary blades swooshing vulgarly and echoing throughout the foothills, announcing itself like the seven trumpets of Hell. It was followed by the desperate ringing of the emergency bell in the crow's nest. Her eyes swelled with panic. She thought about God again. But it was too late for divine intervention. The border patrol was already there.

# TWENTY-THREE

*"Hovership,"* Wade shouted from the crow's nest. *"They're here!"*

The hovership kicked up dust in the valley like a sandstorm, and as the metal bird grew larger on the horizon, Wade dropped the rifle from his shoulder and slid down the long emergency pole. "It's border patrol! They're here!"

---

Croix stood over the open hatch of the underground safe room looking unprepared for what came next. He tossed the duffel bag down to Kid, who caught the bag and handed it off to Gin and looked back up at Croix and asked, "What's gonna happen now?"

"Nothing good," Croix admitted. He looked to Zee's cabin. There was no sign of her, and no time left to wait. "Goddamnit, Zee." He knew she wouldn't make it to the safe room in time, and he had no choice but to accept that now. His stomach began to churn. A helpless feeling in his gut that he'd felt once before, a long time ago. He knew he wouldn't be able to protect her. He looked down at Kid and Gin with a tyranny in his eyes and said, "Don't come out until we say." He slammed the hatch shut and hid the access point with the grill-top. The hovership floated overhead, casting a dark shadow over Revival. He turned and saw Zee staggering out of her cabin, her pregnant belly protruding through her tight shirt and looking unavoidably provocative.

Ru turned to the Revivalists as they gathered around him. "No reactions. No retaliation. Keep your wits. With any luck, we'll get through this unharmed."

They stood together in the open, unarmed with their hands held high to show they were no threat. They watched in fear as the large cargo door at the rear of the hovership lowered and transformed into a ramp. The border patrols walked down the platform with their BP15 assault rifles eager to lay waste. Their Captain was at the forefront, his depraved reputation preceding him.

His name was Captain James Elias Vedder, and everything about him was dark and unsettling. His cropped hair, which was shaved close to the skin. His manic eyes that seemed anxious to hurt someone. The cruel heart beating in his chest, which could somehow be seen by everyone. His intentions were darkest of all, and they were made obvious by the unmistakable look of sadism on his face. A satisfied grin usually reserved for devils and unconscionable monsters. But he was a man of flesh and blood, in his mid thirties, and looking far more weathered and spiteful than his age should've allowed. His face was grizzled like purple mincemeat. There were old burn scars and fresh claw marks on his chin from the scraping of human nails. Some poor victim that was probably dead or dying inside. He walked with boastful pride, as if his presence was something to behold, and why not? He was the leader of the most feared platoon of border patrols in the Rim: *The Warhawks*.

Usually there was an entire platoon of them, but not today. For the past few months a large portion of the Warhawks had been on mining and recovery ops on the east coast. So today there were only seven of them, though that was seven too many. They were dressed in dark olive green fatigues and battle gear, and armed with every Nimbus-issued weapon they could carry. Ballistic helmets, knee guards, elbow pads, military boots, automatic rifles and tactical belts adorned with shock sticks, collars, handguns and sharpened tactical knives that carried many dark secrets. The patch on their chest was emblazoned with the image of an Indian war bonnet, surrounded by orange windswept hawk feathers which encompassed the words *Warhawks* and *Outpost 11*. Below that was the wantonly boastful claim: *In Nimbus We Trust, Never We Fail*. Warhawks had no limits. Truth was, border patrols were just thugs with badges, and the Warhawks were the worst of the breed.

Captain Vedder snickered, "Revival, huh? Ya'll outlaws sure got a sense of humor. I'll give you that. This shit hole looks in need of a complete resuscitation."

His accent was backwoods hillbilly. His words were slightly mispronounced and delivered with a muddy twang. He hocked up some deeply-seeded hatred and spit the phlegm on the ground. He slammed his fists together, rolling them around bone on bone, as if he were charging a pair of electrified paddles on a defibrillator. But this wouldn't be a resuscitation. He had the opposite in mind.

Ru approached cautiously, dragging the damaged

boomerang drone in the dirt behind him. "We have your drone, sir. This was a terrible misunderstanding."

"Where's the boy?" Captain Vedder asked, looking eager to use his knuckles. "The boy from the drone footage. Where the fuck is he?"

"We sent him on his way. He was nothing but trouble."

"You still gotta pay for what he done." Captain Vedder turned to the Warhawks. "That little shit is here somewhere. *Search the place.*"

The Warhawks dispersed throughout Revival, their BP15 assault rifles ready to squash any surprise attacks they may encounter. One of the patrols snatched the damaged boomerang drone away from Ru and dragged it back to the hovership.

Captain Vedder took inventory of the Revivalists as they stood in their orderly line, his bigoted eyes scrutinizing them one by one. His thick unibrow curled with suspicion. "Where's all your runts? Ya'll must have children. Ain't nothin' to do in this shit hole but fuck."

"We don't bear children here," Ru said, trying to sound obedient. "It's our law, sir."

"What'd you call me? I work for a living, you cocksucker. It's *Captain* Vedder. Captain James Elias Vedder."

"I'm sorry, Captain. I meant no disrespect."

Then Captain Vedder spotted Zee, his dark eyes wandering down to her pregnant belly. "You don't bear children, huh? What's that bitch got cooking in there? A mother fucking rat?"

"That baby was an accident," Ru said. "Not something we wanted. But we're seeing it through."

"I don't like being lied to," Captain Vedder said. His eyes flickered with bad intentions. He turned to his Warhawks and said, "These rats need a lesson in proper manners. How they gonna learn that?" He turned back to Ru. "Tell you what… let's break some shit."

"No," Ru pleaded. "Captain, please. Don't do this. It's not necessary."

Captain Vedder drew his sidearm and shoved it into Ru's cheekbone. "Don't get in my fucking way, outlaw, or I'll turn you inside out."

Ru raised his hands carefully. "We're not outlaws, Captain. We make our own way out here in the valley. We're not a part of the black market. We don't have ties to the Bloody Knuckles. None of that. We've shown no disrespect to Nimbus."

"Maybe you didn't understand me." Captain Vedder whacked him in the head with the butt of his sidearm. "Is that more your language?"

Ru staggered backwards, his hand held to his throbbing head. He sensed Croix and the others moving behind him. He knew they'd be tempted to retaliate on his behalf, so he held his other hand up and quietly ordered them to stay calm and let things play out.

Croix grabbed Zee by the arm, and with a subtle motion he pulled her behind him and guarded her pregnant belly. She didn't resist him. She clutched her hand to his arm tightly and secured herself at his back.

Then, like a colony of killer ants, the Warhawks began their purge of Revival, setting out to destroy anything of value, as a punishment for destroying the Nimbus Corporation's boomerang drone. The punishment wasn't equal to the crime, but justice never mattered to the Warhawks. It was about sending a message, just like Ru had said, and these Warhawks were always the corporation's bloodiest messengers. They were young, mostly in their early twenties, and full of blind loyalty. Kassab — a tall sprout of middle-eastern descent whom they lovingly called the *Turban Cowboy* — was the first and only lieutenant. Captain Vedder didn't bother to name a second. Cooley and Chant — two young rambunctious bucks with bleach blonde hair that could've passed for twins — were the master sergeants. They looked like beachcombers, but they'd never actually seen a beach in their lives. Darko and Povich were the pure grunts of the litter, or privates as they were ranked, and they were both still earning their stripes in Captain Vedder's eyes. The more heads they busted, the bigger those stripes got. Then there was the greenhorn, who hadn't even earned the *consideration* of respect among the Warhawks. He was their probationary officer. A newbie. His name was Riley Greenberg. A fitting surname. They called him Greenie, and they treated him like the numbskull rookie he was. Only eighteen years old and still wet behind the ears. The gig didn't come easy to him. After he had flunked out of the Law Enforcement Academy in his first semester, he'd been thrown into the fire at Outpost 11 in the Mojave. Now he was being burned alive. Initiated. A year-long assault of verbal insults, bullying, belittling, and sabotaging, all of which was still going strong.

"*Greenie,*" Captain Vedder shouted. "I want your hands covered in blood this time. And I don't mean your *own.*"

Greenie followed his orders without question. He followed the Warhawks as they stormed the compound, slithering about like something covered in scales, turning their vile intentions on anything that looked valuable, or anything that looked like it would be fun to destroy. They busted up the communications hub, taking their batons to Elmer's precious equipment, smashing the electronics and machinery, in particular a HAM radio, which fortunately was just a non-working decoy. The real one was currently hiding in the underground safe room. Sparks flew like fireworks as the Warhawks took out their dick-swinging rage on several inanimate objects. The little colorful blips and blinks on the HAM radio ceased to blip and blink. They shot at the greenhouse, blasting tiny 9mm holes through the glass. They dotted the plastic sheeting on the hoop houses, laughing and wasting ammo for their own amusement. They set fire to the crops in the garden and watched the precious sustenance burn to a worthless crisp. They raided the cabins and trashed the interiors, ripping cushions from the beds and stabbing them with knives and pulling the crow feathers from the pillows and tossing it around at each other like snow, laughing like school children all the while. They smashed plates and pottery and shattered windows and howled, all while ruining someone else's livelihood. They found the "faux" safe room that was buried partially in the ground. The old yellow school bus.

Cooley smirked victoriously and spoke into his comms, "Cap, we found their safe room. No one here. But there's a crate of weapons."

"Destroy it," Captain Vedder said. "The whole fucking thing."

The Warhawks busted the windows of the bus with the butt of their rifles and kicked the crate of weapons over on its side, spilling them onto the floor. Cooley shattered the old kerosene lantern and stepped outside and tossed a match, setting the entire bus on fire. It went up in flames. They watched and howled and nearly soiled themselves with excitement. Then they turned their eyes on the power station. The source for the electric fence. The hub for the solar panels. Revival's security system. It was the perfect target to send a message.

"Bullseye," Kassab said. He spoke into his helmet comms. "Cap, you're gonna love this."

Captain Vedder approached and saw the main power station glowing in the sunlight like a cache of gold. "This oughta put their lights out for good," he said. "Destroy the fucker."

The Warhawks fired their rifles, blasting the solar panels, destroying the electrifying properties of the photovoltaics, and setting Revival back two and a half decades, to the time of the Collapse when power was nearly impossible to come by. Without the solar panels, there would be no electric. Without electric, there would be no security fence. Without the security fence, there would be no restful nights. No one would be safe.

Ru pleaded, "Captain… *sir*… please… is this really necessary? We're cooperating. There's no resistance from us."

Captain Vedder ignored him.

Ru could do nothing but watch helplessly as the young Warhawks continued to sabotage the power station, blasting holes in the electrical panel and ripping cables from their sockets.

"Please. Stop."

Captain Vedder laughed in victory. The Warhawks raised their rifles and blasted the generator and the car batteries, challenging one another to hit the *O* in the word *OPTIMA*, like young boys in the backyard with BB guns. Revival was no longer a fortress. Now it was free for the taking.

Once the power had been cut, the Warhawks went after the water, raising a few sledge hammers which they'd stolen from the tool shed. They bashed the posts that were holding up the wooden aqueduct. The posts cracked and gave way under the weight and the aqueduct collapsed, crashing down like a devastating tidal wave.

The Revivalists stood there gasping. Thousands of gallons of water flooded the ground around them. The force almost knocked them down as it washed over their feet like the Ganges. They'd have no fresh water for drinking now except for what they'd hidden in jugs.

Captain Vedder watched in amusement. His Warhawks were making a beautiful mess of things. "I'm so fucking proud of you, Warhawks. Flawless. Fucking *flawless*."

———

Underground in the safe room, Kid and Gin heard the unsettling commotion above. They knew the thundering crash had been the aqueduct coming down.

Kid pulled his .380 pocket pistol from the waistband of his pants. "I gotta do something." He started climbing up the ladder without a second thought.

Gin grabbed his leg. "No, stupid. You'll get us killed."

"They need my help."

"No, you fool," Gin said, clawing at his pant leg, "You can't even help *yourself*."

Kid stopped. The sails of his ship had suddenly collapsed. The wind at his back a deadly calm. Gin had called him out for what he always knew he was: a worthless little shit.

———

Cooley and Chant approached Captain Vedder with news of their search. "There's no sign of the boy," Cooley said. "No sign of any children at all."

Then Greenie — the nervous rookie — spoke out of turn, saying, "Maybe these people are telling the truth, Captain."

Captain Vedder turned to him in utter disbelief. "What the fuck'd you just say?"

"Maybe they don't have any children here. It's not unthinkable, is it?"

Captain Vedder charged at him, stopping just inches from his face and poking him viscously in the chest with his finger.

"Greenie, when I want your opinion, I'll shove it down your fucking throat and have you regurgitate it back to me word for word. Now shut your rookie cockhole and burn their fucking storehouse down… *now*."

Greenie gulped at the order, which seemed like a petty act of vengeance to him.

"*Torch it*," Captain Vedder shouted. "Burn the mother fucker down!"

Greenie swung the torch gun into position and took aim at the storehouse.

Ru stepped forward and pleaded, "Captain, Please. We make our own way out here. We don't trouble the corporation for anything. We're not with the black market."

Captain Vedder spun around and punched him in the gut and grabbed him by the neck and forced him to his knees. He put the gun to Ru's head and grabbed him by the chin and forced his eyes on the storehouse. "You're gonna watch it burn, you fucking rat."

"Please," Ru pleaded desperately. "That's our survival. It's everything we have."

Captain Vedder turned to Greenie, who had yet to pull the trigger. "Goddamnit, greenhorn, torch the fucking place already!"

Then Wade limped forward and shouted, "*Wait*. I know where the kid is. *Stop*. I'll tell you where he is."

Greenie took his finger off the trigger.

Captain Vedder turned to Wade. "It don't matter now." He turned back to Greenie. "Burn it down."

Wade rushed towards him. "*Wait*. The kid's *here*! I can show you where he is!"

Captain Vedder spun back around and aimed his gun at Wade. "I said it don't fucking *matter*. Get back in line with the other rats."

Wade stood there baffled, his arms dangling hopelessly.

"This is on *all ya'll*," Captain Vedder declared. "So *you're all* gonna be punished for it. I don't care about that little fuckface kid. Ya'll are the ones in charge, ain't ya? So I'm gonna make sure ya'll remember the Warhawks." He turned to Greenie again. "Greenhorn, for the last fucking time… *burn it down!*"

Greenie pulled the trigger and the flame launched from the torch gun like a jet engine firing up, and the cottonwood storehouse went up in flames.

The Revivalists watched in horror, the fiery blaze reflecting in their outstretched eyes. Croix took an angry step forward. Tavo grabbed him by the shoulder. "Don't, Croix. No."

Croix looked back at him, his eyes darkened by a blank desire for vengeance, and then he looked at the others and they all shook their heads in unison. There was no way through this madness but obedience and mercy, and the hope that one would inspire the other. Croix took a furious breath to calm himself, and then he stepped back in line.

# TWENTY-FOUR

When Greenie took his finger off the trigger the flame returned to the barrel of the torch gun like a candle being doused by a birthday wish. He watched squeamishly as the fire consumed the storehouse and all the life-saving sustenance that was hidden inside, the smoke billowing into a dark cloud of cruelty. He looked back at the Revivalists and offered a silent apology. He panned around at Captain Vedder, who had just witnessed his weak-hearted gesture.

Captain Vedder spit in the dirt and snarled. "Good work, Greenie. These people will hate you forever now. You may prove to be a Warhawk yet."

Greenie's eyes dropped in shame.

Then Kassab approached them with excitement, holding something in his hand. "Cap, look what we found."

Captain Vedder's face turned to stone.

Croix turned to stone too.

Kassab was holding the black *Dagger & Son* flag that Croix had taken back from the kid. The mythical emblem was now an outlawed piece of defiance, and the skull was glaring right at Captain Vedder, as if Billy Dagger himself were taunting him from the grave.

Croix felt a sudden remorse. He'd forgotten to hide the flag properly in the midst of all the chaos, and he knew there'd be hell to pay.

Captain Vedder snatched the flag away. "What the hell is this? Where'd ya'll get this shit? This is a goddamn lie. *All lies*, ya hear me? Fucking lies." He pulled a match from his pocket and struck the phosphorous head. "Billy Dagger *don't exist*. He *never did*. Ya'll are living in a fucking fantasy. This ain't that red, white and blue world." He put the flag to the fire. "This is the *Blaze*." He held the flag as the dull flame began to catch to the fabric and flicker at the bottom corner. "So I say… *let it all burn!*"

He dropped the flag on the ground to let it burn, in hopes of scorching it out of existence. That was his duty as a Warhawk. As a loyalist. The name Billy Dagger was an unspoken insult to his beloved corporation. A terrible lie told by outlaws to undermine Lucian Vanderbon's own heroism. He watched the tiny orange flame dance and flicker, and his eyes danced and flickered with it, but as the corners of his mouth rose up and began to form a pitiless grin, the flame suddenly lost its verve and the bright orange flicker became a dull, yellow glow no brighter than a firefly in the daylight. The fire went dead, as if it were blown out by some phantom breath. The flag sat there on the ground completely untarnished. The menacing skull was glaring at him with ghostly orbits, challenging him from the grave. He rocked backwards on his heels, looking spooked, as if Billy Dagger himself had just whispered in his ear.

"What the *fuck*…" he muttered. "Fucking thing…" He reached down and yanked the flag from the ground and tried to strike another match, but the red phosphorous head wouldn't ignite. He tried again and again, but it wouldn't spark. He threw the match in the dirt and snarled at the flag and shrieked, *"You piece of shit,"* and then he tossed it on the ground and stomped on it with his military boots, digging the rigid soles into the fabric with all his might and trying to shred the flag with his own bitter wrath.

It didn't work.

He turned and gleamed at the Revivalists. "Oh now I'm pissed, you rotten sons a bitches." He turned to the Warhawks and ordered them to, "Collar 'em! Every single one! Choke the fucking life out of 'em!"

The young Warhawks pulled their metal shock collars from their tactical belts.

The Revivalists had never worn a Nimbus shock collar before, but they'd heard terrible rumors about the torturous device, and they'd rightly feared it. It was a flexible coiled necklace that fit loosely around a violators neck and was tightened when prompted by a button via remote control. Once the shock collar was tightened in place, the Warhawk holding the remote control could press a button and send enough volts of electricity into the violator's body to make a grown man shit himself. The unfortunate soul wearing the collar would drop to their knees and suffer an unbearable sting. The zap wouldn't paralyze them like a shock stick would, but it hurt like hell, and that was usually an effective deterrent. No one at Revival wanted to wear a shock collar willingly, but they had no choice. They stood perfectly still as the Warhawks placed the collars around their sweaty necks. The coiled necklaces tightened around their throats. Tight enough to discourage any instinct of retaliation.

"It's time I punish ya'll proper," Captain Vedder declared, his eyes turning from sadism to something beyond. He spun his head around. *"Greenie!* Grab a stinger from the hovership."

Greenie didn't move. He seemed baffled by the order he'd just been given.

"A stinger, Greenie. *Now*."

Greenie snapped from his bewilderment and ran to the hovership in a hurry, scuttling up the ramp in fear.

Kassab stepped forward, "Captain, are you sure we should—"

"Who the fuck asked for your opinion?" Captain Vedder stared him down. "You're as bad as the greenhorn."

"Cap," Cooley said hesitantly. "This… Maybe we should—"

"Another asshole with an opinion?" Captain Vedder clenched his crooked teeth. "Shut your fucking mouth, *Sergeant*, and follow my orders." He turned to the hovership. "Greenie, move your ass with that stinger."

Croix looked at Ru and then Ru looked at everyone else. They'd never heard of a *stinger* before. But they were sure it would be unimaginably cruel, whatever it was.

Ru tried to settle the rising tension. "Captain, we mean no disrespect to Nimbus. We hold onto our memories for comfort. Nothing more."

"Memories?"

"We're no threat to the Republic, sir."

"I decide if you're a threat," Captain Vedder's dark eyes were narrow strips of depravity. He looked to Zee and pointed to her pregnant belly. "*That's* a threat." He pulled his tactical knife, and the serrated blade glistened in the valley sun. "I should cut that little rat out of your fucking gut."

Suddenly Croix rushed forward on instinct, his fists balled up like concrete blocks. "Leave her alone!"

The Warhawks grabbed him by the arms and pulled him backwards. Cooley pressed the button on the remote control in his hand and Croix's shock collar was suddenly engaged, shocking Croix mercilessly. His body stiffened in pain, and the Warhawks laughed as he fell to his knees.

Ru stepped forward, "Punish *me*. I'm the one in charge. Hurt *me*."

Captain Vedder ignored him, keeping his eyes on Croix, who was turning red in the face. Then he thrust the knife towards Zee's pregnant belly.

"No!" Croix shouted, trying to break free from the Warhawks. His eyes inflated like tiny white balloons.

Captain Vedder stopped short of Zee's belly, holding the tip of the blade less than an inch away from the unborn child inside of her. He beamed with satisfaction as he recognized Croix's protective instinct. "So… you must be the daddy?"

Ru closed his eyes and shook his head in distress. This was the very thing he feared would happen. Croix had fallen for the taunt.

"Take your hands off her," Croix growled. "Don't fucking touch her."

Ru could feel the other Revivalists wanting to engage, so he held his hand up like before, ordering them to stand down. They followed his order, but with a boiling hot rage in their eyes. They wanted to fight. Ru knew it. They didn't care about the shock collars that were wrapped tightly around their necks. The Warhawks would have to keep their fingers on the buttons to keep the electricity going. If the Revivalists attacked, the Warhawks would be occupied while trying to defend themselves. The Revivalists seemed to recognize that fact. Their eyes were sharp as tacks and their shoulders were pinned back, looking like a herd of angry buffalo that wanted to charge.

Croix pleaded with Captain Vedder. "Please. Leave her alone." His voice sounded weak and uncharacteristically pathetic. "I'm begging you."

Captain Vedder delighted in the pitiful desperation.

"Please don't hurt her," Croix said breathlessly.

Captain Vedder chuckled and slowly lifted Zee's shirt over her swollen belly and pressed the hot blade harder to her skin. She winced as it dug into her flesh.

"No!" Croix tried to break free again, but the Warhawks piled on top of him.

Captain Vedder began to slice Zee's belly, drawing blood in a dark crimson line across her navel. She wept aloud.

"*Stop*," Croix shrieked, his eyes soft like a beggar. "Look at me, Captain. I'm asking you… man to man… just please… leave her alone."

"Okay," Captain Vedder said with a sudden display of diplomacy. "If you say so." He slid the bloody knife into the sheath on his tactical belt. Then he drew his sidearm. A nickel-plated BP9 handgun chambered in 9mm with a twenty-round magazine. He aimed the pistol at Croix and said, "She'll be alone now."

Then Zee shouted, "No!", and she reached out for Croix.

Captain Vedder chuckled again and rolled his eyes theatrically. "You're an indecisive bunch."

Then Greenie came running down the ramp of the hover-ship with something in his hand and apprehension in his eyes. "Sir, are you sure about this?"

"Shut up, rookie." Captain Vedder snatched the mysterious object from his hand.

Kassab and Cooley traded looks, failing to keep their own apprehension veiled.

Captain Vedder opened his hand for the Revivalists to see the cruel fate that awaited their pregnant friend. It was a needle, attached to a glass vial that was filled with some strange gold-colored liquid. "This is for the disrespect to Nimbus," he said. "Time to pick the winner."

Croix's face went flush.

"Somebody's gotta be punished," Captain Vedder said as he eyed them all. "Who's it gonna be?" He turned his beaming eyes on Ru first, and then he looked at the others, sizing them up one after another as they stood in their row of obedience. "Decisions… Decisions…" He removed his grimy hand from Zee's arm and let her go. He tucked the needle and syringe into his pocket and walked up and down the row of Revivalists. He looked at Tavo and ran his hand across his bicep, tightening his fingers around his bulging black muscle. "Strong boy," he said. "I'd hate to be on your bad side."

Then he turned to Memphis and cozied up to her, pressing himself against her sweaty body. He ran his grimy fingers across the top of her chest, collecting the sweat that was running down into the space between her breasts. "Gotta admit," he said. "I've always had a thing for dark chocolate. There's just something about that bittersweet taste." Then he licked the side of her face, his tongue a slobbering assault, while keeping his eyes directly on Tavo.

Tavo trembled with a molten rage and his lips curled inward as his fist began to ball. Memphis quickly halted him with a shake of her head and hard look. It took a moment for Tavo to back down, but he did. His body kept trembling though. His eyes were focused on Memphis and Captain Vedder's fingers, which were now running along the curves of her hips and down the middle of her backside. Captain Vedder kept his eyes on Tavo as he caressed Memphis and reached his hand up between her legs.

Tavo took an unsettling breath.

Memphis closed her eyes and stiffened her body and took what she was given, knowing that any looks of uneasiness would trigger Tavo's instinct to protect her.

Captain Vedder stared at Tavo, hoping the strong black boy would give him a reason to put him down. But Tavo never blinked. Captain Vedder was vexed. He jerked his hand away from Memphis, no longer interested in his bittersweet treat. He turned his attention on the others, looking for another target. He looked at Skinny and snickered. "You ain't nothin but a bag of fucking bones." He turned to Hickory and said, "You should already be in a hole in the ground." He looked at Elmer and said nothing. He just shook his head and laughed at his unshapely state. He looked at Teardrop and said, "I ain't that desperate." Then he walked back to Zee, making sure that each step he took was a slow, agonizing torment.

Croix was still being held down by the Warhawks.

Captain Vedder grabbed Zee and pulled her close and patted her pregnant belly softly. Then he looked directly in Croix's eyes and said, "Tell you what… I'll make the decision for you." He grabbed Zee by the back of the neck and forced her down to her knees and pressed the gun to her head to keep her there and declared, "*She's the chosen one.*"

Croix lunged forward to fight, but his body was quickly overtaken by the Warhawks again. They pressed him into the dirt on his stomach. He craned his neck upwards, straining to keep his eyes on Zee. "Don't you hurt her. Please don't hurt her."

Captain Vedder holstered his BP9 handgun and said, "You mean like this?" He slapped her across the face, slowly and dramatically, coming down fast and hard on her swollen cheekbone, again and again. CRACK. CRACK. CRACK.

"*Stop,*" Croix shouted. "You fucking coward! Fight *me*! I'm here! Fight *me*, mother fucker! Fight *me*!"

Captain Vedder stopped and smiled fiendishly. "I'm a compassionate man. If you don't want me to hurt her, fine. I won't." He pulled the needle and syringe from his pocket. "This won't hurt a bit. At least not for a while."

"What is that?" Croix asked as he tried to break free from the Warhawks. "What's in there, goddamnit? *What is it?*"

Captain Vedder squeezed a drop of liquid out of the hypodermic needle. The droplet hit the dirt and bubbled up. "It's her fate," he said. "Nimbus controls it."

"Please," Croix winced. "Whatever you're thinking of doing… please don't do it."

"*We* decide," Captain Vedder declared with a celebratory tone. "Not *you*." He pulled Zee closer to him, his grimy hand clutching her waistline as he pressed the needle softly against the skin of her belly.

"*Don't*," Croix tried to rise up again.

Cooley pressed the button on the remote control and the shock collar engaged, zapping Croix with 5,000 volts of electricity. He growled, but he never took his eyes off Zee. Captain Vedder drew back and brutally stabbed the needle into her belly with a loud, excruciating wallop. Zee winced and keeled over in pain, her scream like a wailing siren.

"No, you fucking coward!" Croix tried to break free from the Warhawks, ripping his arms away from their clutches as they pressed him into the dirt. "You mother fucker! I'm gonna kill you!" It took everything the Warhawks had to hold him down. Cooley pressed the button on the remote control again, but the shock collar had no effect. "I swear to fucking God, you coward! I'll fucking *kill you!*"

The young Warhawks could barely keep him down. He clawed and kicked and snapped his jaws at their flesh. Their bodies jostled and bounced around, as if they were wrestling with a wild mustang. They pulled their shock sticks from their holsters and zapped him with the crackling coils and he foamed at the mouth. It was more electricity than his adrenalized rage could tolerate. His eyes went blank, but still burning blue and dripping with tears. He convulsed from the shock and his body went limp, but his eyes didn't close. All he could do was lay there and watch as Captain Vedder emptied the syringe into Zee's pregnant belly. The golden liquid disappeared from the vile and flooded into Zee's bloodstream like water rushing over a broken levee.

Her eyes met Croix's in pity. Something familiar. A bad memory. Captain Vedder let her go. She slid onto the ground and held her hand over her belly, guarding the pierced shell of her womb, and she began to cry.

Croix just lay there helplessly.

Captain Vedder tossed the vial into the dirt and wiped his hands clean. He hopped to his feet and walked over to Croix and knelt down beside him. He reached out and grabbed a handful of Croix's hair and pulled his head up so their eyes met. "You don't have control, outlaw. Don't you forget that."

Croix was still paralyzed, unable to retaliate with anything more than a threatening glare, but even that was no longer electrified.

"Know your place," Captain Vedder said, "and stay the fuck in it." He slammed Croix's face into the dirt and held it there for a moment so Croix couldn't breathe. Then he let go and rose to his feet and boasted with Warhawk pride. "Do we have an understanding?" he asked the Revivalists.

Ru and the other Revivalists stood there in their tamed row of obedience, their bodies all but immovable. They all nodded. There was no choice but to hope and pray it was over.

Captain Vedder turned to his Warhawks and said, "Let's leave these outlaws to their memories. That's all they got left." He looked at Zee's belly. "They sure ain't got no future." He turned and laughed at Croix, who remained motionless on the ground. "You're in for a real surprise, outlaw. Too bad I won't be here to see it."

The Warhawks let Croix go, laughing at his sad state of paralysis.

Croix could feel the nerves in his body trying to speak to him, telling him to get up and crush Captain Vedder's skull with a loose rock or with the indisputable fury in his fists. But he couldn't lift a finger.

As Captain Vedder and the Warhawks boarded the hovership, they looked back and marveled at the mess they'd left behind. All except for Greenie, the rookie, who still had that same shameful look on his face. Captain Vedder put his arm around him and guided him onto the hovership. "You done good, rookie."

The side door closed behind them and the rotors began to spin. The dust swirled in spiraling torrents. A dark cloud of debris curled over Revival like an evil hand about to wrap its twisted fingers around them to squeeze.

Croix felt the tips of his own fingers coming back to life. He could almost make a fist. Then his forearms began to move, and then his shoulders began to loosen at the cuff. He pulled himself across the ground, army-crawling to Zee, who was panting in fear.

The hovership lifted off from the ground and flew away, dusting up the valley before disappearing on the southern horizon.

Croix pulled himself up to a sitting position and wrapped his arms around Zee, pulling her and their unborn child close to him. The feeling had returned to his limbs, but he couldn't feel her warmth. He could only feel her trembling. He held her as close as he could. His embrace was the only comfort he could offer.

She placed her arms around her pregnant belly, her hands cold with shock and shaking in the hot sun. Her imagination began to run wild. If she'd been infected with some kind of abortive drug, the baby's heart would stop beating at any moment. If it was something else, they might both die. She waited on bated breath, each second a harrowing eternity. The baby's heart never stopped, but Zee could feel her convulsing inside. Something was definitely wrong.

Croix looked at the vial that was left behind in the dirt. Captain Vedder's sweaty fingerprints were smeared all over the glass. It was labeled: *Oziacron 1374*. Croix didn't know what it meant, or what it was, but he knew it was meant to make them suffer.

Zee spoke to him through broken sobs, her eyes searching for his, "Croix, what'd they do to us?"

He couldn't answer her. He was too consumed by his own imagination. The worst possibilities were cutting through his mind like poisoned blades. For the first time he felt like a father, and the helplessness of that terrified him. He wondered what godawful torment awaited. That was all he could contemplate. The bleak, colorless thought of uncertainty. He pulled Zee closer to him, his arms tightening around her like a fortified wall.

Their eyes met with terror.

Their bodies trembled as one.

# TWENTY-FIVE

The people of the Blaze called themselves *Freelanders*, but nothing in their land was free. Everything had to be fought for and protected, and the good people of the Blaze had to risk their lives every single day just to keep what was rightfully theirs. The threats were constant. Desperate scavengers waiting to ambush them at every turn, from the shadows of a dark patch of trees, or from the crest of a sunken ravine with their thieving eyes on the prize, which was basically anything of value. Violent gangs roamed in half-crazed war parties, dressed in rags, searching for their next victims and stocking up on new recruits. They desired more than tangible goods. They wanted souls, and they wanted pledges, and if the good people of the Blaze refused, they'd be stabbed, beaten or shot into oblivion. But worse than gangs, there were more sophisticated criminals who'd organized their crimes and built shadowy enterprises to carry out their schemes. They'd established a powerful hold over the people of the territories, with the kind of ambush that was impossible to defend: political ties and power plays and unchecked exploitation. That included sex trafficking, extortion, arms dealing, drugs, coercion, racketeering and debt slavery. There was no universally accepted law in the Blaze, and no established order, and there was no organized enforcement of either. It was every man, woman and child for themselves. A fluid, unstable pecking order that seemed to change hands every few years. Though there was one organization that always had their hand in everything: the Bloody Knuckles. The most formidable enterprise in the Blaze. The controlling party of the territories, at least the western half, from the burnt Great Plains to the scattered beach colonies along the Pacific.

The Bloody Knuckles operated the black market trade network throughout the western colonies and ran their racket in the Brimstone refugee camp just outside of the Republic's border walls. Their operation was run like an old Wells Fargo Express, only they dealt in trade goods, not bank notes, mail or gold. But like the old wild west express, their operators transported their merchandise on horses and covered wagons and repurposed steam locomotives, crossing dangerous territory and crossing paths with scavengers and rival gangs that were waiting to ambush them at every turn. Freelanders lived like settlers in the twilight of the pre-industrial age. But not by choice. There were no working automobiles in the Blaze. There hadn't been for decades. Not since the *Blackout*.

After the Restoration wars, a series of explosions in the sky had created a massive electromagnetic pulse that knocked Freelanders right off the grid. Right off the roads too. It was the beginning of the Nimbus Corporation's *Transportation Control* campaign. Their aim was to limit the Freelander's ability to rise to power. It worked for a while. But the people of the Blaze were resourceful. They always found a way. Especially the Bloody Knuckles.

The organization was formed in '56 by the notorious guerrilla fighter Mannix Lightfoot, known to the world as Lord Mannix. The original "Liberty Boy" himself. The founding leader of the almighty Liberation Army. He'd risen to prominence among the independent militias in '49 after Billy Dagger's untimely death. His pompous war rhetoric had endeared him to the more fanatical members. He merged his own Liberty Boys with the Red Line of Peace, the Oath Keepers, the Southwestern Guard, and several other civilian forces, promising to liberate them all from Nimbus rule. When the bombings of '53 effectively ended their efforts, Lord Mannix was the first to sign the New World Order peace treaty between the Freelanders and the Nimbus Corporation. But he was also the first to break it.

Once the new order of things was established by the treaty, the people of the Blaze made their own way in the burning wilds, surviving on what nature could provide, and with what their own two hands could do with it. But for some, an honest living in the Blaze was harder than expected and much easier to exploit. It wasn't long before Lord Mannix took advantage of the lawlessness of the land, craving the power he'd lost after the wars. He transformed the remaining members of his militia into the Bloody Knuckles crime organization. They set up a black market trade network in '57 and established a shadow economy across the Blaze, fundamentally extorting the people of the western territories.

Then in '58, he and his Bloody Knuckles began operating secretly in the newly formed Brimstone refugee camp outside of the Republic of Phoenix, effectively taking control of the borderlands that surrounded the forbidden city. His shadowy trade in Brimstone undermined the Nimbus Corporation's power and reach, and weakened their once booming economy. The blatant violation of the peace treaty ignited another series of armed conflicts. This time the battlefield was not so clearly defined. Lord Mannix and his Bloody Knuckles used guerrilla warfare and terror tactics from the dark shadows, effectively crippling the Nimbus Corporation's unsteady efforts. Suddenly Lucian Vanderbon's power was called into question by his own people. So to save face, he declared another war.

The Black Market War ensued.

But already, Nimbus was losing. The Bloody Knuckles had implanted themselves in every dark shadow in Brimstone, undermining the corporation's strategy, upending their markets, and making them look inept and unprepared to protect their own city. The people of the Republic began to turn on Nimbus, calling for a change at the top of the corporate ladder. Lucian Vanderbon's grasp was slipping. History was suddenly repeating itself. The tides had to be turned. So Lucian turned to an unlikely hero.

At the height of the war, a young ambitious officer in the Patriot's Defense was tasked with infiltrating the Bloody Knuckles and destroying the organization from within. His mission was simple: discover the location of their secret black market storehouse and turn the tides of the war. After months of working undercover and operating in the dark, the young officer established an invaluable trust among the Bloody Knuckles, gaining unrestricted access to the big bossman himself, Lord Mannix, who took the young officer under his wing and made him an unranked *untouchable* and gave him a highly disputed seat at the council table. The young officer was operating now in the clear, free from the scrutiny of the Bloody Knuckles, and free from the restraints of the corporation. Nimbus trusted him with their assets. Lord Mannix trusted him with his life. One of those two leaps of faith would prove fatal.

On a wickedly hot morning in May, the young officer made his move. He counseled Lord Mannix with falsified intel, coaxing the boss of the Bloody Knuckles into hiding. Lord Mannix chose the hiding spot, fortuitously revealing to the young officer the secret location of the black market storehouse in the process: the limestone caves of the Providence Mountains in the Mojave Preserve. The young officer escaped through the cover of night and gave up the coordinates of the secret storehouse to Nimbus, with a stunning message delivered in morse code: Lord Mannix and his entire counsel were inside.

Lucian Vanderbon seized the opportunity and ordered the immediate bombing. Lord Mannix and his entire counsel were killed in the fiery blast. The smoke plume was captured on film and used by corporate media to solidify the Nimbus victory. In one fell swoop, the Black Market War was over, Nimbus had reestablished control in the borderlands, and the Bloody Knuckles were all but destroyed.

The young officer became a celebrated war hero and a corporate treasure, all before his 21st birthday. He was given the keys to the kingdom and offered numerous positions of power within the Republic. Police commissioner. Corporate judge. Chief. Positions which he subsequently declined. He wanted to protect the Republic of Phoenix and honor the Nimbus Corporation, but with a gun in his hand, not a pen or a gavel. He was given a coveted penthouse in Sky Haven, a decorated position with Border Division in the Phoenix Police Department, and an unprecedented place in corporate history. His heroic exploits had already become legend. So would his name. The most polarizing name in all of law enforcement: Brixton Grace.

Brixton's penultimate place in the sky was more than just a figure of speech. The penthouse that he'd been given 14 years earlier was still his home. It rose high above every other common residence in the vertical city, and he looked down on the inferior neighbors with a god-like supremacy, as if he were some fallen angel who had grabbed hold of a cloud on the way down and was still clinging to his immortality, to the constant envy of mankind. He loved the neon glow of Sky Haven, and the warm embrace of its people. Though his star was fading, they still adored him. He never wanted to leave. Why would he? There was so much to indulge in. His name was like gold there. It could buy him anything. Black market alcohol. Women. Sex. Even forgiveness, which he needed more than anything else. There was always an abundance of sinful opportunities in Sky Haven. The cluster of towering metal inspired sinful thoughts. During the day the glass skyscrapers glistened in the sun like half-naked, sweating bodies, and inspired the same kind of slack-jawed gaze. By nightfall the place came alive with a taunting neon glow and a bold flashiness that called to the Boroughs like some dark, seductive siren song. The two classes of people came together to frolic and play in the soft underbelly of Sky Haven every night. Below the hustle and bustle of the vertical city, at street level, was an even more bustling urban market, open to everyone: the Entertainment Strip. Or simply *the Strip*, as it was commonly known.

It was a three mile run of shady dives, cheap food joints, seedy gentlemen's clubs, and low quality entertainment that appealed mostly to the perceived low character of the Boroughs. But for those residents of Sky Haven who wanted less class, more debauchery, and an element of danger with their indulgences, the Strip was the place to spend their hard-earned Nimbus Coin. Evenings there were more raucous and lively compared to the more elegant breed of establishment in the vertical city above, and Corporate often turned a blind eye to their deplorable activities. *Keep them content.* That was rule number one in the fine art of governing people.

Black market alcohol, some of which was brewed right outside the wall in the dark shadows of Brimstone, was unofficially sold in Sky Haven. It was a clandestine operation with outlawed currency, not Nimbus Coin. The hooch was actually potent enough to get a halfway decent buzz. Illegal drugs, though cheaply made in the slums or smuggled in from the Blaze, were passed around like candy. The pills and powders and pain killers that slipped through the cracks were mostly ineffective, but nobody knew the difference, since Nimbus didn't produce anything of comparable strength. Substance abuse wasn't the only vice. Sex was for sale too. Women in the Haven wore next to nothing and offered almost anything. Food there was fried and dangerously unhealthy. The music was live and loud and unapologetic. It was a party every night until curfew. Then the streets were barren. No one defied curfew. It was Nimbus Law. The consequences of disobedience were often devastating. Loss of Coin, or eviction from residence, or in rare cases, official exile from the Republic and a swift relocation to the refugee slums of Brimstone. There was no jury of peers or due process in the Republic. Only Corporate Tribunals and corporate-appointed judges who convicted and set sentencing based on the evidence of a given case and their own subjective opinion. The system had a lot of room for error, but no accountability. After all, this wasn't really a democracy.

Usually, Brixton would be out there under the neon lights of the Strip, hopping from club to club and dancing and boozing and getting into trouble on his night off. But tonight he was locked inside of his penthouse as if it were a holding cell and he was just waiting for Corporate's final verdict. He swallowed a few colorful pills meant to calm his nerves. The corporate-issued anti-depressants were much easier to swallow than his pride.

His penthouse at the top of Chateau Royale was more luxury than a single man with no real friends ever needed. Four bedrooms. Four bathrooms. A theater room. A game room. An office that he never bothered to furnish. But it wasn't about usefulness to him, or even practicality. It was simply about status. His idea of merit. The vindication of his profesional achievements over the years, or what he called the *spoils of his golden boy reputation*. In his mind, he deserved all that useless space. He was a bonafide war hero. The greatest law enforcement officer in Nimbus history. There were days where he even convinced himself that he was the single greatest asset the corporation ever had.

But things felt different lately. He sat there on the cashmere sofa that night lounging in his purple satin underwear and wondering where it all went wrong. The fake fireplace was aglow with electric flame. His own portrait adorned the mantle. It was a photo of him in uniform. The massive wallscreen flashed with the Nimbus news, but it was muted and being ignored. Despite having a market value of millions in Nimbus Coin, the penthouse was an absolute mess. Too much space for Brixton to keep reasonably clean on his own. Empty food containers were strewn across the couch. Dirty clothes were dumped in piles on the floor. The young maid hadn't been there in weeks. Brixton had made sexual advances towards her, and she had freaked out, and he was too embarrassed to admit to Corporate that she had declined his impulses and refused to come back to work. So the trash can was overflowing in the pantry now. The large, palatial kitchen with trendy hardwood cabinetry could've been mistaken for some trailer park dump at first glance. There were stacks of useless shit on the granite counter top, all in desperate need of sorting. Grimy dishes and scum-soaked coffee mugs stacked carelessly in the sink. The microwave door was hanging wide open on the hinges, the orange light inside burning brightly and wasting precious energy debt.

Brixton held a solar scroll in his hands, flipping through images on the screen with the flick of his finger. Pure ego porn. Old Nimbus press. Glorified headlines. His own professional backstory. But only the glory, not the failures. Just his abundant, overblown successes. Histories of the Black Market Wars. Images of himself as a young officer, clean cut and ready to conquer the world and everyone in it. The headlines read like poorly written propaganda: *The Black Market War ENDS!... Lord Mannix Taken Down By Hero Officer... The Boss of the Bloody Knuckles DEAD... Brixton Grace, Hero of the Republic... A Name No One Will Forget...* so on and so forth. Every word a spit and polish to his ego. He sat there for half an hour scrolling through his past, contemplating his future, and looking rather doomed by the unpalatable possibilities.

How times had changed. He looked so young in those days. So relevant. Now he felt like a parody of himself. A punchline rather than the puncher. *What the fuck happened?* He wondered if he had completely misjudged himself all these years and overshot his landing. He felt like he was plummeting now. A free falling angel, finally dispelled from that immortal cloud that he'd been clinging to, and now he was lost among mortal men. *"Fuck me,"* he shouted as he hurled the solar scroll across the room. The device crashed into the kitchen cabinets.

He suddenly felt irrelevant. Or worst yet, expendable. He'd been pushing Nimbus too far, and now the corporation that always coddled him was pushing back.

## TWENTY-SIX

"Heavy lies the crown," Lucian said with a shuddering timbre. "It only seems to get heavier. Never lighter." He sat at the head of the executive table in the boardroom looking disheartened and crushed by the weight of an awful burden. "So this is your lead? *Brixton Grace*?"

Vice President J.W. Pharaoh and the Inspector General Benjamin Ryker were sitting on either side of him, both on the edge of their seats, pleading their case and looking pleasantly unburdened.

"It's the strongest lead we have," General Ryker said.

Pharaoh leaned on the table with conviction, the woolen elbows of his suit grinding into the lavish, mahogany wood. "Connect the dots, Lucian."

"No," Lucian said in disbelief. "There's no way. He's not involved in that. I know Brixton. He's a loose cannon, but he's not a traitor."

Pharaoh held up the damning evidence: the bag of Sidewinder that Brixton had received in his trade with the refugee known as Gypsy. "But he did break the law. Is that not enough?"

Lucian conceded the point.

"So what's the verdict?" Pharaoh asked. "Do we move forward with this?"

Lucian wouldn't say. He sat there remembering just how hard it was to be king. *Heavy lies the crown indeed.* These were the moments he struggled with. Tough decisions with personal ramifications. Sentencing friends to their necessary penance. It was getting harder these days.

Pharaoh pressed. "There's no shame in it, Lucian. He's done this to himself."

Lucian turned to General Ryker, hoping for some bastardized form of closure. "What do you think, Benjamin?"

"I think Grace is a burn out, sir. I think it's time we light a spark under his ass. See which way he jumps."

Lucian clenched his eyes tightly and ran his hand firmly across his face. The pain in his head was growing intolerable by the minute. He pondered his personal investments in Brixton, both political and emotional. He loved the war hero. He loved the ballsy cop. He loved the guardian that kept his beloved city safe. But he couldn't save Brixton's troubled soul, and the soul of Phoenix seemed in trouble because of that. He sat there for a moment wishing he didn't have to make such a tough decision on the golden boy's future. But that's what kings do. They keep their castle in order. "Alright," he said, distraught over his regrettable decree. "Set the damn thing in motion.

# TWENTY-SEVEN

Zee placed her hand on the painful wound in her belly. The needle stab had been so violent that her abdomen was already black and blue and swollen. The effect of whatever she'd been injected with was already running its course. Her body temperature was on the rise, soaking the sheets of her daybed. Her eyes were pale and encircled by dark purple flesh. She looked like death barely warmed over, or like life accepting its inescapable fate. Gin sat beside her, monitoring her condition and pressing cold washcloths to her body. But Zee paid no mind to Gin's presence. Her mind was on the baby in her belly. On the brutalities of life. On the bittersweet mercy of death. She figured it was time to embrace one or the other.

---

"I never heard of something like this," Hickory said. He stood in the infirmary holding the empty vial in his hand, reading the label to himself, "*Oziacron 1374. Just don't ring a bell.*" His brow line was scrunched up and wavy, like high tide on a shoreline. "It's making Zee awfully sick, whatever it is. The fever's rising by the hour. Fighting off an infection of some kind. I just don't know what it is, and with no meds to control the rapid fever… well… I hate to say it, Croix… but she could…"

"She could *what?*" Croix asked in immediate fear. "She could *die?*"

Hickory didn't say, but the way his eyes shifted downward betrayed every effort to keep the horrible truth from slipping out.

Croix felt a swelling lump in his throat. "Well how the hell do we get it under control?"

Hickory shrugged. "I'm sorry, Croix. It's beyond me. This is unfamiliar territory."

Croix's heart began to sink, forming an empty hole that was shaped like the god he no longer believed in. His mind began to spin, playing tricks on him, searching for any kind of hope where he'd never found hope before: in his deeply cynical mind. It was dark and unwelcoming in there, but he navigated through it, and soon something sparked inside of him. "What day is it?"

"Wednesday," Hickory said.

"No, the *date*. The fourteenth?"

"Yeah," Ru said, stepping forward with a pinch of scrutiny. "Why?"

"The *train*. The Bloody Knuckles smuggle black market meds on that steam engine. They might have something that can help."

"That's a desperate measure, Croix. You know how I feel about desperate measures."

"The train passes through the trading post in two days. No better chance than now. Desperate or not."

Ru sighed. "We don't even know what we're dealing with."

"Maybe they got a cure for it," Croix sparked.

Then Wade stuck his nose in as usual and asked snidely, "Did you forget what happened the last time you went to the trading post?"

"No," Croix said with a forewarning glint in his eye. "I still got the bullet in me."

"It's just not a good idea," Ru said. "There could be drones and patrols all over the Blaze. We don't know what's going on out there. Could be a turf war we don't know about. Nimbus and the Bloody Knuckles are always in conflict. You could be walking right into the middle of it."

Wade shook his head. "Regardless of turf wars or Bloody Knuckles, there's sure to be gangs and scavs and desperate drifters crossing your path. You could lead them straight to us. Then all of sudden we're not the best kept secret in the Sierra no more."

Ru nodded in agreement. "It's true, Croix. It's too dangerous to take that chance."

Croix slammed his fist down on the table, causing Hickory's medical supplies to jump from the pinewood top. "Zee could be dying, Ru. So it's too dangerous not to."

Ru pondered the forceful notion. It was undeniably astute. There weren't many opportunities to get ahead of this mystery illness. In fact, there was only one. Croix's idea sure wasn't promising, but neither was life in the suffocating Granite Valley when the Revivalists first staked their claim under the dying cottonwood trees twenty years earlier.

"You're not gonna change my mind," Croix said.

"Yeah," Ru acknowledged, "I can see that."

# TWENTY-EIGHT

Lucian Vanderbon's office on the fiftieth floor of Tower One was boastfully extravagant, and somehow that was an understatement. It was pure excess. A gold-plated desk worth a king's ransom. Patriotic statues made of bronze. A diamond chandelier that hung from the ceiling with an unapologetic statement of power. An elaborate mural of a fiery Phoenix on the wall, its wings ablaze with a burning halo around its head. It was hand-painted with dark orange and flaming crimson, and meticulously studded with expensive red gemstones. Pure overindulgence. The rug on the floor was lionskin. Rarer than rare. The chairs were made with pink ivory wood from Africa. The rarest. The room was painfully colorful and gaudy-looking. The only consideration when decorating it was stature. Certainly not style. Even the picturesque windows overlooking the city were framed in solid gold. A hideous design clash. Excessive wasn't even the word for that irresponsible touch. They'd have to make up a new word to describe the budgetary negligence. But this was the president's office, so it had to stand above the rest, regardless of cost.

Brixton despised the place. The dizzying motif made him physically ill. Throw in the fact that he was sitting there waiting to receive some kind of lecture, or some ego-crushing punishment, and suddenly he was feeling nauseous and in dire need of a trash can. He knew he was in the shit. He'd shot a superior officer. Shock round or not, he pulled the trigger willingly, against orders from the Inspector General. This was uncharted territory, even for the golden boy. The punishment could be anything. But he automatically feared the worst. *Lucian's gonna replace me as lead inspector. I fucking know it. What a dick-punch. Then Nile will get the gig and supersede me. I'll be taking my orders from him? Jesus fucking Christ. The insult of all fucking insults.*

Lucian sat behind his gold-plated desk with a certain kind of look on his face. Brixton knew the expression all too well. It made him feel like a disowned child. He began to fidget, his leg bouncing in erratic pulses, forcing a confidence in himself that no longer came naturally. Vice President Pharaoh was there too, sitting in a chair beside Lucian and looking as if he was already enjoying Brixton's punishment, before it was even handed down. There was a muted smugness on his face, as if he knew something that Brixton didn't.

That nauseated Brixton even more. *Somebody say something. For fuck's sake. Speak.*

"You've been trouble since the day you joined the department," Lucian finally said.

Brixton had planned to defend his reputation as soon as the first verbal punch was thrown, but the truth of Lucian's words immediately disarmed him. He sat quietly instead, with some strange, almost lethargic sensation pinning his body to the chair. It was humility, and he was as unfamiliar with humility as he was with following the rules.

"You've always walked a fine line between upholding the

law and breaking it," Lucian continued. "But now, you may be more trouble than you're worth."

Suddenly the usual chip on Brixton's shoulder returned. "I'm still worth the risk, sir. I'm the best at what I do. You know that."

Lucian nodded. "You were always my weapon of choice, I'll give you that. Back in the glory days. But what have you done for me lately?"

"Sir?"

"Your past won't save your future, Brix. Not this time."

Then Pharaoh chimed in, all too eagerly. "It's called *former glory* for a reason. You've lost your edge, Inspector."

Brixton shifted in his seat, feeling his pride challenged.

"The Black Market is thriving," Pharaoh said. "Broken Nose and his Bloody Knuckle thugs have taken Brimstone back, right under our noses. They've likely breached our borders with these microchip forgeries, and now we have a possible epidemic within our walls. That's all been happening on your watch."

Brixton turned to Lucian and forfeited all decorum. "Lucian, this is absolute bullshit. What the fuck's going on?"

Lucian didn't answer. He seemed conflicted himself, perhaps by his own interests.

But Pharaoh had no such conflict of interest. "He's finally lost faith in his golden boy, that's what's going on." Then he turned to Lucian with a restless desire. "Let's get on with it, Lucian. Why torment yourself? The decision has already been made."

"What decision, sir?" Brixton looked at Lucian with puppy dog eyes. "What's he talking about?"

Lucian collected his thoughts and slowly processed them one by one. "I've turned a blind eye for you, Brix, one too many times. So I made a vow to the board that I'd never do it again." He paused, as if the words didn't come easy. "We've been watching you."

"We've seen it all," Pharaoh said, interjecting again.

"You've broken every border regulation in the books," Lucian explained. "You've become reckless. Almost beyond redemption."

"You believe you're above Nimbus law," Pharaoh added, "and now you're trading illegal goods with refugees in Brimstone."

Brixton sat there decimated, feeling bombarded by the endless accusations.

Lucian and Pharaoh stared at him with blank anticipation, both waiting for a viable explanation. An argument perhaps. Anything.

"Okay," Brixton said, throwing his hands up in surrender. "You got me. It's Sidewinder, sir. Okay? I fucked up, alright? Is that what you wanna hear? I got strung out like every other asshole in the department."

Pharaoh sneered with obvious sarcasm, "Oh yes, we found the 16 grams of Sidewinder in the console of your police cruiser. How careless of you."

Lucian lowered his eyes to hide his look of grief and disappointment.

"So what happens now?" Brixton asked. "You slap me on the wrist and put me on probation? A stint in rehab? Okay, fine. Fuck it. I'll go if it makes things better."

Lucian sighed. "I wish it were that simple, Brix." He paused, looking quite distraught. "Your bloodwork came back negative."

Brixton didn't blink. His lips didn't move.

"You have no Sidewinder in your system, Brix. Not now. Not ever."

"That's the thing about Sidewinder," Pharaoh said.

"Traces of it remain in your bloodstream until the day you die. If you wanted to effectively carry on this charade, you should've at least taken the drug."

"Charade?" Brixton feigned innocence.

Lucian leaned forward. "The Sidewinder is a cover up."

"To hide your true intentions," Pharaoh added. "What are you dealing in, Grace? Forged microchips?"

Brixton eyed him with a bold contempt, not even bothering to hide it, and then he turned to Lucian looking for mercy. "You think I'm involved in that, sir?"

"You've violated our trust," Lucian said. "Enough with the charade. What are you smuggling across the border? It sure as hell isn't Sidewinder."

Brixton stiffened his jaw proudly, and with a touch of bitterness he said, "It sounds like you've already made up your mind about me, sir. So let's just get on with it."

"So be it," Lucian agreed. The look on his face was pure indifference now, as if he'd fought as hard for Brixton as he was willing to. "As of tomorrow morning, you'll have a new residence. And it won't be within Republic walls."

Brixton felt a sudden sting. "Seriously? I'm being exiled?"

"No," Lucian said. "Not exiled. *Transferred*. Exile requires a unanimous vote, and you still have one executive in your corner."

Pharaoh cocked a disapproving eye at Lucian, who showed no remorse for his decision to keep Brixton on their payroll.

Lucian explained, "You'll be stationed, *temporarily*, at Outpost 11 in the Mojave desert."

"Border Patrol?" Brixton had a look of shattering disbelief on his face. This was beyond insulting. "Jesus fucking Christ. That's not a transfer, Lucian. That's a fucking *demotion*."

"*Inspector*," Pharaoh shouted. "You're in the office of the CEO. Conduct yourself appropriately."

Brixton didn't heed the warning. "Lucian, this is bullshit and you know it. I'm no grunt, sir. You know this isn't right. You're just gonna throw me out with the trash? After all I've done for the corporation? During the worst security breach in our history? Are you fucking kidding me?"

"*Inspector*," Pharaoh shrieked, practically levitating in his seat. "Show some dignity, if not a little class. You're speaking to your President like he's a common thug."

"Outpost 11 is Vedder's crew," Brixton snarled, ignoring Pharaoh's lecture. "Fuck that. I'd rather be exiled."

Pharaoh clenched his bleach white teeth. "I can arrange that."

"*Oh I'm sure you could*," Brixton bellowed recklessly.

He was then startled by a loud *boom* as Lucian slammed his arthritic fist onto the desk. "Inspector Grace, that's *enough*."

Brixton stopped himself and went silent, like a fresh corpse in the graveyard. Perhaps the only place he could go to feel lower than he already felt.

"It's done," Lucian said. "I can't make excuses for you anymore, Brix. Your legacy with the Nimbus Corporation is barely intact. You don't have much dignity left, so I suggest you leave here with some of it." He paused, reluctant to take anything else from Brixton. But alas, he said, "Place your badge and your firearm on my desk."

"This isn't right, sir."

"Do it, Brix."

"I'm not carrying my piece," Brixton muttered brokenly. "Or my badge. I'm off duty."

"Off duty?" Lucian scowled. "That's never stopped you from carrying before."

"I was never under the microscope before, sir. I figured I better follow every rule to a T."

Lucian didn't appreciate the smart-ass remark. "Then

you'll leave your gun and badge with Inspector Wambasa before you leave for your new assignment on Tuesday."

Pharaoh interrupted. "Lucian, this is unacceptable. It's protocol to confiscate his gun and badge upon demotion."

"*Transfer*," Lucian said, his eyes cast imperiously on Pharaoh. "It's a transfer. Not a demotion."

Pharaoh scoffed. "He continues to defy you, Lucian, right to your face, and you do nothing about it."

Lucian glared at him. Pharaoh conceded and turned his eyes away, remembering his place in the current order of things.

Lucian looked at Brixton and said, "I want both your gun and your badge scanned and unregistered before you cross that border wall, is that understood?"

Brixton barely nodded, as if his head was mired in place. There was no feeling of petty vindication. No fight left in him. He was broken, confused, searching for something unknowable. In a word, he was lost. Everything he'd ever cherished, namely his reputation, was suddenly gone from his grasp and drifting aimlessly among his peers now. Something they could shape and mold to their liking. A vague rumor that was vulnerable to judgement and criticism and outright lies. He was no longer a war hero in Corporate's eyes, and he could feel the loftiness of his name give way beneath him. He was no longer an Inspector either, and that made him feel like he was finally sinking beneath the earth.

"You're officially under corporate investigation," Lucian explained. "You'll bide your time... *wisely*... at Outpost 11 while internal investigations builds a case and either clears you or officially charges you with a crime against the Nimbus Corporation. At which time you'll face judgement by a tribunal of executives." He drew a conflicted breath and took a moment to ponder his next words. "Anyone else would be exiled, Brix. This was the best I could do for you."

Brixton wasn't in the mood to offer his gratitude. "That's like kicking me in the balls and telling me to be grateful for it."

Lucian shook his head. "Embrace your new post in the desert. Redeem yourself. Then we'll talk about reinstatement."

Then Pharaoh added, "But if you step so much as one little toe out of line, Grace, you'll be erased from our system and exiled. We know how much you hate the Blaze. And how much you love your place in our history. You'll be nothing."

Brixton recognized the poorly veiled enthusiasm. He could see the corners of Pharaoh's mouth yearning to curve upward into a satisfied grin. "You seem thrilled by all this," he said to Pharaoh, adding a disingenuous "sir" at the end.

Pharaoh inched even closer. "No one is above Nimbus Law. Not even you, *Patrolman* Grace."

And with that smug emphasis on the word *patrolman*, Brixton's uncontrollable hatred for his Vice President was sealed with a big red stamp. He felt a dangerous impulse to hit Pharaoh in the jaw with a bloody haymaker. He could visualize it in his mind. The feeling of flesh and bone crackling beneath his knuckles. The glorious sound of corporate teeth rattling around in Pharaoh's big fucking mouth. The bloody lip and broken jawbone that he would undoubtedly have afterwards. Something he'd have to carry shamefully into his next board meeting. Brixton wanted to stand over him in victory, feeling untouchable, with a smug, shit-eating grin on his face. But that was a pipe dream within a pipe dream, and it would have to remain so. Pharaoh was a true man of power. Brixton wasn't. He was nothing but a grunt now. *A fucking garbage man,* he thought. *The Border Patrol's new bitch.* So instead of throwing a bloody haymaker at Pharaoh and risking a far worse punishment, he went into a shell, coiling up inside and lowering his eyes in defeat like a vanquished enemy on the battlefield. *Some war hero I am.*

Then Lucian ended the meeting with a cold finality. "You're dismissed," he said. "That's all I have."

That's all Brixton had too.

There was nothing left to take from him.

---

An hour later Brixton was blasting down the dark backstreets of the Industrial Zone in his police cruiser. This part of the city was a bleak, concrete and metal dirge where everything unnatural was manufactured. The place resembled a cemetery, but with warehouses and distribution centers instead of headstones and mausoleums. A hot, urban mashup of block and steel-reinforced buildings in neat little rows. No greenery or nature. No life outside. No one there but the workers entombed in their mundane workplaces. Everyone in their right place. Everyone but Brixton. He no longer had a place.

He was heading straight for a massive brick wall at 99 mph with no intention of stopping. His eyes were like two white ghosts finally accepting their demise. His knuckles were even whiter, gripping the steering wheel as if it were his *golden boy* reputation trying to escape him. "*Fuck you,*" he shouted, staring at those two white ghosts in the rearview mirror. He didn't know if he really wanted to die, but the brick wall seemed like a good way out if he did. He figured he had about five or six seconds to change his mind. He counted the seconds in his head, not sure how accurate his calculations were. Three… Two… Then before he reached the final second, he panicked and hit the brake and the tires squealed and the cruiser shuddered violently and came to a miraculous stop with the bumper just barely grazing the brick and mortar. He sucked air into his lungs. His hands shook wildly on the steering wheel. "What the fuck are you doing, man?" He looked embarrassed, even in his own company. "You stupid, crazy fuck."

He sat there in the driver's seat pondering his own mania. He had just lost himself for a fleeting moment, but that moment could've been his last. A permanent vacation from his glorious life. He asked himself, *If I'd cashed in all my chips right then and there, how would the world remember Brixton Grace?*

He didn't like the answer.

# TWENTY-NINE

The armory at Revival was a holy grail of survival. The hill that Revivalists would die on if necessary. It was buried beneath the earth just like the safe room. A manufactured bunker that was placed there before Revival was even founded, when it was just a survivalist's home owned by a militant man named Corbin Rutherford, a founding member of the Southwestern Guard. The armory, and the safe room too, had been put in the ground long before the Collapse, but in sure preparation for it. There was a hidden access point in the trenches, kept hidden by the plywood and corrugated-metal-framing that held the earthen walls in check. It was virtually impenetrable. Reinforced steel doors with analog security codes and a spindial opener like those on a submarine. The old brochure from the bunker manufacturer even claimed it was blast-proof. They called it ballistic steel. C-4 resistant. An 18-bolt system. Nobody was getting inside of that metal beast without the passcode. But the covert location wasn't overkill. If someone even spotted the armory, they would go through hell and high water to get inside of it. They'd kill anyone that stood in the way. There were hundreds of reasons to ensure no one even *found* the armory, blast-proof or not. Hundreds of guns, blades, explosive devices and improvised weaponry. The arsenal inside was once more impressive than that of some of the militias that fought in the Restoration Wars. In fact, most of the weapons had been scavenged from those battles or stolen from the enemies that lay dead on the battlefield. M4s, AR-15s, AK-47s, MP5s, and a grand array of shotguns, revolvers, and automatic handguns. At one point, they even had a handful of military-grade sniper rifles that could take a man's head off from a thousand yards out. Now they only had two. But they still had plenty of guns, with almost every bore possible, from small caliber .22 Winchesters to big game .338 RUMs. Barrels filled with Croix's homemade ammunition. Cast in 44 Magnum, .357, 9 millimeter hollow point, .45 ACP, .380, and whatever else they needed. You name it, Croix made it. They had hundreds of hand combat weapons too, hanging from the walls in neat little rows. Trench bats, tomahawks, throwing stars, swords, war clubs, axes and battle-worn blades. They had boxes of grenades and booby traps and even some explosive contraptions that Elmer had devised in his workshop. They were saving those for a bloody day. The armory was a war chest. But they hoped it would never come to that again. War was a last resort. Something they may not survive the next time around.

---

When Tavo entered the armory he found Croix gathering as many weapons and ammo as he could carry on his body or stuff into his duffel bag. Before he could ask Croix about his intentions, Croix began ranting out loud, as if he'd been possessed by something so troubling that he could no longer keep it to himself. "I always thought the older you get the wiser you get. But that ain't true. You just get more delusional. Then that delusion becomes a habit. Then you accept it as some sort of reality. Then you call it truth and pass it on to your children like it's wisdom. Then the goddamn thing spreads like a fucking disease."

Tavo's face twisted in tight confusion. "Croix, you alright? You sound a little fuzzy."

"It's a vicious circle," Croix said cryptically. "We just go round and round in a goddamn endless spin. From one generation to the next. Making the same mistakes. Making it worse for the ones who follow in our footsteps."

Tavo moved closer to him, this time with caution. "What's going on, Croix?"

"It's a little baby girl," Croix said, his eyes turning and tail-spinning and crashing to the floor. "A little baby girl in Zee's belly."

Tavo stopped in his tracks. He hung his head. He understood Croix's fear now. The world wasn't kind to women, and that was putting it kindly. There was no moral code among men anymore. Certainly no chivalry, if that ever existed to begin with. Men had free rein now. No social standard to keep their vile instincts in check. Humans were just animals without fences, and most men indulged in anything they could get away with. So naturally, women suffered. Little girls didn't have a prayer.

"I never wanted a child," Croix explained fearfully, "because I never thought I could protect it. This world is nothing but chaos and disorder and unspeakable cruelty, and that never seems to end. We're just trying to stay sane in the midst of all that, and I don't even know why anymore." He began loading homemade bullets into the magazine of a battle-scarred Glock 19, shoving each of them into place with his thumb and a wrathful sense of purpose. "I've always felt like I was in control, as long as I just stuck to the plan. But that's unraveling. This world ain't no place for a little girl to be raised. How can I ever protect her?"

His memories began to flash in his mind, flickering like an old black and white movie reel, void of color, but not truth. He could see himself in the desert, as a young boy, under the terrible Mojave sun, a bloody pocketknife in his hand, stabbing another boy to death with the dull blade. The boy screaming in pure agony. Blood splattering from his mouth. He could see the knife slipping through his own hands and landing on the hot sand and gravel like some eternal stain on the surface of the earth. His fingers trembling, the tips of them covered in the boy's blood. The black and white coloration of his memory began to change hues, turning to a blinding crimson. He could hear his own pathetic voice screaming, *"I'm sorry, momma! I'm so sorry!"*

A promise he'd once made.

A lifetime spent breaking it.

Then the reel of memories stopped spinning in his mind and turned to a burning glitch of regret. "I've done a lot of bad things. I think my sins have finally caught up to me." He could see Zee in his mind now, lying there in her daybed with her hand resting on her wounded belly and singing a weeping lullaby to her baby. The vision gutted him, imaginary or not. The thought that he'd caused all her pain was unbearable. He felt responsible for everything that had transpired, as if he'd set the wheels in motion himself a long time ago. He jammed the magazine into the bottom of the Glock 19 and racked a bullet into the chamber. Then he holstered the weapon with the safety off.

Tavo looked spooked by the supernatural conviction of Croix's words. "You're talking like the universe has a purpose

and you're on the wrong side of it. Ain't like you to be superstitious."

"Ain't superstition," Croix said, looking just as spooked.
"It's the law of consequence. Every man's gotta reap what he
sows." He grabbed his triple-barreled Breckenridge *Hydra 300*
and a handful of homemade shells from the ammo crate and
began loading them into the shotgun one after another.

Tavo raised a brow. "Where you going with all them
guns?"

Croix looked him squarely in the eyes this time. "I don't
want Zee and the baby suffering for all the things I've done
wrong. So I'm going to make things right." He pumped a shell
into the chamber and slung the shotgun over his shoulder and
grabbed the duffel bag and headed for the door with his mind
on retribution. Though he feared the ultimate penance would
be his own.

# BOOK THREE

SPIN THE VICIOUS CIRCLE

# ONE

The sun unleashed itself upon the bleak, salt-encrusted wasteland of the Bonneville Flats in former Utah. Thirty-thousand acres of pure white salt stretched to the horizon as far as the eye could see. It was otherworldly, like a frozen lakebed covered with snow in the dead of summer. There was an old wooden boxcar sitting on railroad tracks. It was coupled to a rusty tanker car and a repurposed flatbed which was carrying a mysterious vehicle hidden by a black tarpaulin. The mismatched wheels were the only part exposed and they looked as out of place as the landscape around them.

The boxcar door slid open and a man staggered out drunkenly. He was wearing a yellow chemical suit and a gas mask and holding a mason jar filled with a dark, frothy liquid. His snakeskin boots barely scraped the rungs of the step ladder as he lowered himself to the earth, unable to find his equilibrium. He removed the mask and took a sloppy breath of summer air. His face was bitterly aged and partially hidden by a gray fu manchu. The whiskers were poorly trimmed. His neck was adorned with the blistered remains of an old rope scar. Not the first time he'd escaped the noose. Probably not the last. He placed an old mesh trucker hat on his sweaty head. His so-called lucky charm, with an unfortunate history. There was a Mobil logo on the front, with a red *Flying Pegasus*, or as he always called it, a horse with wings. It was worn to a frazzle and stained with grease and blood and a whole lot of shame. After all, he was the notorious traitor from Dagger lore: Levi Scarborough.

He was seventy-three years old and still serving his self-imposed penance. His limbs were numb and dangling by his side, as if he were untethered from the earth and blissfully detached from the reality that he hated so much. His gut was bloated with liquid courage, but it wasn't working the usual magic. "Billy," he said, as if he'd seen his best friend's ghost. "Where'd you go?" His eyes shifted. Then he realized he was just imagining things again. "Old fool," he muttered, followed by a self-loathing scoff which sounded more like a man choking on his own pride. He was as drunk as a man his age could be without instantly dropping dead. But that was nothing new for Levi. Deathly inebriation was his permanent state of being these days. Life just wasn't bearable when his mind was sharp enough to contemplate it. He took a sip of the dark liquid and stumbled forward, looking at the world around him with baffled eyes, as if it were completely foreign to him. He spotted a lone bison struggling to find its way in the blistering heat. It was lean and starving and looking for water that wasn't there. It had probably been displaced from its natural hunting grounds by the constant wildfires. "Billy? Is that you?"

Levi could smell the smoke on the wind. The heavily-coated buffalo would soon be dead from dehydration and failed organs. Just a rotting corpse to be feasted on by crows and vultures and the nomadic packs of gray wolves that always sniffed out an opportunity to eat for free. Levi thought it was nature's mercy. If only he could be so lucky. Nature didn't seem to like him all that much. Neither did God. He chuckled in amusement, as he often did, and then his legs gave out and he crumpled to the salty earth, his face landing like an airplane plummeting to the ground. He didn't move after that.

Moments later, as he lay there in his regrettable state, a dark shadow crossed over him, like some merciful demon that had come to take him home. But no such luck. It was just a man in a black fedora and dark sunglasses. The man snickered and nudged Levi with the heel of his shiny loafer. "You finally do yourself in, old man?"

Levi casually opened one eye and blew the salt from his lips. "Hell no. But it ain't for lack of trying. Death just ain't in the cards for me."

"We'll see about that," said the man in the black fedora. His real name was Gino Battaglia, but the world knew him as Broken Nose, the kingpin of Brimstone. The current boss of the Bloody Knuckles crime organization. His eyes were a menacing mix of colors. Green and brown and bloodshot. His ears were cauliflowered and his nose was flattened and scarred, as if he'd taken one too many beatings in his fifty-eight years on Earth. He had. But now he was the one giving the beatings. "Show me what I came to see," he said.

Levi sighed in exhaust, realizing he'd have to pull himself up off the ground.

———

As the sun was nearly bursting from its undisputed place in the sky, a strange-looking vehicle was kicking up salt in the flats below, spinning donuts and accelerating wildly and sliding across the earth like something on ice. It was just a heap of random scrap metal from old dilapidated automobiles, but it was fast and powerful and resting on a hardy, all-terrain suspension system, with even hardier tires. Broken Nose sat in a lawn chair under a jury-rigged umbrella that shaded him from the sun. He was bookended by two of his bodyguards as he watched the vehicle perform, his eyes drawn outward with great anticipation.

Levi was behind the wheel in his flannel shirt with a dented flask in one hand and the other hand barely in control. He was still too drunk to be driving, but unsurprisingly, he was more than competent behind the wheel, putting on an impressive display. The vehicle spun, torqued and kicked up salt in every direction like a fireworks show. He pressed the gas pedal to the floorboard with his old snakeskin boots. The vehicle raced towards Broken Nose and his bodyguards, who both took a step backwards in apprehension. Levi hit the brakes and the vehicle shifted and spun forty-five degrees and stopped on a dime, throwing heavy grains of salt into the air around them. Everything went quiet. A moment of calm consideration, and hopefully a happy verdict.

Then Broken Nose stood up from his chair and drew a handgun and fired a single shot at the driver side window. The bullet slammed into the glass near Levi's head with a hard *thwack*. Levi was startled, but the glass didn't shatter. It didn't even crack. The crumpled bullet landed in the salt a few yards away. Broken Nose unloaded the entire magazine and the bullets slammed into the body of the vehicle, one after another, *thwack thwack thwack*, bouncing right off and landing in the salty earth. Levi barely flinched this time, feeling confident in his creation.

Broken Nose chuckled with elation and holstered his weapon. "*Bulletproof*," he exclaimed as he approached the vehicle. "Completely *bulletproof*."

Levi stepped out, grasping at his right arm, realizing that a bullet fragment had just grazed him. "Not completely," he said. "A few sections of the body are just your factory-grade sheetmetal at the moment."

Broken Nose saw the blood on Levi's sleeve. "I winged you?"

"It just grazed the skin."

"You're lucky I'm a bad shot."

"I guess so," Levi scoffed, not feeling too lucky with a worthless flesh wound.

Broken Nose shrugged. "What can I say? I'm out of practice. When you're as powerful as I am, you don't have to shoot your own guns."

Levi chuckled. "The spoils of organized crime, huh?"

Broken Nose took a closer look at the strange-looking vehicle, reaching out and caressing the contours of the body with his hand. "You've outdone yourself, Levi. It's an absolute work of art."

"It's just a prototype," Levi explained. "Made from salvaged scrap parts. It's reinforced with the composite metal foam you spotted me. Besides being bulletproof, it's also a radiation blocker and a heat insulator. So it protects against radiation and makes the driver virtually invisible to the boomerang drone's heat detectors."

Broken Nose was clearly impressed. "And the engine?"

Levi raised the hood and stood there beaming with pride, gazing upon the engine like a father would gaze upon a newborn child in a hospital nursery. "Twin turbo. 8 cylinder big block. 900 horse. Light weight. My design. Runs on a special blend of ethanol."

"Impressive," Broken Nose said. "And the still?"

They made their way into the wooden boxcar, which Levi called his *brew car*. It wasn't the usual breed of rolling stock. It was custom made with electric slide-outs on both sides like an old camper, the sides protruding outwards on a series of intricate metal rails. The whole thing was about sixty feet long and twenty feet wide, significantly wider than the average train car. The roof was covered in solar panels. Broken Nose marveled at Levi's latest bit of ingenuity. A prodigious ethanol distillery. Tanks, filters, pipes, pressure gauges, and copper tubing all interconnected and criss-crossing in a mashup of controlled chaos. It looked like the laboratory of some mad scientist. Levi was no man of science, but he certainly was mad. Maybe even certifiable. He was cooking a batch of ethanol as they spoke. "I brew the fuel right here in the boxcar," he explained. "Run it out to that rusty old tanker car through copper tubing."

Broken Nose smiled. "A Mobile refueling station?"

Levi nodded. "She can go anywhere the rails take her."

Broken Nose was giddy as a schoolgirl, almost forgetting he was supposed to be a hardcore gangster. "With a dozen of these stations scattered throughout the Blaze we could operate an entire mobile fleet." He placed his disfigured hands on Levi's shoulder. "Ingenuity, Levi. That's the only reason I haven't killed you yet."

Levi raised an unsteady brow. "I guess I should consider myself lucky?" He filled a mason jar with ethanol from the tank and took a sip. The fuel was made from sugar beets, with zero hydrocarbon. Safe for human consumption, if consumed in healthy moderation. Of course, Levi didn't do anything in healthy moderation. He took another sip, which naturally turned into a steady gulp.

Broken Nose shook his head. "I see your drinking habit has reached a new low."

"Hell," Levi said wistfully. "I can't do anything right if I ain't drunk. This Dragon's Breath is the only thing that does the trick anymore."

Broken Nose panned around the brew car and spotted

what looked like another vehicle. It was covered with another black tarpaulin. "What's that?"

"Just a side project," Levi said. "Nothing to see."

"You holding out on me, Levi?"

"It's a work in progress. Under wraps for a reason."

"Under wraps? You've never been the modest type."

"If it ever becomes more than junk parts fused together and slapped on top of four shitty tires, you'll be the first to know. I promise."

Broken Nose eyed him suspiciously for a moment, and then he said enthusiastically, "Levi, I want you to build me an entire fleet of these trucks. Bullet-proofed. Ethanol engines. With speed. My smugglers could *outrun* the border patrol."

"No more horses and covered wagons, huh?"

Broken Nose shook his head with glee. "Nope. We've caught up to the past. Now we can take back the future." He looked like a man who'd just seen the light of God. "Grouse Creek is growing," he said. "We have four hundred acres now. Beet fields that spread so far you can't see beyond them."

"I can yield 750 gallons of ethanol per acre," Levi calculated. "So that's 300,000 gallons of fuel per month. If the soil can produce your beets every season."

"We have well water. No reason we can't keep the field red."

"That'll do," Levi said. "But first thing's first. I need to build some cars."

Broken Nose smiled. "You'll get whatever materials you need."

"What I need is in a hidden storehouse down in Box Canyon just south of the Joshua Tree Forest. Got a friend that hoards scrap parts down there, and you know how goddamn hard it is to find automobiles that ain't been destroyed by Nimbus."

Broken Nose pointed south, directing Levi's attention to a long, black train that was sitting on the main tracks in the distance. "Then we'll give you a ride," he said with a chipped-tooth grin.

It was the almighty Black Market Express 311. A repurposed steam engine from the old world. Big and fierce and towing an impressive array of rolling stock. Passenger coaches, baggage cars, and a security car. It would usually be towing several cattle pins filled with prime meat donors, but this wasn't the month for the meat market, so the cattle pins were left behind. Broken Nose and his Bloody Knuckles were on a trade run, heading to the Kelso trading post in the Mojave, where a man like Levi might find more tools to fuel his ingenuity. Levi looked at the mighty train and smiled. He was always opportunistic. It just seemed to work out that way. He called it luck, but oftentimes it felt supernatural, like some flawless highway paved in gold and laid out before him on a predetermined path. The train was his ticket out of the salt flats. He'd been there so long his mind was starting to make sense again. He didn't like that one bit. So he was all too happy to hitch a ride.

# TWO

The Revivalists were gathered around the trade wagon with offerings in their hands. Anything that would fetch a decent barter at the Kelso trading post in the Mojave. Tools, jewelry, plant seeds, medicinal herbs. Even some personal items. All highly valuable. Wade even offered one of his prized military shovels with the folding handle and the proud marine branding on the metal frame. They placed their items in the wagon one by one, in ceremonious fashion. There were more than enough offerings to fill a backpack or a saddlebag, which is all Croix would be taking with him. Tavo and Skinny were set to join him on the journey. A two-day ride on horseback. They would need to travel light and fast. The trade wagon was too big and too slow. An historical heirloom from the old west days. They'd scavenged it from a nearby ghost town in Nevada and reworked it with new steel weldings and retrofitted it with airless tires. The old carriage had survived bullets, rough desert crossings, terrible sandstorms and one very angry bull, and they never made a run without it, but this particular trade run would be for one thing and one thing only: medicine for Zee. So they'd have to leave the wagon behind.

Croix nodded his gratitude. "This is more than I expected," he said, looking at the generous pile of trade offerings. "Zee would be humbled if she saw this." He didn't say anything more than that, but it was more than enough. Everyone understood. It was his roundabout way of saying *thank you*. They all said their *goodbyes* and *good lucks* in short order. Some with words, others with a simple nod. Sometimes in Revival, a simple nod was worth a thousand words anyway.

Croix gathered the most valuable offerings and tucked them into a backpack and stuffed the backpack into his saddle bag. He had already packed some of his homemade ammunition to barter with, which would probably be more valuable than anything else, but for all he knew, he'd have to use the extra ammo to protect himself along the way, so the extra offerings could end up being priceless. He prepped his horse and tack, tugging on the bridle and double-checking the cinch ring. Tavo and Skinny brought their horses around and joined him. He was pleased to see they were ready to run. No slacking. All business. He pulled the heavy *Hydra 300* from the leather scabbard on his saddle and double-checked the tube mags. Thirty shells, all loaded with homemade *tiger shot*. He would be ready for anything.

Ru wandered over to him, looking reluctant to say what was on his mind, but finally saying it. "You watch your ass out there, Croix. Keep that head on a swivel."

Croix slid the triple-barreled shotgun back into the scabbard. "You know I can survive the desert, Ru. I was forged in it."

Ru nodded. He never doubted Croix's ability to cheat death. He'd seen him do it many times before. He just needed to hear it from Croix's mouth. That's how it always was with them. Croix nodded. It meant *thanks for caring.* Ru understood the meaning. It wasn't the first time they'd had this wordless exchange. Then Croix looked beyond Ru's shoulder and saw something that would alter his original plan. It was Kid, sitting alone on the gallows with his legs dangling off the side and his head resting in the palms of his hands. He looked bankrupt, as if he wasn't a match for this odd, formidable world which he was so unwillingly a part of. Croix could see he was feeling outmatched. He recognized the kid's torment. It was the embittered agony of guilt. Not something that could easily be remedied. Croix had been ravaged by guilt his entire adult life. He knew that kind of wound always festered until it was properly rectified, and he knew the only way to do that was the hardest way possible. He suddenly had a maddening thought. A realization which disturbed him so badly he could barely acknowledge it. *The kid was right about Revival,* he thought. *It is a goddamn prison.* He knew he'd been holding Kid captive in every way possible, and captivity was a breeding ground for incompetency. Without the freedom to fail, Kid's fuckups would continue to mount. Without bearing witness to the outside world, Kid would remain naive to its savagery and deception. So he'd always be a victim of it.

Croix turned to Ru, hardly believing his own instincts. "Ru, I... I think we made a mistake with that kid. Sheltering him like we've done all this time. He ain't seen the world at its worst, so how the hell can he be at his best?"

Ru looked heavily burdened. "Why are you saying this now?"

"Because..." Croix said with painful reluctance, "...we're taking him with us."

Skinny nearly choked on his spit. "We're *what?*"

Tavo chuckled as if it were a joke. "Have you finally lost your mind, Croix?"

"He needs to see the world as it is," Croix explained. "Not as he wants it to be."

Tavo's face turned to black stone as he recognized the seriousness in Croix's tone. "You *really have* lost your mind."

"Maybe so," Croix acknowledged.

"No way," Ru said. "Not gonna happen. That's a bad idea."

"He's gotta see it with his own eyes, Ru. I can't make him understand with words alone. He has to be in the thick of it."

"He's not ready."

"Nobody's ever ready. Were we?"

Ru didn't answer. Croix had made an indestructible point. There was no reason to take a sledgehammer to it. "I don't know how I feel about this," Ru said tentatively. "It's a big risk."

"We can't protect him forever," Croix said. "I know you mean well, Ru, but sooner or later he'll face the evil in this world, and he needs to be ready for it when it comes. He'll be alright. I'll protect him with my life."

"I have no doubt about that," Ru said. "But will he protect you with his?"

"That's what we need to find out," Croix said. "For his sake and *ours*."

Ru didn't protest. He seemed to agree with Croix's shaky sentiment. The most effective way to learn anything in life was always the hard way. Easy was easily forgotten. The tough, forbidding experience was etched into your soul with a dull blade, and that always left an impression. No one ever forgot that. The Revivalists sure hadn't. They'd all been etched to Hell and back.

A few minutes later, Croix was strapping Kid into his kevlar vest, making it snug on his slight frame. Kid studied the painted words on the chest plate. "What's it mean? What's Southwestern Guard?"

Croix pulled the vest tighter, partly to make it more snug, and partly to vent his frustration with the endless array of questions, all of which he had no intention of answering. "Keep this on at all times out there, you hear me? It's gonna protect you."

"It's your only vest," Kid said. "You should be the one wearing it."

"Just shut up and do what I tell you to do." Croix was already regretting his decision to bring the kid along. "Surprise me for once."

"I'm the one surprised," Kid said. "Didn't expect you to give a shit."

"About what?"

"About whether or not I get killed."

"Contrary to popular opinion, I don't want anything to happen to you."

"That's comforting I guess."

Croix rolled his eyes. "You don't have to respond to everything I say."

"It just feels wrong not to say something in return."

"It ain't. Trust me. It's better if you just shut up."

"So I should just sit here and say nothing? Like, *nothing at all?*"

"Yes. *Nothing at all.* Pure silence. That's called common courtesy. Hell, you could even call it social etiquette."

"Don't seem right to me."

"There's a lot that don't seem right to you, Kid, but that don't make it wrong." Croix tugged on the vest again to check the fit. It was plenty tight.

Kid gestured his gratefulness with a simple nod and said, "Thanks for bringing me along. I gotta get out of this place."

"Don't thank me yet, Kid. You might be *running* back to this place before it's all said and done."

Kid looked nervous. "Why's that?"

"Just keep the vest on at all times."

Kid didn't say another word, but Croix could see the questions were already formulating in his broken mind. A stockpile of inquiries that he'd be bombarded with later. Then Kid noticed something over Croix's shoulder and his eyes sparked to life, looking like bright searchlights. Croix knew the look. Only adolescent lust could stir such hormonal intrigue. Then Kid waved at someone. Croix turned, and as expected, he saw Gin walking from the headquarters cabin to Zee's cabin. She didn't offer so much as a glance back.

Croix grimaced on Kid's behalf. "What's on your mind, Kid?"

"Nothing." Kid looked hurt by Gin's cold shoulder. "A whole lot of nothing."

Croix dismissed the carnal drama and handed Kid one of his old revolvers and a quick loader filled with an extra round of ammo. "Take this thirty-eight too. It's got more bite than your pocket pistol."

Kid took the .38, reluctantly. He studied the gun for a moment, with a trepidation that he couldn't hide, and then he quickly holstered it as if it were too frightening to touch.

Croix recognized the fear, so he figured he better not downplay what was coming. "There's some real bad shit waiting out there for us." He grabbed both of Kid's hands. They were shaking like the leaves of autumn. "You better steady your nerves. When the shit goes down you gotta have our back. You hear me?"

"I ain't nervous."

"You gotta aim true and pull the trigger, Kid. You can't do that if your goddamn hands are shaking."

"I said I ain't nervous."

"Yes you are," Croix insisted, "and you should be." Then he swallowed hard and admitted, "I am."

Kid was spooked by his rare admittance of fear. Croix never admitted to being afraid of anything, ever.

Croix could see the kid's mind was spinning, and he took that as a good sign this time. It meant Kid's mind was on *what was coming* and not on *what was past*. The look of guilt was beginning to dissipate. The kid had bigger problems now.

Skinny rode up on his horse. "If we're going, then let's get to it. I don't wanna be setting out after dark."

"I like your thinking," Croix said. He hopped into the saddle of his golden palomino and grabbed the reins. "Saddle up, Kid. Time to go."

Kid put his foot in the stirrup and yanked himself into the saddle.

Croix looked around. He was immediately vexed. There was one member of his party still missing. "Now where the hell did lover boy go?"

---

Tavo was standing in front of Memphis in the courtyard with a doe-eyed, apologetic look on his face. She never liked when he left the safety of Revival, and he was sorry to go, but they both knew it was his duty, and he never shirked a task. He mustered a smile and tried to lighten the mood. "I had fun last night," he said, his smile turning flirtatious again. "You?"

Memphis grinned, her eyes soft and welcoming. "You know I always have fun."

Tavo looked proud of himself.

Memphis looked at the fake ring on her finger. It actually sparkled in the sunlight. "You earned it," she blushed.

Tavo chuckled quietly and said, "I gotta confess something. I knew that wasn't no diamond ring."

Memphis laughed. "You think you're so clever. I knew you knew. But it was a win-win for me either way."

They both laughed and embraced like young lovers, and then they kissed each other with more passion than a prudish man would be comfortable with.

"Alright that's enough of that shit," Croix said prudishly from his saddle. "The day is getting away from us."

They ignored him and kept their attention on each other.

He grimaced at the sight of their open affection. It always irked him. Part of him thought it was just them gloating. A way of showing off their perfect union in contrast to his and Zee's imperfect one. He wasn't sure if it was purposeful, but he thought they should have enough respect not to make a show of it every goddamn chance they got. "Let's go, Tavo. We ain't got daylight to waste on your delicate heart. Hell, the whole world don't need to see ya'll swapping spit like that."

Memphis gave Croix a dirty look, then turned her eyes back on Tavo. "Why can't ya'll just wait until morning to set out?"

Tavo gestured carefully towards Croix. "The answer to that question is sitting right there in the saddle of that golden palomino."

Memphis gave Croix another dirty look, letting it be known that she wasn't happy with his bullishness. Tavo kissed her on the cheek and walked away, backpedaling with his eyes still bright and flirty. He blew her a kiss.

"For Christ's sake, lover boy," Croix said. "Enough is enough. Get your ass in the saddle and let's get moving."

Tavo climbed into his saddle and blew Memphis one more kiss goodbye.

Croix turned his eyes on Zee's cabin and immediately regretted it. To his unpleasant surprise, she was actually standing there staring back at him from the porch, barely upright with a blanket slung around her shivering shoulders. Her eyes were indifferent to his. She didn't blink, and neither did he. There was no warmth between them. No goodbye. No good luck. No *go to hell, you bastard* or *I hate you*. Just a cold, dead exchange without words or expression.

Croix whispered to himself. "It sure is good to be loved." Then he gave his horse a little more kick than was needed and the golden palomino bolted for the fading horizon. Tavo and Skinny followed, their horses trotting away at a hesitant pace. Kid's horse stood there at the gate, and Kid sat motionless in the saddle, contemplating every possible outcome. None of them were good. Then he sighed and took a deep breath and said, "Alright then, let's go I guess." He clicked his heels and the horse carried him off without a hint of fear.

# THREE

They rode south following the old crumbling Highway 395 as it curved its way through the Granite Valley. They had no wagon and no packhorse. Nothing more than what they could carry on their backs or in their saddlebags. Croix rode at the head on the golden Palomino, Tavo followed behind on his spotted Appaloosa, Skinny rode beside Tavo on his blue Roan, and Kid was straggling behind on the splash paint horse that Croix had given him for Christmas the year before. They crossed over the derelict concrete aqueduct that once supplied water from their beloved valley to millions of people in the fallen city of angels. Croix always felt a sense of vindication when he crossed over the ruins of the aqueduct. Revivalists were in the business of taking things back. This journey would be no different. But he was looking forward to a calming ride before the retribution. A little time to cool down. A moment to gather his wits again.

Then Kid inspired his horse to a hard gallop and rode up alongside him, uninvited as always, and Croix groaned and rolled his eyes and sighed as loudly as he could to get his point across without actually having to say it outright, and when it was obvious that Kid didn't take the point, Croix hissed and stiffened his neck and growled all in one theatrical motion. He knew what was coming. It was inevitable. More goddamn questions.

"So where'd you get that Billy Dagger flag?" Kid asked. "I mean really. Where'd you get it?"

Croix didn't answer. He looked back at Tavo and Skinny for moral support, or a helping hand, or even some thoughtful interference. Anything that could save him from Kid's tormenting sense of wonder. But they just shrugged and chuckled selfishly. Croix whipped his head back around, his fiery blue eyes looking ahead at the horizon and wishing it was closer than it was. "I told you already, Kid. I found it in the desert."

"I don't believe that."

"Just because you don't believe something don't make it untrue."

"Stop saying things like that. You said he's a hero to you. Why?"

Croix wouldn't answer.

"Did you know him or not?"

Croix still wouldn't answer.

"Did he give you that flag?" All Kid heard was the clacking of horse hooves and a thoughtless breath from Croix. It irked him. "Damnit. Come on, Croix. Did Billy Dagger give you that flag or not?"

"For God's sake, Kid." Croix made a sound like a hacksaw cutting through a tiny metal pipe. "It never stops with you, does it?"

"It's a simple question."

"I regret ever telling you those stories."

"That all they are? *Stories*? You saying they ain't true?"

"I didn't say that."

"Whatcha saying then?"

"I'm saying I don't wanna talk about it."

"Then whatcha wanna talk about?"

"Nothing."

Kid thought deeply for a moment, but not too wisely, and then he asked, "You wanna talk about Zee?"

Croix whipped his eyes at him in absolute disbelief. A familiar response. "*No, goddamn you*, I don't wanna talk about *Zee*. I don't wanna talk about a *goddamn thing*. Is that so hard to understand?"

"Well, *what* then? We just sit here riding in silence?"

"Yes. That's exactly what we do. We sit here in our saddles and ride in silence."

"What's the point of that?"

"To make me happy."

"I've never seen you happy."

"Then keep trying."

"Come on, Croix. It ain't such a hard question. It's a simple *yes or no* answer."

"That's enough."

"Tell me."

"No."

"Did you know Billy Dagger or not?"

"Christ, Kid, your mouth never stops! For God's sake, *Shut the fuck up!*" Croix stopped his horse with a tug of the reins. "What'd I teach you about social etiquette?"

"You just told me to *shut the fuck up*," Kid said. "Don't think that qualifies as social etiquette. Certainly don't qualify as teaching."

"I've taught you everything you need to know, you little shit. *How to ride a horse. How to shoot a gun.* Now I'm teaching you when to *shut the fuck up*. It may save your life someday." He placed his fingers on the handle of his *Crazy 8*. "Maybe even today."

"Fine," Kid said bitterly. "Have it your way, asshole!" He clicked his heels into the paint horse and rode ahead. "We'll just sit here riding in silence then. I won't say another goddamn word."

"Well *hallelujah*," Croix said to himself. "I guess I can start believing in miracles again." He heard Tavo and Skinny chuckle behind him, but he paid no mind to their foolishness. That's all they ever did: laugh like fools. At anything. Didn't even have to be funny. It seemed like they laughed just to be doing something. Croix decided to tune out their noise and savor the peace and quiet for a change. As they rode onward, he sat there in his saddle admiring the rugged landscape. Despite the bloody history in the valley and all the unwanted memories that it stirred within his spartan mind, the land was still beautiful, and a sight to behold, no matter who's eyes were witnessing it. He always marveled at the grand majesty of the mountains, their granite peaks like claws reaching out from the earth trying to grab the sun and squeeze it to death. The red snow-capped tips that were covered in algae during the summer months were so tall that he'd never seen the top of them. Only the birds were so lucky. He watched a bird flying overhead in the pink coral sky. It was a bird of prey. He always envied the hawks of the valley. They flew high above everything else, free from the burden of the earth, watching the world transpire below without ever being touched by its cold indifference. He longed for that kind of peace from the chaos. He watched the hawk glide with its wings resting carelessly on the breeze, floating on air without effort and without ever needing to land. *That's true freedom*, he thought. *If I could only be a hawk. A raptor with sharp talons and a keen eye. If I could only have their perspective.* Hawks had a tactical advantage. One that would serve Croix well if he only had the ability to fly. They were inescapable to their enemies. Their prey was easily spotted from the sky above, and so their enemies were easily conquered. Nothing could hide from them. Nothing betrayed them but their own shadows. For a moment Croix felt their sense of undisputed power, or what he imagined such a thing might feel like. It felt like peace.

Then Kid pulled alongside him again and every microscopic atom of peace he'd felt emerging inside of his body was snuffed out like a midnight candle.

"So, whatcha done to Zee that's got her so pissed at you?" Kid asked. "No bullshit this time."

Croix threw his arms up in sheer exhaustion. "So much for enjoying the goddamn silence. Christ Almighty."

Tavo and Skinny chuckled quietly in the background.

"*Well*," Kid said, "what'd you do?"

"It ain't none of your goddamn business."

"Why not?"

Croix thought for a moment, and then he redirected the conversation. "You should be more worried about yourself, Kid. You're about to find out what chasing tail does to a man."

"What's that supposed to mean?"

"I noticed you got a little hard-on for Gin."

Kid grinned mischievously. "Ain't so little."

Tavo and Skinny burst into laughter. It seemed to echo throughout the nearby canyon.

The comment even forced a healthy grin from Croix, but he was never one to let it show. "Better watch yourself, Kid. Women are nature's most unpredictable creature. Just when you think you got 'em figured, they up and bite you in the ass."

"What do you know about women? Except how to piss 'em off. I don't need your advice."

Croix snickered. "You got *two* hard heads, Kid. You're doomed."

Tavo and Skinny laughed again.

Kid snickered right back. "Oh you know all about doom, don't you?"

"Whatever," Croix said. "It don't matter anyhow. I don't think Gin has any interest in a little boy whose balls ain't entirely dropped yet."

Tavo and Skinny laughed so hard it practically rattled the rocks loose from the canyon walls.

Kid glared back at them, his eyes hawked in anger. Then he turned back to Croix and hissed like a baby snake too afraid to strike. "I don't wanna talk about it no more."

"Oh?" Croix looked victorious. "You lost your will for conversation?"

"It's never a conversation with you, asshole. It's just a lecture or an insult."

"So what's the remedy?"

Kid sulked bitterly. "Silence I guess."

"Now you're learning," Croix said. "Hell, I might make a good teacher after all." There was a certain satisfaction in his voice, as if he were almost happy.

---

They rode in silence for the rest of the evening, each of them harboring their feelings and their deep contemplations and burying their instinct for conversation beneath the surface, especially Kid, who was holding a bitter grudge over Croix's verbal assault. They trotted beneath a canopy of golden clouds as the evening sun crashed into the saw-toothed horizon. It looked as if the fading orb was being cut to pieces. They slept under the stars that night without a fire, to stay hidden from any scavengers that might find their trade goods enticing. They surrounded themselves with ropes and superstition to keep the snakes away, and with trip wire and rattling bells to alert them to any large predators that might be stalking them in the dark. They took turns on watch, their eyes peering through the pitch blackness with uncertainty and their ears straining in the dreadful silence. Kid didn't say a word during his portion of the watch. Instead he sulked with his eyes to the moonless sky and his mind on the kind of things that didn't inspire any wonder. It was going to be a long night.

# FOUR

That very same night within the neon glow of Sky Haven, a young woman was straddling Brixton on the couch in his penthouse. She was naked and glistening with sweaty lust and thrusting up and down on his fading manhood like a buoy in the ocean. A few strands of light blonde hair were poking out from beneath a red synthetic wig. She was still in character, even at that late hour. Just a prostitute playing a part. A sex worker desired by her clients for her exotic red hair and her fiery spirit. Only one was fraudulent. Her name was Roxy, but it wasn't the name her parents had given her. That truth remained hidden, like all truths of the past. She was twenty-three years old and still on her colossal rise from a desperate refugee girl in Brimstone to being the most sought after sex worker in all of Phoenix.

She was giving Brixton all he could handle. That's how it was with him. She had many clients, most of which were undesirable corporate giants and high-rolling businessmen, but she always had a special place in her misguided heart for the golden boy. They weren't together by any means, far from it in fact, but they were certainly entangled, and at the moment they were tangled up in sweaty limbs. Her breasts were dangling in his face where she knew he liked them to be, but he wasn't even looking at them, and they were calling all kinds of attention to themselves. His manhood began to soften beneath her, like the air going out of a party balloon. She tried to stimulate him further, moving herself seductively on his lap, in ways that would make most men beg for more, but Brixton had no intention to beg tonight. He just wanted less. "Stop," he said, grabbing her by the shoulders to halt her momentum.

She stopped and tilted her eyes at him. "What the fuck's with you?"

"I can't do this right now."

She held her gaze with unsatisfied contempt. "You come here to fuck. For free."

"Then I'll pay you, for fuck's sake."

"I fuck *you* for the pleasure, dickhead, not the payment."

He leaned back into the soft cushion and said, "We all pay, darling. One way or another."

She cringed at his forced bravado. "Don't talk shit. You ain't no big shot."

He exhaled as if he knew she was right. "You shouldn't be here, Roxy. I've got too much on my mind."

She grabbed his hands and placed them on her breasts and began to move her body in sexual waves, like oceanic swells. "Well in that case, let me give you something else to think about for a while." It was a simple trick of the trade that never failed to arouse.

But Brixton was only deflating. "Stop, Roxy." He pulled his hands away from her breasts. "I'm serious. *Stop*."

She glared at him. "My God, Brix, what's your deal tonight?"

"I'm in trouble," he said without much thought to preserve

the dark secrets that he held in his heart. His eyes were like those of a newborn baby. Something innocent and frightened all at once.

Roxy calmed herself and studied his face. "Shit, you *are* serious." She rolled off of him and snuggled alongside him on the couch, pressing her naked body against his. "What kind of trouble?"

"You should leave."

"Do you wanna talk about it? It's not *just* about the sex for me."

"Oh wow, I get a mind fuck too?"

"No, you dick, but I heard things."

Brixton whipped his head sideways and glared at her with his deep, penetrating eyes. "What do you mean you *heard* things?"

She shrugged. "People talk."

"Who?"

"I really shouldn't be telling you——"

"Who, goddamnit?" He grabbed her by the wrist before she could explain herself. "Who's talking? You're probably fucking half the executive board. *Tell me.* Is it Pharaoh? Are you fucking him?"

"Let me *go*." Roxy tried to pull away from his grip, but he squeezed even harder. She shouted, "Let me go, you crazy fuck."

Brixton withdrew and let her go and immediately put his hands over his face in shame. He leaned back into the cushion again, as if he needed something to break his fall. He was feeling small, in more ways than one. "Jesus Christ... Roxanne... I... I'm sorry."

Roxy softened her glare. She was always quick to forgive Brixton when he was vulnerable, which was often. Every time he called her Roxanne, it just melted her heart. That was her chosen name, but her clients had always shortened it to Roxy, supposedly because it sounded sexier to them, and the name always stuck. Only Brixton called her Roxanne. She placed her hand delicately on his chest. "Talk to me."

"I'm really sorry," he mumbled. "I'm just... I'm sorry."

"I've never seen you like this, Brix. You're really shaken up."

He tried to shake what was obvious. "No, I... it's just..." Then his mind began spinning with all sorts of aggravating curiosities. One in particular. A real degrading thought. "Wait a second," he said, feeling a sudden punch to his ego. "You're not... *no…* are you fucking *Nile?*"

"Oh my god," Roxy said, rolling her eyes. "I can't with you. Are you serious right now?"

Brixton hung his head. There was so much self-doubt sawing through his mind that he thought he might be cut wide open and exposed.

Roxy placed a hand on his chin and lifted his head softly. "Did you do something?"

He looked at her with suspicion in his eyes again. "Did I do *something*?"

"Something illegal?"

"Who told you to ask me that?"

"What?"

He grabbed her by the wrist again. "Who was it?"

"Stop," she said, trying to pull away. "Let me go, asshole. What the fuck?"

"*Tell me.* Who told you to ask me that?"

"*I'm* asking, you dick. *Me.* Is it so crazy to think I'm just worried about you?"

Brixton loosened his grip, but he wouldn't let her go this time. He scrutinized her with no remorse, as if she were a suspect in his interrogation room and he was close to breaking her down. "I'm not letting go until you tell me the truth."

"People say you're burned out," she huffed defensively. "Maybe they're right. *Seriously*. Look at you. You're losing it, man." She tried to pull away from him again.

But he held her wrist tightly and told her to, "Stop pulling away and answer me."

"Screw you." She finally pulled herself free. "What the fuck is wrong with you, man?"

Brixton held his investigatory gaze on her, staring into her frightened eyes, half-expecting her to break down and confess something. But she was silent and withdrawn. She didn't seem to be hiding anything at all. He looked away, realizing he had miscalculated. He looked around the room for a quick scapegoat. Anything to assuage his guilt. Then he noticed a bottle of pills on the side table. A clustered mix of random, black market anti-depressant tablets. They weren't his. It was just what he needed to turn the whole situation around on her. A trick that he always denied using. "You on that shit again?" he asked, conveniently ignoring his own use of the exact same drug.

Roxy rolled her eyes. "Don't turn this around on me."

"I thought you were gonna stop using that shit. You're better than that."

"Don't lecture me on my lifestyle choices. You're not my daddy."

"Too bad I'm not. You could use one."

"Oh don't you *dare*." She raised her fist like she wanted to strike him.

Brixton shoved her away and leapt to his feet. He pulled his pants up and began clasping his high-dollar belt buckle with the polished sheen.

Roxy jumped to her feet. "Where you going?"

"I'm not going anywhere," he said. "*You* are. Did you forget we're at my place?" He snickered patronizingly. "You've been laid in so many different rooms it's hard to keep track."

"You prick."

"Get out."

"Seriously?"

"Roxy, I'm not playing. Get the fuck out."

"Are we really doing this again?" she asked, calling his bluff. "You know what happens next. I leave and then you come crawling back to me begging me to blow you."

"Not tonight, sweetheart." He tugged on his clasped belt. "I'm all locked up." He grabbed his coat from the couch.

She grabbed him by the arm, accidentally pulling the coat from his grasp, and as the coat hit the floor the wallet that he'd traded for in Brimstone slid out from the inner pocket and onto the floor. She tried to bend down and grab it.

"*Don't touch that.*" He pushed her aside and snatched the wallet up and put it back in his coat pocket.

"What was that?" she asked.

"Nothing," he said, looking away from her.

"What was it?"

"It's just… I said it's *nothing*."

She tried to calm him with her touch. "Brix, let's just crawl back into bed together and—"

"Forget it. You're gonna have to get your kicks with someone else tonight." He walked towards the door and opened it and gestured for her to leave. "I'm sure you've got a long list of clients to choose from."

"Screw you, *golden boy*," she said, emphasizing the tired old moniker. "You're such a self-righteous prick." She grabbed her clothes from the couch and started putting them on in a tantrum. "I'm out of here. I'm not doing this shit with you anymore. Whatever *this* is… it's over. I don't need your bullshit."

Brixton suddenly dropped the charade and closed the door. "Now hold on a second. Just *wait*." He walked back to her and grabbed her softly by the arm.

She pushed him away. "No, you told me to go fuck someone else tonight, so that's what I'm gonna do."

"I didn't mean it. You know I didn't."

"I'm sick of your bullshit, Brix. You're a psychopath."

"A *psychopath*? *Really*? Is that not calling the kettle black?"

She shook her head, as if there was nothing more she could do. "You need help, you know that? And not the kind of help I can give."

Brixton's face turned sour. "That's a little dramatic, don't you think? Stop being so emotional."

She pulled her tight red skirt over her bra-less torso and rolled it down over her curved hips. "I'm going to fuck a big whig tonight. That's what I'm gonna do. Just to spite you."

"That's childish," he said with a scowl. "You should be embarrassed."

She bolted for the exit.

He ran past her and blocked the doorway. "*Hold on.* I'm sorry, okay? I just got a little… *Please, Roxanne*, I'm just having a bad day."

"You've been having a bad day for the past six months. Now *move*."

He wouldn't move. He began his usual plea, as expected, begging like a horny teenager on prom night with his hands cupped in prayer. "Please stay. I'll work my shit out. I always do. I'm sorry, baby."

"*BABY?*" she said with a condescending shriek. "Oh, so now I'm *baby* to you?"

"Roxy, don't… just… *stay.*"

"*Stay?* Screw you. I may like it on all fours, but I'm not a fucking dog." She shoved him aside and opened the door.

He closed it before she could squeeze her tiny little foot through the crack. "Don't leave me, Roxanne." But she didn't stand there melting in the doorway like he'd hoped. She wouldn't even look at him. "Look at me. Please."

She looked at him.

"I said I was sorry." He looked at her with what he hoped was a lovable puppy-dog gaze. "I just want you to lay with me tonight. That's all. Just lay with me in the bed and we can cuddle. Don't leave me alone tonight. I'm not good on my own."

"If you're not good on your own, then why are you such an asshole to everyone who tries to get close?"

Brixton was rocked backwards on his heels a bit, as if the words had punched him right in the chest.

Roxy looked at him with a frown, but it wasn't sympathy. "You're pathetic. You really are. I should've seen this coming. We're just two different people." She pushed him aside and opened the door again. "You can cuddle with your hand tonight, *momma's boy.*"

"Hey!" Brixton shrugged violently. "Why do you have to say something like that? I told you that shit in confidence."

Roxy stormed down the hallway to the elevator with her red stiletto heels in her hands and her tight skirt riding up the left cheek of her ass. The elevator door opened on cue. An older couple exited. They were in their late sixties. Both dressed to the nines. The man was in a sharp suit. His wife was decked out in a tailored purple dress with sequins at the top and bottom. They were startled by Roxy's appearance, probably recognizing her slutty clothes and hooker vibe. They looked at her with a haughty disdain that only the righteous people of the Haven could offer. She flicked them off and turned back to Brixton, who was still standing in the doorway, and she called him the dirtiest name in the golden boy's book. The unholiest of them all: "Burnout!"

Brixton stiffened.

"It's true," she said. "You're a fucking *burnout*. And a worthless fuck."

Brixton could feel his bowels almost give way. The older couple looked at him with a harsh judgement in their eyes, as if he'd violated every single high-classed expectation of a Havenite. He looked at them pridefully. "This is the penthouse floor. You're looking for the gala hall, right?"

They nodded.

"It's one floor below me," he said. "I *own* this one."

The couple looked uncomfortable.

"You don't recognize my face?" he asked.

They turned back to the elevator.

Roxy stood inside waiting. "You going down?" she asked, with her eyes on the old man.

He froze.

She winked at him. "I bet you would if I gave you the chance."

His wife gasped.

Then Roxy looked at him curiously and said, "Wait, don't I know you?"

He grabbed his wife by the arm and said, "We'll take the stairs."

Then they took the stairs, rather quickly.

Roxy turned her scornful eyes back on Brixton. He stood there like a marked man, waiting for the bullet to strike his heart. Then the elevator doors closed mercifully, and Roxy disappeared behind them. He exhaled. He stepped back inside his penthouse and closed the door and stood there with his back pressed against the expensive wood. All he could hear was the word *burnout* being repeated over and over in his mind. Roxy's shrill little voice was still patronizing him, shouting, *Burnout! Burnout! You're a fucking BURNOUT!*

He could hardly breathe.

Then he wondered, *What the fuck happened to Brixton Grace?*

That's how he always thought of himself. In the third person. As if he were something so extraordinary and rare that even *he* should take a step back and admire it from afar. But he could feel Brixton Grace slipping away, leaving his body like some undead spirit not wanting any part of the life he'd ruined. His mind began spinning in its usual fashion: aimlessly. He was always trying to finagle his way out of his own head in these doubtful moments. *Come on, Brix. Do something!* He was feeling a need to prove himself again, and as he pondered his options with reckless abandon, a scenario for a quick redemption sprung to mind. He pulled his SAT phone and dialed Nile's line. "*Nile…* you still at the station?"

"Yeah," Nile said on the other end. "I'm just wrapping up this paperwork. But it's late and I'm about to head home. Why?"

"Don't leave," Brixton said. "I'll be there in ten minutes. Wait for me." He ended the call before Nile had a chance to object.

# FIVE

Brixton arrived in nine minutes and thirty-eight seconds. He walked the long corridor of the detainment facility at PPD with a fresh sense of purpose. He carried himself with his trademark swagger, walking with a confident stride that he'd willfully developed over the years. A sort of social armor. He felt like a rockstar cop again, even if it was total bullshit. He was out to prove something. To restore his ego. "It's good to be back," he said.

Nile greeted him at the entrance to the Quarantine Sector. "What's this all about, Brix?"

Brixton ignored him and just kept walking, barreling his way through the double doors that were labeled in big red letters: *Biohazard. Authorized Personnel Only.*

Nile chased after him. "It's almost midnight, Brix. You're not even authorized to be here."

"You don't know the half of it."

"What's that supposed to mean?" Nile quickened his pace to catch up. "Brix, hold on."

Brixton stopped and turned to him. "Where are they? I've got questions."

"They're still in quarantine. We can't go in there."

"Says who?"

"Says the corporation that employs you. Follow protocol this time, Brix. Please."

"I'm following my instincts."

Nile sighed. "Nothing good ever comes of that."

Brixton raised his biomask in the air. "Relax. I've got a mask. I'll grab a hazmat suit." He started walking to the quarantine chambers. "What could go wrong?"

Nile grimaced and muttered, "Everything." He watched in peril as Brixton slid the biomask over his head and grabbed a yellow hazmat suit from the plastic hanging closet. Then he watched Brixton bully his way through the plastic barrier of the quarantine chambers. His gut began to rumble. He knew he had no choice but to follow.

A moment later Brixton was standing inside of a small quarantine chamber wearing his biomask and his yellow hazmat suit. The small room was framed in hard polycarbonate glass and plastic flooring, with a self-quarantine system that sanitized the environment every few minutes. The refugee woman from apartment 407 sat on the medical bed in front of him. Her eyes were drained from illness, and probably from stress and sleep deprivation. Dark pockets of blood had begun to form beneath her eyes. Her body was weak and being monitored by wired electrodes. She was hooked to oxygen tanks with breathing tubes in her nose, looking like some captured alien in a top secret base. She'd been crying. It was obvious. Her eyes were damp and red.

But Brixton had no sympathy. "You don't belong here," he said to her. "Not in our city. You're not citizens. You compromised our well-being when you crossed that border. Whatever this thing is... *this illness*... it could be contagious. Did you ever think about that?"

The woman refused to look at him. She just stared down at the floor and took deep purposeful breaths to stay upright.

"You're not gonna get treatment," he explained. "The medics just want your bloodwork. They're just gonna run it through some tests to figure out what's wrong with you. To determine whether it's contagious or not. Then Nimbus is gonna pull the plug and let you die. They just want to keep this shit from spreading. They're protecting *us*, you understand?" He paused, allowing the reality to sink in. "It's a shame though. Because you don't have to die. Neither does your son."

The woman looked up at him. Her eyes were deep wells of desperation, but Brixton just saw it as a clear advantage. "We have meds for it," he said. "Meds that would save you both. But you're not entitled to our healthcare." He could sense that she was on the hook. "You wanna cooperate? Tell me what I wanna know. I'll pull some strings with Nimbus and get you those meds. You *and* your boy." He let that linger in her mind for a moment, and then he asked, "Where'd you get those microchips?"

The woman attempted to speak, but her throat was so parched that her voice screeched like air brakes. "Can I... get some... water first?"

Brixton nodded. He stepped out of the chamber and passed through the contagion barrier where the self-sanitizing system blew a fine mist into the air around him and sucked it right back out like a vacuum. He stepped into the observation room.

Nile had been monitoring the interrogation through a

double-sided pane of glass. He predictably had concerns. "Brix, what the hell are you doing?"

"She's gonna talk, Nile. Get her some water. Check on her little boy too. See if he needs anything."

"Brix... *the boy*..." Nile was reluctant to break the news. "*The boy's dead.*"

Brixton was stuck in place. A man trapped in time. "What are you talking about?"

"He's dead, Brix. He died a few hours ago."

"Why the hell didn't you tell me? Jesus Christ, man. I just promised the mother—"

"Meds?" Nile interrupted, scolding him with his usual motherly gaze. "What meds?"

Brixton shrugged in defense of himself. "I didn't know the boy was dead."

"Well it's too late to grow a conscience now. You already lied to her. Lie again." Nile handed him a cup of drinking water. "I told you not to go in there."

Brixton was flush, trying to grapple with a sudden feeling of remorse. A feeling which he was coping with a lot lately.

Then Nile noticed something on the surveillance monitor behind him. "What's that all about?" He saw four Nimbus agents entering the detainment facility. "It's Arroway."

"Arroway?" Brixton turned and saw the watchdog hunting on the screen. "Oh shit… shit shit shit. Stall 'em."

"What do you mean stall 'em?" Nile turned to engage. "What's going on, Brix?"

But Brixton was already making his way through the contagion barrier and back into the quarantine chamber.

When Brixton stormed back into the chamber, he gave the woman the cup of water and grabbed a chair and quickly wedged the backrest under the door handle so it couldn't be pushed open from the outside.

The woman looked at him with concern. "What's going on?"

"Drink the water and talk," he snapped.

She drank, but she was suspicious of his erratic behavior. "Is everything okay?"

"Yeah, everything's fine. Now talk. We had a deal."

"I wanna see my boy first. How is he?"

Brixton froze for a second. "He's… *he's still dying*. So get on with it if you wanna save his life. Who injected you with those microchips?"

"I can't say for sure," the woman conceded. "They had masks on."

"Tell me more."

"They offered us a chance to cross the border and get help. We were desperate, so we agreed."

"Were they with the black market?"

The woman was getting flustered by all the uncertainty. "I… I don't know. I think maybe they were. I heard them say something about the black market."

"Were they Bloody Knuckles?"

"I don't really know. They didn't say."

---

As Nile was watching the interrogation through the double-sided glass in the observation area, Arroway and three Nimbus agents barged in. "Stand down, Inspector Wambasa." Arroway directed the agents to the quarantine chamber. "Get Grace out of there."

"No, you can't," Nile said. "He's in the middle of an inter-rogation."

"He's not even authorized to be here, Inspector."

One of the agents crossed through the contagion barrier and tried to open the door to the chamber, but it wouldn't budge. "He's got the door wedged, sir."

---

The refugee woman saw the door handle being jiggled violently. "What's going on here?"

"I need a name," Brixton said furiously. "A *face*. A fucking *location. Anything.*"

The woman was flustered. "We... we were blindfolded. So I... I don't know."

"Tell me something more or there's no deal."

"We got the microchips in our wrists… then… we…" She stopped, distracted by the door rattling, and by her own fear.

"Then you *what?*" Brixton asked. "Go on. *Talk.*"

"When they were done… they… they left us there. Told us not to remove the blindfolds until we counted to three-hundred. So we counted."

Arroway crossed through the contagion barrier and pounded his fist on the chamber door. "Grace, open the door. *That's an order.*"

Brixton tried to stay calm so the refugee woman would stay calm as well. "It's okay," he said, but the agitation in his voice betrayed him. "Just think… Did you hear anything? A name? A meaningful reference? Any fucking thing?"

She struggled to remember through the stifling anxiety. "They called one of them *Spiral.*"

"Spiral? Did you see his face?"

"No."

Arroway pounded on the door again, jiggling the handle. "Grace, *open this door*. I'm here on orders. You're screwing yourself here, Grace."

Brixton dismissed the woman's story, scolding her with his eyes. "It was probably a bullshit name, lady. If that's all you've got there's no deal."

"Please," she said. "My boy needs help."

Then Arroway rammed his shoulder into the door and breached the threshold, knocking the chair to the floor.

Nile tried to stop him. "You can't go in there without hazmats."

But Arroway and the agents charged into the chamber and grabbed Brixton by the arms. "Stand down, Grace. These people are off limits to you."

The woman pleaded to Brixton as he was being apprehended. "Help my son. Please. He deserves a chance to live. He's a good boy. I'm begging you. Help him!"

Brixton was unsettled by her plea. He imagined the poor boy lying dead in his hospital bed. He tried to pull away from the agents, but they held him tighter. "Get your fucking hands off me!" He grabbed one of the agents by the hair and pulled him down and punched him in the temple. The other agents grabbed him and pinned his arm behind his back, threatening to break it. He finally submitted, and as they pinned his other arm behind his back, he turned to Arroway and asked, "What the hell are you doing here?"

"My bloodwork came back clean," Arroway explained. "I'm back in the field. Corporate signed off on it this morning."

"You're interfering with my interrogation."

"You're not even authorized to be here, Grace."

Then Brixton noticed that he and the other agents weren't

wearing their biohazards. "Where's your biomask? You should be wearing hazmats in here."

"This is my interrogation now," Arroway said calmly. "My rules. Corporate signed off on that too." He showed Brixton the document on his solar scroll. It officially turned the investigation over to Nimbus Security. Signed into law by CEO Lucian Vanderbon himself.

The refugee woman was frightened by all the uncertainty. "Hold on," she said, looking deceived. "*Wait.* What about the meds? What about my son? Where's my *son*?"

Arroway didn't even bother to look at her as he told her the terrible truth. "Your son is dead."

The woman gasped pitifully, as if her soul had been stripped from her body and was leaving her there to die a slow death. She screamed out in agony and roared at Brixton, "You fucking lied to me!"

Brixton felt a sudden drop in his heart. The pressure in his chest began to mount. A sorrow he just couldn't bear. The agents pushed him out of the quarantine room.

Arroway closed the door on the screaming woman and turned to Brixton and said, "We're taking over the investigation."

Brixton looked back through the double-sided glass. The poor woman had just lost her son and now she was dying right along with him. He could see she had already given up on life. The anguish on her face was hard to witness. He turned and glared at Arroway, but he just couldn't find the words to protest. He was speechless, his feelings too mixed for words.

"No questions?" Arroway asked snidely. "No smart-ass remarks? That's a first for you, Grace." He turned to the other agents. "Get him out of here. He belongs in the desert."

The Agents pushed Brixton out of the observation area, but he resisted, planting the soles of his shoes in the rivets of the floor and scraping his heels on the tile as they forced him away. "*Hold on.* I'm still suited. You need to go through quarantine procedures. She could be *contagious.*"

Nile tried to calm him down, even though the questions were more than valid. "Brix, stop! Let's just get out of here."

Brixton shoved him away and tried to fight off the agents who were pushing him through the corridor. "*Arroway, why aren't you wearing your biomask? Arroway! Answer me, you prick!*"

Arroway turned and walked back into the quarantine chamber and closed the door behind him. The agents dragged Brixton out kicking and screaming. Nile followed without putting up a fight.

## SIX

After they had successfully removed Brixton from the station, Nile was ordered to drive the golden boy back to his penthouse at Chateau Royale where he was to pack his belongings and sleep it off and prepare for his transfer to Outpost 11 the next morning. He sat in the passenger seat of Nile's Volt-22 cruiser sulking in silence.

Nile sat behind the wheel, his lights flashing, the sirens wailing, and driving a lot faster than normal. "What the *hell* were you thinking in there, Brix? You trying to ruin yourself?"

"Slow down," Brixton said. "You're driving like a madman. You in a hurry to get rid of me?"

"No. To be honest, I'm in a hurry to get home and get some sleep."

Brixton chuckled to himself. "I bet you haven't slept much in the last four months."

"Yeah, I've been *living* my nightmare. Why bother sleeping?"

"Wow," Brixton said, but without a smile. "You're getting

better with the jabs. I'm impressed. That one actually stung a bit."

Nile cut the flashers off and cut the sirens and slowed down, driving well under the speed limit. "Tell me what's going on with you and Corporate."

"That's a waste of time, Nile. Stop asking the wrong questions."

"What are the right questions?"

"Did you notice something missing from the equation back there in quarantine?"

"Missing? You mean besides Arroway's biomask?"

"Yeah, that's a major fucking problem too, but an obvious one. I'm talking about something else."

"What?"

"No coughing." Brixton cast his eyes on Nile, throwing him a line.

Nile seemed to be on the hook, but he wouldn't let on.

"Not a single cough," Brixton said. "I talked to that woman for ten minutes. She never coughed once."

"So?"

"The white lung is characterized by intense coughing. This mystery illness is supposedly a variant?"

"That's just a working theory, Brix. Nothing set in stone."

"Yeah, but coughing is a basic characteristic of any respiratory illness."

"So what are you saying?"

"Something isn't adding up."

"Okay." Nile looked confused. "So... *what* are you saying?"

"Corporate isn't telling us everything."

Nile shrugged, his eyes on the road ahead. "Why would they keep us in the dark?"

"Obviously I can't answer that. But you can agree that something isn't adding up, right?"

"I can agree."

"Good. Then we both agree that Corporate is keeping us in the dark."

"I didn't say that."

"You won't say it, but you're thinking it."

"Because you put the thought in my head."

"Doesn't matter," Brixton said. "You're thinking it."

"But I'm not saying it."

"Agreed."

Nile huffed. "Can we stop talking about the case?"

"I need to question the landlord," Brixton said, as if nothing had ever happened back at quarantine.

"Brix, you're done. They won't let you set foot in the station. You're as good as gone."

"Then *you* question him."

"No. I'm done talking about the case."

"What would you rather talk about? Life stuff? Should we start off with one of your *get-to-know-each-other* questions?"

"Why even bother? You never answer them anyway."

"I'll go first," Brixton said with a smirk. "Are you *still* a virgin after last night?"

"That's off limits."

"Nothing's off limits. We're partners."

"Not for much longer."

"What was her name? Penelope?"

"No," Nile said with a pout.

"Phoebe?"

"Brix… enough."

"So you're still a virgin?"

"No comment."

"That's a yes," Brixton said. "What happened? Did you blow your wad in your pants before you got the dinner bill?" He laughed.

Nile rolled his eyes. "Have I ever told you you're the biggest asshole I've ever met?"

"No. But I already knew that. If I wasn't, I'd be doing something wrong."

"Well, mission accomplished."

"Yep. It's not easy being public asshole number one. You should appreciate my consistency."

"Something to be proud of."

"Yes it is," Brixton said. "I even have a plaque on my wall at home. *World's biggest asshole.* I hung it above the mantel on my fake fireplace."

"Part of your self-aggrandizing shrine?"

"My self *what*?"

"Aggrandizing," Nile said. "It means... to enhance one's reputation... even in their own mind."

"I knew that."

"Of course you did."

Brixton sat there for a moment. "Aren't you gonna miss me a little bit?"

Nile didn't say.

Brixton wasn't sure how to take it. He himself didn't feel any love loss between them. To be honest, he couldn't wait to be free of Nile's paralyzing caution. But how could Nile not miss him a little bit? He smirked again. "Yeah, you're gonna miss me. I know you are."

Nile had his mind on something else. "You ever wonder why they partnered us up?"

"To ruin my life," Brixton said.

"Seriously. Why the two of us? They knew our personalities wouldn't mesh. We hated each other as far back as the academy. That was well-documented."

"You hated me?"

"Seriously, Brix. It doesn't puzzle you?"

Brixton was impressed. "Look at you asking bold questions all of a sudden. You might make a decent Inspector yet."

Nile shook his head sharply. "Can you ever take anything seriously?"

Then Brixton saw the bright neon lights of Chateau Royale ahead. "Alright, we're *here*. Look at that. Time really flies when you're having a meaningless conversation, doesn't it?"

"Not fast enough."

Brixton laughed. "There you go again. My goodness, Nile, we're breaking some serious ground with you tonight. Getting bolder with your questions *and* your insults? Pretty soon you'll have a pair of balls hanging between your legs and everything. The whole shebang."

Nile had no expression whatsoever. He stopped the cruiser in front of the entrance to the skyscraper. "The answer is *no*, I'm not gonna miss you. Not even a little."

Brixton scoffed arrogantly as he stepped out of the cruiser. "That's a lie."

"You know I don't lie."

"That's true." Brixton shook his head. "You're so lame, man."

Nile didn't even look his way. "Pack your bags and stay out of trouble. I'll pick you up in the morning."

Brixton saluted him mockingly. "Yes *sir*. Whatever you say *sir*." Then he closed the door.

Nile just hit the gas and drove away.

# SEVEN

Croix, Tavo, Skinny and Kid woke before first light and ate hard tack and fish jerky in the foggy blue dawn. As the sun rose they took the ominous Tiger Trail south to avoid the common trade routes and the raiders that might be waiting along the trampled path to ambush them. They passed by Indian petroglyphs carved into the red sandstone. Primitive, child-like etchings of handprints and spiraling circles and unholy crosses and strange creatures with horns that Kid believed to be a poor representation of bighorn sheep. He saw a crudely drawn stick figure holding a mighty spear in its hands and he wondered if he'd ever have the heart to be a hunter like that. He doubted it.

They trotted through the loose gravel of narrow washes and crossed over the unmarked graves of strangers and never once talked about death, nor life. They kept their umbrellas up for most of the morning, blocking the sun and keeping themselves lukewarm in the scorching heat. Soon they laid their weary heads at the water's edge of a small desert spring while the horses filled their bladders. They had lunch under the scattered shade of a desert willow tree, sharing rations of pine nuts that they'd gathered from pinyon trees in the Inyo forest earlier that spring. Croix carried them in a tiny wool sack that Zee had once made for him. A gift from long ago. There was a drawstring enclosure at the top, and the colorful stitching along the side was perfectly intact and stronger than anything that Croix had owned from the factories of the old world. Zee had unmatched dedication to her craft. A soulfulness that couldn't be replicated by robotic arms. She'd even sewn Croix's initials into the fabric, which was now stained with the blood of his enemies. Croix thought nothing of it. For dessert they ate the stalks of a desert trumpet, which left a sour but pleasant taste on their tongues. Croix spotted a black-tailed jackrabbit eating the succulent bits of a barrel cactus, its face crawling with swollen green bugs. Usually he would try to kill such a hearty meal, but they wouldn't be burning a fire on the dangerous trail to the Kelso Trading Post, so the only dinner they'd be having tonight was more rations of hardtack and fish jerky. It irked him to let the jackrabbit go, but he didn't allow himself to be betrayed by his hunger pangs. They'd have to stick to their rations.

After they relieved themselves in a stinking thicket of turpentine broom, they pressed onward, crossing over ancient fault lines where the earth once erupted with an internal fury that seemed to be slowly returning to its core. Croix knew someday she'd erupt again. They rode onward, most of the time riding single file, in a serpentine pattern, Croix at the head with a venomous bite and Kid as far away from him as possible. There was always something to talk about on these long desert treks, but Croix didn't want to talk about any of it, so he kept everyone just out of ear's reach. A strategy of self-preservation. He preferred to ride in silence and study the featureless horizon as he kept a wandering eye out for any possible threats. He didn't like distractions, but the verbal kind was the most intolerable. Conversation was a completely unnecessary pastime to him. So talking was kept to an absolute minimum that morning. At least for the first couple of hours. Then they rode upon an abandoned town, and suddenly Kid was bursting at the seams with questions and unwitting comments, and nothing could stop that boy from talking but a bullet in the head. Though Croix figured that would have to be proven to be believed.

"Hey Croix," Kid said boisterously, forgetting that he was supposed to be holding a grudge. "I got a question."

"You don't say?"

"Why don't ya'll ever go into them towns?"

"Because we've already been there."

"Nothing left to salvage?"

"Nothing we need."

"You think there's bad people in there?"

"I think there's bad people everywhere."

They rode for a few minutes more. Kid never took his eyes off of the town. Most of it had been burnt by the flames of methane gas. The stuccoed corpses that escaped the fire were all broken and sagging in the distance. Suburban ghosts lingering in their eternal misery. The buildings were covered in black mold spores and fungus. The wooden beams had rotted away and collapsed beneath the missing shingles. The plywood roofs were caved in or completely gone, having once been scavenged by the colonists and drifters who used the scraps for firewood or fortification. The homes that once held Christmas parties and summer gatherings were gutted from the inside out, their pasts more of a rumor than a memory. Plastic littered the streets like colorful drops of paint on a torn canvas. That was humanity's greatest contribution: trash, which would never decay. The asphalt roads were buckled and split by the incredible heat. The fabricated stone, and the mortar that kept it intact, was crumbling one chip at a time. A slow death.

Kid wondered if there was anything worth discovering in the town, whose name had been actively forgotten. Maybe snack cakes sealed in their plastic wrappings, which would still be edible even after twenty-five years. Maybe toys from the children who'd once roamed the neighborhoods of the old world. Kid had never had a toy to play with in his life. No RC trucks or basketballs. Not even a single action figure. He'd once made stick figures out of pine limbs that he secretly collected from the foothills while foraging in the Inyo Forest, but when Croix caught him playing with them he snatched them away and tossed them in the fire and told Kid to grow up. Croix could be so mean. Crushing the childhood from Kid's soul seemed to be his sole mission in life. Kid defied the impulse of growing up. He wanted to be a child forever. He imagined himself playing with the children in town, before the Collapse, when things were said to be better. Running in the clean streets. Tossing the ball. Riding bikes. It made him smile. Then he saw a lone wolf trotting down the broken road, nosing through the scattered trash. He thought the white-fanged devil looked dangerous, but Croix didn't seem too concerned, so Kid didn't bother to be concerned either. Wolves usually stayed away from humans anyway. Kid thought Croix was like a wolf. A solitary creature that only roamed in packs when it needed to conquer a rival pack. He looked at Croix and swore he saw fangs protruding from his mouth. Then he looked back at the nameless town and something else caught his eye. A set of broken traffic lights at a barren cross-roads in the desert ahead. He had no idea what they were. Surprisingly, the dead lights were still hanging from their electrical cable, as if nothing had changed since the world ended.

"What are them?" Kid asked.

"*Those*," Croix said, correcting the poor grammar with pettiness. "Those are traffic lights."

"Traffic?"

"That's what they called it back in the old world," Croix said, hoping he wouldn't have to elaborate.

Kid sat there looking at him with a dumbfounded expression on his face, just waiting for him to finish his explanation.

Croix sighed, "It was back when we used to have cars."

"And?"

Croix clenched his eyes tightly and figured he better just explain the whole goddamn thing. "We drove along these roads back in the day," he said with a sigh. "There were so many cars on the road at once they called it *traffic*. They had to make little flashing lights to tell you when to stop and when to go. So there'd be no car accidents. So people wouldn't just plow into one another recklessly like a bunch of damn fools."

Kid waited for more.

"A red light meant stop," Croix said with a grating tone. "Then you had to wait. A green light meant you could go again. That's about all I can tell you, Kid. You satisfied?"

"So hold up a second." Kid looked baffled as ever by such a ridiculous thing. "You had a little flashing light telling you when you could and couldn't move?"

"Yeah," Croix said, looking baffled himself. "Basically."

"Well no wonder the world went mad."

"Yeah," Croix said, "that might've had something to do with it."

Kid nodded, as if they were suddenly bonding.

Then Croix said, "Now can you leave me the hell alone?"

Kid stiffened and blew the hot air from his lungs. Croix sighed epically, flapping his lips like a motor boat. Those cryptic noises had become the markers of their conversation. Hisses and groans and scoffs and the bitter sighs that needed no explanation. Words were just something to pass the time between the noise.

Kid pulled away bitterly. He slowed his pace and rode up alongside Tavo and Skinny, who were conveniently out of Croix's earshot.

"Oh boy," Tavo said, closing his tired eyes, "Now *we're* your target?"

"Croix's a riddle to me," Kid ranted. "Like two different men. One moment he's laughing at the world and making me feel some manner of hope, and the next he's ripping my soul clean from my body and stomping on it."

Tavo made his own cryptic noise. An exasperated huff. "I'm gonna give you some advice, Kid. Don't press Croix like you been doing. There's a line you can't cross with him."

"A line?"

"Once you cross that line, you're on the other side with him, and he won't be the same Croix that you know."

"What's that mean?"

Tavo considered his words carefully. "He's dangerous, Kid. I love the man, but... he really *is* dangerous."

"Dangerous how?"

"Don't be so anxious to find out. You don't wanna be on the other side with him. Take my word for it. I been there."

"I just don't understand him at all."

"Of course you don't. Croix comes from a different world than you."

Kid looked sad. "I don't know the world I come from."

"Well, Croix knows his, all too well."

"I wish he'd go back then."

"He does. A little every day. That's the problem."

Kid scoffed in frustration. "Whatever that means."

"It means he's dangerous," Tavo sassed, losing his patience.

"It means don't press him. It means don't cross that line. You hear me?"

Kid glared at the back of Croix's head. "The bastard's crazy."

"Maybe," Tavo said. "The jury's still out on that one. But you best remember, Croix's the only reason you're still alive."

"And I should thank him for that? He should've left me for dead. I know y'all feel the same way."

"Oh you'll get plenty of chances to die out here," Tavo mused. "Don't you worry." Then he chuckled. A boisterous, patronizing guffaw that was clearly meant to irk. Skinny couldn't help but laugh along with him.

Kid was vexed by their mockery. "I hate all ya'll sons a bitches. I really do." He kicked his heels into the paint horse and rode ahead to be alone, lingering in the middle of the pack, sure to keep a healthy distance from all of them, especially from the crazy bastard at the head.

Soon they rode by the beautiful Granite Lake where the shorelines lay fractured and the rugged earthen walls were striped with rings. Water in the valley had once risen to much greater heights. Kid imagined himself drowning in it, and he thought it might be for the best.

# EIGHT

Brixton had dark circles beneath his eyes that morning. He hadn't slept much the night before. He was all packed up and ready to leave, standing outside of Chateau Royale waiting for Nile to pick him up and escort him to what he now considered to be the gates leading him straight to Hell. He only carried a small bag on his shoulder, with a few valuable belongings inside. Some street clothes. Underwear. A box with some personal items. His SAT Phone. Nothing much beyond that. He didn't intend for this little detour in his illustrious career to be long. He knew Corporate would come to their senses soon enough and fall to their knees begging him to return. He couldn't wait to hear them grovel.

Nile soon arrived and picked him up at the valet entrance and they headed to the border gates where Brixton's escort would be waiting. The two of them didn't say much to one another during the ride, which Nile found curious.

Brixton had an excuse though. His mind was foggy, and so was his future. Humility sucked. He couldn't help but feel internalized. He thought maybe that's how Nile always felt.

Inferior. Insecure. Impossibly vapid. What could he possibly have to talk about?

When they arrived at the border gates, Brixton got out of the cruiser and turned to say a quick goodbye, but Nile was already standing beside him with a look of expectation. Brixton stepped back. "Whoa. This doesn't really call for a hug."

Nile stepped back too. "Hey, don't flatter yourself."

Brixton chuckled softly, feeling his own tension begin to ease. It would be a brief interlude. His escort to Outpost 11 was waiting for him outside of the personnel gate at Immigration Control. They were two young border patrols from Outpost 1 in Brimstone, known as the Gate Keepers, their squad patch adorned with a Spartan guard in a bronze helmet holding a spear and a shield with the iconic Nimbus halo in the center of it. They weren't Warhawks, and that was a relief, but they'd likely be just as insufferable as those notorious bastards from Outpost 11. Brixton prepared himself for the worst. They were all *garbage men* after all, regardless of the patch they wore. Their modus operandi was always the same: douchebaggery. The two young Gate Keepers stood tall and proud in front of a futuristic black UTV with a curved spoiler on the tail that looked like a stinger. The desert rambler was appropriately called a *Scorpion*. It was fast as hell and highly maneuverable, and it was weaponized for combat. But today it was being used as a simple transport for the disgraced golden boy. Brixton approached the gate on foot, with Nile clinging to his side like a suckerfish. They turned to say their stubborn goodbyes, but the words just fluttered in their throats.

Nile looked melancholy. "You gonna tell me what's going on or not?"

"Nope," Brixton said. "I told you to lower your expectations."

Nile made a noise that sounded like an engine shutting down. "Then I guess this is where we part."

"Oh boy," Brixton said. "You're always so dramatic."

"I just want to understand what's going on."

"Then start with the right questions, Nile. What was Arroway doing at detainment? That's the question you should be asking."

Nile sighed.

Brixton kept pressing. "Why the hell weren't they wearing their biomasks? Their hazmats?"

"You're asking me like you're expecting an informed answer. I don't have a clue, Brix. Maybe we're not meant to know."

"Fuck that. It's our job. It's our jurisdiction."

Nile cringed at Brixton's arrogance. "It's all Corporate's jurisdiction, man. We're just tools at their disposal."

Brixton shook his weary head. "You disappoint me, Nile."

"Good. That probably means I'm doing something right."

Brixton hated that side of Nile. The side that always toed the company line and cowered down in the corner whenever the shit really hit the fan. "I want the dirt on those forged microchips. As soon as you find something."

"You know I can't do that."

"Haven't you ever broken the rules?"

"No," Nile said firmly.

Brixton shook his head again. "There's something going on. Nimbus Security took the case over before we could even do our job."

"Brix, you were transferred. They took the case over because you—"

"Ah fuck it," Brixton interrupted. "This gig in the desert is only temporary. I'll come back and solve the damn case myself."

Nile frowned. "You have no boundaries, do you?"

"Not a single one," Brixton said proudly. He turned to walk away, his patience worn thin. He'd heard enough corporate compliance for one day. He thought of Nile's spineless nature and how it was never going to serve him well. Brixton had tried to help Nile for the four months that they were partnered up, but he hadn't even made a dent in Nile's armor of caution. It was hopeless. Brixton decided it was time to give up. Nile was just too damn meek.

*You can't change a man's nature*, Brixton thought.

Then he thought about his own nature and realized that he still hadn't turned in his gun and badge as he'd been ordered to do. "Shit," he said, his eyes tightening. He pulled his gun and badge and turned around. "I almost forgot." He handed them to Nile. "I'm supposed to give these to you. You better have them scanned ASAP."

Nile exhaled. "I'm guessing you were supposed to give them to me yesterday?"

Brixton shrugged. "So arrest me."

Nile took the gun and badge and said, "I hope I never have to."

Brixton hawked his eyes playfully. "You wouldn't have the balls." He turned and walked away with his usual swagger.

Nile watched him walk away for a moment, and then he called out to him, the words escaping his throat in loping waves, "Brix... Should... Should I...?"

"What?" Brixton turned back. "For fuck's sake, Nile, spit it out."

"Should I tell Roxy anything for you?"

"Oh, you two plan on getting cozy while I'm gone?"

"It's not like that."

Brixton blew air through his tightened lips. "Whatever,

man. It's her job. She's a whore. Not my wife." He turned away coldly and started walking again.

Nile shook his head and called out again, "Hey Brix... "

Brixton turned back again. "Can I leave now or what?"

Nile looked serious. "Watch your ass out there, *golden boy*. The desert isn't as forgiving as the Nimbus Corporation."

Brixton gave a cavalier grin and flicked Nile off, his finger as stiff as a board. Nile chuckled a bit, but mostly just to humor his ex-partner. They both offered a lukewarm nod.

Then Brixton turned to greet the future that was waiting for him.

The two border patrols were standing there with mischievous grins on their baby faces and seemingly hard up for instigating. Brixton knew they were planning to taunt him. It was something a couple of petty, unaccomplished grunts might do to garner a little street cred among their braindead peers.

"Fucking grunts," he said.

---

An hour later, the Scorpion was barreling through the Mojave, over the most tumultuous desert terrain imaginable, scraping through the endless sagebrush and trying to find the seemingly non-existent road that would lead them to Outpost 11. Brixton sat in the back seat with his dust goggles on and not looking too happy as the sand and gravel pelted his face.

The two young Gate Keepers in the front seat were amused by his discomfort. "You're gonna love the Mojave," the driver said with a knowing smile. He and the other patrolman shared a good laugh.

Brixton tried not to indulge them, but he had to spit the dust from his mouth, and as the sand clung to his lips it made his effort to dispel it from his mouth far more theatrical than anticipated, like a stubborn hair sticking to a wet tongue, which made him look like the neophytic douchebag that he was sure to become in his new desert post. The Gate Keepers laughed even harder.

"Fucking grunts," he said again, but this time feeling woefully dispirited. The uncomfortable reality was sinking in. He was no longer the man in charge. The Republic of Phoenix was in the rearview mirror now, and it was going to stay there for some time, like a memory sprinting across the desert but unable to catch up to him. His new digs were waiting for him in the desolate fever dream of the Mojave. There was literally nothing to look forward to. Everything he cherished was behind him, wasting away back there in the beautiful glass and metal glow of Sky Haven. He'd once been royalty in that towering city. Now he was royally fucked.

# NINE

Croix, Tavo, Skinny and Kid rode into the late afternoon on bitter terms, each of them communicating only with dirty looks and eye rolls and harsh whistles. Croix was leading, Kid was meandering behind him, and Tavo and Skinny were bringing up the rear, still conversing with each other as if they were being paid to talk.

Then out of the blue, and to Kid's pleasant surprise, Croix whistled for him to come to the head, shouting, "Kid, get your ass up here."

Kid approached on his paint horse. "Yeah?"

"Ride with me for a bit."

Kid nearly fell out of his saddle from the shock. "Okay," he said, looking dumbfounded by Croix's sudden willingness to share his own company.

"Don't speak," Croix commanded. "Just listen." Kid pursed his lips to speak, but Croix cut him off. "Can you do that or not?"

Kid nodded. "Uh… yeah… *yep*… I can do that."

Croix nodded and turned his eyes forward.

Kid's face was as vacant and featureless as a human embryo. A translucent shell, but with nothing pulsing inside, like an unborn creature waiting to receive that mysterious spark of life. But Croix wouldn't be the spark. He was nobody's personal Jesus, and he went out of his way to ensure that. They rode side by side. Kid looked uncomfortable, and Croix just made the discomfort worse by not saying a single word. He rode with his eyes forward as if he'd forgotten he was supposed to speak. Then he finally said, "I'm just trying to help you."

Kid nodded, but it was obvious he didn't get the context, which certainly wasn't made clear in any way by Croix's random declaration.

"You understand what I'm trying to say?" Croix asked.

Kid shook his head.

"I'm trying to help you survive."

Kid nodded, but he looked like he wanted to speak.

"It's okay," Croix said. "If you got something to say, go on and say it."

Kid pursed his lips to speak.

Then Croix interrupted, "Just make sure it ain't something that's gonna rile me up."

Kid decided not to say anything after all.

Croix smirked. *The kid's learning,* he thought.

They rode in silence for a mile or so before Croix said another word. Then one word lead to two, then three, then suddenly he was blabbering on about everything under the sun. Kid could hardly believe it. Croix offered up his knowledge in ways that he'd never done before. Kid figured it must've been the open air and freedom of the land that had loosened his lips. Croix even offered a little bit of history too, which he was always reluctant to share. As they passed by the abandoned naval base at China Lake, he explained to Kid that the base was where the Liberation Army had set up camp back in the days of the Restoration Wars. He told him that the Southwestern Guard — an allied force — used it as a training ground. He told him that Nimbus had bombed the place months later in what they called the Battle of the Mojave.

"So the Southwestern Guard was an army?" Kid asked.

"A militia," Croix said.

"Were you in the Southwestern Guard?"

Croix went silent again, refusing to elaborate.

The history lesson was over.

They rode in silence again.

A while later, as they passed by a strange-looking building and miles of metal pedestals that looked like silver stems without flowers, Croix explained that the place was once a solar farm that powered hundreds of thousands of homes and businesses in the nearby towns before the Collapse. "After the wars," he said, "the people of the Granite Valley took those solar panels and put them to good use, and that's how we thrived in the valley all this time."

When Kid asked how they took the solar panels without conflict, Croix said they didn't. There was always conflict. It was human nature. He didn't elaborate any further. He just said, "War is inevitable, Kid. You're always on one side or the other. Best you figure out which side that is and stick to it."

As they rode further in silence, Croix wondered why he hadn't seen the first sign of trouble. No gangs. No scavengers. No desperate drifters. Not even the first trader on the road. They'd taken an untraveled path, but it was still unusual to be so isolated. When Kid inquired about the gangs, Croix told him about the *Black Lillies*, the *Nightcrawlers*, the *Batshit Crazies* and the *Deadeyes*. "Most of the gangs in these parts," he explained, "have been pruned like weeds over the years. Especially near us in the valley. They all scattered. Found better opportunities to rape and steal elsewhere I suspect. Opportunities that don't come with so many bullets flying back at 'em. It's the scavs you gotta watch out for. Drifters who don't know how to survive without taking what ain't theirs. They're usually desperate, and desperate people are just as dangerous as evil ones."

"You think they're out here?" Kid asked.

"You can bet on it," Croix said. "Especially now during a trade run. That's their cue to hunt. To be honest, I don't know why we ain't seen any yet. It's odd."

"The uncertainty makes you nervous?"

"Nervous? No. Concerned? Yes. I'd expect they're out here somewhere. I just don't like that we ain't seen 'em."

"You think they're waiting for us?"

"I think they're waiting for everybody. But we're hauling a pack horse, not a wagon full of trade goods, so we won't be as enticing as the others. What little value we got on us ain't so obvious to 'em."

"So we're safe?"

"No. Never. Nobody's safe. Nowhere. Don't you ever forget that."

Kid nodded. Then he swallowed fearfully and his eyes began to scan the deceptive surroundings looking for any sign of danger. "How do you know what to look for?"

"Anything that moves, Kid. Nothing friendly out here, I promise you that."

# TEN

When the scorpion finally arrived at Outpost 11, Brixton was exhausted from the strenuous heat and the constant jostling of his tailbone in what proved to be the bumpiest ride of his life, and that was probably by design. Those two douchebag Gate Keepers, who'd introduced themselves as Wiley and Getz, were hellbent on making the ride as miserable as possible for him. They didn't fail. It was two and half hours of endless ass-bruising and sand in his face. But he didn't give them the satisfaction. "That was a delightful ride," he said with an unfazed grin. "Thank you." He climbed out of the Scorpion with his head held high and added, "I'll be sure to request you guys for my escort home in a few days."

The young Gate Keepers chuckled at his legendary narcissism and offered him an insincere *good luck* before driving off into the desert. Brixton shook the humiliation from his soul. It took a lot of shaking. He wiped his irritated eyes and observed his new digs. The place was just what he expected. A total shit hole. A former military base of the Patriot's Defense turned Border Patrol outpost in the furthest reaches of the Forbidden

Rim, or what he'd now have to call the *Kill Zone*. The compound was surrounded by barbed-wire fencing and secured by cameras and blinding flood lights. There was a headquarters building made of concrete block, with a barracks and a mess hall attached. Behind that was a hyperbike lot with rows of bikes. Behind that was a covered training installation with obstacle courses and a shooting range. He panned the grounds and saw a rope hammock that was set beneath the sparse shade of a desert willow tree. He planned to put it to good use as soon as he possibly could. The place smelled like grunt sweat and gunpowder. It reminded him of his days training in the Patriot's Defense. The memory wasn't a welcome one. He saw a concrete landing pad and a metal hangar for the Draco hovership, which must've been gone on a surveillance op. The whole outpost looked empty, as if everyone had hitched a ride in the hovership and left the miserable shit hole behind.

But he wasn't that lucky.

Not anymore.

To him, the place looked like a state penitentiary from the old world, and he felt like fresh meat waiting to be broken in by the hairy, lustful residents. Just a new inmate waiting to be paraded down the corridor and advertised for all the butt-pluggers inside. All he needed was his prison garb, and his rules and regulations, and a hardass warden to tell him when he could speak or blink or even take a piss. As he swaggered his way towards the barracks, forcing each step with what little dignity he had left in his arsenal of delusions, the border patrol's version of a hardass warden was waiting at the entrance.

The man's name was Chief Bad Moon Kadence, but everyone jokingly called him *Bad Mood*, on account of his thorny demeanor. No one had ever heard him laugh or even seen him crack a smile, and it was rumored that the muscles in his lips were paralyzed from a bear attack. Brixton rolled his eyes at that. *Total bullshit.* There wasn't a single scar on the Chief's face. He was a sixty-year-old statue dressed in an olive green Border Patrol uniform with high ranking insignia on the breastplate. He was clean-cut and militant, with a rectangular face and a stoically intimidating presence. He was Native American, or at least he once was, but Brixton didn't know which tribe, nor did he care. Truthfully, Brixton didn't know shit about natives, and barely anything about Americans. He was just a little boy when everything went to shit. All he knew was he didn't like the vibe he was getting from the Chief. The man had an inscrutable countenance that made even the most frivolous men turn serious, and Brixton could feel himself losing his sense of levity around him. That was the only thing that had kept Brixton from losing his mind all these years. Levity. A sense of humor. He used it as his chosen recreational drug. His form of substance abuse. He wasn't about to lose it. He greeted the Chief with his usual swagger. "Chief Kadence, I presume?"

The Chief took a puff from a spicy black market cigar and studied Brixton for a moment, clearly not impressed with what he saw standing in front of him.

Brixton offered a handshake. "I'm Inspector Brixton Grace."

Chief Kadence refused to shake his hand. He continued to size Brixton up, and then he said, "Now that you're officially under my command, I'll be referring to you as *Patrolman* Grace. Is that clear?"

Brixton was vexed by the blatant disrespect, but he accepted it, knowing he had to play the hand he was dealt.

"The job is easy," the Chief explained. "You find outlaws or refugees in the territory, you remove them. Whatever method you use is completely at your discretion. We're not bound by public opinion out here."

Brixton smirked. "What happens in the desert stays in the desert?"

Chief Kadence wasn't amused. He took another puff from the black market cigar. "I read through your file. It says you're hard to work with."

"Is that how they put it?"

"Not exactly." Chief Kadence sighed. "You've buried yourself in a deep hole, patrolman, and now it's my job to resurrect you." He spit in the dirt, as if he were expelling a bad taste from his mouth. "I hate this desert post. I get all the outcasts."

"I won't be here long, sir," Brixton said with bold assurance.

Chief Kadence just laughed. "That's what they all say." It was no more than a condescending chuckle, but it was enough to prove the rumors of his lack of good humor to be false. He offered Brixton a key ring with two keys and a numbered keychain attached. The number seventeen. "You'll have the barracks to yourself tonight," he said. "The pilot, the mechanic and the cook sleep in separate quarters. You'll meet them tomorrow, or whenever they feel like speaking to you. Which may be never. You'll have to get used to that."

Brixton took the key ring, quietly accepting his place in Hell. "Where's the rest of the squad?"

"You're lucky," Chief Kadence said. "Captain Vedder and the Warhawks are on R and R in Brimstone."

"Ah," Brixton said with an air of smug disobedience, "*Captain Vedder*. His reputation precedes him."

"As does yours," the Chief said.

Brixton shrugged. "Mine is a little more polished though."

"Make no mistake," Chief Kadence said. "He *is* your

captain. Like it or not. I don't want you two egomaniacs clashing, so I suggest you take the time to warrior up before they return."

"Warrior up? Is that what you guys do out here?"

The Chief stood tall. "Are you gonna be a problem, Grace?"

"That depends on how you define *problem*… Sir."

The Chief had a deadpan look on his face. "They said you were charming. I don't see it. I just see an asshole who thinks he's bigger than he is."

Brixton felt his pride shrinking, and his knees began to buckle a bit, as if he were actually getting smaller. "Sir, I meant no disrespect."

"Yes you did. But this ain't the big city, golden boy. You don't have a board of executives to clean your linen after you shit the bed. We're in a war zone. Charm wears very thin out here."

"Sir, forgive me. I'm just trying to make an impression. I didn't mean for it to be a bad one."

Chief Kadence took another puff of his cigar. "You'll find I'm not so forgiving. Neither is this bitch of a desert."

"Yeah," Brixton said with an undying chip on his shoulder. "So I've been told."

Then Chief Kadence offered one last piece of veiled advice. "I'm of the opinion that you can't unring a bell. You get my meaning?"

"Look, sir, I'm not here to ring any bells. I don't wanna be here anymore than you want me to be here. I plan to keep my head down and get this over with so I can go back to where I belong."

Chief Kadence tossed the withered cigar to the ground and appeared to consume himself with a troubled thought.

One that seemed to disarm him. "Sometimes," he muttered, "there is no going back."

Brixton didn't like the cryptic notion. Not one bit. He wanted to inquire as to what the Chief meant exactly, but the unfriendly leader of Outpost 11 slammed the door with the same abrupt disregard with which he'd begun the conversation. Brixton was left to ponder the possibilities. Was this place a deathbed? He suddenly felt a familiar affliction. A pressure in his chest. The rapid increase of his heart rate. Clammy hands. Difficulty breathing. A manic need to swallow repeatedly. The station psychologist at PPD always called it a panic attack, but Brixton just called it what he believed it was: weakness. He was feeling humbled by the Chief's blunt assessment, and humility never came easy to him. His comfort zone was shrinking along with his bloated ego. This gig in the desert was going to be an emasculating torment, and he was beginning to question whether or not he had the sand to endure it.

# ELEVEN

As always, Croix rode at the head of the pack with his eyes peeled and his ears perked. He never gave up his place in the pecking order to anyone. There was no better line of defense than himself. So Tavo and Skinny and Kid clung to his six. They rode a few hours through the wasteland without spotting a single living thing. The heat was unbearable, and the sunproof umbrellas were offering very little shade from the burning reflection of the scorched earth. It felt like a gateway to the underworld. They soon entered the part of Croix's map called the *Mojave Preserve,* where death seemed to be a certainty. Kid spotted its cold, wrathful grip everywhere he looked. A lizard impaled on a yucca vine. A pile of coyote scat with the small bones of rodents still intact and stuck in the shiny black mush. A banded Gila monster feasting on a nest of spider eggs. An owl battling with a bark scorpion. An inflated chuck-walla wedged in between a crack in the rocks trying to escape the thunderous pecking of a Raven's beak as it chipped away at the sandstone. Then he spotted a crop of cotton-top cacti and thought they looked like the devil's fingertips reaching up from the fiery dungeon of Hell, with their armature of spines and sharp red hairs that looked like they'd been speckled with human blood. He was beginning to understand why Croix never let him leave Revival on his own. This was no place for a kid to travel alone.

They rode further, wandering through the white, salty crust of a dry playa. They left no hoofprints in their wake. The hardpan caliche was impenetrable. This land was void of anything that might quench a thirsty mouth or wake a sleeping pair of eyes when splashed. Even tears were impossible to form in the Mojave. Their eyes were dry and itching and bloodshot. They trotted through the dead Joshua trees and the burnt sagebrush, the sun cooking their brains and making them feel light-headed and half-lucid, as if they were stuck between worlds, like some fragile life slowly decomposing.

They spotted a defiant crop of yellow wildflowers on the hillside of a steep bajada and it felt for a moment as if they were back home in the Granite Valley sitting on the bank of the river under the shade of the cottonwood trees. But the thought did nothing to boost their sweaty morale. The heat had exhausted more than their nerves. Their minds were turning gray and senseless. Kid began to drift, his eyes closing to the blinding light above. Then out of nowhere a lone butterfly landed on his left shoulder, like some tiny colorful angel come to rescue him. He swore he could hear the insect whisper a warning in his ear: *TURN BACK!* Then it flapped its pretty blue wings and flew away. It disappeared from sight so quickly that Kid wondered if he'd only imagined it. Hallucination was a side effect of heat exhaustion. Perhaps he was already dying from exposure and on his way to that other side of things. He decided that if he was, he wouldn't turn back. He was ready to surrender.

Then suddenly, like a deafening crack of thunder, Croix sat

straight up in his saddle and ordered them all to, "*Stop.*" He whistled and gestured for Tavo and Skinny to come to the head. They galloped forward on their horses and stopped alongside him.

"What's wrong?" Tavo asked.

"Look alive, boys." Croix pointed to the near lifeless playa that stretched out before them like a land of the dead, his eyes sharp as tacks. "Ezekiel's Hollow."

Tavo and Skinny both went stiff, like a pair of fresh corpses.

"The hollow?" Tavo asked nervously. "What the hell we doing in the Hollow?"

"Take a wild guess," Croix said.

"No way," Tavo said. "Ain't happening."

"Oh it's happening," Croix said. "We'll take shelter at the Logas for the night. Won't be many traders taking this path."

"Won't be *any*," Tavo said, "because they got better sense."

Croix eyed him. "You chose to come with me on my terms. So, these are my terms. You don't like it, you know the way back."

Tavo scowled and turned to Skinny for support. Or maybe just for someone to blame. "Damn you, Skinny. Weren't you keeping an eye on the route? He led us straight to the Hollow."

"*Me?*" Skinny said, "Something wrong with *your* eyes?"

"It ain't his eyes that are wrong," Croix said. "It's his mind. It's in the wrong place."

"What's that supposed to mean?" Tavo asked.

"It means your mind is on Memphis and what she's got waiting for you when you get back home."

"What do you know about it?"

"I know a woman's magic can warp a man's mind. His instincts too."

"Yeah, you don't know half as much as you think you do."

"I know a lot more than I get credit for."

"I ain't going in the Hollow," Tavo said adamantly. "That's final. No way in hell."

"Me neither," Skinny said. He was curiously spooked.

Kid was curious to know why. "What's wrong? Why ya'll looking so terrified?"

"The Hollow's cursed," Skinny said.

"Cursed?" Kid asked, his eyes big and round.

Croix quickly stomped the superstition to death, "That's a bunch of bullshit, Kid. Just rumors to keep people out of the Bloody Knuckles' trading ground. Don't buy their lies."

But Kid was already sold. "How'd it get cursed?" he asked.

Croix shook his head at the foolishness. They were all so gullible. Especially Tavo, which always irked Croix beyond comfort. Tavo's superstitions had always gotten the best of him, which brought out the worst in him, and that was one reason that Croix struggled to relate to him all these years. Any man that could be sold such a false bill of goods had questionable instincts.

Tavo pulled alongside Kid on his appaloosa, looking superstitious as ever. "Hundreds of travelers died here decades ago," he explained. "From the Red Death. Their skulls and bones are perfectly preserved. From the dry desert air. Have a look for yourself." He pointed to a sea of ivory remains that were scattered across the flatland like random shells washed upon a lonely beach. "It's a ghostland. Their souls are trapped here."

"What do you mean?"

"They haunt this place."

"They're angry," Skinny added. "If we cross through they'll put a curse on us for sure. Guaranteed."

"Jesus Christ," Croix groaned. "That's another goddamn lie. And by the way, they didn't die from the virus. They killed themselves before it got 'em. It was a mass suicide."

"Same thing," Tavo said. "It was the Red Death that made them choose that fate."

"Why would they do that?" Kid asked. "Kill themselves like that?"

"To stop the cycle," Croix said.

"The cycle? What's that mean?"

"Good people that didn't wanna go bad."

"What do you mean by that?"

"Quiet," Croix snapped, holding his hand in the air. He pointed to the valley ahead. "Look there." He grabbed his binoculars and peered through the glass and saw an abandoned wagon full of trade goods in the flatland. Most of it had already been plundered, but some had been left behind. "Traders," he said.

He saw a scattered mess of dead bodies lying beside the wagon. They'd been recently slain. He couldn't get an accurate count. The bodies were clumped together and far too mangled to tell. Vultures and crows and large ravens were already battling one another for the flesh. He panned the glass and saw two dead men hanging from an old electrical pole that was rising high above the wagon. They'd been strung up to the wood with rope.

He handed the binoculars to Tavo. "Have a look."

Tavo peered through the glass. "Jesus H Christ. My God. I can't..." He looked away.

"They're dead," Croix said. "I can see supplies in the wagon. Let's go have a look."

The horses suddenly spooked, rocking backwards on their hooves and whinnying, as if they recognized Croix's dubious intention. He gripped the reins of his golden palomino as it jerked up on its hind legs. "Calm down, Hop. Goddamnit."

Skinny couldn't control his blue Roan either. "Whoa, girl." He gripped the saddle horn. "They ain't having it, Croix."

Tavo calmed his appaloosa and walked her backwards. "Even the horses got sense enough not to cross through the Hollow."

Croix stepped down from the saddle and placed a calming hand on the palomino's striped face. The horse settled. "We'll stake the horses to the ground here," he said. He pulled a metal stake with a large loop from his saddle bag, along with a lead rope and a large hammer.

"Hold up," Tavo said. "Let's talk about this."

"There ain't nothing to talk about." Croix drove the stake into the ground with a few quick strikes. The desert hardpan was tough, but his will was always tougher.

Tavo dismounted. "Just wait a second. How do you know someone ain't baiting us with those dead bodies? Those trade goods are too good to be true. Could be a trap."

"It's not a trap."

"How do you know? Could be they're just waiting for some fools to tie their horses off and go into the Hollow on foot. Then they're gonna steal our horses and ride off into the sunset."

Croix finished tying the lead rope to the stake, and then he unbuttoned the strap on his holster, making his *Crazy 8* revolver a quickdraw away. "It ain't no trap," he said, "and I ain't no fool."

Tavo didn't argue. He knew better.

Croix walked into the Hollow, his head on a swivel, but not his conviction. It was always steady. He was never afraid of dying. Not the outcome of it anyway. What would it even be like? He often wondered. A sudden jolt into nothingness? A loss of all feeling and perspective of the terrible world around him? That wouldn't be so terrible. A slow fade into oblivion? A state of forgetfulness? That didn't sound half bad. Like sleeping without dreaming. He could handle that. He sure wasn't afraid of nothingness. Living for fear of dying was never his motivation. It was something far less complicated. If he was afraid of anything at all, it was losing, plain and simple. Not losing his earthly possessions. Just losing the fight. Everything was a competition to him. He'd been fighting to survive his entire life, almost out of spite or habit or general principle, and surviving the world always felt like a challenge. A game that he flat-out refused to lose. That was his ultimate motivation: winning. Whether he was fighting Mother Nature or man or God himself, he was going to win. He'd cheated death more often than he'd worried over it, that's for sure, so he figured he had the upper hand when it came to matters of his own mortality.

"Ya'll get those feet moving," he said, expecting them to catch up. They did. They approached the wagon together on foot, and very carefully. Croix studied the fleshy mound of half-naked corpses, making sure they were actually dead and not some kind of elaborate ruse to set an ambush. He knew that Tavo was right to be cautious, and he secretly agreed with that caution, but when he saw the gory wounds on the bodies and the decapitated heads lying on the ground, he was certain this was no ruse. Whoever had done this was long gone, both physically and morally.

Kid grimaced at the mutilated bodies and kept his distance. His eyes turned away, but he was grimly curious.

Tavo and Skinny sifted through the leftover trade goods in the wagon, both keeping their eyes off the dead. "It's already been picked over," Tavo said. "Ain't nothing of value here. Nothing worth leaving the horses for. Let's get back."

Croix stood over the grisly remains, breathing through his nostrils without so much as a grimace. Tavo and Skinny looked on with a much different reaction. The bodies had been savagely butchered, each of them dismembered with a dull blade. Their bones brutally cracked. Two women. Five children.

Kid was fighting back nausea, his hand over his mouth. "Oh my God. What the fuck… What the hell happened to 'em?"

"It's plain to see," Croix said.

Tavo cringed. "Jesus Christ, why would anyone do this?"

The women had been brutally raped and beheaded and no one was sure of the order in which it had happened. Their heads were placed around them in some macabre, satanic circle. A ritualistic element that chilled the hot air of the Hollow. Their dresses were stained with blood from the unspeakable ravaging.

"Someone had their way with the women," Tavo said, his eyes scanning the chopped limbs. "God Almighty, even the kids. Jesus Christ." He jerked his eyes away in disgust.

Skinny covered his mouth and mumbled, "Sick bastards. How could anybody do such an evil thing?"

Kid vomited, unable to control his constitution. His breakfast came out in heavy clumps. He spit and swallowed the stomach acids that had gathered in the pockets of his mouth. Then he wiped the remnants from his lips. "Who would do this? Makes me sick. The thought of it."

"Then don't think," Croix said with little patience for his weak constitution. "Turn away or go tend to the goddamn horses."

"Don't it bother you?" Kid asked.

Croix ignored him. It bothered him in ways that the kid would never understand, so he didn't waste his breath explaining.

Skinny looked at the two dead men hanging from the tree. They'd been hung with a rope wrapped around their torsos and looped under their armpits and pulled tightly to the wood to keep their bodies held in place. Their hands were bound behind their backs. This wasn't a traditional death by hanging. There was no noose. No suffocation. No broken necks.

"Why you figure they hung the men like that?" Skinny asked. "There ain't no rope around their necks or nothing."

"They didn't hang 'em to kill 'em," Croix explained. "They hung 'em to make 'em watch."

"Watch *what*?" Kid asked.

"Whatever was done to those poor women and children."

Kid heaved dryly, his empty stomach causing him to retch and spit up nothing but coarse bile.

"Those men died from exposure," Croix said, without so much as a hitch in his throat. "Let's take what we can use and move on."

Tavo scratched his chin. "You think that radio transmission that Elmer got a hold of the other night was... you think maybe it was this?"

Croix nodded. "I reckon it was."

They looked at each other with unveiled fear in their eyes. Tavo exhaled forcefully, as if he had been holding his breath the entire time.

Then suddenly, a voice from above them shouted out with a high-pitched shriek, "*Kill me!*"

Croix drew his *Crazy 8* and swung around ready to fire, but he didn't shoot.

The voice belonged to one of the men hanging from the electrical pole. He was barely alive and struggling for air, his lungs rattling with every breath. "Please kill me," he muttered, straining to be heard.

Croix lowered his *Crazy 8* and asked, "Who did this to you?"

"They're godless," the man said, his voice like a creaking door hinge. "Kill me."

"I could cut you down," Croix said. "You could go after the men who did this."

"No," the man said, his voice scraping at the cords of his throat. "There's no justice for the evil they done. This is beyond God's wrath. Just *fucking Kill me! Please!*"

"I'll even give you a gun to do the goddamn job," Croix said, puzzled by the man's indignity.

"I don't wanna live in this world no more," the man exclaimed. Tears fell from his eyes in large droplets of emptiness. "I wanna be free of this place. Please. *Please.*"

Croix couldn't understand the lack of vengeance in the man's heart. How could he just let someone get away with such an unspeakable thing? "These men deserve to be punished," he told the man. "I'll even track 'em down with you."

"*No! Please!*" The man screamed. "*Just kill me! I'm begging you! Fucking kill me!*" He was crying uncontrollably now, like a terrified child who had lost his parents in the wilderness and feared he'd never see them again. "You didn't see what I saw! I can't look on my poor girls like this anymore! I can't live in this godawful fucked up world! I can't! I just *can't!*" He began to repeat himself over and over as if his mind had already left his body and nothing remained but some random spark of neurons colliding with their synapses. "*I can't! I can't! I can't!*" As if his soul had already been stripped away and he was nothing but unbearable consciousness. "*I can't! I can't! I can't! I—*"

Then *BOOM!*

Croix fired a single shot and gave the man the peace he'd been begging for. The bullet ripped through the middle of his heart, killing him instantly. His eyes went as blank as his soul.

Kid turned away, unable to witness the death. It was a mercy killing, and that much was understood, but it was just too much for his young heart to handle. There was a mournful silence as the man dangled lifelessly from the pole above them. The blood from his heart dripped to the hardpan below, each droplet sounding like a slow tick of the clock. A countdown to something they all feared: their own death. It felt closer than ever. Nobody said a word to drown out the demoralizing tick. Kid looked to Tavo and Skinny for a touch of sanity, but they looked just as lost as he was.

"Let's get moving," Croix finally said, with a cold stoicism that he'd mastered through the years.

Kid turned to him with mournful eyes. "Shouldn't we bury the bodies?"

"No. I said keep moving."

"You're just gonna leave 'em to the vultures and crows?"

Croix glared at him, his eyes burning with a dark blue rage. "Kid, don't. I'm warning you."

"Come on," Kid said. "It wouldn't take much to bury 'em. We got shovels."

Tavo stepped in quickly. "Kid, you need to shut up. *Now.*"

Kid didn't back down. "It's the right thing to do, Tavo. We should do the right thing. They deserve a proper burial." He turned back to Croix and shouted, "We can't leave them here to be *eaten.*"

Then, like a bolt of lightning from a murderous god, Croix snapped and grabbed Kid by the Kevlar vest and pulled him so close that Kid could feel the heat from his burning eyes. Croix shoved the barrel of the *Crazy 8* under the kid's chin and cocked the hammer back and stared into him with a harrowing blankness, as if he were looking beyond, into some darker realm of life.

Kid froze in fear, the two white orbs in his skull jutting outward from their damp crevices. "Sorry, Croix. I just thought a proper burial—"

"*A proper burial?*" Croix growled. "That ain't gonna change what happened to 'em. Ain't gonna bring 'em back. Who the fuck do you think you are? You got no idea what death is. *No idea.*" He tightened his finger on the trigger. "This world ain't what you want it to be, Kid. Get that through your thick fucking skull and *move on!*"

Tavo inched towards them carefully, keeping his hands in the air and being sure to look as unthreatening as possible. "Croix, take it easy."

Croix kept his burning eyes on Kid. "He needs to learn when to shut the fuck up, Tavo. He's gotta learn before it's too late."

"I know. I know. I get it. I think he gets it now too. You learned, right Kid?"

"Yeah," Kid said frantically. "I *learned.* I *definitely learned.*"

"See," Tavo said calmly. "He gets it. He didn't mean nothing by it. He's terrified, Croix. Look at him. He's shaking like a leaf. He's just a dumb kid that don't know any better."

Croix's eyes were eerily void of any recognizable human emotion. A shocking emptiness. He looked as if he wanted to destroy the entire world. His finger seemed to be operating on its own free will, like it had a mind to pull the trigger itself.

Kid began to cry. "I didn't mean nothing, Croix, I swear I didn't. I'm sorry. *Please. Don't kill me.*"

And with that, Croix suddenly broke, like a raging fever surrendering to a cold defeat. He pulled his finger off the trigger and his eyes seemed to soften and shift, his gaze turning to the ground below in some unaccepted form of shame. He swallowed and stared at the hardpan, slowly coming back to reality. He'd almost done something unforgivable. He'd been on that other side of himself, where anything goes, and he nearly went all the way. He turned his eyes back to Kid, his hot blue irises still ablaze but cooling down. "What's done is done, you understand? The bodies stay where they are. You speak another word and I swear to fucking God you'll be lying there with 'em."

Kid nodded, his body trembling in absolute terror.

Croix shoved him aside.

Tavo grabbed him by the shirt and pulled him close, keeping him safe from Croix's unpredictable wrath. "We're all good here, right?" he asked Croix, keeping his distance and his hands in the air. "We'll just keep moving, like you said. Let's just get back on the trail."

Croix couldn't even look their way. The rage had finally dissipated, and he felt a willful shame creeping up his spine. It began to settle in his throat. A terrible taste. His mind was slowly processing the damage he'd done, like a blurry photo coming into focus. His demons had almost won. He walked back towards the horses, looking unsteady, as if he was out of balance with the world. "You're right," he said softly. "We gotta keep moving."

# TWELVE

They rode in petrified silence for a few hours. A demoralizing hush had washed over them like a rogue wave, leaving them to drown and implode in their own pressurized afflictions. Croix couldn't wait to find a stopping point. A place to recalibrate. He needed a fresh start. A new distraction. Something to make him forget what he'd done.

Soon they came upon an abandoned restaurant in the middle of the desert that seemed wildly out of place. It was crumbling and looked like it might turn to dust if someone blew their breath on it. "We're gonna sleep like babies in there," Croix said.

No one else agreed.

The place was an old landmark on the cusp of nowhere, covered in gang graffiti and dried human filth. Excrement was smothered on the exterior walls and used to write explicit messages with poor grammar and misspelled insults. Croix hadn't seen such a grotesque display of human ignorance and vitriol since the days of the internet. At least these inhuman pronouncements weren't being spread around the world in a matter of seconds with the press of a button, like some deadly social disease replicating itself over the web. He was glad those mindless days of smart phones and faceless trolls were behind them. Now people had to speak to one another face to face again, and if you insulted a man while standing eye to eye with him, he would likely teach you a valuable lesson about respect that you'd be hard-pressed to learn in any other way.

*That's how it should be*, he thought. *No hiding behind some faceless, bullshit name.*

He scrutinized the land around him, which was called Halloran Springs on the old map. But he always called it Logas. The abandoned restaurant was a small block structure with a blue roof that still hadn't caved in yet. There was a stubborn metal sign erected on a concrete post with dull red letters that said: *LO GAS*. Another, less towering sign stood beside it like the shadow of a frightened child. It simply said: *EAT*. But there was nothing on the menu these days but the flesh of unsuspecting fools that didn't have the basic skills to recognize a tiger track or a human ambush.

Luckily, Croix was no fool. There were no tiger tracks, and no tigers inside. But that didn't mean there wasn't a human ambush waiting for them. Nothing was safe until Croix cleared every corner and lit every shadow. He was first off his horse, and first to draw his gun. "Let's make sure there ain't no squatters," he said. "Kid, you stay with the horses."

"Where ya'll going?"

"To book a room for the night."

Tavo and Skinny dismounted and quickly armed themselves. Tavo with a pump shotgun. Skinny with a trusty old Glock. They followed Croix on foot. He crouched stealthily and slid his back against the graffitied wall, and they mimicked his movements, treading lightly towards the open doorway with their guns and their wits fully loaded. Croix stopped short of the entrance and listened for the faint sound of breathing, or any noise that might give him pause. All he heard was the calm, deceptive breeze of the desert. He nodded at Tavo, then he stood and swung his gun and stormed the restaurant in a flash, his finger on the trigger and his eyes scanning for anything that might justify a bullet. Tavo and Skinny stood beside him, their fingers twitching. But the place was empty, save for some overturned tables and scatterings of random trash that were cluttering up the dirty concrete floor. It was devoid of life, but not death. There was another dead woman lying on the concrete, her eyes staring wide-eyed at Croix. Her clothes were bloody and her head had been chopped off. The severing mark was high on her neck. It was a fresh kill. The flies hadn't even found her yet.

"Goddamnit." Croix lowered his gun in a fury. "Fucking savages."

Tavo winced. "What the hell's going on out here?"

Skinny covered his face and asked, "Who's doing this?"

Croix didn't answer either question, but only because he didn't want to share his gut feeling, which was secretly causing the contents of his own stomach to rise into his throat. "We're gonna push on," he said, looking spooked for the first time on the journey. "We'll find a place to sleep under the stars. Might be a risk to leave ourselves exposed, but I doubt ya'll wanna sleep in here with a fresh corpse." He turned and started for the horses. "Any objections?"

"Hell no," Tavo said, following behind in a hurry.

"Nope," Skinny said, outpacing them both. "I love the stars."

"We'll have to hurry though," Croix said as he stepped into the stirrup of his saddle. "The sun is getting low in the sky."

"What's going on?" Kid asked. "We ain't staying here?"

"No," Croix said. "The rooms were all booked up."

---

They rode south at a quick pace, pushing carefully through the sagebrush and deadly spines of jumping cholla, their eyes more focused on the destination than the natural dangers of their surroundings. There were no squabbles or grudges or bitterness between them anymore. They all had the same goal: surviving the night. They trotted softly for a while, in relative peace, which was hard to come by whenever Kid was around. Croix wanted to enjoy it, but he noticed that the weather on the southern horizon was brewing into something fierce, and threatening to turn its ferocity on them. Dark clouds, with a light haziness beneath them, looking like a band of heavy rain. It was rolling in faster than expected. He thought maybe it would push off to the east before it ever reached them, but he knew the weather was no more predictable than God's grace, so they rode a little faster. Thirty minutes of unbroken strides. Croix kept watch, and the clouds just kept darkening on the skyline. They were getting closer, almost deceptively so. Then, as if the world had suddenly grown angry at him, a loud rumble shook his guts. A monstrous thunderclap that nearly scared him right out of his saddle. He saw the storm forming into something terrible, swirling around and changing direction as if it were the fist of God himself, rearing back and anxious to throw another sucker punch.

"That ain't good," he muttered to himself, his eyes locked on the storm like a man watching his own death approaching from afar. It wasn't a summer rainstorm, or even a sudden monsoon from the gulf. It was menacing and devilish and tumbling across the desert like a giant ball of dark cotton.

"Sandstorm!"

Suddenly the wall of dust was barreling at them even faster, as if it had spotted its next victim.

"That came up in a goddamn hurry."

The storm was sixty miles wide now and churning up the earth as it charged. Croix swallowed nervously. It had been a while since he'd been caught in the middle of a dust monster. The last time hadn't gone so well. He'd fallen from his horse in the dark spirals of sand and gravel and landed awkwardly on his feet, twisting his ankle into shredded knots of ligament and bone. He was hobbled for months afterwards. The experience had left him a little spooked by nature's intent. Now anytime the sand was in the air like that he felt targeted.

"We gotta find shelter. I figure we got fifteen minutes at best. And that's my eternal optimism talking."

Tavo and Skinny traded frightful looks.

Kid panned the barren Mojave with terror in eyes. "Where we gonna find shelter out here?"

"I know the perfect place," Tavo said, looking eager to get there. "It's just up ahead a mile or two."

"No," Croix said through clenched teeth. "You know I hate that place."

"But it's always been good for shelter," Tavo said. "I'm guessing it's just what we need right now, considering that storm is about to sandblast our bodies into bone. So take what God gives you."

Croix scowled bitterly. "I've been taking it my whole goddamn life."

Tavo grimaced. "No time to be stubborn about it."

Croix conceded with another one of his wordless but expressive growls. The sucker punches just kept coming. Bolts of lighting throttled inside the massive wall of dust, which stood some thirty-five miles high. There was no time to waste on pride or semantics. "Alright," Croix said, "*mask up*."

They placed their filtered gas masks over their faces and gripped their saddle horns, clamping their fingers tightly around the reins of their jumpy horses.

"We gotta *move*."

They rode at a hard gallop, heading straight for the storm and hoping to beat it to the shelter. They clung to the saddles like rodeo clowns, barely able to stay upright. The outer rim of dust began to flurry around them, clouding their vision and making it harder to navigate. Croix hunkered down, gripping the saddlehorn and the reins so tightly that the threaded seams nearly cut into the skin of his calloused hands. Debris swiped at him in the blistering wind. A thorny piece of sagebrush smacked him in the chest. The hard grains of sand began to pelt the exposed skin on his neck. He strained to see through the dark spirals of dust that were blotting out the sunlight. He wiped the blindness away from his mask and spotted an old crumbling adobe hut just up ahead, standing there in the Mojave like some ancient monolith calling them to safety. A legendary place that needed no introduction. It was the famed church that Billy Dagger had built two and a half decades before. The goddamn thing was still standing.

Croix hated the fraudulent place, but it was their only salvation at the moment, deceptive or not. They rode straight for it, trying to outrun the tumbling ball of dark cotton that was devouring the air around them. The fist of God was about to strike. Croix could practically see the fingers balled up and ready to throw a punch. He pushed the horses harder, trampling across the uneven ground. The church was only thirty yards away when the mighty fist made contact, its knuckles of sand and gravel thrashing their bodies. The wind grew stronger, engulfing them in a blinding squeeze of darkness. Croix signaled to the others to stop before they lost sight of each other. They all yanked their reins and halted their horses.

The sand danced around them like a funnel cloud. Then a sudden downburst plummeted from the sky above. The wind ripped at their clothing and the gravel pelted their skin like bits of shrapnel, notching the flesh of their hands.

"We gotta tie 'em together!" Croix shouted through the mask.

No one heard him. His voice was muted by the mask, and by the howling wind. He signaled his intentions. They all huddled up and began tethering the horses together with a lead rope, struggling to thread the rope through the cinch rings, their hands unsteady and blasted by the granular wind. Everything around them went dark as night, only illuminated by the sharp flashes of lightning that were popping around them in fiery bolts. 7,000 volts of raw electricity. Blue streaks of fire coursing through the clouds above and striking down in threatening judgement. Once they threaded the rope, they pressed on in the chaos.

They were tethered together now, with Croix leading the way. The wind pulled at his body. He felt disoriented. His vision had gone white from the blinding strobes of lightning. The horses kept trying to scatter in all directions, pulling the lead rope dangerously taut. He gripped the rope and pulled with all his might, trying to steer them to safety, and trying to see through the faceplate of the gas mask which was caked with wet sand. The tension on the rope was tightening as the horses rose up on their hind legs, having been spooked by the darkness and the raw fury of the storm.

He finally spotted the entrance to the church. It was just a black mirage in the raging spiral of dust, but he knew it was there. He pulled harder on the reins and kicked his heels into the palomino's hide and the horse bolted forward, pushing through the large black opening of the church and pulling the other horses behind him. The church wasn't much of a reprieve. The sand was swirling inside the adobe walls, coming in from the gaping hole above where a wooden roof used to be. The horses crashed into each other, each threatening to kick their hind legs. "Whoa!" Croix shouted through the mask. "Settle down!"

Then the sky turned loose. A static charge in the clouds. The ice crystals colliding. Suddenly it was raining buckets inside the church. Huge droplets pelting down on the plywood floor. Croix saw a corner where the roofing was still intact. He pulled his mask off and hollered to the others, "Get 'em to the corner!"

They all hopped from their saddles and yanked the reins and hurried the frightened horses to the corner of the church before the plywood floor turned too slick and deadly to walk on. They pulled their blanket rolls and covered their horses' eyes, keeping them calm with their touch as the rain and sand assaulted their hides. The wind rattled the broken rafters above. They huddled together, their arms entwined like spider webs. Kid was stuck in the middle, scared to death and trembling. The thunder struck and rumbled in their guts. The wind howled frightfully in their ears. The lightning flashed and crackled and lit up the church like some holy rapture gone bad. The swirls of sand tore at their flesh. It felt like a thousand bee stings. The rain soaked their clothes and drenched the plywood floor at their feet. The water was already forming a massive puddle around their ankles.

"Stay together!" Croix shouted.

He knew the sudden downpour could turn into a flash flood in a matter of seconds and knock them right off their feet, carrying them out of the church on their backs like a log in a mighty river. They'd be pummeled and knocked unconscious by the rocky terrain, and then they'd all drown in the rough waters before they could even consider begging for

God's mercy. Then, just as he'd feared, the water began to rise to their shins and rush out of the open doorway, cascading away like that mighty river in his mind. Kid suddenly lost his footing and slipped. He crashed to the plywood floor and was swept away, carried off on his back by the raging floodwater. Croix splashed his way across the church and reached out and grabbed Kid's hand. He dropped to his backside and planted his foot in the back of an old church pew that was barely intact, stopping their momentum. The floodwater continued to rise and rage around them, filling up the church like a tea pitcher.

"Don't move!" he shouted, his body lying flat and nearly inundated.

"Don't let me go!" Kid shouted back, trying to find his footing again.

The plywood floor was slippery, and it was shifting beneath them with the force of the floodwater. Croix struggled to his feet, keeping his balance as the water threatened to carry him off. He and Kid turned and pushed against the current, hand in hand, splashing their way back to the corner of the church where Tavo and Skinny were failing to control the frightened horses. The dense swirls of sand and gravel continued to strike their hides. The horses began to lose traction, their hooves slipping on the wet plywood. Croix pulled the lead rope tighter. They forced the horses to their knees. The water rushed around them. Lightning flashed in blinding strobes, its fiery bolts streaking from the air to the ground and back again at 60,000 miles per second. 100,000 amps of certain death. 50,000 degrees of unimaginable heat. The sky exploded above them in brilliant colors. The crackling hiss nearly busted their ear drums. Croix shielded Kid with his body, trying to maintain his balance as the water rose to his knees. Another crack of lightning blinded him. He could feel his mighty pulse threatening to rupture the valves in his heart. If the lightning and the floodwater didn't get him, cardiac arrest just might. He even thought about begging for God's mercy.

But that would be a step too far.

Then as quickly as the storm had come upon them, it began to relent, slowly but surely, as if the fist of God had found another target to strike someplace else. An easier fight perhaps. Someone that didn't punch back. The rain stopped and the water at their feet rushed out of the church and into the impenetrable dirt road outside, cascading its way down the dry path and into the nearest wash where it would settle and evaporate within the hour, leaving a hard, cracked bit of mud behind. They stood and watched the sky turn from a dark funnel of doom to a pretty blue indigo that seemed to welcome them with open arms. Croix was in no mood for nature's sudden change of heart, and in no mood for thoughts about God's mercy. He wouldn't be sharing that deceitful embrace. The howling wind began to sing a more melodious tune, free of the frightening pitch which had haunted them before. The horses settled, and so did the taut rope that was still cutting into Croix's blistered hands. The water receded and the dust fell to the wet plywood floor around them. The dark fog rolled away and the last rays of the setting sun began to shine, piercing through the missing roof and the open doorway of the church.

Kid was sure it was God's mercy. "Thank you," he said quietly.

They removed their masks and wiped the sand from their faces and shook the gravel from their hair. They brushed the horses off, sweeping the mud from their battered coats.

"At least we made it by nightfall," Tavo said, spitting the wet sand from his lips. "We'll get a good night's sleep in here."

"Not me," Croix said, looking vengeful at the thought. "I'll sleep a hell of a lot better outside."

He untethered his palomino from the lead rope and walked the horse outside into the fresh open air, where the dust had fallen to the ground and the rainwater had disappeared with hardly a trace. They were lucky the rains were so brief. The dry bedrock soil was barely saturated. If it had rained for much longer, they would've been carried away and drowned for certain. Croix got to work cleaning his saddle. The setting sun was waving goodbye, but he wasn't one to wave back. He slapped the dust from the leather and prepared his mind for nightfall. Tavo and Skinny followed him outside with their horses, and Kid staggered at their heels pulling his splash paint by the reins. They removed their saddles and brushed the sand from the hides. They shook their bedrolls out and made sure their food satchels and weapon sheaths were spotless and clean.

"That could've been a lot worse," Skinny said.

"Yeah," Croix said with a bitter gleam in his eyes, "but he's probably saving his worst for last."

Skinny wrinkled his forehead in confusion. "Who?"

Croix didn't answer.

Kid walked back to the church and stood there in the open doorway, studying the old adobe shack like some wide-eyed proselyte in awe of its holiness. He saw the cross made of acacia on the wall above the makeshift pulpit. It made him smile. The cross was partially burnt but still incorruptible, and that made him feel incorruptible too. This was a house of God, he was sure of its supernatural prowess. The adobe walls were thick and strong, though the wooden roof was blackened and caving in, and the doorframe was charred and smothered with ash, as if the place had been set on fire at some point. The rafters above hung there like brown icicles, dripping with rainwater and soft mud. The wooden pews were still intact, but dark as charcoal and flaking away like the grisly onset of a slow death.

Kid was inquisitive as always. "What happened to this place?"

Tavo turned his eyes on Croix and smirked with a touch of mischief. "Someone tried to burn it down."

Croix glared at him, hushing him with a threatening gaze.

"Why would someone burn it down?" Kid asked.

Then Croix's words leapt from his mouth without much thought. "Revenge," he said, grinding his teeth so hard the friction could be heard aloud.

"Revenge?" Kid asked. "For what?"

"Forget it," Croix said, wishing he could cut his own tongue out and be done with talking altogether. He suddenly understood the point of Teardrop's silent protest.

"Revenge for what?" Kid asked again.

"I said *forget it.*"

"You can't expect me to let that go without an explanation."

Croix's eyes were bluer now than the hottest part of a flame.

Kid could feel the heat again. "Okay, I'll shut up," he said begrudgingly. Then he turned away and quietly muttered to himself, "That's your answer to everything ain't it? *Shut up. Shut up and don't ask questions.*"

Croix ignored the kid's taunt and walked his golden palomino back inside the church and tied the horse off to the rotting pews and walked back outside as quickly as he could, as if he'd been holding his breath the entire time so not to inhale anything toxic like religion or faith. Tavo and Skinny and Kid walked their horses inside too, and tied them off in the same manner. Then they made their beds for the night among the ghosts of the dead. All those poor souls who had died there back in '49.

Croix stayed outside, breathing the honest air. He made his bed near the threshold where the massive cathedral doors once kept the holiness from corrupting the rest of the desert. The doors were gone now. Disintegrated by the fire that he had once set in his youth, but the stench of God was everywhere, still polluting the stale environment. He sat there with his back against the adobe wall and his *Crazy 8* resting on his lap, with one in the chamber and ready to cut loose if necessary. He knew he'd be exposed to the unforeseen dangers of the night, but he refused to spend another minute in that godforsaken church. He'd rather pull watch duty until sunrise, even if it meant no sleep.

# THIRTEEN

The Vale was the only private sector in the Republic of Phoenix. Fifteen square miles of luxury homes and golf courses, smattered with five-star resorts, high-end relaxation spas, prestigious private schools, renowned medical centers, and first-rate businesses that catered to the wealthy elite. In the old world, before the Collapse, the area was known as Paradise Valley. But it was no longer a paradise for everyone. The Vale was exclusive. Off limits to the general public. Home to corporate bigwigs and white-collar citizens. It branched out into seven communities, or Villages as they called them, each with their own amenities and commerce, and each designated by levels of status. Most of the homes there were leftovers from the old world. Spanish style, Mediterranean, Tuscan, and Tudor resurgence. Some of them were new construction. Lucian Vanderbon always owned the latest and greatest. He collected real estate like others might collect coins or trading cards. He had dozens of flashy pads and elaborate palaces, from resort condos in Paradise Point to penthouses in Sky Haven. He owned the most desirable homes in each of the seven Villages of the Vale. But the custom-built home on the crest of the Phoenix Mountains in Grand Mesa was his most cherished. Everything else felt like an escape. The house on the mesa felt like home.

---

"This place is immaculate," Nile said to himself in awe. He drove through the upscale markets of Central Plaza, which sat directly in the center of the seven Villages. He turned northeast down the winding roads that hugged the foothills of Camelback Mountain. He was amazed at the flawless upkeep. The pavement was pristine and smooth, and the yellow lines were freshly painted everywhere he looked. The meticulous landscaping that danced with the curves of the road was shapely, and the leaves were a healthy shade of green, as if the plants and trees had just been planted that very moment. He couldn't believe the cleanliness. It was a stark contrast to the Boroughs. "I've been living with blinders on," he said.

He could see Lucian Vanderbon's home up on Grand Mesa from the valley below. It was unmistakable. The architecture was grand and imperious, like the CEO himself, but what gave it away for sure was the corporate hovership that was parked on the helicopter pad next to the house. Nile felt a sense of displacement in the Vale, like a stranger in a strange land. He took the road up to Grand Mesa. It was winding and steep, cutting through scattered rock and cacti and the dying yellow petals of brittlebush. As he curved around a line of sagebrush and bright purple lavender, the Vanderbon residence came into clear view. The opulence was jarring to a man of Nile's means. He'd never set foot in the Vale before. Not even on a case. He'd certainly never been to the private residence of the CEO. The reality was sinking in. Questions began to formulate in his mind like a debilitating illness spreading from thought to thought and paralyzing his meager will. *Why me? What could this meeting possibly be about?* His entire body throbbed like a tuning fork. "You're out of your element, Nile," he said to himself. "*Way* out of your element."

He turned into the driveway and marveled at the grand scale of the home. Nearly 7,000 square feet of overindulgence, nesting on the flat peak of the mountains. A contemporary Spanish style home with cream adobe walls, grand arches, a dark tiled roof, and wrought-iron trimmings. "My God," he said, "they really do live like kings."

He was greeted by armed guards and a rather obnoxious security gate, which stood nearly twelve feet tall. He pallidly flashed his credentials. The armed guards opened the gate. He drove through, his limbs still throbbing like a tuning fork. The driveway was lined with a rainbow of wildflowers and mani-cured green hedging. Everything was full of life. No small feat in this lethal desert climate. He parked near the courtyard.

He was greeted by Lucian Vanderbon's head of security, Agent Dorian Robicheau, who opened the car door and said, "Good evening, Inspector Wambasa. Mr. Vanderbon is expecting you."

Nile got out of the cruiser. He didn't know what to say, so he just said, "Thank you."

"Right this way," said Agent Robicheau. He headed for the portico.

Nile followed him on foot through the grandiose Spanish courtyard. It was tiled with dark terracotta squares. There was a stone water feature with a hand-carved statue of the mytho-logical phoenix in the center, with a halo circling its fiery head. The two wooden doors of the entryway were painted Taos blue, a color that Nile was familiar with. The blue was believed by early Spaniards to ward off evil spirits. A curious choice, he thought, considering that Mr. Vanderbon always appeared to have little faith, and even less superstition. Nile thought it must be a coincidence. Or perhaps just a simple novelty. Maybe even a sardonic nod to what Mr. Vanderbon must've considered a primitive culture. It had to be something trivial. The superstition theory was just too hard for Nile to swallow. Then he caught himself overthinking again and made himself stop.

Agent Robicheau opened the front door for him. "After you, Inspector."

"Thank you."

Nile was mesmerized as he entered the house. The views from the foyer alone were breathtaking. Large picture windows lined the living space in a half circle, overlooking the evening lights of the Vale as they twinkled into existence. The sun was just setting to the west and casting a wondrous pink and blue watercolored sky to the east. There was a large wallscreen hung above the stone fireplace and book shelves on either side filled with classic literature, likely from some rare collection that Mr. Vanderbon had obtained after the Collapse and wished to preserve.

"Please make yourself at home," Agent Robicheau said, gesturing to the sofa. "I'll let Mr. Vanderbon know you're here."

Nile took a seat on the sofa. He felt like a random crumb that had escaped the broomstick in an otherwise pristine room. Everything was spotless and bathed in bright orange and turquoise. Pillows, blankets, pottery and art pieces. But surprisingly, the decor was subtle, not indulgent. The walls were ghostly and bare. A minimalist approach which Nile did not expect from someone with Mr. Vanderbon's impeccable means and champagne taste. He half-expected statues carved from gold. He recognized something in his CEO that he would've never expected: a desire for simplicity and modesty. Two words that had never been associated with Lucian Vanderbon.

It puzzled Nile to no end.

The bare walls of the living space were adorned with only one feature: an authentic French oil painting of Madame Adelaide, which was once kept under lock and key in the North Wing of the Phoenix Art Museum. But Lucian Vanderbon could have anything he wanted, so it was there now, on his wall, exposed to the decaying elements of the Sonoran desert and the harsh negligence of time. Nile studied the painting. The lady portrayed was stately and superior, much like Lucian himself. She wore an opulent gold-embroidered gown with a red overcoat, her wide eyes staring ghostly, almost in judgement, as if she were watching Nile from some other world and casting aspersions on the one he was currently living in. He felt a discomforting sense of inhibition as her eyes examined him from across the room. He was curious why Mr. Vanderbon had chosen that particular painting. Female royalty in a world now dominated by men again. Nile had a humble knowledge of her history. He'd learned about her during a tour of the museum years before when the painting was still housed there. Maybe Mr. Vanderbon was simply inspired by her ambition. Perhaps her defiant nature, turning her nose up at expectations and traditions. Perhaps it was her strong will and her reluctance to be controlled by others. Or perhaps it was her spirit of domination. Mr. Vanderbon himself was every single one of those things, or at least he appeared to be. Maybe he just liked the way the painting looked in his living room and nothing more. Nile figured it must be something esoteric. But he would never ask, so he'd never know. He just did what he always did. He formulated his own theory and left it at that. Then he realized he was overthinking again. Such an unbreakable habit. That was another reason he thought Brixton didn't really like him. He was far too internalized for the golden boy's tastes. He couldn't help but analyze everyone in a room, in minute detail, his mind always scrambling for conclusions, which he always kept to himself of course. That made him bad at parties, so to speak, and Brixton was always the life of the party.

"Inspector Wambasa," Agent Robicheau said, "Mr. Vanderbon will see you now."

Nile rose to his feet, his limbs suddenly throbbing again. He followed Agent Robicheau down a hallway and into a luxurious billiards room with a glistening chandelier and a wet bar filled with rare wines and endless bottles of hard liquor. The room overlooked a spacious balcony with a table and chairs and a small hot tub for four. It wasn't a party atmosphere like Nile had expected. It seemed like Mr. Vanderbon had reserved this home for solitude and self-reflection. Nile found that puzzling. Why was a man of such notorious excess, with a history of womanizing and hosting lavish parties, now living in such modest isolation? Sure, he was now at that age where men begin to look back and not forward, and are often consumed with their own mistakes, but it was still quite the contradiction. Reflection or not, Nile thought it was more than the natural progression of growing old. This was an abrupt change of character. It seemed like a self-inflicted form of penance to him. Mr. Vanderbon was in that dark realm of regret, and he needed to be alone to navigate it. Nile was curious to know why. When he arrived at Lucian's study, the dark mahogany double doors were already open, and the smell of sweet cigars and fresh leather assaulted his senses.

"Please wait here," Agent Robicheau said.

Nile stood outside of Lucian's study.

Agent Robicheau hovered in the doorway. "Mr. Vander-bon, Inspector Wambasa is here to see you, sir."

"Thank you, Dorian. Send him in please."

Nile walked through the double doors as Agent Robicheau turned and left.

Lucian rose from behind his desk. "Inspector Wambasa. Welcome. Thank you for being punctual."

"Of course, sir."

Lucian smiled. The charming gesture made Nile less nervous. They shook hands and Lucian said, "Have a seat, Inspector."

Nile took a seat in the massive leather chair across from the desk. It was so big that he imagined himself sitting on a throne in some ancient empire that had been lost to history. All that was missing was a crown. But he wasn't the kingly type. Such heavy responsibility overwhelmed him. He looked around and was struck by the craftsmanship of the study. The elaborate moldings and the dark mahogany cabinetry that looked as if it had been carved by gods, not by men. The desk was made of rare dalbergia wood from Africa. It was unpolished and had a natural richness to the texture that could no longer be manu-factured. Nile had heard of such rare luxuries, but he'd never seen them in person. "This is quite a home, sir."

Lucian chuckled. "You should see my other ones."

"This one is beautiful enough."

"I'd rather have a beautiful woman on my arm," Lucian said with a mischievous grin. "But at my age, the house will do."

Nile laughed, more out of courtesy than amusement.

Lucian took a seat behind the desk and grabbed a bottle of Hawk's bourbon whiskey and thumbed a shot glass. "Do you drink the hard stuff, Inspector?"

"No sir. Not even when I'm thirsty. But thank you."

"I've heard that about you," Lucian said while pouring his drink. "This is my substitute for coffee. My doctor told me to cut out caffeine before bed, so..." He took a shot down his gullet and let it settle to warm his insides. "I'm sorry to call you here at such a late hour. But it was necessary."

"No need to apologize, sir."

"It's your duty, right?

"Yes sir."

"I used to enjoy hearing that." Lucian looked disheartened, seemingly regretful of his lifelong notion of duty.

Nile was puzzled even further. But he didn't press.

"Nile *Wambasa*?" Lucian asked curiously. "That's an interesting name. Was that a name we gave you? Or one you chose yourself?"

"I chose it, sir. It was my mother's..." Nile stopped himself, realizing he was committing a cardinal sin. Reminiscing about the old world was frowned upon in the presence of royalty. "I'm sorry, sir."

"No, please go on."

"I shouldn't."

"I want you to," Lucian said. "Go on."

Nile was careful. "My mother came from a long line of Wambasas who lived near the Nile River."

"Ah, an ode to your mother."

"To her ancestors really, sir. Her maiden name was Clark. She was born in Queens. Three generations there, sir."

"And what was your real name before?"

Nile hesitated. "James, sir. James Thompson Junior."

"Do you remember everything?"

"From before, sir?"

"Yes."

"I remember everything that mattered."

Lucian took another sip of his whiskey. "I'm glad you defied me."

Nile shifted in his seat. "Sir, I didn't mean to—"

"No," Lucian said. "It was foolish of me to think any of you could forget. Or *should*. I thought it would alleviate pain. For all of us. To forget. To move forward and not back. I couldn't have been more wrong. I know that now."

Nile shook his head in disagreement. A habitual response to appease his superiors. But he couldn't muster the words to defend his CEO, so he quietly agreed. It was wrong to steal the past from people. Even the young.

Lucian looked distraught. "You worked on the wall?"

"Yes sir."

Nile reminisced for a moment, remembering his youthful hands placing block after block in the hot Sonoran fall and slapping pounds of mortar in between them. He could still see the Nimbus soldiers at his back with rifles, ensuring he didn't shirk his task.

Lucian took another sip of Hawk's whiskey and let it settle. "That wall is the foundation of this city," he said pridefully. "Paramount to our survival all these years. I've never had a chance to personally thank you for your part in building it."

"That's not necessary, sir," Nile said. "It was my... my duty."

"How old were you when you placed your first block?"

"To my best recollection, sir, I was thirteen."

Lucian frowned. "Just a boy."

"A young man, sir."

"Were they hard on you in the labor camps?"

"The Patriot's Coalition?"

"If that's what you prefer to call it."

"Of course they were hard on us, sir. It was important work."

Lucian hung his head.

Nile was quick to lift his President's wilting spirits. "But we finished the wall, sir. The city survived."

"Indeed," Lucian said, still looking distraught. "It did. "

"When I joined the academy they were hard on me there too," Nile said, feeling an obligation of duty to vindicate the building of the wall and everything after. "But I became an officer, sir. And now I'm an inspector. The job is hard, but I'm good at it. Hardship is life, sir."

Lucian nodded. "That's a truth that no one would deny." He took another sip of his whiskey. The sip turned to a guzzle. "Do you ever have regrets, Inspector?"

"No," Nile said without needing to think on it.

"Not a single regret in life?"

Nile was feeling patronized. "Not to trivialize it, sir, but I see no value in worrying over the past when the future is perplexing enough."

Lucian chuckled. "You're young. I miss that youthful disregard." He sat there pondering for a moment. "Maybe it's more delusion than disregard." He paused, thinking deeply, and looking deeply wounded. "I regret many things now. I wish things had gone differently."

Nile was curious and confused, but growing agitated now, which only made him more nervous. "Sir, with respect, is there a..."

"A point?" Lucian asked.

"No sir, that's not what I..."

"A reason that you're here?"

"Yes sir. Respectfully."

"Yes," Lucian said, looking rather imperious again. "Of course there's a reason you're here. His name is Brixton Grace."

Nile grimaced. "I regret asking."

"You and Inspector Grace are close friends, no?"

Nile could feel the tone of the conversation begin to shift. He was careful not to incriminate himself. "Sir, we work together. Beyond that... well, beyond that there's nothing. Brixton marches to the beat of his own drum, sir. But from my experience, he's a good officer."

"Yes," Lucian said. "He is. Always has been." He guzzled the whiskey until the glass was dry. Then he poured himself another round. "He's under corporate investigation, Inspector. Did you know that?"

"I'm aware of his transfer, sir."

"That was no transfer," Lucian said. "It was a demotion."

Nile was surprised to hear him admit that.

"The Executive Board seems hellbent on bringing Brixton down," Lucian said as he took another sip from his glass. "He's become reckless in their eyes. Uncontrollable. They want to wipe their hands clean. But I want him to receive a fair investigation. I'm not sure the executive board is willing to give him that. I hate to admit it, but the board is — for lack of a less damning word — *corrupt*." His eyes turned downward. "Unfortunately, I'm the one who set that standard all these years." He paused, with a hint of guilt rimming the sockets of his drooping eyes, and then he said, "I want you to run an independent investigation, Inspector. Off the record, you understand?"

Nile was speechless, his empty gut suddenly bubbling up into his throat. The stomach acid was burning his esophagus. Then he found the words. "Sir, why me?"

"Because you're the only one I can trust to be neutral. Everyone else has a vendetta, a grudge against Brixton. I need to know the truth."

"The truth, sir?"

"It's all in Brixton's file. I'm giving you complete access to it. I want you to report directly to me on your findings. And *only* to me. General Ryker and Vice President Pharaoh are not to be consulted on the matter, do you understand?"

Nile felt too overwhelmed to bulk. "Yes sir," he said, looking rather pale for a black man.

"As far as anyone else is concerned," Lucian said, "we never had this conversation."

Nile suddenly lost his ability to move. He even found it hard to blink. He didn't want this assignment. He began to contemplate any excuse that he could use to escape it. "What about Captain Darvish, sir? He'll ask questions."

"No one is to know but me," Lucian said. "You'll have to elude the scrutiny."

Nile nodded in agreement.

Lucian took a final sip of whiskey and placed the empty glass on the desk. "I'll be assigning a corporate security drone to you as well. Special protocol. Fully automated. The signal will come directly to me. It's code encrypted, so it's completely secured. I want the truth. Nothing less."

Nile felt even smaller in the enormous leather chair. "Sir, I'm not even sure where to begin. I don't even know the charges against him."

"It's all in the file, Inspector."

"But sir, I don't—"

"This conversation is over," Lucian said abruptly. His demeanor was much less friendly now.

Nile stopped himself, knowing it was futile to protest any further.

Lucian looked him square in the eyes, and with a certain finality, he said, "Thank you for your service."

Nile could only muster two words. "Yes sir." He pulled himself up out of the chair awkwardly and stood up feeling unsteady on his feet. Everything was so cryptic and unclear. Perhaps the file would give him clarity.

"I'll be eagerly awaiting your report," Lucian said as Nile opened the mahogany doors. "Goodnight, Inspector."

Nile turned around in the doorway and nodded. "Goodnight, sir."

Agent Robicheau escorted him out of the house. There was no conversation this time. When Nile got back in his police cruiser, he shut the door softly and stared at the adobe wall in the courtyard without a single coherent thought in his head. He was burdened by the blunt relevance of his new position. Special orders, from the CEO himself, assigned in total secrecy. This assignment was a bloody cross he never wanted to bear. Investigating Brixton went against everything he stood for. He could only think of one word to vent his nervousness and frustration. Brixton had used the word quite often. The almighty *F* word. But it was vulgar and Nile refused to say it aloud, even in his own company. So he said nothing at all. He just sighed and drove away feeling dreadfully overmatched.

# FOURTEEN

An hour after the meeting with Nile, Lucian was lying in his California king alone, lit by an egregiously expensive table lamp, which had been carved from solid gold. He was wearing silk pajamas, finishing off a cup of hot chamomile tea, and happily engrossed in an old, leather-bound copy of *Don Quixote*. Then his deep concentration was broken by a shallow knock at his bedroom door. "There better be a good reason for this ill-timed intrusion," he said with a sprinkling of humor. "I was enjoying my solitude."

Agent Robicheau entered the room. He'd been Lucian's head of security for the past few years, having replaced Lucian's first head of security who died from heat stroke in the notorious summer of '71. Agent Robicheau was youthful, but only in appearance. Something in the eyes told a much different story. "Sir, it's time for your medication."

"Is it that time again already?"

Agent Robicheau knelt by Lucian's bedside and placed a medicine case on the foot of the bed and opened it. The individual compartments inside were filled with various capsules and colorful tablets. There was a dosing chart for each drug. Lucian's newest medication was meant to slow the effects of dementia. It came in a red, translucent gel capsule. 23mg of Donepezil, a cholinesterase inhibitor that increases naturally occurring substances in the brain which improve cognitive functions like memory, attention, social interactions and clear thought. Lucian thought it was a complete farce. Not just the drug. Everything. The lazy diagnosis. The overkill of medication. The daily checkups. The absurd cognitive tests they'd been putting him through. He hated doctors. He hated being poked and prodded and monitored. He missed the good old days of pissing in a cup and getting penicillin shots. The quick fix for the consequence of a night of fun. No mystery. The simplicity of that was liberating by comparison. This daily monitoring of his health and his cognitive functions was going on for three months now and his endurance for the futile process was beginning to fatigue. "If they're looking for pure sanity," he said, "they won't find it here. Too much sanity may be madness."

Agent Robicheau was straight-faced and unamused. "If you say so, sir."

"Have you ever read Don Quixote?" Lucian asked.

"No sir."

"It more or less reads you, I think." Lucian drifted on a thought. "I wonder how fraudulent my life has been. Striving for a reality that may not exist."

Agent Robicheau removed a red capsule and placed it in Lucian's hand and gave him a glass of water to chase it down. "Sir, please."

"Can I chase it down with some vodka instead?" Lucian asked.

"I wouldn't recommend it, sir."

"Well, too bad," Lucian said, presenting a bottle of his

favored Bloodstone vodka. "I'm the CEO. I'll do whatever I damn well please." He placed the capsule in his mouth and followed it with a generous swig of vodka. The firewater found its way down his gullet and joined company with the remnants of bourbon whiskey that he'd swallowed an hour earlier.

Agent Robicheau shook his head in disapproval.

Lucian never liked when people shook their head in disapproval. It seemed as if everyone was doing that to him lately. *What a condescending gesture*, he thought. It was aggravatingly indifferent, as if whatever dissatisfied thought people had lingering in their mind wasn't even worth the effort to put into words. It irked him fiercely. "You're so serious, Dorian," he said. "I'm growing weary of everyone's seriousness." He stuck his tongue out and opened his mouth wide to prove he had swallowed the red capsule. Then he deftly impersonated a mental patient with dazed eyeballs and an imaginary stream of drool pouring slowly from his mouth. "I'm having an episode," he said mockingly, slurring his speech and acting like a fool. "I think I shit my pants."

Agent Robicheau feigned a smile. The insincerity in his expression irked Lucian further. "For God's sake, Dorian. Have a laugh. What good is life without laughter?"

"I'm laughing on the inside, sir."

"Now you're patronizing me."

"No sir. I'm just doing my job."

"You're my head of security. Not my nurse."

"It's my job to protect you, sir. Even if it's from yourself."

Lucian swiped his hand in the air dismissively. "That's nonsense."

Agent Robicheau closed the medicine case and rose to his feet. "It's my job to make sure you're properly medicated, sir. If I fail you, they *will* have a nurse come here and watch over you. I know you don't want that."

"I hope she's a blonde," Lucian said with his usual mischief. "I have a thing for blondes. I don't know if they really have more fun or not, but I sure have more fun with them."

"I really wish you'd take this more seriously, sir."

"Never," Lucian said with a gratifying smirk.

Agent Robicheau shook his head in a less cordial manner this time and left the room, closing the door softly behind him. Lucian turned serious again. He pulled the unbroken red capsule from his mouth, having kept it lodged beneath his tongue in secret. He tucked it under the mattress next to three other red capsules that he had accumulated from the previous few days. He kicked off his house slippers and took another sip of his Bloodstone vodka and said, "I'm tired of serious."

## FIFTEEN

"Was it Croix that tried to burn this church down?" Kid asked, sitting there among the charcoaled pews and unable to sleep.

Tavo ignored him.

"Was it?"

Tavo nodded reluctantly.

"Why would he burn this place down?" Kid pressed.

Tavo didn't answer.

"Why would he do that?"

Tavo sighed. "He never told me why, okay?"

"Did you ever ask?"

"Yes."

"What'd he say?"

"He convinced me to never ask again."

"How?"

"With a knife to my throat."

Kid sat upright, his eyes bulging. "He attacked you with a knife?"

"*Threatened.*"

"To *kill* you?"

"Yes."

"Why are you still friends with him?"

"Because he saved my life with that knife the very next day."

Kid loosened the tension in his face. He could see an unyielding gratitude in Tavo's eyes.

"That's who Croix is," Tavo explained. "You gotta take the good with the bad, because the good may save your life someday. I don't know much about his past before we met, but I know plenty about who he's been ever since, and I have to say, Croix is probably the most loyal man I've ever known. I can always count on him to have my back."

Kid thought for a moment, and then he asked, "Do you think he has mine?"

"He's had your back since the day he brought you to Revival," Tavo said. "So consider yourself lucky."

---

Croix's dream that night was unusual, and far more terrifying than what usually ailed him in the dark corners of his slumbering mind. He was crawling through the dirt in Ezekiel's Hollow, creeping over the weathered ivory of human remains. The eternal leavings of mass suicide. He knew he was dreaming, but he couldn't wake, and oddly enough it felt more real than reality. The sun was shining brightly, but it was dark as night, as if the sun had lost its will and no longer burned with purpose. The ground was unsettled and soft to the touch, almost like human skin. It was stained red and dotted with pools of blood. As he tried to push forward on his hands and knees, the ground began to soften beneath him, turning to a formless, devouring sludge. He sank into the ground slowly, fighting his way out but failing, gripping at the earth as it slipped through his fingertips like time slipping through an hour glass. The red sludge mired him in place. The skulls around him began to move eerily across the ground, fusing together with bone. Dismantled skeletons began to reform in the blink of an eye. Femurs and fibulae and vertebrae meshing with rib cages, merging into humanoid shapes, and coming back to some grotesque form of life. Reborn into something indescribably awful. He could feel his pulse rising. Their skin formed around bone, looking soft and purplish and maggoty, like rancid meat. Their eyes were blinded by bloody rags, which were wrapped maliciously around their heads, as if it were some cruel punishment in the afterlife. Their legs were jagged like broken limbs and their bodies were bent and crippled, unable to stand on two feet and pulling themselves along the ground like serpents with claws. They grabbed at his body aimlessly, screeching with a deafening pitch, like the ravenous crows of the valley. His ears ruptured and bled. He struggled to break free from their rotten clutches as he reached for something that was buried deeply in the earth beneath him. He had no understanding of what he was searching for, only that he had an inescapable desire to uncover it, as if all would be lost if he failed. He could feel himself yearning for the unknown. He dug frantically, pushing piles of crimson sludge aside. But the ground reformed with every swipe of his hand, covering the mystery that was buried beneath it. Then the rotting humanoids overtook him, slamming his face into the bloody ground and piling on top of him, crushing him and ripping at his flesh with their long misshapen nails. Their stench was repulsive. He could sense it swirling through his nostrils and settling deep into his soul. Bloody saliva dripped from their fangs and onto his neck. It burned like acid rain. They shrieked in his ear as the earth cracked open and began to swallow him whole. He was suddenly weightless and without feeling, like drowning in a waterless ocean. He found himself buried alive, suffocating beneath a dark and terrible nothingness. Then a voice shouted out from the void, "*Croix!*"

He startled awake and drew his *Crazy 8* revolver.

"*Don't shoot*," the voice shouted. "It's *me*. It's *Kid*."

Croix saw Kid approaching him from the side of the church, pulling the golden palomino by the reins. "Goddamnit, *Kid*." He immediately lowered the *Crazy 8* and exhaled the adrenaline that was pumping through his startled heart. "Don't charge at me like that. You're liable to get your fucking head blown off." He wiped the sleep from his eyes and holstered the *Crazy 8* and tried to settle his nerves. He was still shaken by the terrorizing nightmare, sitting there with his back plastered to the hard adobe wall. His shirt was soaked from sweat, and the morning sun hadn't even peeked over the horizon yet. He took note of the time. It was late. Too late. He'd been lost to the world for hours. Not like him at all. He'd left himself exposed to the dangers of the night without proper caution. "Whatcha doing with my horse?" he asked.

"I was walking him," Kid said as he crouched down with a wonderstruck gaze. "Take a look at this. I found something while I was walking."

Croix glanced at the discovery in Kid's hand with very little enthusiasm, figuring to see a dead lizard or a petrified tiger turd or whatever sparked Kid's naive sense of wonder in the desert. But his eyes went into a quiet shock instead, looking quite struck himself. But not with wonder. More like he'd seen a ghost. It was a small, wooden cross. An old world symbol of faith that must've looked ancient to Kid's youthful eyes. Croix's face tightened, heating up with a slow burn. He recognized the unwanted relic from his youth. There were decades of forgotten memories trapped in the splintered fibers of that worthless scrap of wood. He wondered how it suddenly turned up after all those years. As often as he'd returned to the miserable old church, he had never stumbled upon the cross. Not once.

"Looks old, don't it?" Kid asked, holding the cross in his hand as if it were God incarnate. "What's the chances I come across something like this?"

Croix snatched it out of his hand. "Where'd you find this goddamn thing?"

"Buried in the dirt. Ain't it good luck or something? Like from God or whatever?"

"No," Croix said with a flippant disregard. "It's fucking useless." He squeezed the cross tightly in his fist, trying to suppress the demons that were suddenly stirring inside of him.

Kid held his hand out. "You can give it back now."

"No," Croix said sharply. He pulled his bowie knife and pointed the blade at Kid's chest. "Go fetch us some food for breakfast."

"Bullshit, give it back," Kid snapped, reaching for the cross. "I'm the one found it."

Croix pressed the tip of the blade to Kid's sternum, just enough to make his point clear. "I ain't playing, Kid. Go fetch us some fucking breakfast."

Kid stiffened. Croix's eyes were blank. They weren't burning. They weren't even lifeless. They were just lost between worlds. Kid retreated carefully, backpedaling into the church and disappearing inside of the old adobe walls. Croix pulled a hand-rolled cigarette from his pocket and lit what was left of it and took a desperately needed drag. He looked at the discarded crucifix in his hand. It felt like a bad omen. So he took his Bowie knife and began to chip away at the wood furiously with the blade, as if he were trying to etch the unholy amulet out of existence. His golden palomino trotted over to him and stared at him, just watching in some odd, unearthly judgement.

"What are you looking at?" Croix asked.

The horse flapped his gums and spit at him and turned his head and walked towards the church.

"Where the hell you think you're going?"

The horse looked at him once more with critical eyes and disappeared inside the adobe walls. Croix spit in the dirt and called him a traitor.

---

Kid was inside the church pulling food from the saddlebags when the horse walked by and nudged him. "Watch where you're going, *stupid horse.*"

The horse blew his lips and kept walking.

Kid yanked the food out of the saddlebags carelessly, like a child lost in an unconsolable tantrum. Tavo and Skinny were rolling up their sleeping bags nearby and trying to remain indifferent to his presence. Probably to avoid his conversation. Kid didn't bother with them anyway. He was in no mood for small talk, let alone an entire conversation. He gathered some jerky and hard tack and returned outside with a salty demeanor. He dropped the food in the dirt at Croix's feet, refusing to speak to him. Croix was too busy wrapping duct tape around the top of the cross to even notice the disrespect. But as Kid turned to walk back into the church, Croix grabbed him by the arm and said, "Here you go, Kid." He offered him the cross. "Now it's useful."

Kid took the cross in his hand and studied the mangled appearance. It looked much different than before. He was offended by Croix's desecration of it. His eyes scrunched together in dark confusion and rising animosity. "What's this supposed to be?" he asked.

"A weapon," Croix answered.

The bottom of the cross had been carved into a sharp point by Croix's blade, with the duct tape at the top serving as a grip. The crucifix of Christ — a totem of willful sacrifice — had been transformed into a stabbing weapon for self-defense and vengeance. It was no longer an object of blind faith.

"Make your own luck, Kid," Croix said as he took a bitter drag from his cigarette and blew the smoke from his nostrils. "God's dead."

Kid looked at the cross with a blankness now. A fading sense of wonder. Any supernatural curiosities were gone, snuffed out, totally obliterated.

Croix took one last drag of his cigarette and spit the ashes out. "Don't look so broken," he said. "You didn't miss much. I wasn't too impressed with the son of a bitch when he was alive." He tossed the shrunken stub of the cigarette onto the once hollowed ground and stomped out the burning embers.

Kid was drained of all fascination. He dropped the cross at his feet, leaving it there to be buried in the past again. There was nothing left to behold. Nothing left to stir his senses. Faith was truly gone from the world. He could finally feel its absence, like someone unwilling to accept the loss of a loved one and then finally acknowledging their death and succumbing to grief. The world felt cold. He shivered in the morning heat. An insatiable chill. He stared at the empty horizon. Nothing moved in the distance. Not the Joshua trees. Not the sand in the wind. Not a single animal appeared on the landscape. All was still and quiet and devoid of life. He had never felt so lonely.

# SIXTEEN

Brixton stood alone that morning in the locker room at Outpost 11 with a disgruntled heart. He was dressing himself in his disgraceful new uniform. It was actually a painful process, as if spikes had been sewn into the seams and were slicing into his skin as he slid the olive green shame onto his body. But the pain he imagined was just his pride getting the shit kicked out of it. That was something he hadn't even sparred with before. Now he was in the middle of a goddamn prizefight, and he was ready to throw in the towel. Fortunately there was no one there to witness his defeat. The Warhawks still hadn't returned from R and R yet. He looked at himself in the smudged mirror on the locker door and could hardly stand his own reflection. A shell of his former self. A tired, sagging phantom-like face with little resemblance to the man he thought he was. And that was just the surface. What lied beneath was probably far more intolerable. He felt fortunate to be so shallow. He wouldn't have to peer deeper into himself. He hadn't gone to those depths in so long he'd probably drown in them. He studied his new nameplate: *Patrolman Grace*. The sound of that made his pecker shrink.

*How emasculating*, he thought. He didn't deserve such a cruel fate. He may not have been the same man that he once was, and that was becoming self-evident, but he was no fucking grunt. The uniform was an embarrassment. An ugly shade of green that announced his demotion to the world like a bullhorn. He was a Warhawk now. There were amulets on the shirt pocket that meant absolutely nothing to him. He just looked like an asshole. And not the kind of asshole he was proud to be. He felt degraded just wearing it. The border patrol were garbage men. He couldn't be associated with those scumbags. They disposed of human trash for a living, which in his book made *them* trash too. As he glared at his reflection he found himself pulling his newly-issued BP9 handgun from his holster and aiming it at the mirror. A reflexive impulse that he seemingly had no control over. The ghost staring back at him was repulsive, taunting him. It was something to be destroyed. His finger moved to the trigger, almost without will. He wanted to squeeze. The mindless urge was becoming a conscious desire, and suddenly he was lost again. The same kind of lost that nearly drove him straight into that deadly brick wall in the Industrial Zone a few nights before. He needed someone to talk him down, by talking him up. An ego boost. He needed to hear the universe speak to him. To tell him he was relevant. That he had purpose. He always listened, hoping to hear a voice that wasn't his own, but the universe only mocked him, in cryptic mutterings. Some foreign noise, both archaic and unknown, and with nothing in particular to say. That made him feel meaningless. He wondered, *what would the world be like without Brixton Grace?*

*Not much different*, he thought. Then the impulse to pull the trigger intensified. *One squeeze and it would all be over.* As he began to squeeze, he was startled by a loud click. The sound of a locker door being opened. He turned and saw a Warhawk dressed in full battle gear, shoving a black duffel bag into the locker. It was Kassab, Captain Vedder's lieutenant, but to Brixton he was just an unfamiliar face. Kassab didn't even notice the golden boy standing there on the other side of the room watching. Then after he crammed the duffel bag into the locker, he looked around with what appeared to be caution on his face. He noticed Brixton watching him and his eyes suddenly grew wide, like a refugee in the headlights of a Scorpion UTV. Brixton nodded and was about to introduce himself, but Kassab just shut the door to the locker and scurried out of the room without a word. Not a single syllable. No informal greeting. No *go fuck yourself.* Nothing.

Brixton was puzzled by the rude introduction. Either the Lieutenant was a total dickhead with no concept of decorum, which wouldn't come as a complete shock among these Warhawks, or he'd just been caught doing something underhanded and unofficial and wasn't sure how to react. Both seemed plausible. Either way, something was amiss, and Brixton was curious to know what it was. He suddenly felt better about his predicament. Now there was a problem to solve. He felt more like an Inspector than a probationary grunt. He holstered the BP9 handgun and smiled at himself in the mirror and proclaimed with confidence, "You're Brixton *fucking* Grace."

# SEVENTEEN

Chief Kadence was sitting in his cluttered office reading through Brixton's file when Captain Vedder entered without knocking. "Chief, you requested to see me?"

The Chief looked up from the solar scroll in his hand and lowered his reading glasses onto the tip of his nose. "Captain, you're two days late on your report. I wanna know exactly what happened when you recovered that drone."

"Wasn't nothin' to it, Chief. A routine recovery. It'll be on your desk first thing in the morning."

"*First thing*," Chief Kadence said, almost in the form of a question, as if he were giving an order that he knew wouldn't be followed.

"I hear we're bringing in a new guy," Captain Vedder said, feigning ignorance. "Another greenhorn?"

Chief Kadence glared at him. "You know damn well who it is. Don't you give him any shit."

"That's all behind me, sir. I swear."

Chief Kadence wasn't the least bit convinced. Captain Vedder and Brixton had a brief but bitter history with one another. Captain Vedder had been investigated by Brixton a few years earlier for beating a refugee woman to death in Brimstone, and he'd been charged and suspended for dereliction of duty. It was a cakewalk punishment, but he never forgot Brixton's involvement, and he still hadn't put it behind him. That was obvious to the Chief.

"One more thing," Chief Kadence said. "I saw you and the boys took R and R again last night."

"Oh *yes* we did." Captain Vedder grabbed his crotch and tugged on it several times. "I told you, Chief, we had to get Greenie some refugee pussy in Brimstone."

"Uh huh," the Chief said. "That hovership ain't no party bus. It's all fun and games until one of you idiots gets a venereal disease and your prick falls off."

"Ain't happened yet, sir, and we've had hundreds of opportunities. Believe me."

"Behave yourselves when you're in that shit hole," Chief Kadence commanded, scolding his insubordinate Captain with his moody eyes. "It's not our territory. I don't want you tarnishing the Warhawk legacy by acting like a bunch of horny teenagers."

"Well, sir, the boys ain't that far removed from being horny teenagers. Greenie still *is* one in fact."

"You're a company man, Captain. Act like it."

"Don't worry, Chief. Warhawks are the cock of the walk in Brimstone." Captain Vedder raised his chin with pride. "You should see the way the other patrolmen look at us. Like we're fucking royalty. And Corporate knows we're the cock of the walk, too, if that's what you're worried about."

Chief Kadence removed his reading glasses and sat upright. "Don't you worry about my worrying, Captain. You just make sure you don't start any shit with Patrolman Grace. He's gonna require some breaking in."

"Oh I can break him in, sir," Captain Vedder said with a smirk, "don't you worry about that."

"I'm serious, Captain. Shut that bravado shit down right now before it turns into something you can't contain. You two hot heads are destined for a clash of egos, and I'll be the one cleaning up your mess."

Captain Vedder shrugged, playing coy. "No worries, Chief. I'm gonna take the golden boy under my wing. He'll be hollerin' *hoorah* in no time." He grinned like a devil and walked away.

Chief Kadence felt like imploding. "This fucking outpost," he whispered to himself, complaining to the only person who would listen. He pulled another black market cigar from his stash and scrambled for a lighter. "This job is gonna put me in an early grave." He lit the cigar and took a strenuous puff to settle his worried mind.

# EIGHTEEN

When Brixton stepped out of the barracks and stepped onto the hyperbike lot on the eastern side of the compound, the heat of the morning was already forcing a bead of sweat from his temple. *So much for the dry heat*, he thought. He felt like he'd dipped his head in water. Fortunately, his uniform had an advanced cooling function imbedded in the fibers. Highly conductive polyethylene. Something about transferring thermal energy. He didn't bother with the details. He had some clothes back home that claimed to execute the same feat of technology, but those shirts felt like a furnace compared to his uniform. He was impressed, but he still hated the olive green abomination. He wandered the lot looking for his new ride. There were dozens of Nimbus hyperbikes lined in rows, all identical, but numbered and specifically assigned. He found his number: seventeen. He climbed onto the seat and straddled the electric bike carefully, as if it were some wild mustang that could rear back and gallop away at any moment. Hyperbikes were built for speed and for battle, reaching up to a staggering 200 mph on the highway, but designed specifically for rough terrain and even rougher circumstances, with special shock absorption and airless tires that could scarcely be damaged. They ran on solar batteries and stored their energy in small nuclear capacitors. The solar collector panels were protected by a thick anti-ballistic, polycarbonate glass. So they were bullet-proof and practically self-sustaining. The perfect vehicle for patrolling the vast desert of the Forbidden Rim.

Cooley and Chant approached, with premeditated grins on their faces. "Warrior up, Grace," Cooley said. "We're going hunting."

Brixton felt a rare sense of precaution. "Right now?"

"This is what we do," Cooley said. "We're Warhawks. You're riding with me and Chant today. Captain Vedder said we should keep a close eye on you." He looked at Chant with a condescending chuckle. "Maybe to see how a *real* officer of the law operates, huh?"

They enjoyed a hearty laugh at Brixton's expense.

He puffed up pridefully. "Well, don't get lost in the dark," he said with a cocky assurance. "I cast a pretty big shadow." He was comforted by the thought of his glory days.

Then a burly voice shouted out from behind him, "Your glory days are over, Grace."

Brixton whipped his head around to see the source.

It was Captain Vedder.

"You don't cast a shadow, Patrolman," Captain Vedder said. "You *are* the shadow."

Cooley and Chant laughed and hollered *"Hoorah"* in unison.

Brixton could do nothing but shake his head and snicker with contempt, even though he felt a punch to his nuts. He'd seen all this macho bullshit before at the academy. Admittedly, he'd indulged in such childishness himself, quite recently in fact, bullying lesser men and those who were green around the eyes. It was a rite of passage that he had to endure long ago when he was a rookie cop, and technically he was a rookie border patrolman now, so the insults were justified. But he couldn't tolerate the shots coming from a bunch of ignorant garbage men like these so-called Warhawks. They were beneath him, like shit on his boot heels. Something to scrape off with a disposable knife. Taking insults from them was equivalent to having his nose rubbed in it. No way would he stand for that. He was the goddamn hammer, not the nail. "You fucking grunts are ridiculous," he said, struggling to stay composed in the face of his growing inadequacies. "You're walking, talking cliches, and there's not a single ounce of irony in it. How's that even possible?"

He dropped his foot and kickstarted the hyperbike like some kind of badass, hoping the engine noise would growl and overrule Captain Vedder's insults, but the electric motor just wheezed pathetically, sounding more like a sick old man on a deathbed, and that only made Brixton feel more inadequate.

Captain Vedder grabbed the handlebars and beamed. "Careful now. She's quiet, but she's a wild one, and she don't come with training wheels."

"I've had the training," Brixton said.

"That so?" Captain Vedder glared at him for a moment, his dark eyes doing their best to intimidate. But it didn't work. So he turned to his men instead. "*Warhawks*. Gather 'round. We got ourselves another greenhorn."

The Warhawks gathered around like schoolkids about to witness a schoolyard brawl, their eyes anticipating a glorious display of authority by their beloved Captain.

Brixton prepared himself for what he knew was coming. It was always the same bullshit with guys like Vedder. The juvenile bravado was so predictable. He waited for the first jab. He figured it would be entertaining at the very least.

"This is the former golden boy himself," Captain Vedder said with a chuckle. "PPD's finest. Take a good long look, men… and be glad you're a fucking Warhawk."

The Warhawks laughed and howled.

Brixton eyed Captain Vedder intensely, feeling himself fall prey to the taunt despite his better judgement. "That's how it's gonna be, huh?"

"That's just how it is," Captain Vedder said. "And there ain't a damn thing you can do about it. I'm your Captain."

"Then I guess I should salute you," Brixton said. He lowered the visor on his biohelmet and gave his new Captain the one finger salute. It made him feel juvenile, but he didn't care so much. The way he saw it, he was forced to grow up way too fast during the Collapse, so he was just making up for lost time. He cranked the throttle and spun a donut with the wheezing hyperbike, kicking up the earth in a frenzy of dust. Then he blasted off, leaving Captain Vedder standing in the middle of a cloud of his own Warhawk filth.

The young Warhawks stood there speechless.

Captain Vedder wiped the dust from his eyes and turned to them and forced a confident grin. "The golden boy is reckless," he said. "I wouldn't be surprised if he gets himself killed his first day on the job."

The men roared in unison, *"Hoorah."*

Captain Vedder hopped on his hyperbike and shouted, *"Warrior up, Warhawks."*

The engines whirled quietly. Captain Vedder drove off and the young Warhawks followed, howling like wild animals on the hunt and proving themselves to be exactly what Brixton had accused them of being: walking, talking cliches.

## NINETEEN

Croix had been watching the three strangers through his binoculars for the better part of an hour. They were sketchy-looking, hiding up on a hidden ridge on the slope of Kessler Peak on the eastern horizon just a few hundred yards away from the old Dagger church. Croix was partially hidden in the granite rocks behind the adobe shack and raising the glass to his eyes every few minutes to check their movements. The men hadn't moved at all. They just sat there looking right back at him. From what he could tell, they were men of fighting age, which to him meant old enough to make him sweat. These men were late thirties, maybe early forties. Age mattered. Not just physically. Older men would be experienced and savvy. They wouldn't be rash, so they wouldn't be betrayed by their own youthful enthusiasm or by a need to prove something to themselves. They'd be strategic. You'd never see them coming. Croix felt fortunate to have seen them already. He had an unsettling feeling, though that was nothing new. He hadn't felt settled since birth. He took another look through the binoculars. The sun was still waking up and beginning to swell over the eastern horizon, casting just enough glow on the dark side of the peak that he could see the strangers clearly enough, all of them lying on their bellies behind the brush and one of them looking back at him through a long scope. Fortunately there was no rifle attached to it. But Croix never liked being watched. There was nothing more ominous or violating in his mind than men who couldn't take their eyes off him. They always had designs. Those men on the peak wanted something. Maybe the trade goods. Maybe the horses. Maybe both. Or worse yet, maybe they just wanted to hurt someone, just for the hell of it. Croix couldn't see their weapons, so he couldn't take inventory of the possible threats. He couldn't tell if they were gang members. They didn't act like Bloody Knuckles or look like Coyote Clan, and they didn't boast or holler their intentions like Black Lillies or Banshees. He thought they looked like simple drifters. But that didn't mean they were simple-minded. He couldn't see the state of their clothing, which was unfortunate. Clothing was key. Garments could tell a lot about a man's desperation. The more threadbare and worn a man's clothes were, the more he'd want something better suited for his survival.

After a few minutes, the three strangers finally moved from their spot, rising to their feet slowly. Croix watched intently. They took nothing from the ground and carried nothing in their hands. He watched them casually make their way down the mountainside to the foothills. They began their trek across the flatland through the sagebrush and Joshua trees, making their way straight towards him. Their figures appeared as dark silhouettes cast against the burnt hue of the early morning skyline. He couldn't make out their appearance anymore, only their basic shapes. But as they got closer, they became more dimensional, and more real. He could see the details. The looks on their faces. He still thought they looked like simple drifters, not like anyone with means to negotiate a trade. They were dressed in tattered dusters and torn waterproof hiker jackets. More than enough to survive the winter. But it was summer. He still didn't see any weapons on them. But that just meant they were good at hiding them. They wore weathered military boots and old tennis shoes and their cargo pants were filthy and neglected. They looked unbathed and unkempt, their faces softly-bearded and their hair unruly. He watched their hands, making sure they were empty and loose and not looking tense or anticipatory. He watched their eyes as best he could from that distance and studied their manner and tried to guess their business. He had the advantage of knowing bad men and recognizing their intentions. He was confident he would recognize theirs.

As they came closer, he decided he didn't like their look. One was short and pot-bellied, and the dirty t-shirt beneath his jacket was rising up over his navel and exposing a tattoo of a red broken heart and a naked woman on all fours with her backside in the air. Not the kind of thing a decent man would ink on his body. The second man was tall and wiry, with long hair, and he was wearing a long brown duster that could be hiding any number of weapons. The third man was the one to watch out for. He was stout and square-jawed and brooding. He had scars that could only be gotten from fighting. His face was leathered by the sun, and his eyes looked impervious to fear. Croix figured he was the alpha of the pack. He lowered his binoculars and rose from the granite rock and moved into a more strategic position. He stood tall and kept his hand on the grip of his holstered *Crazy 8*, his only salvation. He didn't trust a soul in this world. He wasn't about to start with these three strangers.

Tavo, Skinny and Kid were nearby feeding the horses, totally unaware that three sketchy men were approaching them from behind. Tavo wasn't satisfied with the way that Kid was rigging up his spotted appaloosa. "Kid, I told you to rig her up proper. What is that mess?"

"I done it right," Kid said, shielding his work from Tavo's eyes. "Stop hawking me."

"Let me get a look at it then."

"No, I done it the way Croix taught me. Now stop hawking me, goddamnit."

Then Skinny grabbed at the horses's reins and said, "I should set the riggings for both of you fools."

Tavo chuckled. "If we left it to you, Skinny, we'd be riding backwards on our horses."

Croix dismissed their foolish banter and kept his eyes on the three strangers. They were only fifty yards out now and he figured it was time to alert Tavo and Skinny to their presence. "Boys," he said calmly, "Behave yourselves. We got company."

Kid turned first and saw the men approaching. He dropped the reins and backed away from the horse, making his way behind Croix, where he felt safer. Tavo looked and immediately moved away from Skinny, slowly and carefully. Skinny looked and moved away too, both of them spreading out and making themselves a much harder target.

Tavo placed his hand close to his gun but not close enough to instigate any trouble. "Who are they, Croix? Don't look like common traders to me."

"They're not," Croix said. "Maybe common thieves. They've been watching us all morning from that ridge up on Kessler Peak."

"How come you didn't say nothing?"

"Didn't want ya'll breaking my concentration."

Tavo grunted. "You think they're trouble?"

Skinny tried to reassure himself. "They wouldn't just walk

up on us if they was lookin' for a fight. They'd wanna ambush us or something."

"There's nowhere to set an ambush out here," Tavo said. "Besides, Croix spotted 'em before they could."

"That's right," Croix said.

Kid wasn't so sure. "They look peaceful to me."

Croix narrowed his eyes at them. "They look like wolves that got lost from their pack."

Skinny nervously placed his hand near his holstered pistol. "Croix, don't you do anything unnecessary."

"Yeah please, Croix," Tavo said. "Give 'em a chance to present themselves. It's best we avoid a fight."

The three strangers were only fifteen yards away when Croix swiftly drew his *Crazy 8* revolver and aimed it directly at what he suspected was the alpha of the pack: the man with the square jaw and the brooding gaze. "Keep your hands empty," he warned. "Get 'em up in the air, you sons a bitches."

Tavo winced, "Goddamn you, Croix."

The strangers raised their hands in surrender, presenting themselves as no threat.

But Croix wasn't convinced. "I seen you eyeballing our trade goods. Ya'll see something here worth dying for?"

The stranger with the square jaw spoke first, proving Croix's instinct right. "We don't want no trouble," the man said, confirming his alpha status. "Just came to talk with the Almighty."

"Ya'll come to confess your sins?" Croix asked with waiting eyes.

"I don't know what you're talking about, mister."

"We came across a pile of dead bodies a ways back," Croix explained. "Women and children. They were murdered. Their bodies raped and their heads chopped off like they were animals. Two dead men strung up to an electric pole. Y'all know anything about that?"

"No," the stranger said with a grimace. "That's a terrible thing. Just let us pay our respects to the Almighty. We'll be on our way, and you'll never see us again. I promise."

Croix looked at them with skeptic eyes. He never trusted a promise from a stranger, and he never trusted a man who claimed that God was the source of his earthly inspiration. "I ain't met a true God-fearing man in two decades," he said, "and here I meet three in one day? What are the chances of that? Almost seems impossible." He stared hard at the alpha, reading his eyes, and waiting for a reaction that might betray the man's spoken intentions. The man stared back. His eyes were rimmed in darkness, the lids draped over toneless green irises. Croix had seen the eyes of monsters before. They spoke to him, like the ghosts of their victims screaming out for some bastardized form of justice. He was certain. This was no God-fearing man. So why bother with pleasantries? He fired a shot, sending a bullet ripping through the alpha's chest. Everyone startled and panicked. But not Croix. He calmly fired off another round. The bullet ripped through the short stranger's gut and brought him to his knees. The tall stranger reached for a gun hidden in his coat, but Croix shot him in the chest before his fingers ever touched the handle. In mere seconds the three strangers were on the ground, two dead and one left breathing, on his knees, gut shot and bleeding out. Tavo and Skinny pulled their guns, but the shooting was already done. Kid was paralyzed, his eyes wide and his limbs immovable.

"What the hell, Croix?" Skinny hollered. "Why'd you do that?"

Croix walked towards the gutshot stranger with his *Crazy 8* aimed rather convincingly. "They had bad intentions," he said to Skinny, keeping his eyes on the stranger. "Wasn't gonna end any other way."

"Bad intentions?" Tavo asked.

"They were scheming to get the drop on us." Croix kneeled down next to the stranger and locked eyes with him. "Ain't that right, you son of a bitch?"

The stranger was in shock. He couldn't speak. He just grunted and spit up blood.

Kid was slowly recovering from his own shock, but he mustered enough constitution to speak. "How do you know you done right by killing 'em? Could be they was here to do exactly what they said. Pay respects and all."

"What have I told you, Kid?" Croix asked. "If there's ever any doubt, you shoot first and ask to be forgiven later. Being one step slow out here is the same as having one foot in death's door." He took the stranger's gun from his belt and looked him over. He pulled a two-way radio from the stranger's coat pocket. A walkie talkie caked in dried blood. Then he noticed something hidden behind the man's button down flannel. "Shit. That ain't good."

Tavo lifted an eye. "What is it?"

"Reapers."

"Don't joke. That ain't funny."

Croix grabbed the flannel shirt and ripped the button down, exposing the stranger's chest. There was a tattoo inked over his heart. It was an ace of spades *death card* with a skull of the grim reaper in the center. "I ain't joking."

"Son of a bitch." Tavo sounded irrevocably afraid.

Skinny couldn't believe it either. "Reapers?" He took a step back in apprehension. "Christ Almighty."

"What's a reaper?" Kid asked.

"This ain't their territory," Skinny said frantically. "What the hell they doing this far west?"

"What's a fucking Reaper?" Kid asked again.

"They're a gang of thugs," Skinny explained.

"Thugs, hell," Croix said with a hiss. "They're a goddamn death cult. Murderers. Rapists. Mutilators. Cannibals too. The worst kind of human being on Earth." He turned to the wounded Reaper. "I knew there was something shady about you boys." He put the barrel of his *Crazy 8* in the Reaper's crotch as a warning. He directed Kid's attention to the tattoo. "See that, Kid? That's an ace of spades. The death card. That's all these boys are about. *Death*. Plain and simple. Hell, they'll kill *each other* if they get bored enough."

The Reaper smiled through bloody teeth.

Tavo looked eager to get on with it. "Don't leave him kicking."

Croix stood up and offered his *Crazy 8* to Kid. "You wanna do it, Kid?"

"*What? No.*" Kid held his hands tightly by his side. "No fucking way, man."

"Someday you're gonna have to take a life," Croix said. "It's a rite of passage. Best you get it over with now, when bullets ain't flying around your head."

"No," Kid said. "I don't want to."

Croix softened his tone. "No one who's good ever *wants* to. That's the whole point. If the good people just keep getting killed for lack of fighting back then someday there won't be any good people left." He grabbed the Reaper by the coat and pulled him to his knees.

Kid couldn't bear to witness it. "You don't even know these men, Croix. Or what they done."

"I know 'em all too well," Croix said. He cocked the revolver. It was his way of announcing his intentions. He wanted the Reaper to think about death before he went black.

Kid protested and stood in his way. "You're always lecturing me on right and wrong, Croix. *This ain't right.*"

Croix shoved him aside. "Don't you pity these sons a bitches. They don't deserve the benefit of your doubt." He pressed the barrel of the *Crazy 8* to the Reaper's forehead. "Evil's a sure thing, Kid. It's best to rid the world of it." Then he pulled the trigger and blew the Reapers's brains through the back of his head. The soft tissue exploded in a mass of red particles. The body crumpled backwards to the ground. Croix stood over the bloody corpse, looking completely unmoved. Kid was speechless and clearly sickened by what he'd witnessed. Tavo and Skinny seemed relieved, but they were still harboring an obvious sense of dread.

"Can we just get the hell outta here?" Skinny asked.

Croix holstered his *Crazy 8*. "We gotta hide the bodies first. Drag 'em to the rocks."

"What the hell for?" Skinny asked.

"You want this coming back to us?" Croix asked, as if he were already looking over his shoulder. "Reapers don't forgive. They'd hunt us to the ends of the earth for this."

Tavo quietly agreed. He and Skinny shared a look of pure terror. Even Croix looked like a man on his heels, ready to turn and run, which in their experience had never been the case. This was a box they never wanted to open. Reapers were beyond evil. They were pure chaos defined. Something they just weren't equipped to fight in great numbers. Croix knew these three Reapers weren't alone. They were *Deceivers*: Reapers that were made to blend in and act natural, so they wouldn't call attention to themselves. Ambush predators. Scouts that got the lay of the land and a read on the target before a war party came through to raid and recruit. Croix had carried a strong suspicion ever since they discovered those poor women and children at Ezekiel's Hollow. Only Reapers were demented enough to rape and behead women and chil-dren and hang the men from a pole forcing them to watch it all unfold. Evil like that was beyond human capacity. As far as Croix was concerned, Reapers weren't human at all. Whatever remained of humanity was completely gone from them. Purposely expelled. A fine-tuned emptiness. He'd dealt with their kind before. Long ago. He was always hoping he'd never have to cross paths with them again. He wondered what they were doing this far west, here in the Mojave. It wasn't their territory. They'd come from their stomping grounds on the East Coast. The flooded cities of New York and Boston and Chicago. But why here? This was Blood Ground. Land of the Bloody Knuckles. A force far more powerful than Reapers, or so it was thought. Croix wondered if they'd come west out of desperation, to rob the traders on the trade routes, or if they'd simply come to start a war and claim the territory for them-selves. That thought truly frightened him. Reapers were more of a cult than a gang. *A death cult,* bred to be evil, from blank seedlings to blackhearted murderers, all ingrained with a vile sense of purpose, and molded to have no conscience. That human flaw was beaten out of them before it could grow and fester. By the time young Reapers were old enough to hold a weapon and take a human life, they'd become unnatural purveyors of death. Hunters of goodness. Killers of the soul. Even the devil himself couldn't have authored a more vile and vicious creature within the dark chambers of his imagination. Croix knew he'd have to face them again. That was inevitable now. The Reapers were here to stay. So he'd be keeping his hand resting on the grip of his *Crazy 8* from here on out. That would be his only salvation.

# TWENTY

The sun was burning in the desert as if it had a grudge against humanity. One-hundred and ten degrees of pure vengeance at high noon, according to the hyperbike's onboard thermometer. Brixton was trailing behind the Warhawks. They were hunting in the Forbidden Rim, thrumming across the lifeless Dutch Flat. Brown patches of brittlebush. Leafless ironwood trees that were sulking in self-pity. Barrel cacti that would've prayed for rain if only they were sentient and capable of such futile solicitation. Captain Vedder was keeping a watchful eye on the golden boy. Brixton recognized the scrutiny, so he returned the gesture, keeping his own curious eye on the Captain. He could sense the notorious Warhawk leader scowling at him through the tinted visor of his biohelmet. This so-called hunt felt more like a transport to a shittier version of Hell. Brixton felt like chained chattel, as if he were being escorted to his next place of enslavement, and Captain Vedder was the one holding the whip. Brixton aimed to play it cool, even in the unbearable heat. So he just followed the Warhawks and did what Border Patrols do: ride around aimlessly, apparently. "We going anywhere in particular?" he asked through his helmet comms. "Or are we just collecting a paycheck?"

Captain Vedder didn't respond.

They were back in the Sonoran Desert now, heading further southeast than expected, and pushing the boundaries of established law.

"That was a real question," Brixton said. "Do you even recognize where we are?"

Captain Vedder still didn't respond.

Brixton shook his helmet. "Is this fucking thing working or what?"

Then Cooley said, "Cap, we got wagon tracks."

Captain Vedder studied the tracks on the ground ahead. "Two wagons," he said. "Side by side. Southbound." He signaled to the men. "That's our cue, Warhawks."

He turned due south. They followed him.

"Where are we going?" Brixton asked.

This time Captain Vedder was all too eager to answer. "To disrupt the order of things," he said.

"In case you hadn't noticed," Brixton said, "the Warhawk boundary line ended about a mile back. You're out of your jurisdiction."

"The jurisdiction lines have been redrawn."

"Redrawn?" Brixton didn't buy that. "By who?"

"I bet it kills you," Captain Vedder said with an overt satisfaction in his voice.

"What?"

"Me having information that you don't have."

"Tell me what's going on," Brixton said.

"You're dying to know, aren't you?" Captain Vedder snickered. "But you don't need to know, Grace. All you need to do is follow my fucking orders. Is that clear?"

Brixton didn't respond.

"I didn't hear you, patrolman."

Brixton didn't bite. He stayed quiet, with his mind on this new revelation. He had a hard time believing the jurisdiction lines had been officially redrawn. For what purpose? If only he could contact Nile and find out what was transpiring in his absence. But what good would that do? Nile was probably sitting behind a desk by now with his head stuffed safely up his own ass.

"Grace," Captain Vedder said. "Did you lose your ability to speak when Corporate took your balls? I asked if you heard me?"

"I heard you," Brixton snapped. He could feel himself wanting to push Captain Vedder on this new jurisdiction thing, but he decided to remain obedient and ride it out, against his nature, to see where the Captain was taking them, and what it might lead to next. He could feel his investigative curiosities peaking. It felt like home. He could almost feel the bright neon lights of Sky Haven warming his skin. But that feeling turned out to be the brutal sun cooking his body. It was burning through the cooling mechanisms of his uniform. "Fuck this desert," he said softly. "I'd rather be in Hell."

Soon he would be.

They followed the tracks for nearly two hours before they reached the end of the wagon's trail. Brixton didn't like where the tracks had led them. To a known Bloody Knuckle storehouse. A place called Vulture City. It was an old ghost town from the days of gold mining and cowboys and wild Indians and the bullshit claim of manifest destiny. The town was once a mining operation, established in 1863. Home to 5,000 residents back then. They had produced half a million ounces of silver and gold until it was closed and abandoned in 1942, to ensure that resources were focused on the war against the

Nazis, and not on citizens getting rich and becoming self-suffi-cient. *Some things never change*, Brixton thought.

They rode under an old wooden entryway which still had the words *Vulture City* painted in fading white letters at the top. The town looked like an architectural graveyard. There were tumbledown shacks that were slinking to the ground on all sides. The rotted beams were twisted and the roofs were leaning and surrendering to the undefeated hands of time. Defunct mining equipment dotted the hills around it. The ancient skeletons of jack pumps were covered in rust. The place still smelled of metal and oil. Monstrous saguaro cacti and leafless velvet trees were the only life sprouting from the earth, and they looked more like the earthly embodiment of death. Most of the man-made structures had lost their outer shell, leaving nothing behind but gutted haunts of the past. Brixton felt like he'd wandered into a time warp.

There was an ironwood tree that was once used for legal hangings in the mining days. It had a sign above it that announced its purpose. The noose at the end of the rope was still taking names. Anyone who broke the Bloody Knuckles' law in the area was dealt with swiftly. Beneath the limbs of the ironwood, with a short drop and a sudden stop. There was an old Wells Fargo Post made of stacked stone, a gas station made of tin walls that had been scavenged and hollowed out by drifters, and a large scrapwood cabin that was still in proper shape with a solid roof and shuttered windows. It was kept in decent condition. Brixton knew why. The old cabin was used as the bunk house for the Bloody Knuckle smugglers. Inside they had proper bedding, well water, a place to cook, and an outhouse to move their bowels after they ate.

But today, the usually bustling Vulture City was empty. The whole town appeared to be vacated and occupied only by the ghosts of those who'd built it long ago. The vacancy was not unusual for this time of year. The season was peak for the black market, and the smugglers were living on the move, staying mobile, making their way to and from the outer sprawl of Phoenix on covered wagons with valuable shipments of trade goods. But it was still unexpected to see no Bloody Knuckle guards watching over the storehouse. Brixton figured the gang must've solidified their standing in this part of the Blaze, so drifters and scavengers knew better than to trek across their Blood Ground. No sane person fucked with the Bloody Knuckles. Unfortunately, Captain Vedder wasn't sane. He had designs on the place.

"Jackpot," the Captain said, making Brixton cringe.

The wagon tracks led straight into the wooden portal entrance of an old horizontal mineshaft. That was the storehouse. It was cut out of the hillside and cordoned off by sliding barn doors which were painted a fiery red as a warning to curious minds who didn't belong. The doors were wide open. That likely meant someone was inside. Captain Vedder followed the wagon tracks to the portal entrance, and the Warhawks followed after him like armed ducklings. The tracks were fresh. Hours fresh. Maybe even minutes. So if there was anyone in Vulture City, they were currently in that mineshaft, and they'd be armed, and they'd be in possession of a large shipment of trade goods, which meant they'd be in a protective state of mind.

Captain Vedder got off his hyperbike and gave his orders. "Scout team, come with me."

Cooley, Chant, Greenie, and Kassab got off their hyperbikes and drew their weapons. Brixton was content to stay behind with the leftovers: Quan, Darko and Povich.

But Captain Vedder had other plans. "Grace, you're coming with us too."

Brixton suddenly felt immovable. He didn't want to follow them into the hidden storehouse. The entire operation felt shady. He didn't trust any of the Warhawks. They were just delusive thugs with badges. A facade of law enforcement. They sure as hell weren't lawmen. They just wanted to hurt someone. They didn't abide by any jurisprudence or code of ethics. They abided by their own savage impulses and nothing more, and they indulged those impulses every chance they got. But Brixton had to play the hand he was dealt, and he had to play it right if he was ever going to get through his punishment and return home to where he belonged. He stepped off his hyperbike and hopped over the muddy leavings of a recent flash flood. He spotted a dead ringtail cat trapped in the deadly flow, its body being eaten from the inside out by parasitic intruders. Pesky bot flies and red-headed harvester ants, crawling on top of one another in mindless gluttony, looking like the grand opening of some all-you-can-eat buffet in the Boroughs. He feared he would end up just like the cat: devoured and forgotten. He knew he didn't have nine lives to spare anymore. As he followed the Warhawks into the mineshaft, he kept his distance from them, lulling behind at his own pace, watching them carefully as the dark earthen corridor became even darker. They turned their tactical lights on to illuminate the drift. Brixton was sure to keep everyone in his line of sight.

Greenie slowed his pace and turned back to Brixton and nudged him in the half-light. "You scared?"

Brixton shrugged dismissively.

Greenie studied the surrounding darkness and said, "Cap, we gotta watch for tigers out here. Especially in these mineshafts."

Captain Vedder snickered. "You scared of a little pussy?"

The Warhawks laughed.

Brixton shook his head and said, "Tigers should be the least of your concern. This is Blood Ground. Bloody Knuckle territory. I doubt they'll be too hospitable."

"It's Warhawk territory now," Captain Vedder snapped. "We're taking it back."

The Warhawks quietly howled in mock celebration, being sure not to make too much noise.

"Taking it back?" Brixton asked. "Who gave those orders?"

"You're forgetting your place, patrolman," Captain Vedder said. "You don't get to ask those kind of questions anymore."

Brixton was beginning to realize that.

They moved cautiously through the half-lit dark of the mineshaft, following the wagon tracks, their fingers resting eagerly on their triggers and primed for any foe that might require a bullet.

Greenie was breathing heavily, his eyes big and shining with fear. "You smell tiger shit?"

Kassab sniffed the air. "Maybe you shit your pants again, Greenie."

The Warhawks chuckled quietly.

Then Cooley said, "Greenie, you might get eaten by a tiger before your nineteenth birthday. These big cats don't just eat men. They eat little boys too."

They chuckled again. Until they heard a rustling noise echoing throughout the chamber. They stopped. It was an abstract sound, but it mimicked the quick pattering of footsteps.

Chant swung his gun around, his light illuminating a dark offshoot. There was nothing there. Just earthen partitions and wooden posts. He squirmed. "Now you got me thinking about it."

"Hey tiger," Kassab said. "Eat the new guy. He's fresh meat."

Cooley laughed. "Ya'll are jumping at shadows. Don't ya'll know tigers run for their lives when they hear the Captain coming?"

"*Shut the fuck up*," Captain Vedder ordered.

The men went silent. Captain Vedder pointed to the load cavern. A hint of light flickered up ahead. They heard a commotion in the distance. Muddled voices in conversation. It sounded like men arguing over logistics. Captain Vedder signaled to the young Warhawks and they turned their flashlights off and moved stealthily towards the flickering light. As they entered the more expansive area of the mineshaft, there was a kerosene lantern illuminating the cavern in orange fluctuating strobes. It was firelight. They stayed at the rim of the cavern, stalking quietly in the dark shadows cast by the giant rows of stored goods, all of which were in wooden crates.

Brixton followed, staying low and ambling behind.

They stopped in the darkest shadow and took inventory. There were five Bloody Knuckle smugglers unloading goods from two canvas-covered wagons and storing the wooden crates among the numerous rows that had already been established.

One of the smugglers ordered the others to, "Unload everything."

Captain Vedder quietly signaled to the Warhawks. A three-finger countdown. Two fingers… one… Then they charged, blinding the smugglers with their flashlights, and shouting, "Border Patrol! Don't fucking move!"

The smugglers didn't.

Captain Vedder pressed his gun to the lead smuggler's temple and said, "Ya'll thought you could escape the Border Patrol?"

The smuggler didn't seem overly concerned with the predicament. "Easy now," he said. "We're Bloody Knuckles. With the black market. We work for Broken Nose. I got papers." He offered Captain Vedder a piece of hand-crafted papyrus with hand-written orders, legitimized by signatures. In the world of the black market, it was as official as any document could get.

"Oh wow," Captain Vedder said. "The bloody knuckles gang? Well *shit*, my mistake."

"That's right," the lead smuggler said with a confident gaze. "Your *mistake*. We have a deal with border patrol to cross this part of the map unharmed. Signed by both parties. This is Blood Ground. You should know that."

"I'm so embarrassed," Captain Vedder said. He took the papyrus in his hand and acted like he was reading it in earnest. Then, with a self-indulgent smirk creeping across his face, he tore the paper in half and let the pieces oscillate softly to the ground like the feathers of a dead bird.

The smugglers didn't look so confident anymore.

Captain Vedder pulled his shock stick and grabbed the lead smuggler by the throat and pulled him close and shoved the stick into his solar plexus. "Unfortunately for you," he said to the lead smuggler. "I'm Captain Vedder. Outpost 11. You know what they call my crew?"

The lead smuggler scowled with defiance and said, "Warhawks."

"That's right. *Warhawks*. You know *why* they call us that?"

The lead smuggler knew, but he wouldn't say.

"Because nobody ever escapes us," Captain Vedder boasted. "We can't be bought and paid for by the Bloody Knuckles like some of them other outposts. We don't turn a blind eye for nobody. We're company men. *In Nimbus we trust*." He turned to his men. "Whatcha say, Warhawks?"

They hollered "*Hoorah*" in unison.

The lead smuggler snarled and said, "You're out of your jurisdiction. What the hell is this?"

Captain Vedder tugged at his coat and zapped him with the shock stick. The smuggler's body jerked and stammered.

"This is the new order of things," Captain Vedder said. "Let's take a walk, shall we?

# TWENTY-ONE

The Warhawks escorted the smugglers and their horses out of the dark mineshaft and into the blinding sun. "Get 'em on their fucking knees," Captain Vedder ordered.

They forced the smugglers to the ground.

The lead smuggler resisted. "You're fucking up big time, man. You have no idea what you're doing. You're gonna start a fucking *war*."

Kassab shoved the barrel of his gun into the smuggler's back, and that was all it took to shut him up. Captain Vedder walked along the row of kneeling smugglers and announced, "You're in the kill zone. That's an illegal trespass on Republic territory. And you're smuggling illegal trade goods to boot. These unlawful acts will be punished..." He signaled to the Warhawks. "...with a lawful execution."

The Warhawks shot four of the smugglers in the head, execution-style. The lead smuggler was left alive, in a panic, with the dead bodies heaped around him in a bloody mess. He held his hands high, pleading, "Wait! Stop! Don't shoot me!"

"*Grace*," Captain Vedder said, "that's *your* man."

Brixton refused to shoot. His gun was still held safely by his side.

"You'll follow my orders out here, Grace. When I tell you to pull the trigger, you pull the trigger, even if it's aimed at your own fucking head. You understand me?"

"I'm not a murderer," Brixton said.

Captain Vedder laughed. He looked at the young Warhawks and said, "So this is PPD's finest? My goodness. Makes me proud to be a Warhawk." He kicked dirt over the dead smugglers. "I commit these bodies to the dust. Ashes to ashes."

The Warhawks laughed.

Cooley raised his gun to the back of the lead smuggler's head and asked, "Should I kill 'em, Cap?"

"Nah," Captain Vedder said. "There's an ironwood tree and a noose that looks lonely. String 'em up and wait for my order to set 'em swinging."

This was the psychopathic Captain Vedder that Brixton knew. The violent sadist that was aroused by his own cruelty. Brixton never claimed to be a saint, but this was an unlawful massacre, and he wouldn't be a part of it.

"Burn the wagons," Captain Vedder ordered. "Kill the horses."

"Kill the horses?" Brixton asked. "Why?"

"Article number fourteen dash two of Nimbus Border Law," Captain Vedder said. "We call it transportation control."

The Warhawks aimed their guns at the horses.

"*Hold your fire*," Captain Vedder shouted in anger. "Don't waste bullets on those stinking beasts. Just cut their fucking throats and let 'em bleed out."

The Warhawks holstered their guns and pulled their blades. Brixton grimaced. The horses whinnied as the knives cut deeply into their throats. Blood gushed from their jugulars. Brixton looked away. He was never fond of animals, but this was cruel and unusual punishment. Completely unnecessary to the cause. He didn't like hearing the horses in pain either. Their wincing made him nauseous. Fortunately their pain didn't last long, and neither did the noise. The animals staggered and crashed to the ground and spit the blood from their mouths and stopped breathing.

Captain Vedder grabbed a small bag of explosives from his hyperbike. "Gonna blow the storehouse," he said to the Warhawks. He looked to Cooley and Kassab with a subtle nod and then turned to Brixton. "Grace, you come with me."

Brixton froze. He didn't want to follow the sadistic Captain anywhere, especially into that dark cavern again. He had zero trust in Captain Vedder's motives now, and zero trust in his mental stability.

"*Grace, now!*" Captain Vedder waited, his eyes lingering on the golden boy.

Brixton obeyed the order, if only to avoid any further conflict. He kept his mind sharp and his eyes focused as they entered the dark mineshaft together.

Captain Vedder stopped and gestured. "After you, patrolman."

"No," Brixton said. "You're the Captain. I follow you."

Captain Vedder looked at him for a moment and then started walking. Brixton followed. They made their way through the long dark drift to the lode cavern with the covered-wagons and the rows of trade goods. The kerosene lantern was still flickering.

"Let's blow this bitch," Captain Vedder said.

Brixton handed him the bag of explosives, keeping his hand within quick reach of his sidearm. "What the hell are we doing out here?"

Captain Vedder wouldn't say. He began pulling the explosive charges from the bag.

"Why'd you kill those men?" Brixton asked. "They're Bloody Knuckles. This is a legal trade route. You're not even supposed to be conducting operations here."

Captain Vedder pressed on in silence.

"Tell me what's going on, Vedder," Brixton insisted. "Do you even know whose supplies these are? I don't think you realize the ramifications of what you're doing."

Captain Vedder said nothing. He just kept setting the charges. He placed the explosive devices on the wagons and on the wooden crates filled with goods.

"*Vedder*," Brixton snapped, refusing to call him *Captain*. "I asked you a fucking question."

Captain Vedder turned and looked at him calmly. "I think you're gonna catch on quickly out here, Grace. You got the instinct. I've seen it before. I know you're fighting the urge to accept your place among us, but there's a grunt in you, I know it. Maybe not a Warhawk. But a grunt nonetheless."

"I'm no fucking grunt," Brixton said. "I'm sure as hell not a Warhawk."

"We've heard that before," Captain Vedder said with a chuckle. "You might be surprised to find that uniform suits you."

Brixton was thrown by his calmness.

Captain Vedder pointed to the roll of fuse line and gestured for Brixton to pick it up. "Unspool that line and run it alongside the charges."

Brixton stepped forward instinctively and grabbed the roll

and began to unspool the fuse. He just wanted to get it over with. But as he was pulling the line from the spool, he suddenly felt the hairs on his neck stand up. A sudden premonition, as if something bad was about to happen. Then he was startled by the sound of Captain Vedder's walkie. The booming voice of Chief Kadence was bristling through the speaker, saying, "Captain, we've got red level orders from Corporate. Return to the outpost immediately."

Brixton spun around on his heels and saw Captain Vedder's left hand fumbling with the walkie that was clipped to his belt and his other hand clinging to his gun, which was aimed directly at Brixton's face. Brixton pulled his sidearm and aimed it directly at Captain Vedder. The two men locked eyes. The standoff seemed to linger for a lifetime. The tension so thick the air around them felt like an invisible fog of humidity.

Then Captain Vedder loosened his posture and softened his glare and chuckled again. "You startle easy, Grace."

Brixton didn't loosen his posture or soften his glare. He kept his gun aimed. "I guess it's gonna have to wait," he said carefully. "The explosives I mean."

Captain Vedder eased off the trigger and lowered his gun. "Yeah," he said. "It can wait. Some other time."

Brixton nodded and eased off the trigger, but he kept his finger on it. He lowered his gun, but not his eyes. Captain Vedder holstered his weapon and walked towards the tunnel exit as if nothing had happened. Brixton stood there wondering if he'd just been the target of a foiled attempt on his life, or if it was truly just a misunderstanding sparked by two very jumpy, agitated men. He followed the Captain carefully, his flashlight illuminating the dark of the tunnel, but struggling to shed light on Captain Vedder's true intentions.

When he and Captain Vedder exited the mineshaft together, the young Warhawks were standing guard over the lead smuggler, who'd been strung up to the ironwood tree with the noose slung around his neck. He was balancing on a tree stump to keep the rope slack. Captain Vedder wasted no time. He kicked the stump out from under him and the smuggler's body dropped. The noose went tight around his throat. The fall wasn't long enough or sudden enough to snap his neck. He was left choking. His legs kicking. His eyes bulging and threatening to burst.

Brixton cringed at the sight.

Captain Vedder hopped on his hyperbike and announced to his men, "We got red level orders. Let's head back to the outpost."

The Warhawks were thrilled. Red level orders were rare and always coveted. Something big was brewing, and they'd be right in the thick of it, whatever it was. They didn't even take the time to holler *Hoorah* or watch the smuggler meet his gruesome end. They ran to their hyperbikes and started the electric engines.

"What about the smuggler?" Grace asked. "He's not dead. He's just choking."

"Well," Captain Vedder said, watching for the golden boy's reaction. "If he chokes to death he's lucky. Otherwise we'll just leave him for the tigers. They gotta eat too."

Brixton clenched his teeth at him.

The visceral reaction seemed to please Captain Vedder. "Unless you wanna be the hero, Grace, and shoot the fucker in the head?"

Brixton didn't budge.

"I didn't think so," Captain Vedder said as he kickstarted the hyerbike. He and the young Warhawks took off, leaving the golden boy behind with the choking smuggler at his mercy.

Brixton stood there watching the man suffer. He felt compelled to end the suffering, if for no other reason than to end the godawful noise that the man was making as he gagged to death. But he didn't want his registered bullet to be lodged in the smuggler's head. Somebody could dig it out. The man's blood would be on his hands. His concern had nothing to do with morality. He'd done worse than shoot a dying man in the head. But this particular trade route was *legal*, and shooting a Bloody Knuckle here was very *illegal*. Vulture City was different than other black market storehouses. The goods inside were not the usual fare. They were boxes of alcohol and drugs and cigars and rare treasures. They weren't meant for Brimstone at all. They were meant for Corporate.

This was the *phantom* trade, as they called it. The covert, unspoken part of the black market trade that citizens of the Republic knew nothing about. Corporate indulgence. Conducted in secret. Outlawed goods and outlawed sex, to quench the everlasting desires of the Nimbus suits. Even Lucian Vanderbon himself indulged, quite often. The black market was a necessary evil for Nimbus. Their phantom trade had always been flawless. Brixton didn't want them to know he was there when the Warhawks disrupted it. So he didn't use his bullet to end the man's suffering. Instead, he watched the smuggler choke to death, forcing himself to watch it happen, as if he were punishing himself for allowing it to happen in the first place. He cringed with guilt. He didn't like this whole conscience thing. It was a foreign invader. He didn't know how to fight it, so he didn't. He just let the guilt take over.

Once the smuggler drew his final breath, Brixton took a deep breath of his own to calm his rising anxiety. He hopped on his hyperbike and followed after Captain Vedder and the young Warhawks on their way back to Outpost 11. He was sure to keep everyone in plain sight. He also kept his sidearm close, though his hands were shaking uncontrollably and his aim would undoubtedly be no more effective than his once-heralded reputation. This was going to be a long, worrisome ride.

# TWENTY-TWO

The black market train slithered down the tracks of the old Union Pacific railway like some dark metallic ophidian. The big S-2 locomotive was an old 2-8-4 Berkshire steam engine that was salvaged from a defunct railyard in Fort Wayne, Indiana years earlier. Once named Nickel Plate Road 765, the locomotive was repurposed and renamed the Black Market Express 311. The engine was painted pitch black with a red horizontal stripe and branded with the notorious red fist that let everyone know who owned it: the Bloody Knuckles. The old railway slogan of *Safety First* was rewritten to say *SHOOT First*, with the word *shoot* painted in big, red letters. That was the undisputed law of the land. *Shoot first*. The Bloody Knuckles always did.

The 311 was their premiere engine. The one that carried the boss and his henchmen and all the valuables that were transported to the trade market in Kelso. Today it was pulling a long line of rolling stock. There was an observation car for security watch, covered in a glass dome that was cracked in several spots and even missing a few window panels. There was a royal coach with amenities and table services so the boss and his henchmen could ride in comfort. It was the only car that was maintained, with refurbished fabrics and working headlamps and curtains that didn't have blood or mold on them. There was a passenger coach for the guests, but it was disgusting inside. There were three baggage cars filled with trade goods and armed guards. Then there was Levi's recent contribution. A flatbed carrying his strange hybrid vehicle, which was hidden beneath a black tarpaulin, followed by his brew car and a massive rusty tanker that stood out like a sore thumb. The caboose was at the tail end, occupied by armed guards who were watching their six. The Bloody Knuckles had eyes everywhere. They could never be too careful. The Mojave could be littered with drifters and gangs who might be desperate enough to do something foolish, like try to steal from the most powerful organization in the Blaze.

⁂

Levi was wobbling around on his feet in the brew car as the train shifted from left to right on a curvy stretch of track. He was wearing his yellow chemical suit and the old gas mask again, cooking up a batch of ethanol in the distillery. The gauges were ticking. The tubes were pumping. He removed the gas mask and filled a metal flask with ethanol from the spout and took a sip to test the mix. It was so potent he cringed when he swallowed. "Perfect," he said, as if he'd never brewed anything better. He stuffed the metal flask into his snakeskin boot and rolled the jeans back over the worn shaft. He grabbed a mason jar and began filling it with fuel. When he was done he removed the chemical suit and staggered out of the brew car across the flatcar and into the baggage car. He was sporting a yellow and blue sleeveless flannel over an old greasy t-shirt with the endearing image of Jesus Christ wearing a crown of thorns and a pair of dark sunglasses with a swag expression on his face and the words *DEAL WITH IT* printed in quotations below, as if it were some forgotten passage from his Sermon on the Mount. Levi had always tried to do just that: *deal with it.* He wore thick silver rings on his fingers, some of them skulls and some of them crosses, and he had a fake gold tooth that no longer sparkled when he smiled. His black leather pants were too tight even for his skinny old frame, and his crotch was bulging with an unyielding vigor. *A man of passion never relents until the day he dies*, he always said, unapologetically. He planted his lucky Mobil hat firmly on his head, though he wasn't feeling too charmed in the moment. The jar of ethanol in his hand was sloshing around, and so was his brain. The lid was rattling loosely on the threads, and so were his thoughts. He struggled to steady himself as he passed by a few armed security guards in the baggage car. They were dressed in black uniforms with red arm bands that had the Bloody Knuckle branding stitched into the fabric. He smiled inconspicuously. "Fellas," he said, raising the jar. "Ya'll need some liquid courage?" They didn't find it the least bit amusing. He frowned. "Lighten up, boys. It's a long ride."

The baggage car was filled with weapons, food, medicine, tools, bags of seed and numerous trinkets. Anything marketable.

Levi took inventory. "Ya'll got lots of quality merchandise. I might have to consider a trade."

Then one of the humorless guards raised his gun and said, "Keep moving, old man."

"I'm going, I'm going," Levi said with a dispirited frown. "Calm your tits. Just a man trying to conduct a little business is all."

He left the baggage car and crossed over the coupling

outside as it rattled beneath him. He staggered through two more baggage cars before entering the passenger car where he wobbled along the aisle. He saw more people onboard than expected. "Christ Almighty, where'd ya'll come from?"

The seats were full of warm, sweaty bodies, all reeking of human filth. They were traders, workers and guests of the Bloody Knuckles. Levi took another sip of ethanol and looked for an empty seat. One that wasn't cluttered with excess baggage. One that was actually functional. The passenger car wasn't luxurious by any means. The maroon upholstery was stained with blood and punctured with bullet holes. The cushions were ripped and barely intact. The white stuff was poking out of the torn crevices. The springs and other mechanisms were broken. The arm rests were falling off or missing. There was trash and broken glass in the aisle and the headlamps above didn't work. Some of the pull shades were still working, but most of them had been torn up by overuse or completely obliterated by gunfire and left dangling in unsightly scraps. Just mangled polyester. But compared to riding horseback or bouncing around inside of a covered wagon, the train was pure opulence. So Levi didn't complain. He finally spotted an empty seat. It was perfect timing too. The ethanol was beginning to work its magic, fuddling his mind and screwing with his equilibrium. He waddled over to the empty spot. But just as he was about to take the seat he saw a feral boy in the seat right next to it, and suddenly he had a mind to keep waddling. The boy was a scraggly little turd with matted hair that was clumped together with grease and dirt. He looked like he hadn't bathed in months. His clothes were tattered and mismatched. He seemed tired, probably from the world kicking the living shit out of him. But beneath all that bad life experience was a decent boy that was probably just looking for a friend.

Levi didn't want any part of him.

"Hi," the boy said. "The seat's free if you were wondering."

Levi was never one to turn down an empty seat or a friendly conversation, but this opportunity for both came with a caveat. He didn't like children. He hated them in fact. They talked more than he did, and made even less sense. The boy sat there staring at him with total disregard for common courtesy. It made Levi feel uncomfortable. He thought the boy looked like a royal pain in the ass, and though he couldn't exactly justify why he felt that way, he didn't want to stick around to prove his instinct right.

The boy shrugged, "You gonna sit down or what?"

"I'd given it some thought," Levi said. "But it ain't too enticing to be honest."

"Why's that?"

Levi began searching for excuses. "Well for starters, the seat's all busted. The arm rest is missing. Hell, the cushion's worn down to the metal frame."

The boy looked puzzled by the reluctance. "Well standing there thinking about it ain't gonna turn it into a lounge chair, now is it?"

Levi sighed. His instinct was proven right. The boy was a royal pain in the ass, just as predicted. But to make matters worse, he was also a crafty little smart-ass. Levi looked around for someplace else to sit, but he didn't see anything promising. He grimaced and sat down cautiously, and as he did the broken chair immediately buckled under his weight, shifting on the loose screws of the framework, and the jerky motion sent him into a frenzied recovery that almost threw his back out of alignment. "This sure as hell ain't no *lounge chair*," he declared as he steadied himself in the seat.

"I told you," the boy chuckled.

"Well maybe if I'd stood there and thought about it a while longer. You *rushed me.*"

The boy was amused. "I'm Badger," he said with his hand out waiting for a shake.

Levi grimaced. *Of course that's your name*, he thought. *How appropriate is that?* He ignored the boy, already regretting his decision to sit down.

"I said *I'm Badger*," the boy repeated.

Levi looked at him and said, "I'm drunk," and then he dismissed the boy's outstretched hand and laid back in the rickety seat and covered his face with his lucky hat and passed out before he even made himself comfortable. He hated to sleep, because as soon as he closed his eyes he'd begin to remember, and remembering was a goddamn torment, but before he could wake himself, a dream began to take shape. A bad memory. He found himself sitting in the dark, surrounded by the emptiness of his thoughts. A dream he'd had before. It was pitch black and silent. He could feel his own presence, and someone else's too. He was much younger in this dream, bouncing around inside of a Nimbus cargo trailer as the wheels hit potholes in the crumbling desert highway. There was a potato sack over his head, blinding him to his surroundings. He could feel the coarseness of it catching the stiff hairs of his beard. Then he heard someone say *it's time*, and there he was, back in August of '49 about to betray the one and only friend he ever had. The sack was ripped from his head and he saw a Nimbus security guard with a gun aimed at his face and a walkie talkie in his hand. The guard shined a flashlight in his eyes and said, "Call him."

Levi wanted to wake himself from the living nightmare, but like always, he couldn't.

The security guard placed the walkie in his hand. "Call him now."

Levi took the walkie and lifted it to his mouth. He put his thumb to the button and pursed his lips, but he couldn't speak.

The security guard pressed the gun to his head and said, "Do what I tell you to do, or I'll put you out of your misery and we'll take your friend down the hard way."

Levi took a deep breath and pushed the button on the walkie and said, "Billy, it's me. Do you copy?"

There was no response.

"It's Levi. You there, brother?"

"I'm here," Billy answered. "Go ahead."

Levi cringed, wishing Billy hadn't answered. His heart began to break. This dream was no dream. It was the cruelest of memories. He could hear himself saying, *Wake up, Levi. Wake up!*" But this was a moment from his past that he could never escape. "They're on the move," he said through the walkie. "Westbound. A big rig and a four Humvee escort." He fumbled through his words, feeling drunk and only getting drunker. "They should reach the mark within the hour."

"The vaccines?" Billy asked.

Levi hesitated, and then he lied. "Got a full load of 'em." It was such an unbearable deceit.

*Wake up, Levi! Wake up!*

Then Billy said, "Let's go make it right, brother."

Levi wanted to cry, or come clean, or put a bullet in his own head, if only he had the courage for self-sacrifice.

"Levi?" Billy asked.

Levi clenched his eyes tightly and forced the words from his lips. "I'm with you, brother. Guns a' blazin."

"Just get your ass here," Billy said.

"I've got it to the floorboard," Levi declared with tears in his eyes. He ended the transmission and dropped the walkie at his feet.

The Nimbus security guard smirked and said, "He really does trust you, doesn't he?"

Then Levi's world went dark again, his head covered by the potato sack, and his eyes blinded. Then in a sudden flash, as if he'd leapt straight through time, he found himself standing in the bright sunlight of the Mojave, with the godawful moment of deception flashing around him in painful colors. He saw Billy on the highway in front of him with his eyes broken by the betrayal. Then gunfire erupted and he saw Billy being massacred by Nimbus bullets, with blood bursting from his chest. Levi startled awake and pulled his lucky hat from his face and screamed out, "Billy, no!"

The feral boy named Badger looked at him. "You alright, mister?"

Levi looked at the boy in drunken confusion. Then he looked around the passenger coach and saw he was still on the black market train. The other passengers were staring at him with concern for their own lives, as if he'd gone completely mad and might be a threat to their well-being. He shook the panic from his pickled brain and feigned a smile and said, "Sorry, folks. Nothing to see here. I just had a little too much to drink is all." He blew the air from his lungs and lay his head back on the broken headrest and placed the hat back over his face in embarrassment. He whispered to the void, pleading, "God, just take me away. Why won't you just take me away?"

When he closed his drunken eyes again he immediately drifted off to another living nightmare. He saw little Bo Dagger in the driver's seat of the Moon Runner, sitting there scared to death and already in ruins. He saw Billy in the passenger seat, bleeding out and dying and wondering how his best friend could ever betray him like that.

*Wake up, Levi! Wake up!*

# TWENTY-THREE

When Brixton and the Warhawks arrived at the barracks of Outpost 11 on their hyperbikes, they were immediately ordered by Chief Kadence to board the hovership and fly into the Blaze to investigate the black market train that had been spotted by a boomerang drone and was now being tracked by Nimbus Security. Brixton was all kinds of confused. What was a boomerang drone doing out there in the Blaze? Who the hell ordered that? He was realizing that things were conducted much differently in the Forbidden Rim. Different standards and different rules and certainly different loyalties. He wondered if he'd always been kept in the dark about this side of things. He began to question his own relevancy. Was the golden boy just a pawn in a larger game? The doubt blind-sided him. He would usually want to revolt and fight for his place in the order of things, but he was completely devoid of that impulse now. The driving force that always propelled him forward was replaced with a paralyzing fear. He feared he may not have the self-control needed to survive his penance. He'd have to do something that he was no longer good at: proceed with caution.

The young Warhawks boarded the hovership on the tarmac in single file order. They were hyped up on pure adrenaline. Brixton would have to play the part. As he followed them onboard, he began to feel an unsettling tightness in his chest. Dizziness. Shortness of breath. Difficulty swallowing. Issues he hadn't truly dealt with in years. He reached in his pocket and scrabbled a couple of loose pills and tossed them in his mouth and swallowed them down without water. They would mask the problem.

Chief Kadence approached the hovership and grabbed Captain Vedder by the arm before he boarded. "Captain, this is just a surveillance op. We need intel on that train. You're going over the red line. With that comes great responsibility." He looked at Captain Vedder as a father might look at a problem child just before sending him off on his first day of school. "Resolve is necessary."

"There you go worrying again," Captain Vedder said gleefully. "You gotta stop that." He turned and boarded the hovership.

"Don't start a war," Chief Kadence said.

"I wouldn't dream of it, sir," Captain Vedder said. He closed the hatch and the hovership rotors began to spin.

Chief Kadence began to worry.

Inside the hovership, the Warhawks took their seats and strapped themselves into their harnesses. There were four rows of passenger seats, updated with the latest crash-rated safety features. The overemphasis on being strapped in made Brixton nervous. He didn't like to fly, and if the damn thing was gonna crash, he'd rather not be strapped in for it. He saw several gun hatches with RPG launchers and .50 caliber machine guns, each bolted onto a turret stand. He didn't expect to see that kind of firepower onboard. This hovership wasn't built to be a war machine. It was built to be a platoon transport for special ops. But the Warhawks had repurposed it to serve their desires. As the electric engine whirled and the rotor blades began to spin, Brixton stood by the side hatch and grabbed the safety bar and braced himself for liftoff.

Cooley offered him an empty seat, patting his hand lightly on the cushion next to him with a slippery demeanor. "Grace, have a seat and strap yourself in."

"No thanks," Brixton said, keeping his eyes on the young Warhawks. "I gotta watch my back around this crew."

The Warhawks laughed. It only validated Brixton's concern. He looked at Captain Vedder as the hovership lifted off. The two men locked eyes. Every instinct Brixton had about the Captain had proven to be true so far. The Captain was vile and sadistic and borderline psychotic. Brixton wasn't about to turn his back on someone like that, or on the young impressionable Warhawks who followed him so blindly. They were beginning to reveal their own slippery nature. Brixton suddenly remembered a mantra that he'd learned at the academy: *People are never what they appear to be. They're most often defined by what they're hiding. And everyone is hiding something.*

*Everyone*, he thought, catching a distorted glimpse of his own reflection in the metal safety bar. *Absolutely everyone.*

# TWENTY-FOUR

Croix was leading the pack on his golden palomino in the burning heart of the Mojave. He was sweating out his fluids and hoping he wouldn't have to break his own rules on rationing the water. But the deadly sun and his own thirst weren't the only concerns he had. He was scanning through channels on the walkie that he'd taken from the dead Reaper. Nothing but white noise. Abrasive static. Channel after channel. Then as he spun the knob, a swirling high-pitched spectral of radio waves broke through the crackling hiss and he suddenly heard voices. He toggled the dial until it became clear enough to comprehend. There were two men in the midst of a conversation.

*"You got the monkey wrench in place yet?"* — *"Copy that. Got the monkey wrench on the sticks."* — *"Good. Clock's about to strike."*

Croix stopped the horse in its tracks and listened more intently. Tavo, Skinny and Kid huddled their horses around him.

The voices on the radio were hiding their true intentions. Speaking in a sort of code. *"They may barrel through."* — *"We'll intercept. If they don't jump the sticks."* — *"That would screw it all. We'd be picking up scraps."*

Croix raised a brow with suspicion. "Ya'll hearing this?"

Tavo shrugged cluelessly.

Then a train whistle shrieked in the distance and the conversation on the radio grew more urgent. *"I hear thunder. — Copy that. Right on schedule."*

Croix suddenly put it together. "That's what they're doing out here," he said with a spark in his eyes. *"Thunder. Monkey wrench. Jumping the sticks.* They're gonna jack the train!"

Skinny was baffled. "What? Who?"

"The Reapers! They're gonna jack the goddamn train!"

Without another word, Croix dug his heels into the golden palomino and the mustang bolted off in the direction of the train whistle. Croix shouted back, "Let's go, boys. Move your asses."

Tavo finally put it together. "That's what they're doing out here." He looked to Skinny and Kid, who were both slow to process. "Dig in, boys. Whatcha waiting for? Let's go!" He dug his heels into the appaloosa's hide and the horse took off, following after Croix's golden palomino.

Skinny and Kid looked at each other, both a little confused. Then Skinny nodded frantically as if he'd suddenly put it together himself. "So that's what they're doing out here." He kicked his heels into his blue Roan and the horse scurried away.

Kid grimaced and shrugged, "I have no idea what's happening right now." He closed his eyes in apprehension. "God, please don't let me die. That's all I ask." He kicked his heels and followed after them.

## TWENTY-FIVE

Levi was still sleeping like a dead man in the passenger coach of the Black Market 311, and his lucky hat was still clinging to his face like a suction cup. The feral boy named Badger sat beside him with a bored expression on his face, watching the barren landscape pass outside the dirty window. When he heard Levi's mason jar rattling around in the lone cup holder, his eyes whipped around to investigate. He hovered over the drink curiously. The thick, dark liquid inside the jar looked like something that might taste good. Like syrup from a maple tree or a bitter sarsaparilla made from sassafras root. He looked carefully at Levi, who hadn't moved an inch for the better part of an hour, and then he poked him with a stiff finger to ensure he was really lost to the world. Levi didn't budge. The boy reached over and quietly unscrewed the lid from the jar. He leaned in and sniffed the contents and his nose ruffled up in disgust. It wasn't sarsaparilla, and it sure as hell wasn't maple syrup.

Then like a whirlwind of greed, Levi grabbed his wrist and said, "That's pure ethanol, boy. Dragon's Breath. Don't touch." He removed the hat from his face and looked at the boy with bloodshot eyes and snatched the lid from him. He raised the mason jar to his lips and said, "Only two kinds of man can drink this fire. You know which?"

The boy named Badger shook his head nervously.

"A dead man..." Levi answered as he took a sip and exhaled what he always called the flames, "...and *me*." He offered a sip to the boy. "You wanna die?"

The boy promptly shook his head, looking creeped out and no longer curious.

Levi screwed the lid back onto the mason jar and set it back down in the cup holder. "I'm going back to sleep," he said. "Don't badger me, boy." He rested his pickled dome on the headrest and placed the hat back over his face.

---

As the train thundered down the track heading west through the burnt sagebrush and fallen Joshua trees of the Mojave, smoke billowed from the engine's stack, spiraling in dark funnels like a tornado in reverse. They were only a few miles out from the Kelso trading post. The fireman in the locomotive was shoveling more hot coals into the firebox. The flame practically roared, like some sleeping beast being rudely awoken from its slumber. The engineer sat there in front of all the pressure gauges and levers with his eyes on the path ahead and his hand on the regulator. A security scout stood guard behind them, keeping a watchful eye out the window for any possible threats. The cramped space inside the locomotive was scorching hot, and their sweat-drenched bodies were a testament to that. Heat stroke and dehydration were common factors. This job was not for the faint of heart.

Suddenly their hearts jumped inside their chests as a loud

*bang* erupted from beneath the locomotive. They recognized the sound: a torpedo detonator. A small packet of powder placed on the tracks that exploded when the wheel struck it, emitting a loud bang like the one they'd just heard. It was a common warning to the engineers. It meant *look out ahead!* Usually it was a friendly heads up. In this case, not so much.

The engineer looked out the window and spotted something nefarious on the rails ahead. "Holy Hell. The rail's blocked!"

"*Oh shit,*" the scout shouted, his neck craning out of the window to see for himself. "It's a jack. Push through."

The fireman looked out the window and saw a large, man-made barricade on the tracks ahead with a jury-rigged de-railer attached to the front, just waiting to flip the train on its side. "We can't push through," he hollered back. "That's a de-railer. We'll go flying right off the tracks."

The scout turned his gaze to the south and saw dozens of Reapers rising up from behind the dark sagebrush outside. They were armed and colored up in war paint and likely high on Sidewinder, which would make them feel invincible and push them beyond their usual limits. The scout gripped the shotgun and shouted, "*Don't you stop.*"

"*We have to,*" the fireman hollered.

"*No, it's an ambush.* They're *Reapers.*"

The engineer looked frightened. "*Reapers? No. Can't be.*"

The fireman turned to the engineer and shouted, "*Dyna-mite.* There's no more time. *Drop the air. Now.*"

The engineer pulled the vacuum brake lever and the train screeched and howled as the metal brakes were engaged. The scout cursed them both. "We're as good as dead." He sounded the master alarm. It echoed throughout the train.

Inside the passenger coach, Levi and Badger fell forward in their seats as the train shuddered on the metal brakes. Levi startled awake and pulled his hat from his face and immediately looked out of the window. He saw a cluster of armed Reapers approaching the train on foot. "Oh fuck us all," he muttered. "From one goddamn nightmare to another."

The other passengers panicked when they saw the Reapers coming. Reapers were notorious killing machines, made up of all colors and creeds, but they were instantly recognizable by their unmistakable body adornment: painted up to look like skeletons, with white skulls on their faces and deep black circles around their eyes. They looked like walking death. They were carrying a startling array of weaponry. Handguns, rifles, machetes, swords, knives, sawblade axes, shields made from stop signs and bats with rusty nails protruding from the wood like thorns from Hell.

---

The scout in the locomotive grabbed the onboard radio and shouted, "We're *jacked*. *Code red*. We're being *hijacked*. Security to the engine. I repeat, we're being—"

But before he could finish his warning, a bullet ripped through his skull and his body dropped to the floor. A Reaper jumped up on the locomotive's coupling rod and stuck a pistol through the open window. The fireman grabbed the other shotgun and blasted the Reaper in the face. The train hissed and sparked. Steam from the cylinders engulfed the locomotive in a white fog. The fireman heard a volley of gunfire erupting around him. Bullets thumped the metal frame of the engine.

---

Inside the passenger coach, the glass windows were ruptured, sending broken shards hurtling through the car. The passengers were shredded by sharp glass and bullets. Levi stumbled to his feet in a panic as the bodies began to drop in the aisle around him. His mind was still fuddled by the ethanol and his feet were still uncoordinated and feeling detached from the rest of his body. He struggled to conceive an escape, his brain pickled and aimless. He grabbed the feral boy named Badger by the back of his shirt and pushed him through the passenger coach, trying to shield the boy from the raging onslaught of bullets. Fragments of glass exploded in the air around them and blood splattered the car, staining their clothes with little red spots. "Stay down, boy."

Levi was struggling to stay upright, his equilibrium in grave disorder. The chaos swirled around him with dizzying effect. He guided Badger forward, trying to protect the boy with his own body, but he stumbled in his drunkenness and fell to the floor and lost his grip on the boy's shirt. The boy wandered frantically into the path of a Reaper bullet. Levi looked over and saw him lying dead in the aisle. His eyes were white and lifeless, staring back at Levi with the worst kind of questions. The passengers trampled his body in their desperate attempt to flee.

Levi moaned in sorrow. He wasn't drunk enough to escape the immediate remorse of his failure. His heart sank in his chest, and then he gazed upon the boy for a moment as the world exploded around him. Bullets punctured the metal framework and thumped the seat cushions. The white fluffy stuff inside was flung into the air like snow flurries. Levi thought about standing up and taking one in the chest, but the impulse didn't have wings. He shook the desolate feeling and stumbled to his feet and scrambled through the passenger car, hobbling over the dead bodies. He made his way to the exit as

Reaper bullets narrowly missed his head, as if he were protected by some supernatural hand. He pulled an old revolver from his hip holster. It was Billy Dagger's gun from the old world. The Ruger Redhawk .357 with the handle made from buffalo bone. He'd kept it by his side all these years, possibly for a moment just like this. He fired back, but his bullets were as aimless as he was.

---

Inside the royal coach, Broken Nose took cover behind his bodyguards, who fired on the Reapers, killing several of the painted maniacs before more bullets pierced the shell of the train from outside. The bodyguards dropped for cover, pulling Broken Nose down with them and shielding his body. Bullets ransacked the coach, ripping through the metal framework and rupturing the flesh and bone of the bodyguards who were unfortunate enough to be on the outer ring of the human shield. The surviving bodyguards piled on top of Broken Nose and slunk to the floor as bullet after bullet hissed by their heads.

---

In the observation car, the Bloody Knuckle Railroad Security was overwhelmed by the assault. The glass dome shattered above them and the shards rained down onto their heads. They fired back recklessly as Reaper bullets shredded their bodies. Then the Reapers stormed the car, stomping over the broken glass, some with bare feet, their eyes bloodshot and raging from the Sidewinder that was pumping through their veins. They were dripping with sweat. It was clear that they were being adrenalized by the black market drug, which in high doses caused a homicidal madness known to the world as Slay Fever: a psychedelic effect that was currently fueling their murderous rage. They charged the remaining guards and massacred them with knives and machetes, bludgeoning them beyond death, and decapitating them for the pure joy of it. They stood over the pile of bodies, sweating and howling in victory.

---

Reapers swarmed the locomotive from every direction, hiding in the fog of steam that was still rising up from beneath the engine. The fireman raised the shotgun and blasted a Reaper that was trying to climb through the busted window. Then he heard a chorus of vicious howls and turned to see a dozen armed Reapers scrambling across the coal car and heading straight for him. The engineer picked up the dead scout's shotgun and turned to fire, but the Reapers dropped down inside the cab so fast he couldn't pull the trigger in time. They cut him open with blades and put a bullet in his head for good measure. The fireman picked up the shotgun, but the other Reapers charged at him, raging on Sidewinder, with their hearts pounding and their bodies sweating profusely. They struck the fireman with several blows to his gut, and then one of them dug a deep trench into his throat. The fireman dropped to his knees grasping at his neck. His body hit the floor, and death soon followed. The Reapers had control of the locomotive now. The engine was theirs.

# TWENTY-SIX

As Croix blazed through the open desert on horseback, he saw the train under siege and charged at a hard gallop. He pulled his *Crazy 8* and fired every single bullet in quick succession. His aim was true, taking out seven Reapers in his path and lodging the very last bullet in the spine of another. He holstered the empty revolver and charged hard at a Reaper that was blasting the passenger coach with an AK-47. He leapt from the saddle and tackled the Reaper to the ground. He hopped to his feet and pulled his tomahawk and struck the Reaper in the top of the skull. He wrenched the blade from the bone and slid the bloody tomahawk back into the sheath. He grabbed the Reaper's AK-47 and an extra magazine from the Reaper's belt and rose to his feet. He smacked the horse on the ass and shouted, "Get out of here, Hop. Run, boy!"

The horse ran for a large cluster of granite rock nearby, escaping a flurry of bullets. Croix swung the AK-47 and started blasting every single Reaper he could see, with calm and calculated precision. His hands were steady, and every single bullet he fired found a viable target. Heads. Hearts.

Guts. The chaos of war never hindered his instincts. It was unexceptional to him. Battle wasn't complicated. No matter the field, it was always the same. There was an evil that needed to be stopped and he was trying to stop it. Plain and simple.

———

In the field, Tavo tackled a Reaper to the ground and beat him to death with his war club. Then another Reaper nearby fired a shot from a pistol, striking Tavo in the side of the Kevlar vest. The jolt knocked the air from Tavo's lungs, but he swiftly pulled his Glock and fired, blasting the Reaper in the chest. The Reaper keeled over. Tavo screamed out in a rage. An uncharacteristic cry of war that punctured the air like thunder. He turned his eyes on the field, looking for his next target.

———

Skinny had found a hiding spot among the granite rock, and he was firing the sniper rifle and taking out any Reapers he could find in the crosshairs. Kid was hunkered down beside him, balled up like a clamshell in the sand, watching the battle unfold through the binoculars. He could see Croix running alongside the passenger coach, firing the AK-47 at the Reapers that were trying to board the train. He panned the binoculars upward and saw a Reaper following Croix on the rooftop of the passenger coach, aiming his gun at him.

"Croix's in trouble. A *Reaper. On top of the train.*"

Skinny caught the Reaper in the crosshairs and fired a quick shot. The bullet struck the top of the coach, distracting the Reaper just long enough for Skinny to rack the bolt action and take aim again and fire another round. The second bullet struck the Reaper in the gut and his body crumpled and rolled off the train and hit the ground.

Kid turned the binoculars on Tavo in the field and saw him being overtaken and pinned down by three Reapers, one armed with a massive blade. *"They got Tavo."*

Skinny spotted them and steadied his aim and shot the bladed Reaper in the chest. Tavo tossed the Reaper's limp body aside and swiftly overtook the other two, swinging wildly and beating them to death with his war club. He screamed, looking half-crazed and holding his weapon high in victory. Kid watched the madness through the binoculars. Tavo was covered in splotches of blood and his eyes were menacing in a way that Kid had never seen before, the whites big and round and looking anything but human. Kid lowered the binoculars and looked away. War made monsters of men. Even the best of them.

---

Croix tossed the empty AK-47 aside as a Reaper charged at him with a machete. The blade was glowing with sharpness. Croix pulled the bloody tomahawk from the sheath on his belt and lunged forward. As the Reaper swung the machete, Croix dodged the blade and somersaulted right past him and spun around and struck the Reaper in the spine with the tomahawk, all in one swift, calculated move. He finished the Reaper off with a quick strike to the skull. Another Reaper charged at him, wielding a battle axe. Croix spun around and threw the tomahawk end over end, striking the Reaper in the chest and knocking him off his feet. He ran to the Reaper and wrenched the bloody tomahawk from his black heart and slid it back into the sheath. He pulled a Glock from his back holster and quickly shot two more Reapers that were trying to board the train. They dropped dead at the boarding steps. He looked around for his next target. Everything was happening so quickly. His eyes had to be quicker. He spotted a Reaper and fired. A perfect head shot. He spotted another and fired again. The bullet struck the Reaper in the shoulder. The Reaper spun and looked at him and howled in a drug-fueled rage. Croix shot him right between the eyes.

A dozen Reapers stormed the royal car where Broken Nose was still being protected by a human shield of bodyguards. The Reapers and the Bloody Knuckles exchanged fire, eviscerating each other and shattering the bottles of homemade whiskey on the tables. Bodies dropped and bled as glass shards filled the air. The bodyguards put up a good fight, but the Reapers outnumbered them. The maniacs just kept coming. When one Reaper dropped, another one took his place. The bodyguards were shot to pieces and stabbed furiously. Broken Nose crawled away and rose to his feet. He drew a Colt .45 and fired. The Reapers took cover behind the seats. Broken Nose limped towards the passenger coach in a panic. The Reapers rose to their bloody feet and charged after him.

Levi was on the flatcar making his way past the covered prototype as bullets bounced off the vehicle's metallic foam body. He pulled a small remote control from his pocket and pressed the button as he passed. The vehicle went up in flames. He quickly stepped over the coupling rod onto the exterior railing and barreled his way through the door to the brew car, which was now extended on the metal slides. As he barreled into the car, bullets burst through the wooden walls. He was struck in the shoulder. His body jerked sideways. He stumbled but stayed upright. He headed for the mystery vehicle inside. It was still covered by a black tarpaulin. He flipped the tarp up and pulled it over the rooftop and quickly opened the driver's side door of the vehicle and slid into the seat and slammed the door shut as bullets struck the window. They bounced right off the glass and didn't even leave a mark. He squirmed in the seat, hoping his bullet-proof *"side project"* would keep him safe from the Reaper bullets.

---

Inside the passenger coach, Broken Nose ran out of ammo. He'd been shot in the gut and was looking weak and defeated. Five Reapers entered the coach and charged at him, all raging on Slay Fever and eager to kill. He stared them down and balled his fists and charged them like a bull, swinging with a youthful tenacity. "Come get some, you fucking animals." He bashed several of them in their heads before they overtook him and beat him to the ground. They piled on top of him, kicking and punching and stomping at his head with their bloody feet.

---

Croix and Tavo met at the entrance to the passenger coach just as a bullet from Skinny's rifle struck a Reaper who was standing in the doorway in front of them. The Reaper's body dropped to the ground at Croix's feet, clearing the way for him and Tavo to board the train. They carefully took the steps, their guns preceding them. When they entered the passenger coach they saw the Reapers beating the boss of the Bloody

Knuckles to death. Croix fired a shot, then Tavo fired another, and they repeated that volley until they killed every single Reaper in front of them. Five shots. Five dead Reapers. No wasted time or ammo. They stepped over Broken Nose who was lying unconscious in his own blood. Croix didn't bother to check his pulse. "Keep moving," he said.

They walked over the mass of dead bodies in the aisle. The soles of their boots splashed through the puddles of blood. They saw the feral boy named Badger lying dead on the floor. Croix grimaced at the sight. He felt a swelling lump in his chest. "Goddamnit," he growled. Innocence was always the first casualty of war. He shook the distraction and refocused. He pressed on, squeezing the trigger of his Glock to the break, and ready to kill anything that moved. "We ain't safe yet."

# TWENTY-SEVEN

Inside the brew car, Levi sat in the covered vehicle, which was partially hidden beneath the tarpaulin. He was trying to stop the bleeding from his wound, pressing his hand against the hole in his shoulder, but the blood was still gushing. He removed his flannel shirt and tied it around his torso and shoulder and pulled it tightly to stop the bleeding. He looked at his gut. It was hurting too. But there was no wound. He figured something had been busted or bruised inside. The image of Jesus Christ in shades on his old greasy t-shirt was splattered with blood. The words *DEAL WITH IT* caught his eyes and struck him in such a way that made him laugh out loud. "Don't that just say it all," he chuckled as he looked skyward. "Goddamn your twisted sense of humor."

Then a loud buzzing noise caught his attention. It was coming from just outside the brew car. His eyes drifted slowly in that direction. He heard the buzzing noise again, and immediately recognized the distinct electronic whirl. He knew the high-pitched sound all too well, and like everyone who'd ever heard it, he was deathly afraid. He looked out the window, through the shattered siding where the bullets had blasted a large hole in the wood, and he spotted a boomerang drone hovering just outside, its electric blue eyes searching. He quickly opened the glove compartment and pulled out a strange-looking gun. It looked like something straight out of an old science fiction movie. Two glowing cylinders, one on each side of the barrel, and a button near the trigger that was lit up in red. It was called a *Pulveriser*. It fit in the palm of his hand like a pistol, and it even had a sight and a laser for accuracy. It didn't fire bullets though. It fired an acute electromagnetic pulse that could knock out the circuitry of any electrical device known to man. An outlawed EMP gun. He pressed the red button and the primer engaged. The gun made a swishing noise, like a miniature washing machine on a spin cycle. He turned his attention back to the boomerang and whistled, "Here little birdie. Come and get me, you little fucker."

The drone was staring back at him with demonic blue eyes. He was startled by the evil in its artificial glare. It seemed to have its own mind, and its own desires. An inexplicable sentience that spooked the shit out of him. He looked down at the Pulverizer, which hadn't primed itself yet. "Come on, you little son of a bitch. Prime, goddamn you. Prime!"

The boomerang drone turned sideways and slid through the hole in the wood siding. It moved towards Levi with a spine-tingling stealth, like a cunning predator moving in slowly for a kill. The blue eyes flashed and scanned the vehicle.

Levi shook the Pulveriser. "Come on. Prime, goddamnit. *Prime!*"

The boomerang heard him and suddenly charged. The primer light on the Pulverizer turned from red to green and Levi quickly took aim. The boomerang whirled through the air, its coils crackling with the feared *kiss of death*. Levi pulled the trigger and the Pulveriser hissed like a snake. The boomerang was hit with a short-wave electromagnetic pulse. It dropped to the floor like a dead bird. The onboard electronics were completely fried.

Levi breathed a sigh of relief. "Still lucky," he said. He took the old Mobil hat off of his head and gave it a big sloppy kiss.

---

Croix and Tavo entered the first baggage car quietly and saw three armed Reapers sifting through the trade goods. They were vicious psychopaths with vile tattoos depicting rape and murder inked in vainglorious color on their bodies from head to toe. They had proud battle scars trenched into their flesh, and shiny piercings in every possible spot on their body. Their veins were bulging with Sidewinder, which had similar effects on the body as PCP from the old world. Blocking pain receptors and emotion. Causing manic behavior and a feeling of detachment. As if a Reaper needed anymore reason to feel detached. The killing machines turned their bloodshot eyes on Croix and Tavo and raised their guns to fire. But Croix was faster. He shot one of them in the chest. As he fired another round, one of the Reapers took cover behind the stacks of wooden boxes, leaving the other Reaper exposed. Tavo shot that Reaper in the back. The Reaper that was hiding behind the boxes fired wildly, his gun raised above the trade goods and his head down. Tavo took cover from the wild bullets, crouching down behind a large metal freezer. Croix stood tall in the aisle without a hint of fear, as if he knew those wild bullets weren't meant for him. He raised the Glock 19, waiting for the Reaper to make the inevitable mistake of blowing his wad. The Reaper fired a few more wild rounds and the bullets bounced around the baggage car and hit nothing of consequence. Then Croix heard a series of revealing clicks. The Reaper's chamber was empty. The Reaper stood to confront Croix, pulling a machete from his belt and shouting, "Fight me fair."

Croix just shrugged and said, "Why the hell would I do that?" Then he took steady aim and shot the Reaper in the forehead.

There was a cold silence after that. The dust and chaos from the battle had settled around them. No commotion of any kind. Nothing was stirring on the ground outside. Dead bodies lay scattered in the field and piled on the train. A massacre on both sides. Croix didn't like the ghostly calm. It was eerie, and to a lesser mortal, it could be deceptive. He and Tavo appeared to be the last men standing, but that couldn't be trusted. Croix listened carefully, his finger on the trigger of the Glock. There were no gunshots being fired in the distance. No scrambling across the train cars by warring Reapers. No celebratory howls. But he felt the hairs on his neck stand up, as if death was still near. The calm after a battle was always jarring to him. Going from pure chaos to an unsettling peacefulness in the blink of an eye. It could give a false sense of victory. Croix knew better. He grabbed his walkie. "Skinny, how we looking out there?"

"No movement," Skinny said through the walkie. "Far as I can tell they're all dead."

"Any movement in the train cars?"

"Not that I can see. Looks clear from my view. But there could be some Reapers crawling around somewhere."

"Keep a watch," Croix said. "We're gonna find the meds."

He scanned the goods at his feet. Mostly tools and household items. They exited the first baggage car and hopped the coupling and entered the second baggage car with their heads on a swivel. Croix saw food stores that had been destroyed by bullets. Herbs and dried meats on the floor. Barrels of rice spilled out. Water leaking from the barrels. Then he saw the medicines. They were all scattered across the floor like a puzzle, and totally unrecognizable to his uninitiated eyes. Most of it had been destroyed in the cross-fire. Glass jars were busted. Vials lay shattered on the shelves. Pills lying there in colorful confusion. He had no idea what he was looking at. "No no no," he growled. The liquid meds were pouring out and mixing with the pools of blood on the floor. "*Fuck.*"

"It's all shot up," Tavo said. "I can't tell what's what."

"*Goddamnit.*" Croix was struggling to remain hopeful. "Just grab everything you can. Anything we can salvage. Hickory might know what's what." He pulled his walkie. "*Kid, get your ass on this train.*"

There was no response.

"Goddamnit, Kid. Do you hear me?"

Then finally Kid asked sheepishly, "Just me?"

"Just you," Croix said. "Skinny has to watch our back."

Kid's voice shuddered, "How do you know them Reapers are all dead?"

"Because we killed 'em," Croix snapped. "Now bring the duffel bags and move your ass."

---

Kid climbed down from the granite rock and ran past the blood-soaked clumps of dead Reapers. The two empty duffel bags were strapped to his back and his gun was drawn, but he had no intention of using it. He kept his eyes on the baggage car ahead, trying not to look at the bloody carnage at his feet.

When he finally arrived in the second baggage car, Croix grabbed him and removed the bags from his back and said,

"Next time don't question me. Just come running when I tell you to."

"Is everybody dead?" Kid asked.

"Everybody but us."

Croix emptied the shelves with a sweep of his arm, dumping all the meds into one of the bags, spilled liquids and all. Time was not on their side. They took anything viable from the floor and stuffed it into the bags too. It wasn't a promising endeavor, but it was all they had to go on.

"Alright," Croix said, "let's take any weapons and ammo that we can carry. We gotta check the rest of the train."

They collected a few extra handguns, a rifle and some extra rounds of ammo and made their way out of the baggage car. Tavo carried the heavy bag. Kid carried the light one. Croix led the way with his finger on the trigger of an AK-47. They walked through the last baggage car, which was filled with dead guards and random supplies that were either ruined by bullets or worthless to begin with. They stepped onto the flat car where the prototype vehicle was still burning. The flame danced in the air. The tarpaulin was a melted tangle of black plastic and the engine was still puffing black smoke. They passed by carefully, avoiding the sudden arcs of flame. Croix stepped over the coupling and onto the exterior railing of the brew car. Tavo followed quickly behind him. Kid staggered at their heels. Croix entered the brew car with caution. He knew a Reaper could be in there waiting to ambush them. Maybe two or three. It appeared to be empty upon first inspection.

The wooden train car was unusual, extending on both sides like an old camper with electric pullouts, each side protruding outwards on a series of intricate metal slides. The whole thing was about sixty feet long and twenty feet wide. Significantly wider than all the other train cars.

"I never seen a train car like this one," Tavo said.

Croix nodded. "I'm guessing there's never been one like this."

The ethanol distillery and all its frenzied mechanisms and copper tubings had them all feeling bewildered. It looked like a giant spider's nest.

"What's all this about?" Tavo asked.

"Looks like a distillery of some kind," Croix said.

"Alcohol?"

"I'm guessing so. But not for drinking."

"For what then?"

"I'm guessing fuel."

Kid was stumped. "Fuel for what?"

Croix pointed to what he suspected was the answer. A black tarpaulin was covering what appeared to be a truck, with the shape of a high cab and a low bed extending behind it. The wheels were exposed and glistening like polished chrome. Croix recognized the ornaments on the rims: crossed daggers. "I'll be goddamned," he said. They sparkled as if they had just rolled right off the factory floor. He reached out and pulled the black tarpaulin from the frame, exposing the truck that was shrouded beneath it, and his eyeballs ballooned in disbelief.

There it was in all its mythical glory: the black '63 Chevy C10. Billy Dagger's legendary ride from the old world. The *Moon Runner*.

Tavo stepped back in surprise. "I don't believe what I'm seeing."

Kid moved towards the truck, his eyes lit with awe. "Is that... is that the Moon Runner?" His childlike wonder had suddenly been restored. "Is that the real thing?"

Croix didn't speak. He couldn't. He was transfixed by the sight himself, as if it were an absolute impossibility. It felt like witnessing a miracle. Like something returning from the dead.

He studied the emblem on the side of the truck. The skull and crossed daggers were still inked in bone-colored brightness. Not a single blemish. The truck looked new, as if it had never been blasted by a thousand bullets, or scraped by the sharp foliage of the desert, or dented by the chaos of the outlaw life. The black paint was flawless. The words *Dagger & Son Kustoms* looked freshly painted. "How could that be?" Croix asked himself.

Then a rustling noise captured his attention. He raised the AK-47 and narrowed his gaze. He moved closer to the truck where the noise was emanating from. He reached out and opened the passenger side door and raised the rifle to fire.

Levi sat there in the driver's seat, still bleeding like a stuck pig, but with his eyes bright and hopeful, as if Croix was the living embodiment of God's mercy.

Croix loosened his trigger finger and asked, "Who the hell are you?"

Levi stared at him like he was his own personal Jesus. "Better question is, *who are you*? Please tell me you're *him*. Tell me you've finally come to collect."

"I don't know what you're talking about, old man."

Levi was loopy from the loss of blood, and from the ethanol that was still fuddling his brain. "You look like him," he said with eyes that just wouldn't keep still. "I think, maybe... Hell, I don't know... That part of the memory's faded."

Croix was puzzled by the cryptic nature of his words. The old man seemed crazy. "You're shot, old man. You've lost a lot of blood. You may be losing your mind too."

Levi forced an odd smile. "There ain't no need to stand on ceremony," he said calmly. "Go on and do it, boy. I want you to. Finish the goddamn job."

"Your wounds ain't fatal," Croix said. "Ain't nothing to finish."

"*Do it,*" Levi shouted.

"I said *no.*"

"Shoot me, goddamn you."

Croix lowered the AK-47. "I ain't gonna shoot you, old man."

"Why the hell not?"

"Because you ain't a threat to us."

Levi looked broken by Croix's refusal. "Then you ain't him," he said defeatedly, as if the final gasp of life was all that he had to look forward to and he knew it wasn't coming anytime soon. "That means I gotta go on living. Goddamn you. Whoever you are. Goddamn you to Hell!"

Croix was suddenly struck by an idea. "Does this truck actually run?" he asked.

"You're goddamn right it runs," Levi said, looking insulted. "Like thunder and lightning. Why wouldn't she? Billy left her in my care. You don't think I can take care of a goddamn truck?"

Croix suddenly had a deep suspicion. "What's your name, old man?"

Levi scowled, "What difference does it make?"

Tavo leaned in and whispered in Croix's ear, "This old man's dying, Croix. Let's help him die with dignity or get the hell out of here."

Then Levi hollered, "I ain't dying, you dumb shit. I *can't* die. God won't let me. Can't you see that?" Then he answered a question that nobody asked. "Because he wants me to *suffer*. That's *why*. For *my sins*. Christ Almighty! Get with the program!"

Tavo looked at Croix with a frazzled expression. "We don't have time for this. He's batshit crazy."

Croix studied Levi and couldn't disagree with Tavo's assessment. But he still had an idea, and it was still gnawing at him. "Look, old man. We're on the clock here. No more bull-shit. My name's Croix. I came here to find—"

"I don't care," Levi interrupted. "If you ain't here to kill me then I don't give a shit who you are." He took a long swig of ethanol from his flask and closed his eyes and seemed to lose consciousness before he even swallowed a drop. The ethanol streamed from the corners of his mouth and his head cocked to the side and his arms went limp.

"Is he dead?" Tavo asked, sounding hopeful.

Croix placed two fingers on Levi's neck, searching for a pulse. "No. His heart's still pumping. He's alive. The sombitch is piss drunk." He took a closer look at Levi's shoulder wound. A brutal entry, but no exit. "The bullet's still lodged inside of 'em. He's losing a lot of blood. Let's dress his wounds."

"What the hell for?" Tavo asked.

"We're taking him with us."

"Like hell we are. That ain't happening, Croix."

"We ain't leaving him here to die."

Tavo huffed. "What's got you all sympathetic? Sounds to me like he *wants* to die."

"His wounds ain't fatal," Croix said sharply, and then he looked at Tavo with the usual threatening gaze. "He goes with us and that's final. Unless you wanna fight me over it?"

Tavo shrugged in defeat, letting his anger turn to indif-ference.

Then Croix looked at the Moon Runner with a spirited glow in his eyes and said, "We're taking that truck too."

Tavo blew the air from his tired lungs. "Let me guess… you got a *plan*."

Croix looked at him and sort of smirked. "Don't I always?" There seemed to be a real hopefulness in his eyes, as if he had a feeling of predetermined victory. A quicker way back to Zee. A better chance to save her life. For a minute, it looked like he just might smile. He was almost happy.

---

But little did he know, beyond the domed hill to the south, another horde of armed Reapers were making their way on foot towards the train. They were painted up like death and raging on Sidewinder, scurrying through the dark sagebrush with guns and blades and the worst of intentions. They weren't simple men with simple grievances. They were living devils, with Hell in their veins, and there were no angels on Earth to stop them.

# TO BE CONTINUED
## IN VOLUME 2

Dear Reader,

Due to the epic scope of Mojave Run, the story has been split into three separate volumes in order to preserve the author's complete and original vision. *The Team* at Blackwing Books will always strive to publish content that is extraordinary and without equal, and we are proud to push the stubborn limits of traditional publishing with Mojave Run, which we feel is a literary odyssey unlike anything we've ever read. After all, our official motto at Blackwing Books is: *Break the rules. Defy the odds. Never let them tell you no.* We are an independent press for fearless authors, and our very own fearless author Jared Martin perfectly embodies that rebellious spirit. We couldn't be happier to share his boundless imagination in all its unabridged and unfiltered glory.

Thank you for your support,

*The Team* at Blackwing Books

# NOTE FROM THE AUTHOR
## A THANK YOU TO MY READERS, AND A FAVOR TO ASK

Dear Reader,

Thank you for taking the time to read Mojave Run: Volume 1. I hope you thoroughly enjoyed it. Writing this emotional odyssey took me to the edge of my own existential boundaries and forced me to explore the greater depths within myself, and I hope it has had the same profound impact on you. I hope to make a long, productive career of writing, with many more novels to come, and I hope I have earned your trust and your desire to follow me on that journey. I value your support above all else. Fans are everything! Thank you!

Please follow me on social media for updates, and please subscribe to my author newsletter on my official website: byjaredmartin.com

Also… Please take the time to:

<u>WRITE A REVIEW</u>: Reviews — no matter how brief — are incredibly helpful to new authors. If you have enjoyed the story so far, and you don't mind sharing your opinion on Mojave Run: Volume 1, then please consider leaving a review on Amazon or Barnes and Noble or Goodreads. A review for each volume will really help me a lot!

<u>SHARE WHAT YOU'VE READ</u>: If you share Mojave Run on social media with friends or family, or hype the story by word of mouth, you're letting more readers discover my work, and that is the best marketing available to new authors. Your support is truly invaluable to me.

<u>CONNECT WITH ME</u>: I'd love to hear from you. Feel free to reach out to me by e-mail via my website or on social media. SEE "About the Author" for more details.

# ACKNOWLEDGMENTS
## A TRIBUTE TO THOSE WHO SET ME ON MY PATH AND HELPED ME ALONG THE WAY

I'd like to take a moment to thank my family and friends for their unconditional love and support through the years, even when those years were emotionally tumultuous, or physically grueling, or spiritually challenging. Your support is a blessing. A man can survive anything when he's surrounded by people who care.

I want to thank my mom and dad, *Sandy* and *Richard*, for a lifetime of counsel and encouragement, even when I was attempting to break the mold or blaze my own trail in the face of insurmountable odds. You taught me to work hard, to fight for what I believe in, and to never compromise my integrity. You taught me perseverance and self-worth. You taught me the importance of family. You taught me those things — and how to incorporate them into my own life — by living them yourselves. I've never met two people who have fought harder for their family. You are truly the unsung heroes of my life, and I know you'll always be there for me — in this life and the next.

I want to thank my two older brothers, *Jason* and *Justin*, for a childhood of adventure, loyalty, freedom and camaraderie — riding our bikes to "Pot Lake" and running through the woods like wild things, armed with nothing but BB guns and our own boundless imaginations — where we "fought the enemy" together and built forts and built a bond that will never be broken. Our brotherhood is set in stone, and only *we* can break it apart. Blood is blood, and brothers are forever. You both have helped to shape the man that I've become.

I want to thank *Danielle*, my partner in life — and the mother of my two amazing children — for allowing me to follow my dream without the fear of losing the dream that I've already been living. You've worked so hard all these years, providing your love and support and ensuring that I can bring my imagination to life on the black and white pages of a novel, and I've never once had to explain myself for pursuing a dream that sometimes seemed impossible. I'm forever grateful to you for your faith in me.

I want to thank my two amazing children, *Averee* And *Wyatt*, who have truly taught me more than I'll ever teach them. You've always shined your light in my darkness, *every single day*, and you've been lighting my path ever since you entered this world. Everything *I do* is for the two of you, but know that everything *you do* makes me grateful to be alive. I love you both forever, and no matter the time or place or situation, I will always answer the call. I'm your father, your dad, your friend, your teacher, your student, your shoulder to cry on, your heart to break, and hopefully, your unsung hero.

I want to thank my grandmother — whom we always affectionately called *Nanny* — for giving me the creative spark which has defined my entire life. Her passion for thinking and doing things outside of the box set me on a path to do the same, and I will hopefully live up to her exceptional precedent from this day forward. I know you're out there somewhere watching over us, *Nanny*. I miss you. Always.

I want to thank my extended family (whether bound by blood or by common law) for all the support, belief, unforgettable childhood memories, old stories told at family gatherings, new stories made, and the blessed kinship that we all share in this wonderful thing called life. Family is a saving grace for many a lost soul, and because of my family I'll never fear losing my way. My *in-laws, sisters-in-law, nieces, nephews, cousins, aunts and uncles*. You've all played a crucial part in my life, and I'll never forget that.

I want to thank the "Wolfpack" — my friends for life — who have kept me entertained all these years with your unfiltered and unapologetic humor. Laughter is truly the best medicine, and without you guys, perhaps this life would be insufferably dull. Thank you *Joe, John* and *Rene* for the enduring joy of unintentional comedy — even when it's at my expense — and for putting up with my stubborn and reclusive nature. After all, a lone wolf is only as strong as the pack from which he comes. You've helped me to discover that *friendship* is just another word for family.

I want to thank my book cover designer, *Jair*, whose work and creative vision I greatly admire, and of which I'm proud to share with the world.

And last but not least, I want to thank *you, my readers*, for trusting me as a writer, for offering me your precious time, and for sharing the adventure, conflict, tragedy and ultimate triumph of the characters in my boundless imagination.

Thank you all, with overwhelming love and respect,

Jared

# ABOUT THE AUTHOR
## A LIGHTING-QUICK "BIO" AND MY CONTACT INFO

My name is Jared Martin. I'm 45 years old going on 13, and the latter part of that equation is never going to change. To be young at heart is to be free of spirit, so I *try* to stay young, even though my weary mind and aching body put the shackles on me every day. I'm an author, a father, a brother, a friend, a partner in life and a grateful son. I love stories and music and creating them both. I'm obsessed with the pop culture of my youth, i.e. the glorious 80s and 90s, and I believe that a writer's contribution to socicty is only as significant as his or her readers wish it to be. It's a collaborative effort — *this strange, whimsical thing called storytelling* — and *you, the readers,* are the ones who make or break the story. So thank you for taking my story from the black and white pages to the colorful depths of your imagination and bringing it to life.

If you'd like to follow me or connect through social media, my handle across all platforms is *byJaredMartin*. All social media links can be found on my official website: www.byjared martin.com. You can find me currently on X, Instagram, Facebook, YouTube, and TikTok. Just look for my official logo:

**by JARED MARTIN**
AUTHOR OF FICTION

**Twitter/X**: www.x.com/byjaredmartin
**Instagram**: www.instagram.com/byjaredmartin
**Facebook**: www.facebook.com/byjaredmartin
**Youtube**: www.youtube.com/@byjaredmartin
**TikTok**: www.tiktok.com/@byjaredmartin